# Incognito: Preternatural Pedagogy

Edgar Washburn

Incognito: Preternatural Pedagogy
By Edgar Washburn
Copyright 2020 by Edgar Washburn
Cover art by Germancreative

**Author's Note**
This book is a work of fiction. Names, characters, places, and incidents are products of the author's imagination or are used fictitiously. Any resemblance to actual events or locations or persons, living or dead, is entirely coincidental.

For Marsha, my loving (Sonnet 116 kind) wife

# Prologue

Dr. Joseph Corman reread the resignation letter. It was probably a blessing, and it wasn't really a surprise. Betsy Burns just hadn't had the heart for the job, and he'd known she'd been applying for other work since returning from winter break last January. He wouldn't miss her, but the situation would have been easier if she'd gotten her new job before mid-August.

Not that she'd admitted that a job offer was her reason for leaving just before the new school year began. Because it would be unprofessional to accept a job from one employer after having signed a contract with another. Not only would it be unprofessional, it would show a complete lack of consideration for the people who would have to scramble to fill the void she'd left.

Corman inhaled deeply through his nose, held it, and released it slowly and completely through his mouth. He imagined his frustration being expelled with his breath. He repeated the process a few more times and felt ready to interview another applicant. He looked down at the next resume and cover letter on his desk. Maybe Sean Brannon would be a good fit. He certainly hoped so.

He stood and straightened his blue tie and smoothed the creases out of his burgundy waistcoat. He retrieved the jacket of his medium-gray suit from the closet and slipped it on and buttoned it. There was a full-length mirror on the inside of the closet door, and he examined himself. Though he was well into his forties, he was lean and athletic, and his clothes fit well. His dark hair was neatly cut and his hands manicured.

He paid a great deal of attention to his appearance, but it wasn't out of vanity. There was deliberate intent in how he presented himself. His look was classic, right down to the pocket watch with the carefully-draped gold fob chain. The bright waistcoats he wore with his subtle suits were intended to give him a little flair within a traditional

1

mold. It was important to stand out but not be gaudy. His continuing success depended a great deal on how people perceived him. Professional, intelligent, confident, competent, compassionate, polite, modest. He worked at it all. Earnestly.

Once he had himself squared away, he turned his attention to his office. He genuinely believed that where a person spent his time was also a reflection of him, so his professional space was deliberately organized and decorated. Framed diplomas, tasteful landscape paintings by a local artist, dark-wood furniture, bookshelves holding both educational and medical texts, dark medium-pile carpets, and matching drapes were all chosen with a particular effect in mind. The Mannaz School might have only been five years old, but this room exuded venerable solidity. The parents who met him and spoke with him in this office would trust him to save their children when no one else had. So far, results had borne out that trust.

There was just one object in the room which did not fit his preconceived model of a headmaster's office. He'd had it since he was five years old. It was not a strategic accent like the waistcoats. He loved it and felt compelled to display it.

On the front right corner of his desk, the corner closest to the door, a crystal ball rested on its polished bronze stand. It was a little larger than a grapefruit. Light from the window created a rainbow starburst in the center of the sphere and gleamed dully on the serpentine coils in which it was nestled. The bronze coils eventually curved downward into three legs ending in curled dragon claws.

It was a good piece, historically and financially valuable. It just wasn't the sort of thing one expected to see in a headmaster's office. Visitors probably just thought it was an eccentric knick-knack and didn't give it much thought. Corman himself found it endlessly fascinating and its presence comforting.

He stood next to the desk, absently brushing the backs of his fingers along its hard, smooth surface. It would remain where it was whether it fit the décor or not. Its presence relaxed and centered him more than his breathing exercises or his morning yoga or anything else he'd discovered.

There was a knock on his door. He automatically checked his pocket watch. It was a habit developed from an affectation. There was a perfectly good clock on the wall opposite his desk.

Hilde Fitzwilliam opened the door before he answered her knock. She did that sort of thing. She was large and blond, and her rosy-cheeked face was pleasantly plain. Her blue, floral-print dress looked strangely feminine on her blocky body. There was nothing fat about her. She was what Corman's mother would have called "good peasant stock."

She said, "Your ten o'clock called from Gracie's Market. Said he might be late."

Corman gave his pocket watch another glance and slipped it back into his waistcoat. His sigh was a little gusty, and he regretted it immediately. Hilde loved to complain and gossip, and he had just given her an opening.

She said, "I hope that today's applicant isn't another dud." She shook her head and looked downward with a mournful air. "Where do these kids come from?"

"Hope springs eternal," Corman said. It was a noncommittal thing to say. The kind of thing that didn't invite further conversation, but Hilde needed little by way of invitation.

She leaned a substantial hip against the doorframe and said, "The dorm parents have been complaining to Matt about having to cover the classes." The mournful tone was still there, but she couldn't quite hide her eagerness for drama.

Matt Raymond was the head of the residential program. He was good at his job. Corman knew of the complaints already. He and Matt had spent a couple of late nights coming up with a viable plan which wouldn't inconvenience anyone overly much.

Corman picked up Sean Brannon's resume and cover letter from the desk and looked over them hoping to give Hilde the impression that he had things to do. She continued to stand in the doorway, either unable or unwilling to take the hint.

Finally, he said, "There's nothing to be done for it. The dorm parents are being fairly compensated, and it hasn't been more than

3

five extra hours a week for any of them. Teachers are giving up prep periods as well. It's all part of being a community."

Hilde was good at spotting openings and slipped in another complaint. "Brenda says that the extra hours these last two weeks have thrown off her salary calculations. She's had to refigure everything. If you ask me, I think that you should have made more of an issue about Betsy breaking her contract. The problems that girl has caused. You're too nice to these kids. They take advantage." Hilde referred to the young faculty as kids.

Of course, he'd also talked to Brenda, the bookkeeper, at length about payroll issues. That sort of thing was part of his job after all.

He tried not to feel offended. He knew that Hilde didn't believe him incompetent. She simply wanted to get nostalgic about the "old days" by complaining about this new generation. It was one of her favorite subjects. Corman didn't think that young people in the '80s were any more irresponsible than they had been when he was young, but he wasn't going to get pulled into a debate. Not that it would be a debate in the true sense of the word.

He simply said, "We'll get by, Hilde."

Unlike his secretary, Corman didn't like to wallow in the injustices of life. He was an unashamed optimist. He tried his best to avoid negative thinking. Hilde was actually a good foil for him. His mood often improved because he naturally reacted against her doomsaying. That didn't mean that he wasn't about to make good his escape from her now, though. There was no reason to suffer needlessly.

He put Betsy's letter away in a desk drawer. It would have to be filed soon. After scanning Sean Brannon's resume one more time, he said, "Thank you, Hilde. I think I'll wait for Mr. Brannon outside. It's a lovely morning."

"Of course," she said. "I've got so much work to get though." She wasn't good at hiding disappointment and lingered in the doorway for another few seconds. Corman said nothing, and after a gusty sigh of her own, she returned to her desk.

He was smiling when he descended the steps of Oak House, the main building on the Mannaz School campus. All of the buildings were

4

named for trees which grew in the surrounding woods. The "House" part of the names was also appropriate because all of the buildings, residential and academic, were large, repurposed country houses.

Oak House had once been the sprawling mansion of a railroad millionaire. When the railroad began to fail in the 1950s, the millionaire sold the building and surrounding property. The mansion was then inexpertly converted into apartments. Poor management caused them to fall into disrepair. In 1980, Corman bought the building from the bank for a song. Fortunately, the original structure was still solid, so the greatest renovation challenge was removing the shoddy new construction. Within two years, it looked pretty good again, and everything worked the way it was supposed to work. The year after that, the Mannaz School opened.

From the foot of the main steps, Corman breathed in the warm September air and looked over his school. He'd put all of his mental, emotional, and financial resources into this experiment, and after five years, it was still going. It was a marvel considering all of the factors against it. But his school was still running. His school. Not perfect by any means but very close to what he wanted. He knew that he would find a new English teacher. It was just another of the endless hurdles which this particular race would involve. If he hadn't been an optimist, he wouldn't have started the school in the first place.

He walked along the sidewalk which marked the center square. It wasn't really a square. It was rectangular and nearly an acre and a half in size. The houses around it made up most of the academic school buildings, and the residential buildings were no more than a five-minute walk away. The campus looked less like a school and more like a wealthy rural neighborhood because that's what it had been during the boom. Until the bell rang for class changes, little would indicate that it was a school at all.

Noah, the head of maintenance, had recently mowed the grass, and the scent of it hung in the air like a promise. That smell and the breeze and the soft sun continued to ease the tension he had been feeling earlier. Being in the woods was possibly the best thing that the school had going for it. There was something soothing about the closeness of nature. He worked his shoulders a little as he walked to help loosen his muscles.

He'd made it halfway around the square when the rumble of a big engine rolled across the distance. In moments, an old, black muscle car appeared on the curving driveway approaching the square. Corman was impressed that the driver obeyed the ten-mile-per-hour speed-limit sign, but he wasn't thrilled about the loudness of the car. Assuming that this was the potential English teacher, he walked toward the parking lot.

He was nearly to the lot when the door of the car opened with a pop and a groan of hinges. Corman's eyebrows rose when the occupant climbed out. The young man's hair was red. Not orange. Not auburn. Red like the plain red crayon in the Crayola eight pack. It was a little long, covering the tops of his ears and falling past his collar. He shrugged into the jacket of his navy suit. The darkness of it emphasized the fairness of his skin. There was something of the nineteenth century poet about his appearance. Maybe a little like John Keats. How appropriate for an English teacher.

There was a clear quality of physical competence about him, though, which spoiled the Keats comparison. His movements were deliberate and precise, graceful like a dancer who was going over a familiar routine. He retrieved a soft black leather briefcase from the car and closed the door with the same pop and groan of hinges. Using the glass of the window, he straightened his tie and finger-combed his hair.

When he saw Corman, he smiled and shifted his briefcase, so they could shake hands. Corman was startled again when he saw the man's eyes which were a bright, electric-blue. They were almost unnerving in their intensity. His appearance would take some getting used to. Striking was too mild a term.

"Dr. Corman, I'm Sean Brannon. I recognize you from the Mannaz brochure." His grip was firm but not aggressive. After they released each other's hands, Brannon looked at his wristwatch, a simple black-faced Timex. "I know I'm cutting it close. I got a little turned around. Wow, this place is really out in the woods."

6

Corman nodded to indicate that yes, the school was indeed out in the woods and said, "I like to start interviews with a little tour of the main campus. If you don't mind?"

"Sounds good."

Gesturing widely, Corman said, "The school owns over four hundred acres of Western New York woodland. We won't venture far today, so there will still be plenty to explore later. Feel free to ask any questions, and I'll answer all that I can."

They began with the residential areas. Brannon was shown inside one of the student dorms called Elm House. Only the bulletin board in the kitchen indicated that it was anything but a regular home. He also saw the tiny studio apartment which would be provided to the new English teacher. It was a mother-in-law-type apartment in the basement of Willow House, one of the academic buildings. The rest of the tour consisted of a lap around the square so that Corman could point out all of the other academic buildings. They ended up at Oak House where they planned to look in on classrooms after the interview proper.

Hilde's eyes widened and her mouth made a little "o" when they entered her office. She very overtly looked Brannon up and down. He didn't notice or pretended not to. Corman thought that the young man would never go unnoticed, not with that hair and those eyes. He would probably be quite popular with the ladies, as well, though truth be told, his features were not especially handsome.

Corman directed Brannon to take one the of the two visitor chairs facing his desk, and he took his own seat. The crystal ball clearly caught the young man's eyes as it did anyone's who entered the room. The concentration of his scrutiny was not typical, however. It was almost as if he expected to see something in its depths. Maybe the light was just up to its tricks again.

When the young man pulled his eyes from it and focused on Corman, he said, "That's an interesting piece. It looks old."

"It is," Corman said.

"Are you familiar with its history?"

Something in Brannon's examination of the crystal ball and his evident curiosity about it made Corman feel suddenly protective. By way of polite redirection, he said, "Perhaps if we have time later. For now, we should remain focused on our purpose."

As a man of science, Corman felt decidedly uncomfortable talking about his grandmother who had been a genuine Romani fortune teller. He remembered little of her appearance, but the sense of her kindness and strength remained undiminished, especially when he was near her crystal ball. She had specifically instructed that he should receive it when she passed away, and it was special to him. Talking about it would diminish it somehow, make it a mere curiosity. At the same time, he felt the need to display it. One of the many contradictions in life, he supposed.

"Okay. I look forward to hearing about it. Now, let's focus on our purpose." Brannon's smile was charming and easy-going. A lack of ego, maybe, or at least a thoroughly tamed one.

"The job you have applied for is a difficult one, Mr. Brannon," Corman steepled his fingers in front of his mouth, the index fingers touching his lower lip. Long practice made the pose seem less affected than it was.

"Thank you for your candor," said Brannon. "I can appreciate a challenge."

Corman placed his hands palms down on his desktop and leaned forward slightly. His gaze was direct and a little intense. "I had been a practicing physician for fifteen years when I founded the Mannaz School. That was five years ago. We have a certain way of doing things here," he said. "I need to clarify this, in general terms at least, right from the start."

Brannon said, "Okay. I'm all ears."

Corman leaned back slightly and began his speech, not necessarily rehearsed but familiar ground. "There is an increasing trend in our society to medicate difficult children until they are docile. The long-term effects on their health are often unknown, and they usually don't learn to cope with challenges on their own. They become dependent on the medication. With few exceptions, we wean the students from their medications. We teach them to acknowledge their situations and to plan ways to take control of their own actions. Personal responsibility is a key concept in our community." Corman

8

paused, allowing time for comment. Brannon waited for him to continue. "Our students have not found success in more traditional settings, and their initial period of adjustment to any new place or situation may be difficult and prolonged. We offer patience and assistance instead of punishment. There are, of course, natural consequences to certain behaviors, and we must maintain a safe environment, but our main tools are guidance and support."

In the pause which followed, Brannon said, "So, I should expect some bad behavior."

Corman smiled and nodded.

"And I'm expected to ride it out, not just send the kids to the office or give them detention and whatnot."

Corman nodded again.

Brannon said, "I thought it would be something like that. I did read the Mannaz brochure and some other materials I found at the placement office. The tone in all of it is pretty positive, but there is also a lot between the lines. I was intrigued."

Corman nodded again to acknowledge the effort Brannon had taken to learn about the school. "While I am headmaster, the school will never have more than sixty students. Current enrollment is forty-eight. That's about where I like it. We must give guidance and support so that each student succeeds. If you are offered the job, we will try to catch up your training, but the unexpected vacancy has made a last-minute hire necessary."

"I can do it. If you give me the job, I will do it."

Corman noted that Brannon didn't say that he would try. He said that he would. The statement sounded confident, not arrogant. The young man had a self-assurance, a poise that made him seem older than his age. Corman felt that he was a good judge of character, and he liked Sean Brannon.

After a short nod, Corman continued. "We can't fix the world here, but we can help some young people. Maybe ourselves too. Things move very fast in the '80s. Many students who don't adjust to the world are medicated or marginalized. This is where those students can come and take the time they need to become the best people they can be, and they will do it without drugs. That means that we expect to weather storms. It is a difficult path, but I believe it is worth the cost."

Corman grinned sheepishly, which for a moment, gave his lean face a boyish quality. "I'll step from my soapbox now. I just want to be certain that you understand that all of your experience may not be applicable here. Our approach is deliberate and unlike what you have probably seen before."

"I'm a pretty quick study," said Brannon.

Corman was about to suggest that they look in on some classes when a crash sounded from somewhere outside the door. A shrill voice screamed, "Goddamn piece-of-shit motherfuckers!" There was another crash.

Brannon moved decisively through Hilde's office and into the hall. Corman was right behind him, hoping that the young man had the sense not to get in the way. He intended to tell him to stay where he was but, for some reason, didn't. Corman was never able to figure it out and eventually rationalized it as intuition.

A first-year seventh grader named Charlie came striding across a student common area. He was undersized and wore jeans and a torn Spiderman t-shirt. His face was red and tear-streaked. His sandy hair was in wild disarray. He stopped at a table set with two chess boards ready to play. He grasped the edge and strained against the table, his small body trembling with effort until it went over, and chess pieces scattered across the tile floor. He screamed, "Mother fucker!" and kicked and stomped at any chess pieces still near the table.

The boy saw the adults and stalked toward them. It was impossible to know what he intended, but his manner was aggressive. When he was still ten feet away, Brannon knelt and held up a hand. At first glance it looked like a gesture to halt, but Corman had the sense that the man was somehow testing the air.

*Oh no*, Corman thought. *This could be bad*. Again, he intended on interfering, and again, he didn't. He wasn't being indecisive. He was deciding to hang back and watch the drama play out in front of him. More intuition?

Something strange happened then. Corman would never be able to clarify it, even to himself, but he felt a change in his perceptions.

Things seemed to become soft around the edges. There was a quietness like there sometimes was on snowy nights when the falling flakes were fat and heavy. A stillness.

Charlie slowed and stopped three feet short of Brannon. He blinked and rubbed his eyes like an overtired child, which is really what he was. He looked around him as though he had lost his train of thought, maybe forgot where he was going.

Brannon said, "Hey, is that Spiderman?"

The boy looked down at the picture on the front of his t-shirt. He fingered the torn neckline absently.

"He's one of my favorites," Brannon continued.

The boy sighed. His shoulders slumped a little, and he said, "Wolverine is my favorite, but I can't find a Wolverine shirt."

"I love the X-Men!" said Brannon.

The boy looked skeptical. "Who's your favorite?" he asked.

"I like Nightcrawler."

The boy smiled. "He looks like the devil."

"Looks can be deceiving, right?"

"Yeah," said Charlie. "He goes to church and stuff."

Corman shook his head slightly, once left, once right, back to center. That stillness gradually bled away and sounds gained clarity. It was a little like waking from a doze. A residual sense of strangeness still hung in the air, but as a practical man who dealt in concrete data, he thrust the feeling aside. But regardless of the dreamy, muffled perceptions, he couldn't deny what he'd just witnessed. He'd never seen a child who was that angry calm down so quickly, so completely. If it wasn't a fluke, Brannon could be an invaluable asset to the Mannaz School.

"You kind of look like Banshee," said Charlie to Brannon. "That's a dumb name for a guy, though, 'cause a banshee is a girl ghost." He yawned and asked Corman, "Who's this?"

"This is Mr. Brannon. He might like to work here."

Charlie's mouth gaped at first then transformed into a smile. He said to Brannon, "Really? Why?"

Brannon stood from his kneeling position and shrugged. "Well, it would be nice to have someone I could talk to about comic books."

11

Conrad Novak, a history teacher, entered the common room, moving with purpose but not hostility. He said, "Hey, Charlie, are you coming back to class?" Novak gave the impression of being as wide across as he was tall. He was short, but his shoulders and chest were heavy with muscle which strained against his yellow sport shirt. His black hair was cut in a flattop, and he was a man cursed with permanent five-o'clock-shadow. Corman had always thought that he would look at home in a '30s gangster movie. He'd just need a fedora and a cigar.

Corman said, "Mr. Novak, I think that Charlie should spend some time with Ms. Gallaway." Ms. Gallaway was a counselor, and her room was a safe place for students to decompress. It seemed that Charlie had decompressed already, but there was no need to deviate from standard operating procedures.

Novak and Charlie walked calmly away together. Brannon called after, "It was nice to meet you, Charlie."

The boy waved absently without turning to look. Novak did spare a quick glance and nodded once.

Corman said to Brannon, "You don't work here yet, you know."

Brannon looked embarrassed and said, "Yeah, sorry about that. I didn't think of my. . . status. I just acted."

"It's best to act deliberately here. The students are more than impulsive enough for everyone." Though Corman was criticizing, he had a smile on his face. He would go through the rest of the applicant interviews, but he thought that he would likely hire Brannon. Strange or not, the situation with Charlie showed that Brannon had great potential, and there was something markedly likable about him.

"I will be more mindful in the future."

It was another good response. Corman said, "Shall we look in on some classes in progress?"

"Let's."

# Chapter 1

"Jesus, Mr. Brannon, I don't even know why I'm here! I didn't do nothin' wrong!" Duane slumped back into his chair and groaned at my staggering stupidity as only a fifteen-year-old could.

He was a good-looking boy but prone to either smirking or scowling. Both looks were chock full of condescension. But now, he was sulking. His seated posture was closed, his arms firmly crossed, and his chin tucked to his chest. He was mostly still except that his long blonde hair repeatedly fell into his eyes, and he repeatedly twitched his head to swing the hair away.

I took a moment to psychologically unclench and reset. I had to do that every time he spoke, it seemed. After thirty years at the Mannaz School, I would have thought this would be easier. I knew what I was doing. . . mostly. Well, a lot of the time I did. I found that student rationalizations for bad behavior were really just variations on a few themes. Countless similar interactions unspooled in my memory as I searched for some finesse points which might work with Duane. He'd been pretty resistant for over two years now.

Even when my mental script was in place, I remained silent. Silence usually worked in my favor. In most cases, kids who had done wrong knew that they had done wrong, and that knowledge undermined them, ate away at their confidence. This was the "stew phase." I was waiting for the undermining-confidence part, but Duane's pigheadedness was adamantine. So far, at least.

I decided to go with a compliment. A little respect could go a long way.

"You're not dumb, so I won't treat you that way, alright?" I said.

Duane's chin jutted, and his eyes narrowed. "There's nothin' wrong with sayin' evolution."

"In and of itself, no," I said. "Well, now that I think of it, speaking out of turn probably disrupted the class. Unless, of course, you were discussing evolution in math class."

"There's nothin' wrong with sayin' evolution," he said stubbornly and twitched his head. The longer his stubbornness persisted the younger he seemed.

I thought of this particular game we were playing as "find the loophole." Basically, the student does something he knows is wrong, but he rationalizes it according to some technicality. Compassion and the good of the community don't come into the thinking. It was a game that made school life difficult.

"Saying evolution upsets Marty," I said quietly.

Duane leaned forward, chin first, flicked his hair, and said, "That's unreasonable."

"Maybe so, but that's not what we're talking about."

The wall clock ticked for a half minute and Duane twitched his head several times. His hair swung back and forth like a pendulum every time he did it. I wondered how he would look with a barrette, but I kept that thought to myself.

Then, Duane practically threw himself against the seat back. "Just because he's some holy roller who doesn't believe in science, doesn't mean I can't say evolution!" He crossed his arms tightly over his chest again, and his lower lip trembled. "It's my First Amendment right."

The corners of my mouth twitched. It was the old First Amendment chestnut. I said, "You realize that all speech is not protected by the First Amendment."

The boy hunched his shoulders and tucked his chin again. He probably wasn't listening, but there was no reason not to try for a little longer. "For example, you're not allowed to threaten people."

"I didn't threaten him!"

"You're not allowed to incite people to riot."

"I didn't incite a riot!"

"Why did you need to say evolution in math class?" I waited patiently for the answer, but I didn't expect one, not a legitimate one anyway. What the hell. I could always dream. When it was clear that he wasn't going to answer, I continued. "Ms. Hart stated that you said evolution repeatedly throughout the class before Marty stormed out."

"There's nothin' wrong with saying evolution."

I leaned in to give him the full force of my eyes. They can be pretty unnerving. I wasn't proud of the satisfaction I felt when he flinched, but the satisfaction was there nonetheless. I knew that a pissing contest with a fifteen-year-old kid was pointless. Even though I had that in mind, a little tension had creeped into my voice when I spoke. "Did you know that Marty would react badly to hearing the word evolution?"

"It's stupid," he muttered. "Marty's stupid."

"Did you know that Marty would react badly to hearing the word evolution. . . repeatedly?"

Duane flicked the hair out of his eyes. If the frequency picked up any more, he would look like he had Parkinson's. "How the hell am I supposed to know what that psycho preacher is going to do?"

Two blue memo slips sat on the corner of my desk. I picked them up and looked over them for a moment. "Mr. Samson reported an altercation between you and Marty yesterday in science class. During a discussion about evolution, you called Marty a 'backward Bible-thumping fuck.'" Profanity rarely shocks kids, and Duane was clearly not shocked or embarrassed by what he had said. I waited for him to respond. When he didn't, I continued. "Marty cried and ran out of the room then too. Sounds a like the beginning of a pattern to me. We need at least three occurrences, right?"

Duane said nothing.

I put one of the slips down. The other I held between my index and middle fingers. "Mr. Brown reports that you said evolution repeatedly in the dorm last night. Ms. Willis took Marty to an impromptu music lesson, so he didn't have to be in the dorm with you. That was nice of her to use her own time to help defuse a hostile situation."

Duane smiled unpleasantly. "I had to ask for extra help on my science homework. . . on evolution."

I resisted calling him a liar. Name calling never helps, even if it's accurate. I said, "There wasn't any science homework last night because Mr. Samson was unable to get through his lesson." I accepted that I was probably wasting my time, but I wanted to finish my play just in case. I tended to indulge hope.

Sometimes students responded well when they were given a voice in problem solving, so I asked, "How can we fix this problem?"

"Make the freak stop spazzing whenever he hears evolution!"

I had to clamp down on my immediate response like a beartrap. I felt proud of myself. Less so when I heard the tone of my own voice. It was pretty tight. "If I can't make you stop saying evolution for the sole purpose of upsetting Marty, I doubt that I can make Marty stop getting upset when he hears you say evolution for the sole purpose of upsetting him."

Duane was still. Even his hair stopped moving.

I took a moment too and tried to breathe out some of my tension in a slow exhale. "Whether Marty's reaction is reasonable or not, you know it's going to happen. You are acting with intent. Your schoolmates, teachers, and dorm parents are all collateral damage in your pointless campaign against Marty. Everyone suffers, not just Marty."

Duane's jaw muscles bunched. He spoke each word deliberately. "There. Is. Nothing. Wrong. With. Saying. Evolution."

My shoulders slumped. I had no words left. I would need Moe.

If you're a mundane human, which I'm guessing you are, this is where the story gets weird. To start, Moe needs some explanation. I guess I do too, but Moe is mostly what makes me special. Understanding him will go a long way toward understanding me.

Okay. . . Moe is my familiar. His actual nature is debatable. There are two schools of thought among the Talamaur. That's what I am. Well, specifically, I am a Talamaur-Moroi, a European variety of my race. I only look human. Anyway, one of the schools believes that familiars are symbiotic entities attached to us from birth. They act as servants of sorts. The other school believes that we simply project an invisible, mostly intangible aspect of ourselves, sort of an astral projection.

I lean toward the entity belief. It gives me someone to talk to when I'm lonely. In either case, the entity or the projected aspect of ourselves is referred to as a familiar. To my knowledge, no Talamaur has ever named his or her familiar, though. I didn't name mine until

1933 when I first saw a Three Stooges short. I figured, if the familiar wasn't me, he should have his own name.

Moe is handy for innumerable reasons, but he goes way beyond being handy. I would starve without him. I need regular food like humans need food, but I also need more. Moe helps with that. I had a tough time visualizing what he did until juice boxes came out. The metaphor isn't exactly right, but it's as close as I can come. Anyway, Moe is the pointy straw, and people are the boxes. Figurative language only goes so far, though. A person, especially a young one, will regenerate life force, and a juice box only has so much juice. Also, people will reseal in a fairly short time. Juice boxes just stay punctured.

I wasn't going to spear Duane with Moe though that was an attractive thought at the moment. When I first came to the Mannaz School, I learned that my familiar could be much more versatile than a pointy straw, and that the school enrolled a relatively large number of very rare kids. Most of the students are sealed juice boxes like everyone else, but many of the more extreme cases get so overwrought or angry or stubborn that they rupture their seals and leak life force. It just floats around them like their own personal storm clouds. All I have to do is have Moe mop it up like a, well a mop, before it eventually dissipates.

A normal Talamaur feeding is invasive and unpleasant to victims. Yeah, they're victims. There's no denying it. They don't understand what they're feeling when it happens to them, but it's not good. Symptoms vary, but they are usually things like stomach cramps, headache, and fatigue. Taking life force isn't necessarily fatal to humans, but it's always dangerous. Take too much and there's not enough to regenerate. Something about the process can also make people more susceptible to sickness and disease. Diminished lifeforce equals weakened immunity, I guess. There's no way to tell how much is too much either. A fragile-looking granny might bounce back without a hitch, and a burly lumberjack might waste away after just a sip.

My kind usually don't worry much about it. Emptying the whole box is not a general practice, but it can happen. There's no way to trace the death to the Talamaur, so the possibility of being caught isn't a deterrent. *Hey that guy across from me on the bus just collapsed for no*

17

*reason! I was just minding my own business. Must have been a bad ticker.*

If we don't get greedy, the victim might feel a little out-of-sorts for a while then be fine later. The other possibility is that the victim might go home and die in his sleep of unknown causes or develop pneumonia and die. That kind of thing. I spent my life before coming to the Mannaz School being as careful as I could. Except when I wasn't, but those people had it coming. Rationalization is another one of my powers. But now, I don't have to worry about it. Moe just acts like a sponge or the saucer under a teacup, and we use what would normally go to waste. It's pretty green of me, right?

My relationship with the Mannaz School turned out to be symbiotic. I got to eat for free, and there was a beneficial side effect on the leaky-seam students and, by extension, the whole community. Clearing away the spilled energy of a kid who's throwing a tantrum or being a stubborn ass seems to remove a, sort of, metaphysical blanket of strain. It's like he can breathe and see more clearly with it gone. That lessens stress and the pressure on the seams. Over time, many of the leaky kids can become regular juice boxes.

Everyone benefited. In the early years at least.

The last three decades had done wonders for my conscience, no need to rationalize endangering the lives of innocents, but the smorgasbord was over after about fifteen years. I originally came for the free food. Now, I stayed because I'd found a purpose or something. It certainly wasn't for the money or prestige. No, now it was borderline starvation and abuse from bad-tempered children for me.

I watched Duane flip his hair a few times and then brought my fingertips up to the wrinkles at the corners of my eyes. I was proud of them, but I liked the white in my hair best. It was mostly at my temples, so I had this red-haired Reed Richards/Doctor Strange thing going on. I'd have to be careful now, or I'd mess up my work.

Moe moved invisibly across the desk. Duane's defiance surrounded him like a dense fog, insulating him from everyone. So much lifeforce went into his pointless insubordination that I wondered that normal biological functions were able to continue. He probably wouldn't back down from this confrontation if there were a gun to his head.

Moe absorbed energy until he was saturated. He couldn't hold much because he was intended to be a conduit, not a vessel. You know, like a straw. The little bit of excess crossed the short distance to me, and I had to suppress a shudder of pleasure. Moe then zipped outside and dumped the energy which dissipated quickly. I felt a sense of waste. This sort of thing did little more than whet my appetite, but it had been standard procedure for a lot of years now.

After two more trips outside to dump energy, Duane's arms, which had been crossed over his chest like a vice, loosened and dropped to his sides. He took a deep breath and visibly relaxed. He blinked slowly a few times and seemed slightly dazed as though he'd dozed off in the middle of the day and was trying to reorient himself.

As though nothing metaphysical had just happened, I said, "You can be an asset or a liability to the community. I don't want to argue with you about rules. I would like you to help your teachers and your classmates to be successful."

He nodded. Clearing away the fog of spilled lifeforce around him had enabled him to hear me in a way he couldn't before. Communication was possible, not just confrontation. I knew that he was more suggestable at this stage, and I decided to press my advantage.

"I can't make you do anything," I said. "I'm asking for you to help."

Duane looked like he was considering the words, not just waiting to counter them. He was still oppositional by nature, but that aspect of his personality wasn't being supercharged at the moment. He nodded again, and I happily accepted that small victory.

"What class do you have now?" I asked him.

Duane looked at the quietly ticking clock, squinted as he drew the memory, and said, "I'll have history in five minutes."

"Why don't you take a few minutes to get a drink of water or use the bathroom. Go to class. Be an asset." I knew that Marty was in a different history class, so I didn't fear immediate problems. I would send Moe to check up on both of them later in the day.

Duane didn't look dazed anymore, but his posture and carriage were much more open and easy when he left the room.

I withdrew my smartphone from the top drawer of my desk. I flipped the image on the camera, so I could see myself. Nothing looked markedly different to me, but I snapped a picture for comparison anyway. I opened the gallery app and put the picture in my selfie album. Anyone who saw it would think I was the vainest guy in the world. I flipped back and forth between the one I'd just taken and the second-most-recent one. Feeding was a balancing act these days. I decided that I didn't look any younger. Each time Moe had absorbed lifeforce from around Duane, I'd gotten a little taste, just like when you fill up a straw by sucking on it. I now really felt that special kind of hungry, and I wondered again why I was doing this. I was going to need to spend some time with less-douchey students to remind myself. I did like most of them. With some, I had to pretend.

I knew that my life at the Mannaz School couldn't go on forever, and I asked myself how much longer it should go on. Fifteen years was an awfully long time to be on a starvation diet. If other Talamaur knew what I was doing, they'd think I was crazy, and they'd probably be right. As far as I knew, it'd never been done before, but who in his right mind would get old on purpose?

There was a knock on my door. I said, "Yeah?"

The door opened to reveal Conrad Novak. His shoulders and chest were still as heavy with muscle as when I'd first met him, but a round, hard belly strained equally at the material of his shirt. His hair and the beard he now wore were shot through with gray, and wrinkles cut lines around his eyes and mouth. He'd gotten old too but probably not intentionally.

"Lore?" he asked.

I felt a tiny bit of joy leap in my chest. Lore was the greatest place on earth. I said, "I have creative writing last period, but I'll meet you right after."

He said, "Learn 'em to write good," and walked back out of the door.

20

My teaching space in Oak House was something midway between an office and a classroom. My desk was a big black metal thing with a pressboard top. The woodgrain veneer was peeling in places. Six one-piece student desks were wedged into a fairly small space, and the closet at the back of the room held school supplies and textbooks. I tried to give the place some character and hopefully inspire some conversations with my students by hanging posters which I changed every couple of months. The current selections were a *Highlander* movie poster and a blowup of Django Reinhart playing one of his Selmer-Maccaferri guitars.

I was no longer an English teacher. My current position was a little hard to categorize. I did some administrative work, but mostly I was a resource for students. Even with my restricted diet, I was good at dealing with especially problematic kids. My room was a safe place for them. I helped them with school work. I gave teachers a break when they needed it and helped to mend fences later on. I also taught occasional "elective classes" when the schedule needed padding. Some kids signed up for them because they wanted to take them, but the classes tended to be catchalls for students who might be too disruptive elsewhere.

My current creative writing class consisted to three boys and a girl, ranging from grades seven through nine. With one exception, none of them liked writing or were particularly talented, so the project objectives were modest. Today, they were inventing their own comic book characters. Comic books were not just for nerds any more. Even Karen, the ninth-grade girl in class, liked the new Marvel movies. Guys like Chris Hemsworth and Chris Evans probably had something to do with it, but converts are converts.

I had my back to the students as I wrote on the chalkboard. That's a risky proposition for a typical teacher, but I had Moe. He hovered like a helium balloon near the ceiling at the back of the room. Karen had asked a good question about subject and verb agreement, and I wanted to share the explanation with the whole class. I didn't think that everyone would pay attention, but a little validation for Karen was warranted.

Brett and Andy were a couple of boneheads who always sat in the back as though it made a difference in such a small room. They weren't paying attention. Brett had written a note which he was sharing with Andy. Moe investigated. The note read, "Karen, you got little tits!" Grinning like an ape, Brett folded up the note and tried to toss it onto Karen's desk.

Moe's ability to influence the physical world was limited. He could carry about two pounds worth of anything, knock over lamps, slide books across a table, and that sort of thing. Skimming the note from Karen's desk as though it had taken a bad bounce was easy for him. He even managed to get the note to skitter underneath my desk.

Annoyed at the distraction, Karen turned to glare at Brett. He paled, his eyes flicking to the dark space beneath my big black desk.

I'd been experiencing the world through Moe for over a hundred years, and processing information from him and my mundane senses simultaneously is no problem. It never was. It's not like watching two TVs. It's more like looking and listening at the same time. Or smelling and touching. I get a lot of data from him, but it's not as though he has his own eyes and ears. It's different than what I get from my human senses, but I guess I do sort of think about what he shows me terms of sight, sound, and smell.

Not all lessons are academic, and I thought I saw a good opportunity to instruct Brett. Moe could sense the anxiety rising in him. By that, I mean that Moe could observe increased heartbeat, sweaty palms, and that sort of thing. See, he's really handy. I couldn't help but to smile.

When I said, "Brett," the boy flinched like I'd jabbed at him.

"What?" he said in a tight voice. His eyes jittered between me and the space under my desk.

"Do you understand subject/verb agreement when using collective nouns?" I asked.

"Yeah," Brett answered. "Yeah, you explained it good."

Karen turned around and said, "Well."

Brett looked confused and a little like he might bolt. "Well what? I didn't do nothin'!"

She said, "Anything."

22

Karen could be a little snotty, but I liked her.

Brett looked at Andy and me and Todd, the fourth student in the class, for aid. When no one said anything, he turned back to Karen and said, "What?"

Apparently, she thought him a lost cause because she shook her head and turned her back on him.

The students spent the rest of the period with their planning notes. I knew that it wasn't high-literature, but I enjoyed helping the kids come up with origin stories and super powers. It was a pretty popular assignment, and with the exception of Brett, the students were engaged with their work. Brett kept looking at the space under the desk and even tried the "dropped my pencil" routine twice trying to retrieve the note. He was unsuccessful because Moe had already put the note in my pocket.

When I wasn't thinking about comic book heroes, my mind drifted to the Green Man IPA or the Old Shuck Schwarzbier I would be drinking at the Lore Brewpub after class. It was a happy place. If heaven existed, I hoped it would be like Lore.

# Chapter 2

Less than ten minutes after I dismissed the creative writing students, Novak was at my door. His smile was broad. "Do you mind if Allie comes along?"

"Have I ever minded Allie's company?"

He pulled his Buffalo Bills cap so low on his forehead that his eyebrows disappeared. His massive shoulders rose and fell in a shrug, and he said, "I was just asking to be polite. She's probably already waiting in the parking lot."

Alejandra Park was a twenty-eight-year-old English teacher at the Mannaz School who, for some unfathomable reason, liked the company of a couple of old guys more than the other faculty who were closer to her own age. She was smart and fun and more than a little quirky. I'll play the shallow card here too: she was gorgeous.

Her own good looks didn't seem to impress her much, which was a rare quality in someone who looked the way she did. She was like Salma Hayek and Lucy Liu rolled into one. Well, Allie was half Korean, not Chinese, but my point is that she won the genetic lottery as far as exotic features go. Yeah, it's pretty obvious. I was smitten.

She was great company in any case, but her presence on a visit to the pub was doubly beneficial. Although she liked beer, she didn't drink more than one or two on an outing. Whenever she went along, she was the designated driver. For appearance's sake at least, being a teacher with a DD was a must.

It was too warm for my old bomber jacket, but I loved to wear it, battered and scuffed as it was. After I shrugged into it, I said to Novak, "It's important to remember that even though neither of us is driving, we can still drink in moderation."

"What? I don't understand what you're saying. Sometimes you talk crazy." He smiled again. "Don't worry. Allie and Coop will have good judgment for me."

"What about me?" I asked.

"Ha, you're funny." He punched me lightly on the shoulder. "Come on, Mr. Comedian, let's go."

He walked off. I said to his back, "I have good judgment."

He didn't turn around but said, "Ha, see what I mean? Funny."

I followed.

On the way, we saw Brett walking toward the square, which often doubled as an athletic field. I said, "Watch this," and called out, "Hey, Brett!"

He jumped and executed a move that was something like a sloppy pirouette. He looked around, eyes wide. When he saw me, he said, "What. . . uhm. . . what?"

Although he didn't say, "I didn't do nothin'," it was clearly on the tip of his tongue.

I said, "Have fun playing soccer."

"Uhm, yeah. . . yeah, see ya," he stammered and hurried away.

"What was that?" Novak asked.

"He wrote a douchey note that didn't reach its intended recipient but ended up under my desk. I thought it better to let him stew instead of call him on it. Since he couldn't find it, he figures that I will eventually. He's waiting for the other shoe to drop."

"You are a devious and heartless man."

"Thank you, sir."

Allie waited next to her little blue Hyundai. Even though it was mid-October, she wore denim shorts. Her legs were muscular, maybe a little thick in the thighs, but absolutely feminine. I had asked her once if she'd ever played field hockey. She'd said she hadn't, but she had that look. She wore a purple and gold Alfred Saxons sweatshirt in deference to the weather. Her glossy, black hair lay loose across her shoulders, and her coffee-and-cream skin caught some golden tints from the fading afternoon sunshine. Yeah, my thoughts tended to get a little poetic about her.

I knew I should feel like a dirty old man what with the hundred-year age difference and all, but the point was really moot. I would still be robbing the cradle if I looked for dates at a retirement home.

When I passed my old Nova, I patted her fender lovingly. I would need to put her into storage soon. I had no doubt that a single New York winter would turn her into a 1966 pile of rust. She wasn't a showpiece, but she was in awfully good condition for a vehicle which had been in regular use for over fifty years.

"That thing kills the environment, you know," said Allie when we reached her.

"That thing is art," I returned. "I barely drive her anyway." My year-round car was a red 1991 Subaru Loyale. What can I say? I like to preserve things. The Subaru wasn't a pile of rust either. That's because it was mostly Bondo, and few of the body parts were actually original.

Allie said, "Why do guys refer to their cars as girls?"

I shrugged.

Novak said, "Boats, too."

"Huh," I said. "I just realized now that the Nova is a her, and the Subaru is an it."

"Why?" Allie said.

I shrugged again.

She blew out a breath and shook her head.

To Novak she said, "Christie will kill me if I bring you home as banged up as you were last time." Christie was Novak's tall, slender, blonde wife. The two of them were a study in physical opposites. They were well-matched in all other ways, though, except that Christie didn't drink. She didn't see the point. Novak loved her anyway.

"I wasn't that bad," he said.

Allie looked at him, her eyes narrowed.

"Okay, I will show restraint even though you are driving." He held up three fingers in a boy scout salute and then crossed his heart. "I still don't think I was that bad."

Allie smiled. "No, you just got a little loud and talked to my boobs all night."

Novak ducked his head in a small bow of acknowledgement. "Okay, that is probably an accurate observation."

"Let's go," I said. "That beer's not going to drink itself."

The drive to Lore was a little over three miles mostly along Route 19A. The country was beautiful. Fields opened out on either side of the road for much of the short trip, but in several places the trees

26

came out all the way to the road. The autumn had been fairly mild, so many of the red, orange, and yellow leaves still clung to them.

In only a few minutes, Allie's little blue car pulled into the brewpub's gravel parking lot. The low brick building rested easy with its back to the forest. There was a deck where patrons could drink and eat and watch the deer which regularly came out of the trees to watch the humans. The building was plainly visible from Route 19A, but the sign was small and well back from the road. It was a word-of-mouth kind of a place.

The brewpub's success was surprising to me because most of the locals from Geary and surrounding areas preferred mass-produced domestic pilsner, loud cover bands, and weekend brawls. Lore's clientele clearly wanted something else and were fiercely loyal. Seven or eight of the dozen taps were dedicated to Lore beers, and the others carried guest craft brews and at least one cider. If you wanted Bud or Coors or Michelob, you had to go elsewhere. The kitchen produced simple bar food, but it was locally sourced, and the cooks knew what they were doing. There was no jukebox, no TV, no pool tables, and no pitchers.

The main entertainments were conversation and beer, but there were a few acoustic groups who played on weekends. The Genesee Three played blues and jazz selections. The Bards played Celtic and folk. And the Jake Wolfe Group played unplugged versions of '50s and '60s rock songs. I had been known to sit in occasionally with the Genesee Three. I didn't want to commit to a group, but I did enjoy playing out sometimes.

When we entered the pub, Jeannie, the bartender, called out to us. "Hey, guys!"

There were only a few other patrons, but the place would fill up as suppertime neared. The only person sitting at the bar was Vernon, an old guy who always seemed to have a book at hand, most often a Louis L'Amour or Zane Grey novel. He was short and slight and mostly bald. The hair he had was white, but a few red-gold strands still hung on here and there. He wore old black-framed glasses and was partial to dark-blue slacks and khaki work shirts. He looked up from *Silver Canyon* and nodded to us as we neared.

Jeannie distributed coasters. As we were settling into our spots, she said, "I'm supposed to yell downstairs before you order."

She went to a green door to the right of the bar, opened it, and called down into the basement, "Coop, the teachers are here."

She was an attractive woman just into her forties. Her hair was somewhere between blonde and brown, and she changed styles regularly. Today, she had a Mary Tyler Moore style going. Combined with her little square glasses, it made her look like a hot '60s librarian. She wore a white button-down and blue skirt which showed off well-formed calves.

She came back to her place behind the bar. "He's got something new that he wants you to try." She turned to look at the beer board, which was a big blackboard not unlike the one in my classroom. "Red Cap Copper and whatever he just hooked up need to be added."

"Nice," I said. "Red Cap is awesome."

"Oh, and the Pixie Party Pilsner is out," she added.

"Summer's over," I said.

I loved a good beer. Prohibition had killed most of the character and variety for decades after repeal. Pilsners were pretty much it back then. Thank God for the craft beer revolution. It made this the best time in my life to be a beer drinker.

Footsteps thumped up the stairs from the basement, and Brian Cooper came out of the green door. He was a massive man. He stood 6'4" and his double extra-large Flogging Molly concert shirt could barely contain him. He had the same combination of muscle and beer belly that Novak had, but he was nearly a foot taller. Coop's head was shaved, but his dark beard was full and grew down to the top of his round belly.

"Hey, guys. I've got something for you." He maneuvered behind Jeannie, so he could get to the taps. He placed a plastic bucket beneath one of the taps and let it spit and sputter until first foam then dark beer flowed. He filled three whiskey tumblers halfway and placed them in front of Allie, Novak, and me. "I want you to tell me what you think?"

We all sipped, and Coop stood and watched us with his "proud papa" expression. I knew not to make a judgment after the first taste, and I had been trying to teach Allie and Novak to appreciate the subtleties of their beer. Results of my instruction were mixed. Allie was coming along. Novak would probably be just as happy to drink Genesee, but he was trying to stretch.

Surprisingly, after our second and third sips, Novak spoke first. "The flavors come, kind of, one after the other."

Coop nodded.

Allie said, "Yeah, at first I just noticed the malt. It's kind of sweet, but it's roasty, almost smoky too."

Coop smiled broadly. I did too because I was proud of my students.

I added, "It's got a pretty bitter hop finish, earthy or piney hops. Northern Brewer?"

Coop shot me with a finger-gun and said, "And Liberty." Spreading his hands, he asked, "So does it work?"

We all indicated approval, but I guessed that Novak would have a Pooka Pale Ale. He wasn't terribly adventurous. He found a beer he liked and generally stayed with it.

"What do we call this malty, roasty, hoppy nectar?" I asked. Coop's beers were all named after people or creatures from folklore and fairytales, and it was interesting to hear his naming process.

Coop leaned on the bar. "Have you guys heard of Brownies, the helpful house fairies?" he asked.

We all nodded.

"Do you know what happens to a sweet, kind, helpful brownie if someone pisses it off?"

"The brownie turns into a boggart," I said. After a moment's thought, I added, "That's pretty brilliant, Coop."

"A boggart, like in Harry Potter?" Allie asked.

Coop made a seesaw gesture. "It's more like a prankster. It's as harmful as the brownie is helpful. It's like a bipolar fairy. So, the brown ale starts out sweet and ends up bitter."

"So, the name is?" asked Allie.

"Boggart Brown!" Coop made a dramatic bow and gesture like a stage magician.

Allie said to Jeannie, "I'll have one."

29

Coop said, "The ABV is seven four." He said to Jeannie, "Be sure to write that in the red or orange chalk."

Allie considered for a moment, eyes narrowed prettily. She held up one finger. "I'll have one, just one."

I started with the Red Cap. It's my favorite of Coop's beers, but I hate the real things. Red caps, I mean. Of course, there are more kinds of supernatural things in the world than just Talamaur. Faeries among them. They can be pretty damn scary, and red caps are some of the scariest. They live to inflict pain and fear. A red cap midst torture, murder, and mayhem is a happy red cap. What a bunch of pricks. Oh well, most of the faeries went back to Faerie anyway. Glamours don't fool cameras, and cameras are everywhere nowadays. Unless their true forms look human, there's not much use in trying to blend.

I pulled my thoughts away from my other life. Sometimes memories and musings came on all of a sudden. It's not as though I forgot who I used to be or what I used to do. Normally, those things were just pushed to the back of my mind. Living as a human made me feel human, I guess. I had friends and a job that felt significant most of the time. I was helping people in my small way, and most importantly, I wasn't hurting anyone. It was a good, simple life. I knew it couldn't last, but I would enjoy it while I could.

Lore patrons generally knew each other. There was a pretty wide range of characters, but they were all willing to pay premium prices for quality beer and food. In Geary, New York, that made them a select group. There were two more-typical Western New York bars right in town. One was called The Bar. Catchy, right? The other was called Silver Creek, but the locals just called it The Crick. If there was a sporting event that Novak wanted to watch while drinking, he would sometimes insist that we go to one of them, probably The Bar.

Many of the men who frequented Lore liked to flirt with Jeannie. It was harmless fun, and I'd never seen anyone take it too far. She would tell them if they did, and Coop would give them the boot, probably forever.

I was enjoying the view as Jeannie stood on a chair which she'd dragged behind the bar so that she could remove Pixie Party Pilsner and add Red Cap and Boggart Brown to the beer board. She looked over her shoulder and said, "Don't tell OSHA about the chair." She saw me looking at her legs and cleared her throat. I lifted my eyes to her face, eyebrows raised.

"Yes?" I asked. I knew what she was getting at, but it was fun to play dumb. With Moe around, there was no reason for me to get caught checking out a girl. Sometimes I could be careless, though, and sometimes I got caught on purpose. It was part of my flirting technique.

She continued to look at me.

I pretended to just then get her point and said, "It's just science."

"Science?"

"Eyes tend to follow movement, and you're moving around all in front of me."

She wiggled the fingers of her free hand, and I looked at them intensely like some kind of spaniel pointing at water fowl. She laughed and turned back to her writing.

I added, "I am also a healthy heterosexual male, and it's natural that I would be interested in well-turned female legs."

Jeannie faced me, hands on her hips, the pose lifting her breasts against the material of her blouse. The orange chalk in her hand left a streak on her dark skirt, but she didn't seem to notice. She said, "I knew it. Your science talk was just a ruse."

Allie leaned nearer, affecting a conspiratorial stage whisper, and said, "He was looking at my legs before we left school, and Con's going to start talking at my boobs any minute now."

At hearing his name, Novak disengaged from a conversation with Vernon. He said, "Allie, everyone looks at your boobs. The beer just robs me of my subtlety, and you catch me at it."

Allie looked the question at me. I shrugged.

Vernon didn't say anything, but I could see him grinning as he studied the cover of his book. He clearly wasn't that old.

Allie said to Jeannie, "I would think that these guys would be mature enough to have their hormones under control by now."

31

"It's not just hormones," I said. "When I go to a museum, I look at the art. Right? I sometimes watch the sunset, but I'm not going to try to have sex with it."

Novak snorted a laugh. "It's just hormones with me. No sex with sunsets, though."

Jeannie groaned good-naturedly and turned back to her work. As she wrote, she said in a lilting voice, "I'm like art in a museum." She stood on her toes even though it was unnecessary, and her calves rounded nicely. She turned dramatically when she was finished writing and struck a pose, one leg out slightly, toes pointed downward. She overbalanced, though, and began to teeter.

Moe crossed the intervening distance in an instant and steadied her until she could regain her balance. It was as instinctive for us as reaching out a hand. Moe couldn't do much to help, but Jeannie didn't need much. Once she stopped wobbling, she said, "Shit, I really thought I was going over just then."

"OSHA would fine you for standing on the chair," said Novak.

"Perhaps the wisdom of OSHA is greater than I suspected," Jeannie said as she climbed down and carried the chair back around the bar.

We stayed for four pints and dinner. Well, Novak and I had four pints each. Allie, true to her word, just had the one brown ale. The little stresses of the day melted away as we enjoyed each other's company and our food and drink. Jeannie and Coop talked to us when they weren't occupied, and we exchanged greetings with the regulars who came and went. It was what a pub ought to be. Our conversations followed a meandering path which covered beer, of course, DC versus Marvel comics, renewable energy, progressive rock, and the Celtic calendar. Though we had never made a specific agreement, we usually didn't talk about work when we were at Lore. It was an escape for us.

When it was time to go, I felt a sense of well-being but no real buzz. One of the side effects of my aging experiment was that my alcohol tolerance had dropped a bit, but it was still pretty damn high. When I had been operating at my prime, my metabolism burned up the booze at a really accelerated rate. Back then, getting drunk required some fairly serious intent. It was a little easier to catch a buzz now that I had aged my body to fifty-something, but four pints sure wouldn't do it.

Even if I got drunk, though, even seriously drunk, I could still pass a field sobriety test. Moe's perceptions were absolutely unaffected by alcohol or drugs or toxins. If I passed out, he couldn't operate me like a marionette or anything. What we could do was switch entirely from my mundane senses to his. Camera one to camera two. Even if my eyes were seeing double, Moe saw true. My reflexes and balance as good as ever. Information pathways were rerouted around the muddled bits somehow. I sort of had a designated driver for my body. See how handy Moe is. But I still liked having Allie drive anyway.

It was pretty dark on the drive back to the Mannaz School. Sunset comes early in October. We followed the little cones of light. Allie sat straight and alert, hands at ten and two. She'd nearly hit a deer the year before, and it made her cautious. For the first mile, there was only the sound of the heater and our breathing.

Then, Novak leaned forward from the backseat so that his head was between Allie's and mine. He smelled like beer and bacon cheeseburger. He said, "You guys hear that we have two more darlings showing up this weekend?"

"What grades?" Allie asked.

"Both seventh," said Novak.

"Dammit!" she hissed. "Things were just beginning to calm down."

I smiled even though no one could see it. Novak was too far back and Allie wouldn't take her eyes from the road. I felt no need to comment, but it was a common understanding that when students arrived late to our school, it was because their other options hadn't worked out. Yeah, I mean expulsion. Being kicked out only six weeks into the school year was pretty quick work, but if other schools didn't want them, the Mannaz School would probably give it a shot. With a school as small as ours, it was amazing how much individual students could influence the tone of the community. Each new arrival was met with a certain anticipation which was not necessarily good or bad, but it was significant.

We were silent for the rest of the trip, probably all thinking about how our plans would need to be altered for Monday. Even when teachers aren't teaching, they seem to spend an awful lot of time thinking about teaching.

Back at the school, Novak and I congratulated each other on our restraint. Allie rolled her eyes and said she'd make a chart and give us both gold stars. I learned not to assume that she was joking about things like that. I figured that there was a better than average chance that I would find the chart on my desk come Monday.

Novak and Christie lived in a little cottage which was about a five-minute walk from the main campus. It was a perk. Thirty-five years of faithful service and all that. I was single and needed no cottage. From the parking lot, Novak went his way, and Allie and I walked toward Birch House, the building which contained both of our apartments.

At the place where our paths should have diverged, Allie took my arm and said, "Invite me in for a drink."

It wasn't yet seven o'clock, but it was full dark. The area lights on the surrounding buildings washed out the lovely, warm tone of her skin and cast dark shadows over her eyes. Light or its absence was no hindrance to Moe's perceptions, though. I could see in her expression that something was up. She often came to my place to hang out. We were pretty casual about it. The request for an invitation seemed forced, artificial.

"Sure," I said. "Come on in."

I'd graduated from a studio to a one-bedroom apartment, but there still wasn't very much to it. The kitchen and living room were the same room. The only thing that indicated where one ended and the other began was the carpet. The walls were off-white, the carpet was beige, and the linoleum was a beige and white checkerboard. The curtains were beige too. I guess that was the theme.

There was only enough room for one print on the walls, something that I found in a bookstore in Buffalo called *Across the Poppy Field*. In it, a dark-haired woman in a sunhat and dress walked down a flower-dappled hillside. I don't know what was special about it, but I sure liked it. The rest of the wall space was covered by

34

bookshelves which contained mostly used paperbacks. One held cartons of DVDs. The cases took too much space, so I'd discarded them in favor of little paper sleeves. My movie collection was vast. I still hadn't quite gotten comfortable with streaming video. I watched them but never depended upon them. I wanted something physical to own if it was a movie I liked.

In the corner next to my hideous green couch sat my pride and joy, the only thing I was more attached to than the Nova, my Gibson ES-175. Tobacco sunburst. 1959. I usually played it unplugged, but a little 40-watt Fender tube amp and my pedal board were in the same corner waiting to be fired up.

Allie pulled the Alfred sweatshirt over her head and kicked off her tennis shoes as soon as she walked through the door. The yellow t-shirt beneath the sweatshirt drew tightly across her full breasts as she lifted her arms. What a sight. Did I imagine that she held that pose a little longer than was really necessary? She tossed the sweatshirt onto a little blue Ikea chair in the living room and brushed the hair from her face.

The hair thing was pretty wonderful. She had the kind of straight, thick black hair that seemed to shimmer like satin. She pushed it back with both hands which caused her breasts to rise and push against the cloth of her shirt again. When she released it, the lustrous dark hair cascaded down and settled around her shoulders in a display worthy of a shampoo commercial. It fanned out like it was trained to move in formation.

"Are you doing that on purpose?" I asked.

She smiled and said, "Yes."

"Why?"

Her smile widened, turning her eyes into crescent moons, and she struck a Wonder Woman pose, fists on hips. Her breasts did their thing in her little yellow t-shirt again. She said, "It's my superpower."

"Yep," I said. "It is that. Mind control, I think."

Allie's figure was fairly generous in the bust, hips, and bottom, but not exceedingly so. Her waist was not exactly narrow or her tummy entirely flat, but the lines of her formed a subtle hourglass. She was soft lines over solid muscle, sturdy and entirely feminine. I knew, objectively, that she wasn't society's physical ideal, but I was hard-pressed to think of anyone whom I found more attractive.

To avoid staring, I turned to hang my jacket on the back of a kitchen chair and went to the cabinet where I kept my booze. There was normally beer in the fridge, but I needed to restock. Over my shoulder, I said, "I only have whiskey. You can have Maker's Mark bourbon or Tullamore Dew Irish."

"What do you have to mix with them?"

I turned with a bottle in each hand and said, "Uhm, ice, I guess. Water?"

"I'll have whatever you're having."

"I usually just pour it into a glass," I said. "But sometimes I drop in a couple of ice cubes."

"Sure, sounds good."

Allie dropped onto my ugly green couch. Anyone who sat on it seemed to become fond of it instantly. She sat sideways and stretched her legs out, crossing her ankles. Her leg muscles beneath the silky, dark skin moved smoothly as she pointed her toes downward. She was definitely doing that on purpose.

I poured some Tullamore Dew into a couple of rocks glasses and dropped ice cubes in each and brought them over. I gave one to her, and we clinked them together. I said, "Sláinte," and she repeated it. We sipped. She didn't make a face, so I gave her points for that.

She swung her feet back onto the floor, so there was plenty of room for me on the couch. She didn't pat the cushion next to her or anything, but her intention was clear. When I sat on the blue Ikea chair on the other side of the coffee table, she pursed her lips and narrowed her eyes. The expression made me think of a wet cat, feline and annoyed.

"Why are you sitting in the ten-minute-chair?" she asked. We called it the "ten-minute chair" because it was only comfortable for ten minutes at a time. It was usually where people threw their coats.

"You've got a funny look in your eye," I said.

"You're wrinkling my sweatshirt."

"Sweatshirts wrinkle?" I took it out from under me and draped it over the back of the chair.

She stared. "Are you going to sit over here or not?"

"What's going on?" I asked.

"We sit next to each other whenever we watch a movie and most other times too. This is the most comfortable place to sit in your whole apartment." She did pat the cushion next to her this time. Really, it was more like a whack, whack, whack—or else.

"My Spidey-Sense is tingling."

She stared at me. "Really?"

I sipped my drink and said nothing.

"Fine," she said and took a longer pull from her drink. She looked like she was going to put it down hard but restrained herself and lowered it with exaggerated care. She looked me right in the eyes again and said, "You like me, right? I haven't been misreading that."

"I like you quite a lot," I said.

"We've known each other for over a year now. We drink together. We go to movies. We hang out." She waited, giving me time to deny it or something.

Finally, I said, "Yeah."

"Do I need to come on to you?" she said. "Because I'm really not used to that."

I knew it was true. She'd spent her first few months at the Mannaz School gently refusing the attentions of the younger faculty men. She'd done it so artfully that it must have come from long practice.

"You probably shouldn't?"

"Shouldn't what?"

"Come onto me."

"Why?" She drew out the word in a tone that packed it with meaning. It felt like a trap.

"I'm kind of your boss."

"Are not," she said. "Con's my boss. And I guess Dr. Corman too because he's everyone's boss. You're your own thing." She thought for a moment. "Come to think of it, I don't think you're the boss of anyone."

I shrugged. "I'm a lot older than you."

"I've been legal for ten years. Anyway, I didn't say that I wanted us to get married and have your babies and live happily ever after. Hell, you're probably ten years from the nursing home." She smiled then, but it was a little tight.

"What do you want then?"

Her smile fell away, and a contemplative line appeared between her eyebrows. "I don't know. Right now, I want to punch you on the nose. But I really like spending time with you. You keep inviting me, so you must like spending time with me too."

"I really do."

She continued. "I can tell that your feelings for me aren't chaste. I see the way you look at me. You're not very subtle."

"Everyone looks at you like that," I said.

"What's that have to do with anything?"

"I guess I assumed you were used to it."

"Of course, I'm used to it." She gestured at her own bustline like she was revealing a magic trick. "I started growing these things when I was ten. Guys look. Mostly, I don't care. I ignore it." She leaned forward making sure that she had my attention. "But sometimes it's. . . really important to me."

I had no idea what to say, so I didn't say anything. That's usually safe.

She sighed and sat back against the couch cushions. "It seems like there's a natural progression that just isn't progressing, you know?" The corner of her mouth turned up a little and she said, "I've never spent this much time with a guy without him putting some kind of moves on me. You're making me feel insecure about my sex appeal."

I drank again to give myself time to think of something to say. I considered a funny comment about my advanced age but decided that she probably needed me to be straight.

"I just don't want us to do something that we'll regret later," I said.

"What would we have to regret?" she asked.

That was a question that I absolutely couldn't answer. There was a very clear line that I couldn't cross. I wasn't human. I was just playing at it. I was a supernatural predator, a silent killer. The freaking boogeyman.

I don't want to give the wrong impression. I'd had plenty of sex in my life, mostly with humans. Supernatural types are much rarer and much more dangerous. Sex was actually one of my favorite things in the whole world. I'd been at my sexual peak pretty much through the entire twentieth century. Lots of fun.

I did have rules about sex which basically boiled down to being a decent person, but I had mostly had sex of the casual variety. Longtime relationships with humans were problematic, what with not aging and all, though my aging experiment opened up some new possibilities, I supposed. But not with Allie. She'd met me when I was already pretending to be older.

I think I cared for Allie too much to be casual about it. What if we fell in love? It's not like I could tell her the truth about myself. That could get both of us killed.

She was watching me like she could see the cogs turning in my head. Apparently, I took too long to answer her question because she downed the rest of her drink in a gulp and put the glass back down on the coffee table. She did make a little face that time.

She stood and said, "Well, I guess I've embarrassed myself enough for one night."

I put down my own glass and blocked her way when she moved to retrieve her sweatshirt. I'm not sure what I expected to happen. I just didn't want her to leave. Not like that. I hated to see her upset and know it was my fault.

She looked up at me, her soft brown eyes unsure. I'd never seen that insecurity before, and I didn't like it. She was a sassy world-beater, not timid, not uncertain. Damn it.

We were standing close. I could smell apples in her hair and whiskey on her breath. It was then that I noticed that her breathing had quickened. I put my hands on her bare arms. They were soft and warm, good muscle beneath. I thought, for a moment, that she was going to pull free, but she didn't. Her eyes dropped, focused on my chest. She just stood quietly, clearly waiting for me to do or say something.

I gave it a go. "I'm old and cautious. I do like you. You are beautiful and sexy as hell."

She didn't say anything, but she worked her lips like women do after they put on lipstick and want to even the color. I realized that I was staring at her mouth.

I said, "Getting involved with a coworker, a much younger coworker, when I am in some sort of vague position of authority, seems like a minefield to me. I want to think a little."

She dropped her forehead to my chest. There was a little force to it, not quite a headbutt. "Figures," she said.

I said, "May I kiss you?" I was surprised to hear me say the words because I don't remember telling my mouth to make them. Apparently, I was still young enough to be impulsive.

She lifted her head and looked into my eyes, making sure I was serious, I suppose. Then, she said, "You're not supposed to ask. You're just supposed to do it. It's manly."

I said, "I don't take something without asking first. It's just polite."

"Yes," she said.

"Yes, it's polite or yes I can kiss you?"

"Jesus, Sean."

I kissed her. Her lips were soft and the kiss was slow. There was something exploratory in it, like savoring a fine drink. Appreciating each subtle flavor and texture. There was heat but nothing wild or manic. Well, at least not at first. Things began to build.

As the kiss lengthened, she pressed against me, the softness of her breasts flattening against my own chest. Then, her stomach. Her hands found the small of my back, and she pulled me even closer so that parts of us even lower. . . Well, you get the picture.

I may have been in a middle-aged body, but it was the halest and hardiest of middle-aged bodies. She began to move against me, and her tongue pushed into my mouth. I realized that my own movements were mirroring hers, my own tongue exploring as well. We were both breathing hard, and I had the sudden impulse to carry her into my bedroom and let the consequences be damned. It was a close thing. Self-control is good, right? It sure felt pretty crappy just then.

40

My hands were still on her upper arms, and I held her away. The kiss ended. She made a sound, something like a groan and something like a growl, and pushed a little against my grip. It was a good sound. Her eyes were still mostly closed and her lips slightly pursed.

I wondered again why I didn't simply take her into the next room. She wanted it. I wanted it. But there was something else that I wanted more.

I just needed to figure out what it was. I knew it was important.

She sighed and dropped her head against my chest again. "You're such a bastard." Her voice was thick and soft at the edges. We stood that way for a while, the only sound our heavy breathing.

Then, saying nothing, she took a single backward step. My arms dropped. She retrieved her sweatshirt and put it on again. There was no seduction in her movements this time, just function.

I noticed that her eyes were a little shiny, and I felt like a heel. I'd initiated the kiss, which I shouldn't have. Then, I'd stopped it, which was an asshole thing to do. *Way to send mixed messages, dumbass.* I didn't mean it to seem like a rejection. It was a timeout until I could make sense of the misgivings which undermined my more basic desires. I really should have learned to be smoother by now.

She began to turn away. Then, I saw her jaw muscles bunch, and she squared off with me like we were going to have a pushing contest or something. She held up a finger like she was going to scold me, which turned out to be pretty accurate. She didn't wag the finger, though. She poked me in the chest, a little hard but mostly for emphasis. "The first time in my life that I come on to a guy, and he shuts me down."

"Allie—" I began.

"If you didn't have such a boner right now, I probably would have cried. You're a jerk!"

She was, of course, correct in her observation. Both counts.

I didn't know what to do. My mixed-message quota had already been filled for the day, so I said, "We'll talk later, okay?"

"You're damn right we will." She punched me on the shoulder, pretty hard, and turned abruptly and headed for the door. I watched her grind her feet into her tennis shoes without unlacing them. Before she left, she pointed a finger at me and said, "If you hear *Magic Mike* playing from my place all night long, it's your own damn fault."

The door didn't slam, not quite.

# Chapter 3

I stood where she left me for quite a while. Not hours or anything crazy like that, but long enough that I eventually had to ask myself what the hell I was doing. If there was anything coherent, like a real thought, moving around in my head, it was *Holy crap, that was a good kiss*.

Then, I realized that I was actually listening for the sounds of *Magic Mike* coming though the wall. I don't know why I would do that because I'd never heard much of my neighbors before. The walls were solid. I'd also never watched *Magic Mike*, so I didn't know what to listen for anyway.

I decided that I should do something besides stand in my living room with my mouth hanging open like some kind of doofus. But what? I needed a brain reset.

Playing guitar was usually able to distract me when I needed distracting, so I poured myself another whiskey, no ice this time, and sat down on the couch. After a little fortification, I put the glass down and picked up the guitar. There was a great deal of comfort in its familiarity. I knew every ding, scratch, and wear mark. It was mine. I was a light player, so it had only been re-fretted once. Like the Nova, it was in excellent condition for seeing so much use.

I picked at some chord progressions for a bit, just noodling. Something that sort of sounded like the rhythm part of "Minor Swing." Then, something that sort of sounded like "Take the A Train." It was playing born of years of noodling around. It was normally relaxing, easy but engaging enough to reset my thought pathways. I guess that this evening just wasn't normal enough because my mind kept circling around to where I didn't want it.

I'm less at home with classical pieces, so I stumbled around "Danza Andaluza No. 5" for a while. I didn't really have the guitar for it, and the Super Strat and the Breedlove steel-string acoustic in my bedroom wouldn't be any better. Maybe I needed to buy a nylon-string guitar. Yeah, one of those high-tech Godin numbers. Hey, retail therapy might work to distract me. I imagined myself sitting up all night in front of my computer scouring Ebay for a good-quality bargain, and I dismissed it as an option. I'd accumulated too much stuff already. And truth be told, a classical guitar wasn't going to help me play classical music any better. The only thing that would do that was practice.

There was a strong part of me that kept saying, *Just pick up and leave, dumbass.* I'd done it often enough before the Mannaz School snagged me. It was certainly the path of least resistance, and I was going to have to leave soon anyway. But I guess that *soon* is relative when you're almost a hundred twenty-eight with no end to the years in sight. I'd brought this whole situation on myself. We supernatural types are supposed to live secret lives, not make significant connections with humans. Sure, your bartender or your barber or the cashier at the supermarket might recognize your current name, but living with the same group of people for years and years is just foolish.

And, no, my name isn't Sean Brannon. I'd never had an alias so long, though. It kind of felt like my name.

My agitation kept growing, and I was sure that I didn't have enough whiskey to mellow me out. I kept thinking about her. Sure, a lot of what I thought about was how she looked and felt and smelled. But, dammit all, I did really like her. We spent a ton of time together. Frankly, I was surprised that this latest development took so long to develop. Now that it had, I felt lost somehow. I needed direction. For direction, I needed information.

I try my best to respect people's privacy, which is not a common trait in the Talamaur. We tend to be nosy types, but I tried to resist the impulse to spy on everyone. What's one more aspect of my basic nature to resist? I tried, but the temptation was too great, and I sent Moe to check on Allie. Yeah, I know. Skeevy, right?

She was watching a movie, but it wasn't *Magic Mike*, and she wasn't doing anything naughty to herself. She wore plaid flannel pajamas, which made her look younger, more vulnerable. She was hugging a small fleece blanket like it was a teddy bear. Her legs were drawn up, so her knees were against her chest. She wasn't crying, at least, but the light flickered on eyes more moist than usual.

I wished I'd curbed my curiosity.

44

The movie she was watching was *Casablanca*. I didn't even know that she had a copy. I didn't even know that she had a DVD player. *Casa*-freaking-*blanca*! That was the first movie we'd watched together. I'd given her a hard time about never seeing it, so she'd sort of invited herself over to my place to watch it. That was a little more than a year ago and the start of our friendship.

The fact that she was watching *Casablanca* and not *Magic Mike* after our. . . thing. . . meant something. Rejection is never pleasant, but this seemed like more than a bruised ego. Not just vanity about her sex appeal.

Damn it all to hell.

Without really thinking about what I was doing, I stood up and went into my bedroom, found my overnight bag in the closet, and began to pack. Was I leaving forever? I had no fucking clue. The need to escape was sharp, though, irresistible. I had to get away. Next, the Gibson went into its case. That proved that somewhere in my mind a permanent exit was an option.

I had great fondness for the stuff in my apartment, stuff I'd accumulated over thirty years. None of it was irreplaceable, though. I slipped on my worn old bomber jacket, hung my bag over my shoulder by its strap, picked up the Gibson, and walked out the door.

I stowed the guitar and the bag in the trunk of the Nova. But once behind the wheel, I hesitated, looking out the windshield at the other cars and the more distant buildings. My birthday was coming soon and Halloween, which was a big deal at the Mannaz School. There would be a costume party and trick or treating with the kids. Ghost stories. The whole deal. The damn holidays! Thanksgiving with Novak and Christie. Christmas sing-a-longs and my yearly screening of one of the *Christmas Carol* movies. I liked Alistair Sim as Scrooge even better than Patrick Stewart. The kids seemed to like CGI Jim Carrey.

I almost sent Moe to look in on Allie again, and that did it. I had to get out, or I'd end up watching her all night and feeling like a bigger and bigger louse. I pulled away as quietly as I could with a fifty-year-old V8 and headed toward 390. I considered using no headlights until I got to the main road. I didn't need them. But really, what would draw more attention? A rumbly old car with its headlights on or off?

The Nova is mostly original, but I had added an iPod dock. I wouldn't have if it was a show car, but it wasn't. There were fine cracks in the dashboard and tiny pits in the windshield that had a way of catching sunlight or oncoming headlights. Maybe I would get the windshield replaced this winter. The car didn't smell bad necessarily, but fifty years of habitation had built up a certain kind of aroma. The floormats were new, though. Their rubbery smell combined with the vague body funk to make something. . . difficult to describe. Maybe I should look into an air freshener. The knob on the end of the gearshift was long gone. I'd replaced it with a blue twenty-sided die that was the size of a baseball. I'd drilled the hole into the one so that the twenty faced up. I guess it was the nerd equivalent to four aces.

Once I got on 19A, I picked a playlist with a lot of AC/DC, Scorpions, and Ozzy—no ballads though. The volume was high, and I drove too fast. Moe raced about fifty feet above the car. He can't see in all directions at once, but he could see as far as any human could see from that height as if it were broad daylight. It was a wide enough perspective for my reflexes to handle just about anything.

Even Ozzy and company couldn't keep me from thinking. My mind seemed to be firmly on a track, not like a crazy train at all. I had Allie on the brain.

Maybe it seems like I was over-reacting to a kiss. The kiss wasn't the problem. The problem was where the kiss might lead. For a regular guy, love and marriage would be just peachy. For me, it just couldn't be. Not unless I met a nice Talamaur girl, maybe a faerie or vampire. No joking. Well, not much anyway. Supernaturals, as a general rule, aren't really into marriage. The whole idea of marrying someone out of love is a pretty new concept, not much older than I am. And how long would a successful marriage last between individuals who could live for centuries, millennia, or potentially. . . well, forever? Might as well just shack up for a couple of decades. Stay together as long as you want and no longer.

I suppose that I could marry a human, but I'd have to keep my nature a secret. How long could that possibly go on? You might be thinking that I should be able to trust my hypothetical wife completely, right? But it's not my trust which is the issue. It's the Venator Ex-

Hominibus Council that would take exception. It isn't an organization founded on trust.

So here is this particular can of worms. We'll just take a peek under the lid. It had to come up sooner or later. Supernatural creatures are absolutely forbidden to reveal their existence to mundane humans. Who forbids? The Venator Council. It's made up of the oldest, most powerful supernatural creatures, especially the ones who prey upon humans in some way or another. Thus, the title, Hunters of Men. Latin always sounds weightier. But other supernaturals can be on the council too because all are held to the same standard whether they eat people or not. The council members are the police force, the judges, and the executioners, but there is just the one law that the council cares about.

If a supernatural type does anything to reveal the existence of the supernatural world to anyone in the mundane world, some heads will roll. That's not figurative. Decapitation kills just about everything. Any humans who know what they shouldn't will be dealt with in the same way. Probably not decapitation for the humans, though. It's unnecessary, and it's hard to make a beheading look like an accident.

Because Talamaur are so rare and our abilities so highly prized, it's possible that I might escape execution. I'd probably have to go through some torture to make an impression on me. Have to make some bargains to use my talents. Mostly, it would depend upon my father, whom I have never referred to as Dad, by the way. Actually, I haven't spoken to him since the mid-eighties. We're not close. He's not an officer on the Venator Council because that's not the way that Talamaur operate. That doesn't stop him from having immense, if subtle, influence, though. He pretty much runs the council, but I doubt that the others fully understand that.

I don't mean to imply that the council discourages killing humans or preying upon them or using them in other ways. Humans are a resource to be maintained. That's all. Beyond that, the council doesn't give a shit about people. If a body turns up completely drained of blood with puncture wounds in its neck, though, they're going to be pissed. If there's an article in *The Inquirer* where a woman says that her lover is a werewolf, the council will check it out. Sure, it's probably a crackpot or outright fiction. If it's not. . .

47

See? If I told Allie everything and she didn't freak out, we still couldn't play house. Maybe we could get away with it, I suppose. I don't think it would be much of a life. Anyway, that's assuming that she doesn't freak out. I couldn't tell her everything and then take it back if she did, freak out I mean, and who the hell wouldn't. That's a lot of faith to put in someone.

So, that's the crap that was going through my head as Brian, Klaus, and Ozzy screamed through the stereo speakers.

The Nova was well-maintained and tuned regularly. She ran as fast and handled as well as she ever did. Not that old American muscle cars are known for their handling, but she always did right by me. The feel of the engine and the sound of tires on the road did something that the whiskey hadn't. It allowed me to unclench despite my dire thoughts. By the time I reached 390, I knew where I was going.

It was a good thing that my brain hadn't shut off like I wanted it to because I'd made a decision. I wasn't going to leave my friends hanging this far into the school year, and I wasn't going to leave Allie the way I left her. That doesn't mean that I had a plan. I didn't know what I was going to do. I just knew what I wasn't going to do.

Well, I did know what I was going to do in the next few minutes which was get a room.

I called ahead to the East Avenue Inn in Rochester. Sometimes I went to the city for a weekend when I needed to be anonymous and get a little urban atmosphere. I liked to listen to jazz at Powell's Lounge and order old-timey cocktails. I was partial to Manhattans. So, my immediate plan was to take two days away from the school and a certain curvy Asian Latina. Hopefully, some insight would come to me by Monday morning.

I checked in at the East Avenue Inn, parked the Nova, and brought my bag and the Gibson to my room. It was a pretty lavish room, but as a general rule, I never could quite buy into an extravagant lifestyle. It was always an option. My family was as rich as they come. And anyway, Moe and I could easily support ourselves in high style with periodic trips to Vegas or Reno. We'd just need to remember not to overdo it in any one place.

Before I caught a cab to Powell's, I had to touch base with Allie. So, you see what I mean, right? I was almost a hundred twenty-eight years old, and I had to touch base with a girl I'd just kissed for the first time two hours earlier. You must imagine that an old guy like me has a ton of romantic stories to tell. The truth is, not so much. Sex, yes. Romance? No matter how often I watched movies with Tom Hanks and/or Meg Ryan, I just couldn't tie my own experiences to that sort of rom-com story. Not really.

Yet there I sat on my hotel bed, staring at my smartphone. I texted, "Hey Allie, I'll see you on Monday. I just need some time."

Immediately—kids these days—she returned, "Jerk!" It seemed that she was still miffed. About thirty seconds later, my phone chimed again. Her message this time was a smiley face with its tongue out and two different sized eyes. Was I forgiven? I chose to go with that interpretation of the crazy-looking smiley face. I speak several languages, but I hadn't gotten the hang of emojis yet.

I would go listen to the jazz quartet Liquid Moonglow at Powell's Lounge and then do whatever came later. I would worry about Monday when it arrived. Good ideas often came when we weren't looking for them. That's what I hoped would happen.

# Chapter 4

There was some pretty good jazz and some pretty good cocktails but no ideas at all. Nothing. Zip. Zilch. On Monday morning, I decided that my first baby step would be to go to work and do the best job I could do. After work? Well, hopefully something would come to me during the day.

At least I felt a lot more relaxed on my drive back to Geary on Monday morning. I hadn't planned on staying at the hotel on Sunday night, but I was improvising. The Mannaz School was home, but everyone needs a break from home sometimes, right?

I really liked driving at night, but the wee hours of the morning were even better. It was still dark as I took the Geneseo exit from 390, but a line of gray was bleeding from the horizon by the time I hit Perry. The little towns along the way were just waking up. Golden squares of light from houses along Route 19 looked especially warm and inviting in the chilly autumn pre-dawn. I came really close to making the right onto Route 246, so I could have a good diner breakfast at a place I liked, but I just didn't leave myself enough time. Not to really enjoy it. And if I didn't enjoy it, what would be the point. It was going to be sliced banana in instant oatmeal in my apartment for me. Woo-hoo!

The campus was still quiet as I drove up the driveway. Well, it was quiet except for the Nova. I loved the way she sounded, but it could be pretty obtrusive. I was careful with the doors. They could be pretty loud too. First, there's a pop. Then, a groan like Dracula's coffin lid in a Hammer movie. Yeah, I should get the doors looked at too.

Once back in my apartment, I had a coffee and some instant oatmeal. I was drinking Starbucks Café Verona lately, so I enjoyed that. I especially liked the way it made my place smell. The oatmeal was only functional, but it was a good vehicle for brown sugar, cinnamon, raisins, and a banana.

I washed the dirty whiskey glasses from Friday night along with my breakfast dishes. Dirty clothes went into the hamper. The Gibson went back onto its stand. I put on a standard, Sean Brannon ensemble: a dark-blue sweater-vest over a light-blue button down, gray pants, and brown brogues. I thought of it as teacher-professional. My hair was a little on the long side, but it was clearly a style choice, not inattention or neglect. I held my bomber jacket up to the light before putting it on. The leather was looking a little dry. I'd need to treat it again soon.

I could see Oak House from my window. That was my commute to work. Fifty yards, maybe. The students were having their breakfasts in the dining room, so I didn't see any of them as I headed up the stairs to the teachers' lounge. The light was on but it was empty. There was about a quarter inch of sludgy coffee at the bottom of the coffee pot, but the burner was still on. Grr.

I rinsed the pot, emptied the old grounds, filled the tank, and put in a new filter and grounds. Folgers. Meh. Allie came in just about when I pushed the brew button. I was a little startled and clenched involuntarily. She either didn't notice it or didn't comment on it.

You might wonder why a guy with an invisible familiar who can float around and go through walls and all that would ever be surprised. The truth of the matter is that Moe usually just hung around with me unless I sent him on a task. I suppose I could have had him patrol regularly like a guard dog, but I didn't think about it much. I worked at a boarding school. It wasn't exactly an atmosphere of danger and intrigue. Well, there was some intrigue but not the type that would get you assassinated or excommunicated.

Allie wore a cream-colored cardigan sweater over a calf-length dark green dress and penny loafers. Her dark hair was pulled into a long ponytail so that the clean line of her neck was emphasized. There was nothing unprofessional about her outfit, but she walked with this rolling stride that was both athletic and sultry. It was just the way she moved.

I was leaning with my back to the long counter which held a dish rack and a little sink and the coffee pot. Allie walked up and stood next to me but facing the counter. I didn't know exactly how to interpret her position until she bumped her hip into mine and said, "Shove over."

I did, and she retrieved a mug from the cabinet above the counter. She was partial to a cream-colored mug with a stylized brown tree on it. Everyone understood that the mug was Allie's and left it alone. I'd been at the school forever, and if I wanted to use the same mug all the time, I'd have to chain it to my wrist.

We stood next to each other with our butts against the counter waiting for the coffee to finish brewing. We were quiet for a while. Then, she hip-bumped me again and said, "Sorry for coming on like a cat in heat the other night."

"Sorry for flaking out and running away," I said. "We'll figure it out."

"Or we won't. Not every mystery can be solved."

I snorted a laugh. "What?"

She smiled her big smile. I know it's totally un-PC to say it, but that smile made her look a little like an anime character. I thought of it as the Hello Kitty-Kawaii smile.

She said, "Yeah, it just came out. It was pretty bad. Sorry. I was going for 'serene' and 'wise-beyond-my-years.'"

"That's totally what I was getting." My smile was as broad as hers but probably not Kawaii.

Just like that, we seemed to be okay again. I didn't think that the kiss was just going to go away, but it also seemed that there wasn't going to be any awkward drama about it. We'd see.

The coffee pot made that gurgly, hissy sound that indicated that it was just about done. I ripped open a sugar packet and poured half of it into my cup and gave the rest to Allie. She put my unused half and another packet into hers. Usually, I put my unused half packets in a corner of the cabinet, and one or the other of us would use them. If there wasn't an unused half in the cabinet, Allie just put in two. I put a dollop of cream into mine and then poured some into her cup. I knew about when she'd say "when" but I waited for it anyway.

She poured the coffee after the machine dripped its last drop into the pot. She replaced the pot and asked, "Why do you use cream and sugar at school and not at your apartment?"

"I drink better coffee at my apartment."

"True."

"You dump cream and sugar into my good coffee too."

"Don't you say that people should take their drinks the way they like them and not be embarrassed about it?"

"Even when I find a merlot in the fridge."

"Jerk," she said, but she was still smiling. "I like it to be kind of. . . viscous."

The door to the teachers' lounge was usually closed, but Allie had left it open when she'd come in. Maybe she didn't want me to feel cornered. Anyway, the open door was probably a good thing, because Maggie James may have crashed through it like Kool-Aid Man if it had been closed. Instead, she gave a kind of locomotive vibe, and her track went right to the coffee pot.

Maggie wasn't big, but she was no shrinking violet either. She was a former-college-athlete type. The Mannaz School got quite a few. There were plenty of places to hike, bike, and canoe on campus and at Letchworth State Park, which was just a few miles away. That was a big selling point for the sporty types. She was wearing jeans, a red sweater, and hiking boots, which was a standard outfit for her. Dorm parents were allowed to be more casual than the teachers during the school day.

The coffee mug in Maggie's hand was huge and pink with little red hearts all over it. She nearly emptied the coffee pot into it. I might have given her a hard time about it, but the look on her face stopped me. She didn't look mean or angry, but there was something very tightly wound about her. Very focused. She moved to the refrigerator like she was on rails and brought over a quart container of Reese's Peanut Butter Cup coffee creamer which she poured liberally into her mug.

I guess if you're going to do that, it doesn't matter what the coffee tastes like.

She replaced the creamer and took a big gulp of coffee. I guess all that creamer must have cooled it off enough for her to do it. She nodded to Allie and me and left the way she had come in. I hoped that no one got in her way. I wasn't sure that she would go around.

"Huh," I said. "What's up with that?"

"I hope that your weekend away was restful," Allie said. She smiled sweetly, but there was something of the imp in her voice.

"Okay, spill," I said.

There was an orderly, steward part of my personality that couldn't bear the mostly empty coffee pot, so I set about to make another.

Allie didn't say anything right away. I had the feeling that she was considering whether or not to make a game out of it. I guessed that she didn't want to waste the entire fifteen minutes before she had to teach class, so she went ahead with the tale.

"One of the new kids is named Howie Tragger, and he caused quite a hubbub during his first couple of days."

"I guess he's in Maggie's dorm then."

"Yup." She sipped at her coffee and put it back on the counter, still too hot. "He broke two windows."

"At the dorm?"

"No, at Willow House. There was a soccer game on the square, and he freaked out. Threw a couple of rocks through the windows. It's going to be pretty dark for the fourth and fifth graders today because Noah had to take out the broken glass and put plywood up until the window guy can come."

"Glazier," I said absently.

"I don't think he actually cuts the glass," she said. "My point was that Howie broke windows."

I set the new pot to brew and sampled my own cup. It was passable if un-inspirational, and the temperature was just about right.

I said, "That kind of behavior isn't exactly unprecedented here."

"No. No, it isn't, but Con is pretty unflappable. When I talked to him about it, he seemed a little. . . flapped."

"Con was there?"

"Yeah, he had to restrain the kid. He said it was like wrestling a bag of snakes."

"That was Saturday?"

"Yeah," she said and checked her watch. "The kid spent all day yesterday with Dr. Corman. Refused to go to any activities. Only went to his dorm after bedtime when the other kids were already asleep."

"He's coming to classes today?"

54

"He was in the dining room when I walked through. I guess Corman really had to put some pressure on him to come." She picked up her mug. "Can you believe the nerve of that man?"

"That bastard, convincing kids to go to class."

"I know, right?" She just looked at me for a beat, held up her cup, and said, "Gator."

I said, "Crocodile."

I watched her walk out the door with that catwalk stride of hers and wondered how any of her male students could concentrate on their school work. Guys of all ages could be pretty dumb about pretty girls. I wondered if Allie would consider her appearance more of an asset or a liability. She was one of the most talented teachers I'd ever seen, and she was a good friend, but, at that moment, I was mesmerized by the way her bottom moved.

With an effort of will, I wrenched my thoughts onto a more constructive but less pleasant track. Howie Tragger sounded like a kid whom I would be meeting soon. Might as well be proactive. There was nothing to do then but to go to the supreme fount of wisdom, also known as Joe Corman. With my unremarkable coffee in hand, I headed to the door.

Moe went ahead to Corman's office to make sure that he was in. Heaven forbid that I'd have to walk all the way downstairs to find out. Lazy ass? Me?

He was standing by his desk with his hand on his crystal ball. His eyes were closed and he was breathing slowly and deeply. He never did tell me where it came from. I'd mentioned it a few times over the years, but I wasn't going to press a reticent guy out of basic curiosity. Mostly, I wanted to find out who the ghost was. I don't think that Corman knew the thing was haunted, not on a conscious level anyway. The ghost was friendly to him at any rate.

Oh, right. Yeah, Talamaur can see ghosts too. It's a thing, and it gets complicated too.

On my way to Corman's, I saw some students outside of the dining room, completing last minute tasks before class or generally milling. I said hey or gave them the Bruce Campbell point-and-grin.

Good cheer rarely goes wrong. I like when people greet me pleasantly, so I operate under the assumption that others like it too.

After some general futzing, I stuck my head into Corman's outer office. Pam Wesley looked up from her computer and smiled at me. What a smile. She said, "I was just going to buzz your office, Sean. Dr. Corman wants to talk to you." Her eyes narrowed in a dramatically inquisitive way. Sometimes she even rubbed her chin like she had an invisible goatee but not today. "You don't read minds, do you?"

"I only receive when the Doctor sends a summons."

She shook a finger in the air. "That's what he uses the crystal ball for, am I right?"

I smiled knowingly and said, "You have yet to reach the true inner circle."

"The inner-inner circle?"

We often had goofy, melodramatic exchanges. Creative types like that kind of thing. Not many people had much real curiosity about the crystal ball, but Pam and I liked to make up stories to go along with it. It was pirate booty or Corman's way to communicate with the rest of the wizards or an alien artifact. They weren't original ideas *per se*, just cribbed from whatever we were reading. We both read widely, so our scenarios varied.

She was fun and cute, a real girl-next-door sort. When Pam replaced Hilde Fitzwilliam eight years ago, it was a definite trade up. Hilde had been good at the nuts and bolts of the job, thoroughly competent. . . just really unpleasant. Novak and I used to refer to her as the Black Hole or the Doomster. Only to each other. Usually when we were drinking. Pam was about as good at the nuts and bolts, but it was the change in the atmosphere around Corman's office that made the difference. Pam welcomed people, made them feel valued, comfortable. It was a great way for a headmaster's administrative assistant to be.

She had a way of mitigating her cuteness with classic business suits. She and Corman seemed to channel the same spirit of fashion. Today, she wore a charcoal skirt suit over a satiny peach blouse. Her hair was blonde and cut in a slightly-spiky pixie style, and modest-sized gold hoops hung from her earlobes.

56

Her suits were cut well, and they emphasized rather than hid her pleasant figure. She was attractive, no doubt about it, but the smile is what people remembered about Pam. The smile was like sunshine.

Corman opened the door to his office then and said, "You received my summons?" He must have heard us talking about telepathic communications and whatnot.

Pam made a face and pointed at him with her thumb.

I said, "Yes, my liege."

He said, "Enter," and stepped aside.

Corman wasn't prone to playing around, so I felt pretty fortunate for the rare treat. He was a straight-laced and double-knotted kind of guy. Not without humor, but reserved in his interactions. He was a careful person, and humor could be tricky.

I winked at Pam and walked into the office.

I sat in the chair I always used when I saw him in his office. Come to think of it, it was the same one I sat in for my interview thirty-something years earlier. In that time, I'd pretended to age, but Corman had gotten old. As always, he was impeccably dressed and groomed. Only a fringe of gray hair remained on his head, but what he had was neatly trimmed. He'd always been lean, but at some point in recent years, he'd edged into the gaunt end of the spectrum. Not cadaverous, but with a severe, colonial-puritan kind of a flavor. He moved a little more slowly nowadays, and he lowered himself into his chair with care.

The crystal-ball ghost was emanating some concern just then, and for the first time, I had the impression that the ghost was family. Corman brushed his fingers absently once across the sphere. It seemed to wink in a stray beam of sunlight. On some level, I thought he could sense the presence of the ghost, too. Humans came with a varying range of sensitivities, and I often found his intuition to be highly developed.

So, just to be clear, I don't really see ghosts. Moe sees ghosts, which in many ways comes to the same thing. It's not like Caspers and Patrick Swayzes are floating around everywhere I go. Really, Moe doesn't "see" at all. I don't want to get too complicated about it, but I get all kinds of data from Moe: energy, physical forces, the makeup of matter. It's crazy. I don't understand all of it, much of it really. Mostly, my brain translates this data into the kind of stuff I would pick up from my mundane senses, but there's a ton more. I should work on a physics degree and a chemistry degree and biology degree, and I could make better use of Moe. I've got a good instinct for most of it, though, like playing music by ear.

At any rate, there was a ghost in and around the crystal ball. I knew it because Moe knew it. Something that I couldn't quite translate made me think that Corman and the ghost were from the same family. There, now you know basically what I know.

"So, you want to talk to me about Howie Tragger," I said.

Corman's eyebrows raised. "Do you have a crystal ball of your own?" he asked.

"I have an Allie Park."

"Probably better," he said. "Yes, Howie's first couple of days were challenging."

He tended to understate less-pleasant aspects of life. "Challenging?" I said.

He waved a hand. "Broken windows can be replaced."

Despite his casual dismissal, something was troubling him. After a moment, he said, "I'm good at reading the students I accept at the Mannaz School. Obviously, my assessments are not perfect, but I'm usually quite accurate. This weekend, I was truly surprised by a student's behavior.

"I met Howie and his father when they arrived. We all went to the dorm together where I introduced them to Ms. James. He was shy and quiet, which I expected. The greatest challenge I thought would be getting him to come out of his shell."

He stopped talking, his eyes looking into the middle distance.

"Broken windows," I prompted.

"Plenty of windows have been broken here over the years. The thing what bothered me most was Conrad's reaction to the incident, and what I observed for myself. He was. . ."

Corman was rarely at a loss for words, so I listened extra-close.

"He was beyond comprehending, just rage. I've seen tantrums. They're expected here. Some can be quite dramatic, but this was something quite different."

58

"Can we help him?" I asked. Occasionally, we had to admit that a student was beyond the Mannaz School's ability to help.

"I would like to. I must admit that my pride is at stake here as well. I believed. . . no, I still believe that he is an ideal student for us. When he was much younger, he had problems with fits of temper. He was able to get them under control, but in doing so, he withdrew, closed himself off. In recent years, when he felt overwhelmed, he shut down, became non-communicative. It seemed that he'd trained himself to first, clamp down, then, disengage."

"You spent the day with him yesterday. How was he then?"

Corman smiled at me and said, "For a man who returned to campus not an hour ago, you certainly are informed."

I held my hands palms-up in surrender.

"He was embarrassed," Corman said. "No, he was ashamed. I tried to get him to talk, but I also didn't want to press too hard. Mostly, he stayed in my office and read or drew pictures while I went about my business. We played some chess, and he opened up a little. The only thing he would say is that he suddenly 'felt too much' and 'couldn't think.'"

I raised my eyebrows at that, wondering again if he might be too much for us.

Corman continued. "He's had counseling, of course. Nearly all of our students have, but there was no indication of psychological breaks, nothing even close."

"Do we treat Saturday as a fluke?" I asked.

"We watch him like a hawk. You are good at your job, Sean, excellent really. I want you to make Howie Tragger your first priority. I know that we cannot save all of them, but I want to save this one. I truly hope that I am not speaking out of hubris, but if I am wrong about this boy, it will be a blow to my pride."

"I'll keep a close eye on him."

"Thank you, Sean," he said and stood.

That was my cue.

I realized that I'd left my coffee on Pam's desk. Actually, I realized it when she cleared her throat and point at the cup when I was walking by.

"Oops," I said. I say cool things like that. I sipped it. It was pretty cold. Oh well.

Pam said, "So, is it the beacon so that an alien rescue party can come for him and take him home?"

"Naw," I said. "It's the dwelling place for a ghost who gives him comfort and guidance."

"Ooo, that's good," she said.

"I know, right?" Truth in fiction.

I drank the last of my cold coffee at my desk and pulled up Howie's schedule on my desktop. Normally, I wrote the schedules, so either Corman or Novak must have plugged him in. I saw that the second student who arrived over the weekend was named Morris Starr and made a mental note to look in on him when I had time. My memory is excellent, which makes sense for a guy who may just live forever.

I sent Moe to look in on the new students. One of the benefits of working at a school with only fifty-two students, sorry, make that fifty-four, was that I knew all of them well. It was easy for Moe to find Howie and Morris. Their schedules only intersected a couple of times, but Howie was my priority, so my trusty familiar planted himself with him.

Howie was in Spanish class with Señora Catalina Diaz who paced like a jungle cat at the front of her room. She was as kind and nurturing as a person could be, but she had a hard time sitting still, and something in her manner of movement seemed. . . assertive? decisive? Surely, not predatory. . . like a jungle cat. Howie alertly followed her back and forth with eyes that had dark circles under them. He looked exhausted, but there was also a tension in him, like a rabbit about to bolt.

Aside from the signs of strain in Howie, he looked like the posterchild for prep school. He was of average height and build, but he looked fit and generally healthy. His medium-brown hair was cut in a timeless style that would have looked as natural in 1918 as it did in 2018. He wore khakis, a blue button-down shirt, and brown loafers which perfectly matched his belt. It was hard to imagine that this boy could "flap" Novak and make Corman question his judgment.

Moe stayed with Howie throughout Spanish class where the boy was quiet and attentive. He avoided eye contact with everyone. The shame that Corman had seen was still plainly visible. Other students glanced at him covertly, sometimes not-so-covertly. His episode on Saturday must have really been something to make such an impression on Mannaz students. They tended to become desensitized to that kind of thing.

Howie's second class was just as uneventful. He was especially withdrawn and tense at the start because the art students were working on a group project, and their interpersonal patterns were pretty clearly established. The teacher, George Ryan, had an excellent sense for classroom dynamics, though, and he had placed Howie with a super-nice group of kids. They were so welcoming that Howie seemed to have relaxed, at least a little bit, by the end of the period.

Even though I was in constant contact via Moe, every twenty minutes or so, I took a stroll through the halls and peeked in on Howie. I was surreptitious up to a point, but the main reason for my circuits was to be seen doing my job. My familiar was much more efficient than I could ever be in person, but being invisible, he didn't offer much by way of encouragement to anyone. I made high signs to the teachers whenever I caught their eyes through the windows in their doors. I didn't want to disrupt classes, but I wanted people to know I was around if they needed me.

I admit that I became less attentive as the morning wore on. Everything seemed to be going smoothly, and I had paperwork to do. Moe stayed with Howie, and I continued to receive data from him. But sometimes we all become distracted, right? So, when third period came around, I was only halfway paying attention.

Howie was in Novak's history class, which was another factor contributing to my inattention. On some level, I thought Novak could handle whatever came his way. Normally, that would have been the case. This wasn't normal though. Even Moe and I were surprised, so Novak was really out of his depth.

My reaction time should have been better, but I didn't immediately recognize the presence of magic. Moe doesn't really sense "magic," but he senses energy, and magic can move energy around in strange ways. There are all different kinds of energy, some more noticeable than others. Lifeforce energy is right in Moe's wheelhouse, though, so he should have sensed that something was amiss earlier. I guess we'd both been too sedentary for too long.

Regardless of our slow start, I was up and moving before Novak or any of the students in the class knew that anything was amiss. I was trying to make sense of it as I ran down the hallway. Whatever was happening, I'd never seen it before.

I have described some Mannaz students as leaky juice boxes. It usually works pretty well as a visualization, but it fell short this time. Howie's seams were not just leaking. Lifeforce was jetting from them like pressurized steam, and I had no idea how that could possibly happen.

Students began to notice when Howie went rigid. Their expressions turned to fear or concern or embarrassment when his back arched, lips drawn away from gritted teeth, eyes bulging. Then, he stood in one surging movement, and his desk crashed onto its side. He still held his textbook in a death-grip. He was as motionless as a statue except for the shudder which ran through him like a current. The sound came then, something like a buzzing growl. It grew in volume, building into a full-fledged roar.

Novak said, "Howie," and moved toward him in that quick but unaggressive way that he had. Students were getting up from their desks and moving away except for those who were closest. They seemed frozen in place like deer in headlights.

Howie's eyes, which had been unfocused, suddenly locked onto Novak, and the boy went silent. With a movement that looked almost spring-loaded, Howie flung the book at Novak. It was a hard throw and may have struck him if the covers hadn't flopped open, as often happens with thrown books. I've seen more than my fair share. The drag of the increased surface area slowed the book and altered the trajectory, and Novak was able to duck away. The book continued on past and cleared half the stuff from the top of Novak's desk with a crash.

Howie moved fast, and while Novak was still a little off balance from the dodge, Howie landed a good punch right in his round belly.

Novak grunted but wasn't incapacitated in any way. He caught Howie's flailing wrists, and he turned his torso sideways to present less of a target for the kicks which inevitably followed.

The boy kicked and thrashed and even tried to bite. But Novak was a veteran of decades of tantrums, and in a move that would have made a professional wrestler proud, he wrapped Howie up. The boy's arms were immobilized across his own chest, and Novak had crouched in a way which kept Howie's mule-kicks from getting any real momentum.

I entered the room just as Howie brought the back of his head into Novak's collarbone. Novak winced in genuine pain and shifted slightly so that the second attempt caught him on the slab muscle of his shoulder. The boy roiled and squirmed in soundless struggle. The intensity of the effort was disconcerting. That kind of thing is exhausting and can't be maintained for long. That's true normally at least, but there was nothing normal about this. He just kept twisting and thrashing.

Novak's eyes caught mine, and I could see the fear in them. He would hang on, and let the boy wear himself out. That's what he thought anyway. I didn't know if he could last that long. I had to do something. But what?

Howie had way too much lifeforce. Where the hell did it come from? I knew it couldn't blow him apart physically, but it would damage him regardless. I would figure out causes later. Now, I had to release that pressure. It had been thirty years since I speared anyone with Moe, and I didn't like the thought of it, but the kid was clearly in a lot of pain anyway.

Clearly frustrated with his inability to break free of Novak's hold, Howie began to wail. It sounded like an old police siren, pitch rising and falling and rising and falling. He only stopped long enough to catch a gasping breath and began again.

Without knowing what would happen, I shifted Moe into pointy mode, and he lanced Howie. Any sign of discomfort the boy might have shown was lost in his thrashing and keening.

Normally, an effort of will is needed to draw lifeforce from a victim, like sucking on a straw. That was not the case now. Imagine the straw in your juice box shooting like a firehose. Yeah, it was like that. If you're not careful, you're going to get soaked, even knocked right on your ass. I had no ability to dodge, though. There is a direct conduit between Moe and me. Feeding range is about ten feet, and I was within it. Lifeforce surged into me. It was only for a fraction of a second, but I did compare it to a firehose, right? Moe disengaged instantly, but I'd already absorbed more energy at one time than I had in a decade.

Then, I had another first-time observation. So many surprises today. The lifeforce continued to erupt from the puncture wound. There was no way that anyone could contain that much energy. It just kept coming.

Whatever I did next had to be fast. Dithering was not an option.

We Talamaur can heal from anything that doesn't kill us right out, provided that we have the reserve of lifeforce. And what is aging but damage to cells as a body deteriorates? The healing process is not instantaneous, though. Our bodies have to assess the damage. It's like a diagnostic before resources can be distributed. The more complex the problem or the more extensive the damage, the longer the diagnostic takes. Ironic, right? The more desperately we need healing, the longer it takes to start. I was counting on that now. The damage from aging seemed like it must be more complex than cutting a finger with a paring knife or stubbing a toe.

Of course, the aging I'd experienced in the last fifteen years was all part of an experiment. Without precedent as far as I knew. There was no telling what was about to happen to me in front of a class full of kids.

The lifeforce eruption from Howie tapered to a trickle. The expended energy hung like a cloudbank that no one but Moe and I could see. With Moe disconnected, I was in no danger of absorbing more, but seeing it all just hanging there in the metaphysical air was bizarre.

Howie slumped in Novak's arms, eyes fluttering, barely conscious. The energy ceased even dribbling because he seemed to have reached some sort of equilibrium.

Novak looked at me, and he seemed shaken. I couldn't blame him. I was too. I held out my hands and took Howie from him. The boy was able to stand, but he was wobbly. I kept a good grip on his shoulders. I think he would have dropped without the support.

Novak said, "Thanks," and rubbed his collarbone and shoulder absently. "Are you okay with him?"

I said, "Yeah, you mind your other students. I'll take this guy with me." I smiled, but I wasn't fooling anyone.

I started feeling the tickle then. It was the first stage in the healing process. The "tentative fingers" stage. It was less obvious when there was a painful injury. The maddening itch would be coming soon. Then, the show would start.

I moved toward the door as quickly as I could without dragging Howie. The energy floating around was beginning to dissipate, but it was still pretty thick. One of the students righted the overturned desk and the other students began to move back to their own desks. Mannaz students built up a pretty high tolerance to dramatic displays though this one had been quite a doozy. A boy named Paul held the door for us. I thanked him, and as soon as the door closed behind us, I picked up Howie and made a beeline for the nurse's office. Sure, it might have looked weird if anyone saw me carrying a kid like a sack of potatoes but not as weird as a guy aging in reverse at high speed.

Moe scouted to make sure that the coast was clear.

# Chapter 5

I headed for the nurse's office, but I came to an abrupt stop near the top of the main staircase when Moe found that there were students in the common area playing board games. To get to the nurse's office from the main stairs, I would have to go through the common area. Dammit. I was well into the itchy phase of healing. It was strange to feel it over my entire body instead of around an isolated injury. I was pretty sure that I didn't look fifty-five anymore, and Moe quickly confirmed my suspicions. What he showed me of myself was not specifically visual, but it was close enough.

I noted that the students should have been in Laura Hart's math class. Everyone has an off day or a spacy day once in a while, but the woman seemed constantly adrift. She needed to be rescued a lot. If I wasn't running away from the school to hide my altered appearance in the very near future, I would be sure to ask her why her whole class was out of class. There weren't any adults at all nearby, which really pissed me off. Oh, well. I had to keep my priorities in order. You know, maintain the secrecy of my supernatural nature first. Correct the irresponsible teacher second.

For lack of a better option, I decided to take Howie to my classroom. It wasn't far, and hopefully, I could get a few minutes of privacy to come up with a plan. I was about to round the corner to my hallway when Moe let me know that Noah was coming up the stairs at the opposite end of the hallway. The old guy was pretty slow, but I knew I couldn't make it to my door before he topped the stairs.

Noah was carrying a caddie which held basic cleaning supplies. He had it with him most of the time. No telling when you might find something to clean, right? I hated to do it, but I needed to buy a few seconds. The supply caddie hung from his hand by a single wire handle shaped like an inverted U. The brushes and rags and spray bottles were distributed evenly, really well balanced. There was no way to make it seem natural, so Moe just artlessly overturned it. Noah still had a grip on the handle, but all the supplies went tumbling down the stairs making quite a racket.

Noah started like someone had goosed him. Then, he looked around for the culprit, whomever it was who had tipped his caddie. There was nothing to see, though, but his scattered supplies and the gently rocking supply caddie in his hand.

He said, "Aw, hell," and descended the stairs to pick up the mess.

I got Howie into my room. He was no longer semi-conscious. He was all the way out. Whatever had happened had really exhausted him. Well, that made one fewer thing I had to worry about. I didn't have much floorspace, but he wasn't very big. I lay him down on the floor in front of the chalkboard. There was nothing by way of cushions in my room, but I rolled up my bomber jacket and put it under his head. He never woke or even stirred very much.

Now what?

I retrieved my smartphone and looked at myself with the camera app. Looking back at me was a guy who could pass for forty. There were wrinkles around my eyes, but they weren't very pronounced, and my hair was almost entirely red again. In a fraction of a second, I had absorbed enough lifeforce to reverse fifteen years of aging. Holy shit.

For an instant, I considered flight again. That impulse didn't last long though. My shock and dismay were overcome by curiosity and outright anger. Something seriously weird was happening to Howie Tragger. I didn't know much of anything about magic, but I could recognize it. And in Novak's room, just a minute ago, I'd seen some damn potent magic. There was no way that I was leaving my friends to fend for themselves against whatever it was. I was the only one equipped to handle this sort of thing. I hoped I was anyway since I really didn't know what exactly this sort of thing was.

It seemed like I stood for a very long time trying to make my brain come up with something, but it was probably less than thirty seconds. There was really no way for me to know definitively what to do. I could try any number of things to burn away the energy I had absorbed, but I didn't know if that would make me look old again.

See, I'd been low on lifeforce before. Normally, that sort of thing followed significant injury, acts of prolonged peak-human physical activity, or both. That never made me look old, though. It made me look more like a heroin addict, all pale gray and sunken, dark circles under my eyes. I'd only managed the aging thing by tapering my sustenance over several years. I hadn't known that it would work. I was just testing a hypothesis.

The only thing I could hope for now was that my body had gotten used to being old, and that a significant expenditure of energy would cause it to revert. I might end up just looking like a forty-year-old junkie, but I was willing to give it a try.

I could try to race a train or bend steel in my bare hands, something like that. But I would have to venture out to find a train or some steel to bend, and I really didn't want to be spotted by anyone. What I had in mind was far more unpleasant, but I could do it in private.

I shut off the light and locked the door to my room. I almost laughed aloud at the first thought that came to mind. *Oh my God, I shouldn't be alone with a student in a locked room*. If the other monsters found out that I was concerned with such things, they might revoke my status. I might be demoted to bad influence or something.

Gray autumn light came through the windows and made everything seem softer. The room was warm, the baseboard heater making gurgling sounds as it worked against the October chill. Howie had begun to snore quietly. It seemed like a good time to take a nap instead of do what I had decided to do. But nothing good would come of putting it off.

I kept a gym bag in the closet at the back of my room, right underneath the shelf with the loose-leaf paper and the manila folders. My body is much like a human body, you know a human body which is totally efficient, immune to sickness and disease, and able to heal from every injury completely with no scarring. You know, like a human. Before the aging experiment, there was no need for working out. I just naturally had a Jason Statham kind of build, which pissed Novak off to no end. It was pretty awesome. Now, I had to put in a little work to keep the paunch at bay. Well, it was that or give up the beer.

I put the bag on my desk and unzipped it. The smell that emanated reminded me that I hadn't washed my workout clothes very recently. I took out a big fluffy white towel and a gray t-shirt that had a Jim Lee picture of Wolverine on it. Too bad I would have to wreck it. I liked the shirt.

I rummaged through my desk. Well, not exactly rummaged. I'm too organized to have to rummage. I mostly knew where to find everything. Everything, in this case, was a new roll of duct tape and an old pair of tailor's shears.

I'm a tough guy and all that. I know how to be. I've watched all the Stallone and Schwarzenegger movies. I even have this huge leg up in the tough department. I know I'll heal. I get to avoid that aspect of pain which is the fear that an injury has caused irreparable damage. That fear of being permanently crippled or maimed. That being said, pain hurts and I try to avoid it. As far as I know, my nerve endings are at least as sensitive as anyone else's.

That was the gist of my internal pep-talk. It wasn't very peppy. Mostly, I just looked at the long stainless-steel blades of the scissors and felt a queasy sort of dread.

I sent Moe to watch the door and patrol the hallway. Then, I flipped off my shoes and dropped my pants. Yeah, the whole "what-would-this-look-like-if-someone-walked-in" scenario played through my head again, but I kept on with my plan. I folded the towel over twice and put it on the floor in front of the closet, and I sat down so that my right thigh rested on it. I tore off four long strips of duct tape and stuck them to the closet door within easy reach. I actually ended up tearing off seven strips because the damn things kept wadding up. Stupid tape made me mad in that way that only inanimate objects can make me mad. I folded the Wolverine t-shirt into a neat square and placed it within easy reach as well.

I didn't look forward to what came next, but it had to be done. After another glance at the little boy who needed me here to protect him, I got a firm grip on the long, tapering shears and drove them into the meat of my thigh. Each blade was pretty thick, and I had the shears closed, so both blades were side-by-side. That was really thick. So thick that my skin and muscle did more stretching and tearing than actually being cut. That was calculated. Tears are harder to heal than clean incisions. I managed to sink in three inches, right about up to the screw which holds the two blades together.

I made a sound that Stallone never would have made. It was a little kittenish. I might have been embarrassed if there was anyone to hear it. But just to prove to myself that I wasn't embarrassed by the kitten sound, I made it again when I yanked the shears out. Before I had time to think about it, I drove the shears in again, yanked them out, drove them in, and yanked them out. The second and third wounds were shallower. It was all I could manage. My hand trembled and I let the scissors drop to the floor.

The blood didn't exactly gout, but it came out fast. I folded the edges of the towel over so that my thigh was completely encircled, and I pushed down on the wounds hard. They were close together, so I was able to apply solid pressure to all of them. I was glad that I'd had a light breakfast. Ultimately, I didn't puke, but it was a little touch and go for a bit.

It seemed like forever until I felt the buzz of healing begin. Until then, I got to enjoy the pounding throb in my leg that mirrored my heartbeat. I was a little lightheaded too, but since I was already sitting down, I didn't worry much about it.

When I thought that enough time had passed, I eased the pressure on my leg. There was a little blood still oozing, but it continued to slow even as I watched it. I used the few white areas I could find on the towel to wipe away the remaining blood. Then, I pressed the folded Wolverine t-shirt over the wound and wrapped the duct tape around it all. Do it yourself pressure bandage.

Talamaur heal fast, but it's not instant like the Crow or Wolverine in the X-Men movies. My leg would be fine by mid-afternoon. There would be no evidence of injury at all by the end of the school day. In the meantime, the pain would fade and be replaced by a maddening itch. I'm not sure which is worse, the pain or the itch. The question is not as silly as it sounds. I know that humans feel an itch when a cut or puncture is healing, but for Talamaur, all that itching gets compressed into just a few hours. Like a month's worth of itching in an afternoon.

I climbed unsteadily to my feet, keeping most of the weight on my uninjured leg. Getting my pants back on was a feat. I didn't want to bend the leg much until the healing progressed a little more, but I also didn't want to be *sans* pants any longer than necessary. The pain throbbed like a house-music bassline, and another wave of light-headed nausea caused me to wobble. I braced myself on the closet door until it passed. It only lasted a few seconds. I noticed a small smear of blood on the closet doorframe when I took my hand down and reminded myself to be careful about cleaning up.

I wiped my hands off with my gym shorts before tucking in my shirt. I also used them to wipe at the blood on the door, but it had already gotten into the woodgrain. I doubted that anyone would be able to identify the stain as blood once it had a chance to dry. No time to worry about it now.

I put the bloody towel back into the gym bag. The bag was black nylon, so I didn't worry that the blood would leak through. I also tossed the shears into the bag. They would need cleaning. I zipped the bag and carried it back to the closet. I just tossed it on the floor to avoid bending down. I kicked the roll of duct tape into the closet too and made the mistake of trying to kick the wadded balls of tape in as well. Of course, they stuck to my sock-clad foot. Hated the tape. Stupid sticky tape.

I was still looking at my feet when Corman appeared at the end of the hall. There wasn't time to check my face with my phone or to put on my shoes or even pluck the tape from my toes. I closed the closet door and Moe unlocked the classroom door while I got myself situated behind my desk, injured leg as straight as I could manage. I was shuffling creative writing assignments when he knocked. Props can sell a scenario.

I said, "Come on in," and acted casual.

He entered and surveyed the room. Though the lights were off, it wasn't really dark. Plenty of soft light came in through the windows. My shoes and one of the wads of duct tape were laying on the floor by the closet, and Howie was sleeping on the floor at the front of the room. It wasn't all that strange. Was it?

First things first. Moe showed me, basically, what Corman could see from his perspective. It turns out that I was mostly silhouetted by the light from the window behind me. Moe could perceive that changes were taking place to my face, but I didn't think that Corman could. He didn't act as though he couldn't at least.

He didn't seem to note the shoes or the tape, but he looked pretty intently at Howie. His lips tightened into a line.

I said, "I thought it best to let him sleep as long as he needs to." That seemed like a good reason to have the lights off.

"How is he?"

I realized at that moment that I hadn't really checked Howie over. I was too busy dealing with my own situation.

I said, "He's fine, just worn out."

I sent Moe to see if that was the truth. His pulse was strong and regular, and his breathing was deep and even. Temperature normal. Just a sleeping kid.

"Okay," Corman said. "We'll talk later. Let me know if I have to take him after school. Ms. Hart is ill, so I'll need to cover her afternoon classes."

"I'll keep an eye on Howie," I said.

"Thank you, Sean," Corman said and left, closing the door behind him.

I liked that he called me Sean. Novak and I were the only ones who got first-name treatment. Corman addressed everyone else at school by surnames. I hoped that it was more of an esteem thing and not just seniority.

Using my camera app as a mirror, I examined my face and verified with my eyes what Moe had already told me. It really was interesting to watch my wrinkles deepen and the white in my hair spread like spilled cream over my ears. It seemed to me that the white should have appeared as my hair grew out, not that the pigment would bleach from the hair that was already there. Curious.

My luck was holding out. Hopefully, I would look like the Sean Brannon everyone expected when it was time to show myself again. In the meantime, I had some thinking to do.

I didn't know about magic, so I'd need to find someone who did. A downside to my time at the Mannaz School was that I'd dropped my associations with the supernatural world. Not that thirty years was a terribly long time for many of us, but it was more than a "see ya later." My contact information with everyone was doubtlessly out of date.

I would have made a list of possible resources, but really, there was only one person I could call. Well, two if I counted my father, but I wasn't.

I was having a tough time coming up with any cohesive plan. Outside of the domestic use of my familiar, I was horribly out of practice dealing with the supernatural. I would have to fall back on the "one-foot-in-front-of-the-other" method. I'd keep moving forward, focused on individual tasks until I could see a clearer path. Moe and I were going to stick to Howie Tragger like glue. He seemed to be either the source or the target of whatever was happening. My gut said that he was the victim. In the absence of any other data, I would proceed according to that premise.

The pain in my leg began to fade, replaced by a pins-and-needles sensation that was really just another type of pain. The itching phase was really just a different kind of pain, too. I kept track of each stage because it was important to know how things were progressing. Knowing would inform my movements.

The pin-and-needles were my cue. I retrieved my shoes and unlaced them so that I could put them back on. I figured I could do some bending without causing my wound to ooze, not much anyway. My pants were a dark charcoal, so the blood probably wouldn't show very much, but why chance it? While I plucked the stupid tape from my socks and put my shoes back on, I sent Moe to check on Howie again.

He'd barely moved since I put him down. It was like someone had hit him over the head with a giant cartoon mallet. The only things missing were the little yellow birds flying in circles around his head.

About halfway through fourth period, Howie sat bolt upright and almost clipped his head on the chalk tray. He looked around in a panic, and I was reminded again of a cornered rabbit. The way that he sprang to his feet fit the image too. He moved too fast and swayed like he was light-headed.

I said in a tone as casual as I could make it, "Howie, how are you feeling?"

"Uhm, how did I get here?"

"Don't you remember when you and I left Mr. Novak's room?"

Howie shook his head and said, "I don't remember much."

Sometimes kids say that sort of thing after a blowup because it disconnects them from the incident, but I thought that Howie was telling the truth. He still seemed pretty out of it.

"Uhm. . . who are you?" he asked. His eyes swept the room.

"I'm Mr. Brannon," I said. "Have a seat if you want. Or you can go back to sleep if you're still tired."

He shook his head and sat down at one of the student desks. "How long did I sleep?"

I checked my watch and said, "About an hour."

"I feel beat," he said and sounded like it. "I did that thing again didn't I?"

"Like on Saturday."

He put his face in his hands. I thought he might cry, but he just sat that way for a minute or so. It doesn't sound like long, but it really seemed like it. I was going to wait to let him talk if he wanted to, but now that he was awake, I wanted to keep him moving.

I asked, "Has this kind of thing happened before?"

He took his hands down and shook his head, but he said, "Not since I was a little kid. I worked really hard to stop it. I didn't want to be bad. I don't want to be bad." He put his face in his hands again, and this time, he did cry. Quietly. I let him.

I brought a box of tissues to him, putting it on the edge of his desk. I didn't want to crowd him, so I went back to my own seat and waited.

Finally, he said in a small voice, "Are you going to send me home?"

"I doubt it."

His head whipped around and he looked at me through puffy eyes. I think he thought I was messing with him. He couldn't see me well because I still had that dramatic silhouette thing going on. That didn't discourage him from looking, though.

After he'd looked enough, he wiped his eyes with a tissue and said, "Really?"

74

"Really." I added, "We should probably try to figure out what's going on, though."

His face started to crumple, and I thought he was going to cry again, but he didn't. His jaw muscles flexed and his eyes got the intense look you might see on a weight lifter right before the concentrated exertion. There was nothing of the scared rabbit in that expression of will power.

"We'll figure it out," I said putting a lot of confidence into it. I didn't really feel it, but if he could be brave, so could I.

The bell, really a tone, sounded to indicate the end of fourth period. It wasn't very loud, but Howie jumped enough that his legs bumped the underside of his desk. His fingers gripped the edges of the desk tightly, and I could actually hear him swallow.

Brave or not, he was still twelve and full of anxiety.

The thumping feet and chattering voices of students passed by the door. The teachers would wrangle them to the dining room in just a few minutes. The diligence and mindfulness of the teachers varied, so either Novak or I would normally make a sweep of the usual hangouts to give the stragglers a nudge in the right direction. It would have to be him today.

I didn't want Howie dwelling on his episodes. I've found that riding out hard times requires moving forward, so I said, "Let's get some lunch."

"I don't know. . ." he began.

"So, what, you're just going to hide?"

"The other kids. . ."

"They all have their own stories if difficult times. It's part of being a Mannaz student. You can compare notes once you get to know them."

He looked at me, searching for something. "Okay," he said, but it sounded uncertain.

I stood up decisively, hoping that my show of confidence would inspire him. I felt a little jolt from my leg and wondered if the gesture was worth it. I decided, yeah. Yeah it was.

Moe showed me that the changes to my face had stopped, but I wasn't entirely confident that they had gone far enough. I hadn't had a chance to take a comparison picture. I would have to trust Moe's perceptions, but eyes were eyes, and I would have liked a look at myself.

I crossed the room and held the door. I didn't even limp a little. Tough guy.

Howie looked at me for a three-count. Then, he got up and walked into the hall.

# Chapter 6

Howie walked so close that we bumped lightly every few steps. If my proximity gave him comfort that was fine by me. He was my mission after all.

More than a few eyes turned in our direction when we entered the main dining room. There were two smaller dining rooms that upperclassmen and other students who had earned the privilege could use. Sometimes school clubs used them for special meals.

The meal was underway, and there wasn't much of a line at the serving window. It was quesadilla day, so we stopped off at the sideboard for salsa and sour cream. Howie was very cautious about the heat of the salsa, so I went with the mild as a show of solidarity. I could live with the disappointment. Normally, I stopped off at the window and asked Ron, the kitchen manager, for this green El Yucateco sauce which he generously shared with me.

A broad-shouldered blond student named Paul said, "Hey, Mr. Brannon," as he stepped up to the sideboard next to us. Howie looked on in horror as Paul proceeded to load his quesadilla with the hottest salsa and liberally sprinkle sliced jalapeños on top. He was only a seventh grader, but he'd been at the Mannaz School for four years. He wasn't the best student, but he was about the nicest kid I'd ever met. He was also a proud nerd, and we could talk comic books, D&D, and *Star Trek* all day.

I said, "Hey, Paul. Can we join you for lunch?"

His eyes flicked to Howie for the briefest moment He seen the episode in Novak's room firsthand, but he said, "Sure. I'm over here with Scott and Jan."

The three of us walked across the room to a corner table where a slightly-plump, mousey-haired girl and a tall, thin boy with wild brown hair sat waiting.

Scott's hair bore a striking resemblance to a bird's nest. I don't know if his Woodstock t-shirt was in sticking to a theme or if he hadn't made the connection. It was easy to imagine the little yellow bird flying up to Scott's head to nest.

Jan didn't get much romantic attention from the guys. They hung out with Jan because she was fun. A goofy nerd girl who, on occasion, might imitate the Ministry of Silly Walks walks or other random slapstick.

They watched us approach and smiled. Their smiles made my chest unclench, and I felt such a rush of gratitude to them. Howie really needed to be welcomed now, and these were the kids to do it.

Before we even had a chance to sit, Scott said, "Okay, Mr. Brannon, is Captain America's shield made out of adamantium or vibranium?"

I put my tray down and said, "Both, kind of."

Scott and Jan looked at each other. Then, they looked at me, and I thought I picked up a little annoyance in their expressions. They had apparently expected me to settle an argument.

The five of us talked about the Marvel Universe versus the Marvel Cinematic Universe. The kids listened raptly as I told them of Dr. Myron MacLain's metallurgical experiments involving vibranium and iron which resulted in Captain America's unique shield. Attempts to recreate the material resulted in the development of adamantium. Kids never listened so closely when I was trying to explain gerunds. Admittedly, verbals just weren't as interesting. Scott and Jan were clearly not happy about both of them being sort of right, but not so unhappy that they were actually mad.

Howie really didn't do much talking, but he was engaged in the conversation. Paul, Jan, and Scott were pleasant and didn't try to exclude him in any way. It didn't seem to matter to them that he was new or that he had had a couple of very dramatic explosions in the last few days. By the end of the meal, Howie was actually smiling, and much of the tension had gone out of his posture. I also noted with some pleasure that he'd eaten most of his lunch.

When the bell rang for class, he didn't flinch, but I saw his shoulders hunch the slightest bit. We continued to sit while Paul, Jan, and Scott headed to the dish room with their trays. They waved in that offhand, adolescent way kids have, not dismissive so much as on-the-move.

Howie said to me, "Can I stay with you instead of go to class, Mr. Brannon?"

Looking into his face, which was starting to look a little rabbity again, I almost said yes. I didn't for two reasons, and one of those reasons didn't totally reflect well on me.

First, I knew that he did the same thing on Sunday by staying with Corman and avoiding activities. It was understandable to want to hide from stressful situations. Hell, I'd been doing the same thing in Rochester over the weekend. At the same point, I didn't want to reinforce his tendency to withdraw. I was fine with that reason. Howie and I could be brave together.

The second reason didn't rest so easily with me. It demanded a cold pragmatism that I appreciated but no longer had a taste for. I had to identify the threat and deal with it whether it was a supernatural bad guy or Howie himself. If Howie was the target, being in the open would draw out the attacker. If he was the source, there were likely more catalysts to set it off while interacting with others.

Keeping Howie under wraps might cause the bad guy to shift targets. It would be easier to watch one kid than fifty-four of them. Yeah, that was a Howie-as-bait scenario. Not very noble.

The other possibility was that Howie didn't have an attacker but was the source of the phenomenon. He didn't feel like a bad guy for what that's worth, and I couldn't think of what would motivate a bad guy to throw epic tantrums in a school intended to weather tantrums.

I also had to acknowledge the extremely unlikely possibility that Howie was some kind of a supernatural half-breed but didn't know it. Relations between supernaturals and humans happened, but they very rarely resulted in offspring. Unlikely or not, I didn't suppose I should dismiss the possibility.

I needed to know more at any rate, and I probably wouldn't learn with Howie hiding in my room.

I said, "Howie, you have a super-awesome teacher for fifth period English, and I would hate for you to miss out on her and her class."

"But, what if—" he began.

I knew it was rude to interrupt, but I did anyway. "I'll introduce you to Ms. Park. We'll work out an escape plan. Give class a try. If you need to leave, you can."

"Won't I get in trouble?"

I poked my thumb at my chest and said, "I'm boss."

He bobbed his head, and we got up to take out trays to the dish room. As we were walking up the main staircase together, I said in a stage whisper, "Don't tell Ms. Park I said I was boss, okay?"

He grinned, and I saw the truckload of potential he had. I renewed my resolve to root out the problem, the source of whatever nastiness was going on here.

Allie hadn't closed her classroom door yet. We stood just outside in the hall while she gave stacks of paper to the first student in each row of desks. When she saw us, she said to the students, "Name and date at the top. Read the directions." She came to the door, a smile on her face.

I said, "Ms. Park, this is Howie Tragger. He's feeling a little anxious, and I told him that he could come to me whenever he needs to. Is that okay with you?"

Howie was looking at the floor between his shoes. Allie's eyes locked with mine for a moment, and I nodded once.

She said, "Howie, it's absolutely okay for you to go to Mr. Brannon if you need him. Just get up and go, and I'll know where to find you."

His rabbit eyes came up to meet her for the barest moment. Then, he bobbed his head and looked down again.

Allie said, "Thank you, Mr. Brannon." She put her hand on Howie's shoulder and began to guide him toward an open desk in the front of the room. Then, she stopped and looked back at me. Her eyes narrowed, appraising me. Her head actually cocked to the side a little like the RCA Records dog.

She saw something that piqued her curiosity. I smiled and waved and made my escape.

Moe stayed right where he was, though. He was actually sharing space with Howie, acting as a sort of monitor. Heartrate, respiration, perspiration. He observed all of it. There would be no distractions this time.

I left the lights off in my room when I went in and sat behind my desk. I had a good set of Sony headphones in one of my bottom desk drawers. They weren't noise-cancelling, but they would help to quiet my audial perceptions. I closed my eyes too. I didn't do any kind of Shaolin meditation or anything. I just tried to focus all of my attention on what Moe observed.

It was kind of weird.

I think that my mind is like a human's in most respects. It's just wired a little differently. I often refer to what Moe sees and hears and smells, but he really does none of those things. That's just the easiest way for me to think about the data. There is a scene in *The Matrix* when Tank is looking at seemingly endless lines of code. He's looking at 1s and 0s, but he's seeing the Matrix. It's kind of like that for me. Not exactly right, but it's the best I can do. You know, like juice-box people.

I wonder how Talamaur explained this kind of thing before packaged food and movies. I suppose they didn't condescend to explain anything to anyone.

Howie had a good English class, and I was reminded again about Allie's intelligence and abilities. She really knew her shit, and the students all seemed to be pretty thoroughly engrossed and actively participated. There was also a solid "cool" factor in teaching *The Invisible Man* by H. G. Wells. I thought it was fun to be a sort of invisible man sitting in on class, too. I'm easily amused.

Nothing even mildly supernatural took place though. Well, aside from a student being guarded by a familiar, I mean.

As the English class neared its conclusion, I took off my headphones and headed to Allie's room. Howie didn't know he was guarded every moment of the time, so I thought he could use some more material assurance. I waited at the door, and most of the students said, "Hey, Mr. Brannon," or some variation of it as they walked past. I greeted each of them by name. It's the little things.

Howie had had a good lunch and a good English class, and they had clearly affected him positively. There wasn't quite a smile on his face when he met me at the door, but it was close to the surface. Allie stood by his side. She was smiling.

"Howie had an excellent class," she said.

Howie's smile surfaced.

"Brilliant," I said to him. "Are you ready for math class?"

"Yeah," he said. "I am."

I was about to turn away to take Howie to Laura Hart's room, when Allie said, "Whatever you've been doing today agrees with you, Mr. Brannon." Her head did that little tilt again.

"Thank you, Ms. Park." I guess I looked a little younger but not enough to seem unnatural. Allie was more observant than most, though, so I thought I was okay.

Howie and I barely had to take five steps to get to the math room. It wasn't quite across the hall, but it was close. I stopped for just a minute when I saw Corman behind the desk. Then, I remembered. Laura was sick, and he was covering.

We walked over to Corman, and Howie said, "I had a really good English class. Ms. Park is really funny, and she said that I can draw a comic for my *Invisible Man* project."

Corman said, "That's wonderful, Howie."

Howie didn't seem to notice that Corman wasn't looking very well. But when kids aren't being super-perceptive, they're usually oblivious. He made a bee-line for the front and center desk.

I said to Corman, "Are you okay? I can take the class if you need a break. I'd be right here with Howie."

He shook his head. "I need you mobile. Thank you for getting to Con's class so quickly. He said that you showed up almost as soon as anything happened."

"My Spidey Sense."

He said, "Keep it turned on. . . if it's something that goes on and off. I'll be fine. I like math."

"Okay." Who was I to argue with the headmaster?

Back in my room, I took up position at my desk again, eyes closed and headphones on.

Class was going well. I let my concern for Corman override my commitment to having Moe connected to Howie every moment. It would only take a few seconds to give the old guy a checkup. His pulse was good and strong, but he was a little warm, and there was a slight tremor in his hands. It wasn't a fever, just a little elevated temperature. I was no doctor, but I had the suspicion that Dr. Corman was mostly just old and tired. It was a strange experience to watch someone get old. I didn't like it.

I returned all of my attention to Howie. Specifically, his possible reactions to whatever power might affect him. This was only a starting point, though. As soon as I knew anything was happening, Moe was going to go through a series of wavelength adjustments. Whatever had happened in Novak's room took us off-guard. We didn't know what was happening until it was well underway. That was only because we didn't know what to look for. Moe can't see everything at once, but he can cycle through frequencies quickly. Given time, I don't think that much is beyond his powers of perception.

About twenty minutes into class, Howie's muscles began to spasm. Just those little ticks that sometimes happen. A flutter of the eyelid. A little wiggle of the pinky finger. He didn't seem to notice at all, but Moe did. My familiar's regular perceptions didn't pick up any energy out of the ordinary, so he adjusted.

The more obscure the wavelength, the less likely I am to understand it. To understand, I have to think in the simplest terms. Moe dialed through settings like someone scanning for radio stations. Flick, flick, flick, flick. In less than three seconds, we could see it. It was lifeforce, but it had been altered somehow. The texture was off. It was drifting from the other people in the classroom and soaking into Howie.

That shouldn't have been able to happen. People are vessels. Vessels don't work if they're so porous that whatever they contain can seep through. Somehow, the "particles" of lifeforce had been shrunk or divided so that they could pass through the physical shells of everyone in the room, and all of that lifeforce was passing into Howie. It didn't seem to be coming out again. Maybe he was only porous going in, or maybe he contained some sort of gravity which drew and held the lifeforce.

A thousand questions flashed through my mind, but they would have to wait.

I moved as soon as I witnessed the weird phenomenon, but things happened fast. Howie went rigid, a white-knuckled grip on the edges of his desk. I hated to do it, but I sent Moe to lance him right away. Energy jetted out of him at it did before. I was still well out of range, so I wouldn't absorb any of it.

Howie whimpered and doubled up like he had stomach cramps. His whole body trembled violently. When I'd lanced him that morning, relief had come quickly. This time was different. The energy that shot from him into the atmosphere didn't fill the room like a cloud. It changed course and surged into him again with more violence. The suction or gravity in Howie was continuing to draw.

I was almost there.

Howie was beginning to draw attention. Doubtlessly, some of the kids had been in Novak's class that morning and saw the signs. No one exactly leaped up, but they looked ready to make a break for it. Corman was up, a look of concern on his face.

Moe disengaged when I reached the door. There was no cloudbank of lifeforce this time. Howie had sucked it all up.

At that point, I cared little about appearances. I just charged into the room. The door slammed against the rubberized stopper screwed into the floor as I charged through. I scooped Howie up in my arms like he was a baby and was back out the door in three long strides. I was alarmed when Moe showed me that tendrils of energy were following us into the hall. They were reaching out for Howie like giant squid tentacles.

Moe slammed the door with all the force he could manage. That would look weird to the people in the room. Maybe they would assume that a random gust of air did it. I didn't care. Thankfully, the tendrils were snapped off. They hung for a moment having lost their momentum. Then, they drifted away like smoke.

Howie's muscles were taut as cables, and he began to spasm. I tried to put him down, but he was bucking and squirming so violently that it was more like I dropped him. He writhed as I backed away. I needed to put some space between us, so Moe could do his thing.

84

In the seconds it took me to move, something changed. Howie went still. The change was so abrupt that Moe and I stopped too, just watching. Then, Howie sprang to his feet. His eyes were wild, and he showed his teeth in either a grimace or a silent snarl. I didn't know if he would attack me or not, but I had no desire to find out. I was out of feeding range, but I wouldn't be if he charged, so Moe lanced him yet again.

It needed to be done. I know that, but I didn't feel any better about stabbing a little boy with my familiar for the third time in one day. The sound that he made began as a roar but lost volume as the stolen lifeforce jetted out of him. As before, Moe only needed to jab. The pressure inside Howie kept the energy spraying until he reached some kind of equilibrium. His knees wobbled. Then, he collapsed bonelessly to the floor. His eyelids fluttered, and he looked like he was going to pass out.

The classroom doors had little windows in them which were reinforced with mesh. They weren't very big, but I could see student faces peering out from the closest three classrooms. The noses smooshed against the glass might have looked comic in another situation. Now, it annoyed me. I couldn't really blame the kids, though. They didn't know what was going on. Hell, I didn't know what was going on either.

Instead of venting my frustration on curious students, I went to Howie and helped him to his feet. He couldn't stand on his own, so I kept a good grip on his shoulders. We made it a few steps before Corman opened the door to the math class.

He said, "Do you have this under control?" His voice quavered just a little, very un-Corman-like.

I turned to face him, preparing my most encouraging smile. But it never made it to my mouth. I might have gaped a little if it's possible to gape a little. Corman had looked tired and a little sick before. Now, he looked worse. In the space of seconds, he'd gone paler and grayer, and there was a light sheen of sweat on his forehead.

I said, "I've got it."

He nodded and returned to the classroom and students without another word.

Did I really have it? No, I didn't, but I hoped I would.

I took Howie to the nurse's office. Missy Waters, the nurse, was her normal hospitable self. She was a little past forty, but she had the kind of elfin features that made her look younger. There was a vitality about her and a no-nonsense attitude that managed to avoid being brusque or dismissive. Her auburn hair was still without a trace of gray, and her green eyes sparkled.

"Is there room at the inn?" I asked as we came through the door. I had gotten my expression under control. Anxiety off. Boyish charm on.

"What's up?" she asked.

"I've got a boy who needs a nap."

She was small enough that she didn't need to kneel down or even stoop that much to look into Howie's face. I noted the crease that formed between her brows. She touched his cheek and his forehead. His eyelids quivered, and he tried to focus on her.

"Okay," she said, but there was something in her tone that sounded unsure. She steered him into the room with the cots. He sat down heavily on the closest of them. She said, "Shoes off."

Howie kicked off his shoes, pulled up his legs, and lowered his head onto the pillow. In a handful of seconds, he was asleep. His face went slack and his breathing deepened to a light snore.

Missy put his shoes at the foot of the cot. The thoughtful crease remained on her brow. She came back out into the office where I stood, and said in a matter-of-fact way, "That boy looks like he's been sedated. He didn't get a hold of something did he?"

I shook my head. "He had a bit of a blowup, and it took a lot out of him."

She looked very directly into my face with a probing kind of intensity. If I weren't so manly, I might have felt a little intimidated. Was she looking for deception or omission? Whatever it was she was looking for, she didn't find it, or maybe she did and chose to ignore it.

She said, "Okay. I'll keep an eye on him. But he seems more than just tired to me."

"Thanks. I'll stop in later," I said.

I left Moe to stand guard, and I returned to my room. I had to do some figuring.

# Chapter 7

My leg was still sore. The pins and needles were beginning to fade and be replaced by the super-itch. Back in my old life, I was good at ignoring that sort of thing, but I'd gotten soft since then. The intense sensations drew too much of my attention. It would have been great to take a nap and wake up all better, but that wasn't in the cards for the rest of the afternoon. By then, the healing would be done.

I sat at my desk with the class schedule up on my computer. I'd looked it over and jotted some notes on scrap paper. The notes were really just a list of students. Howie had had three episodes, two of which I had witnessed. Without talking to the dorm parents who led the soccer game over the weekend, I had no way of knowing the particular students present during that one. That left me with Novak's third period and Hart's sixth period classes. Which students overlapped? There were six, but only one of them stood out to me.

I hate to be lazy in my thinking, making assumptions and that sort of thing. I also know the danger in blaming the "outsider" for things that go wrong. Even with those thoughts in mind, I couldn't help but to believe that Morris Starr was the most likely candidate for bad guy status. I'd circled his name so heavily on my list that graphite dust powdered the page.

Three of the overlapping students had been at the Mannaz School for over a year. Two had been at Mannaz for six weeks, seven counting the orientation week. It seemed strange that any of them would have waited this long to start mischief. It made more sense for the new trouble to come from a new source.

That left Morris.

And, of course, Howie himself was a common factor in all of the occurrences. Moe had given him a thorough going-over and found nothing out of the ordinary. Of course, we didn't know exactly what we were looking for, but we should have found something if there was anything to find. For the time being, that was my premise.

I was going to meet Morris and see if any bells went off.

I got up from my desk chair and flexed my leg. The super-itch was decreasing. I would be whole soon, maybe an hour or so. The duct tape tugging on my leg hair was now nearly as bothersome as the injury itself. I considered removing my makeshift bandage, but decided to wait until after school. That way I could throw the hairy duct tape and bloody t-shirt into my private trashcan.

I debated whether or not I should separate Moe from Howie so that my trusty familiar and I could get a look at Morris. I would hate to make a mistake. Caution was important, but some action had to be taken. While Moe was my best resource, he wasn't all I had. I had me too.

I like detective fiction, and I have read a good deal of it over the last eighty or so years. There are a number of things that guys like Philip Marlowe, Lew Archer, and Mike Shayne have in common. One in particular is that none of them have a familiar to do their investigating for them. They pound the pavement and use their eyes and ears to find clues. I figured that I could do the same.

Morris was in art class with George Ryan last period, so I put on my bomber jacket and headed over to check him out. The art room was in Willow House which was really just across the lawn, like fifty feet. The temperature hadn't climbed much since the morning, and the chill was invigorating. It was slightly overcast, and the light had the blunted, washed-out quality I associated with autumn and winter in Western New York. The little walk across the grassy lawn with that nip in the air did something to center me. I was alert. I had a plan.

The art room was on the first floor of Willow House, but the first floor was actually halfway below ground, so it had somewhat of a basement vibe. Entering made me feel like I was going into Cheers except that there was no beer inside.

I knocked to announce myself even though I would have been completely visible from the window as I came down the steps. It was strange for me to go through a door without Moe to tell me what was on the other side. I felt vulnerable. If you wore a blindfold or even earplugs, you might have a sense of it. My knock wasn't of the waiting-to-be-invited variety. It was a heads-up knock, so I just went in.

Seven students and George Ryan were spread around the available space, a still-life in the center of the room. Each kid had an oversized drawing pad on a desk easel and was trying to render the random objects which George had carefully arranged on a high table.

I heard a chorus of "Hey, Mr. Brannon," and the kids continued to draw.

George said, "Have you come to see some art?"

He was a big blond man in his early thirties, but he didn't give the impression of physical strength the way Novak did. Something about him made me think of a St. Bernard but less drooly. He dressed well, but it was impossible to tell most of the time because he usually wore a thigh-length, white painter's smock.

He was drawing too. Most of the time, he completed the same assignments that he gave the students. That was generally more difficult at the start of the year because students required more minding before they learned and accepted his classroom expectations. This class, with the exception of Morris, was made up of returning students, and everyone seemed to be riding easy in the reins.

"I like to check in," I said.

I moved from student to student looking at their charcoal renderings, but I wasn't really looking all that closely at the pictures. I was looking at Morris.

He was pale and plump, but not quite plump enough to be chubby. His hair was dark and unkempt. It stood up at the back of his head where he'd slept on it, and he hadn't bothered to comb it down. His cheeks were full and he had light freckles that made him look healthy despite the whiteness of his complexion. His eyes were bright green like spring grass. He wore jeans and a t-shirt with a green shamrock on it. Was it some kind of a retro Care Bear shirt? I didn't think that bad guys were allowed to wear Care Bear shirts.

Without Moe, I couldn't sense anything more than a normal human could. I had more experience than a normal human, though, and I'd hoped that I might spot some tell-tale sign. But he just looked like a twelve-year-old boy who needed more exercise.

So, yeah, it's weird on some level to look at a little kid to figure out whether he's a monster or not. It's that weirdness that makes the whole scenario so brilliant, though. It's pretty common for supernatural predators to appear either very attractive or very harmless, maybe both. They may or may not really look the way you see them, but it comes to the same thing. They want your guard down. For example, big, tattooed people wearing skulls and black leather and whatnot tend to make people wary. Not so for cute little children.

Morris noticed me standing beside him as I pretended to look at his picture. He grinned up at me. There was a slight gap between his front teeth. That and his freckles and chubby cheeks and messy hair made him look like he'd stepped out of a Norman Rockwell painting.

I said, "You must be Morris."

He held out his hand for me to shake and said, "Everybody calls me Morrey."

I heard a slight lisp at the end of "calls." Jeez Louise.

I shook his hand despite the charcoal dust. All in the line of duty. He pumped my hand up and down like he was trying to get water to come out of me.

I took my hand away from him and asked, "How are you liking the Mannaz School so far?"

His eyes grew serious and he covertly looked around the room at the other students. He whispered, "I like everything but the scary boy who gets so angry all of the time."

None of the students seemed very interested in what he said, but Morrey's eyes kept darting around to spot any possible eavesdroppers. He added, "I don't feel safe when he's around."

"We'll keep you safe," I said.

His head bobbed a couple of times, and his brows drew together. "You did seem to get there really fast both times today." His eyes overtly appraised me.

Did I see something a little too aware behind those eyes or was I projecting, thinking of him too much as a suspect?

Back in Oak House, Moe heard the voices of students as they entered the nurse's office. They were low and mumbling, but I heard a "feel like crap" from one and a "stomach hurts" from another. Something was up, and I decided that my physical self should probably check it out.

I said, "Keep up the good work," to the class in general and made my escape.

The voices of the students in the nurse's office had awakened Howie, and a moment later, Missy looked in through the door at him. She saw that he was awake and entered. After a quick appraisal, she asked him, "How are you feeling?"

He said, "Just a little tired, I guess."

"Can you give up the bed?"

"Sure."

Howie swung his legs over the side of the bed and looked around for his shoes. Missy picked up his shoes from the foot of the bed and put them by his feet as she knelt in front of him. She touched his forehead and looked into his eyes and felt along his jawline. The crease appeared between her brows again.

She stood and said, "You look just fine. After you put on your shoes come out to the office."

A girl named Kate entered the cot room as Howie was tying his shoes. She lay down on the other cot without taking off her own shoes and was sleeping before Howie finished wrapping the second bow. There was concern on his face as he watched her sleep for just a moment.

Kate had been in class with Howie both third and sixth period. Was there a connection? I had a sinking sensation in my stomach.

As I approached the nurse's office, I saw Todd standing outside of the door, leaning against the wall and appearing to be hung over from a world-class bender. He'd also been on the list of students who'd been with Howie both third and sixth period. He looked up at me as I approached but didn't say anything.

I asked, "What are you doing in the hall?"

He smiled slightly and said, "Full house."

"What's the matter?"

Todd shrugged. "Don't feel good."

"Hang in there," I said and entered the office.

Missy had her back to me with her phone in her hands. My phone chimed and she turned to face me. The corner of her mouth quirked, and she held up her phone to show that she had been texting.

She pointed at the pocket where I carried my phone and said, "That's me. Can you take Howie? I need the bed."

"Yeah, I actually came here to check on him anyway," I said.

Andy was sitting on Missy's office chair with his legs stretched out in front of him. He looked a little peaked but not too bad. He noted my look in his direction and waved vaguely.

Howie appeared in the connecting door and asked me, "What's going on, Mr. Brannon?" He was clearly anxious, worried.

I looked to Missy.

She said, "I'm not a hundred percent sure. I haven't taken much of a look at Todd yet, but Katie and Andy look exhausted. If I didn't know better, I might say that they're hung over."

Andy grinned a little at that and held up his hands in a mock warding gesture. "You can't prove a thing."

Missy said, "I think that this wise guy can relax in the common room. I'll keep an eye on Kate and Todd for a while." She gestured to Howie, "Howie's recovery was quick, and I bet theirs will be, too."

"Does it look like the same thing?" I asked.

"Not quite but similar." She looked at the doorway to the hall and said, "Let me get Todd before he falls over."

Howie crossed the room to stand by me while Missy got Todd situated on the recently vacated cot. Howie didn't say anything, but Moe could feel that his blood pressure was high and his breathing a little quick. I squeezed his shoulder and said, "None of this is your fault. Relax if you can." I hoped it was true. You know, that it wasn't his fault. It was difficult to imagine that he'd worry so much about the other kids if he'd hurt them. Well, if he did it on purpose, that is.

When she came out of the cot room, Missy said, "Will you stay here for a minute while I get these guys settled in the common room?" She indicated Howie and Andy.

Howie looked at me with some alarm, and I said, "I'll be out to get you as soon as Ms. Waters and I have a chat." I couldn't very well add that Moe would be guarding him, comforting as that may have been.

The two boys trailed along behind her as she walked toward the common room. Moe stuck with Howie. She got them settled into comfortable chairs with magazines and said, "Come see me if you feel any worse. Go to after-school activities if you're up to it. If not, check in with Dr. Corman. He'll be in my office."

As soon as Missy left, Andy said to Howie, "So, do you got some kind of seizure issue or somethin'?"

Howie shook his head, and I didn't think he was going to say anything aloud, but he did. "I never have before."

"That sucks, man." Andy looked serious and added, "You can't really swallow your tongue."

"What?"

"You know, when you. . ." Andy widened his eyes and showed his gritted teeth and flopped around in his chair for a few seconds. ". . . you know, like that."

Howie's mouth was hanging open slightly when Andy finished his performance. "Do I look like that when the thing happens?"

Andy shrugged noncommittally. "I used some artistic license."

Missy returned to the office and she fixed me with that penetrating stare of hers. I withstood it until she finally said, "Okay, Sean, do you have any idea what's going on?"

I lied. "I have no idea whatever." But it wasn't lying by very much.

She looked at me for a couple of beats longer. Then, she sat down on her desk chair. "If the kids didn't come in all at once, I wouldn't feel much concern. Mostly, they seem really tired. The fact that four kids came in in that state at about the same time seems very unlikely."

I didn't say anything.

She continued, "Howie, was a little different. Well, not so much different as more extreme. Now, he seems okay again."

"What should we do?"

"If Dr. Corman wasn't an MD, I would feel more reluctant to go home. I'll talk to him. . ." She looked down at her wristwatch. ". . . in fifteen minutes when seventh period is over. Then, I'll leave it in his hands."

"What's your professional opinion?"

She shrugged and made a sort of motor boat sound. "Something sucked the energy out of them all at the same time."

I held up my hands and wiggled my fingers making a ghostly sound. "Ooohooooohooo."

She shook her head at me, an amused quirk at the corner of her mouth. "Get out of here, wise guy."

Andy was asking Howie if he heard voices that told him to kill people or anything like that, but he stopped talking well before I came into hearing range. I walked directly up to Andy and pointed down at him. He looked up at me innocently.

I said, "Andy, be nice. Sensitive to others. You know, the stuff I've been asking you to do for over three years now."

He kept up the innocent expression and added raised eyebrows. "What do you mean, Mr. Brannon?"

I smiled down and said, "I can only resist the voices in my head for so long, Andy."

His expression changed from innocent to awed and a bit nervous. He said, "Dude."

I pointed both index fingers at him and made that clucking sound horse riders make when they want the horse to giddy up.

I abruptly turned to Howie who wore an expression similar to the one that Andy had. I said, "You want to help me with a project this afternoon?"

"Uhm. . . sure."

"Come on, then," I said, and we left the common room together.

I heard Andy's voice say behind us, "You bugged the place."

Howie followed me to my room. I flicked on the lights and said, "Grab a seat for a minute. I have to make some arrangements."

I called Allie's classroom line. It rang twice and she picked up. "Ms. Park's room."

"Hello, Ms. Park. This is Mr. Brannon."

"What can I do for you, Mr. Brannon?"

"Will you take my creative writing class in ten minutes?"

She paused briefly and said, "Is anything wrong?"

"Not so much. Howie and I just have a project to work on."

"Okay," she said. "Do you have sub plans in your room?"

"That's the thing. We're going to need my room, so I was hoping that you could keep the students in your room. If you have anything fun for them to work on, you can do that, or we can drop off the sub plans."

"Bring the plans over," she said. "Who will I have?"

"Karen, Bret, Andy, and maybe Todd."

"You'll owe me," she said.

I made another couple of calls to make sure that the students went to Allie's room instead of mine at the end of the regular school day. Missy let me know that Todd would be staying in the nurse's office to sleep, and Dr. Corman would be in to relieve her. That left only Andy in the common room to inform. I hoped he wouldn't try to play sick.

With the sub folder in hand, Howie and I went to Allie's room. Her door was open, so I waved to get her attention. Her students were clearly finished with their work and socializing at their desks, and they didn't even seem to notice us. She walked toward us, and I recognized the look on her face. She was worried.

She looked directly into my eyes and said, "Something's going on."

"Nothing big," I lied.

"You'll tell me later," she said. There was clearly no doubt in her mind that I would spill. She was rarely wrong about things like that, but this was one of the times when she was.

She held out her hand, and I gave her the folder. She slapped it against her thigh absently, and the green of the dress and the red of the folder made me think of Christmas. She said, "Is it seatwork, or do I need to teach anything?"

"I give them the first page of a story, and they need to continue it. It's pretty straightforward."

I thought that she was going to say something. Then, she decided not to. She held up the folder and said, "I'll leave this in your mailbox after class. I hope your project goes well."

Howie and I had to hustle to get downstairs before the end-of-day bell. When we entered the common room, we found that Andy had tipped three chairs upside-down and as examining them closely. He looked at me with narrowed eyes, his lips pursed.

"Okay, where is it?"

"You look like you're feeling better," I said.

"How did you know what I said about the voices?"

I noted that Howie looked at me curiously, too, and I regretted giving in to my impulse to mess with Andy. I considered telling the truth so that they would dismiss my answer as a crazy fabrication. Sometimes kids believed crazy things, though. I went with a reasonable fabrication instead.

"It was just a trick of acoustics. I've got good hearing."

Andy looked unconvinced. Howie appeared skeptical as well.

Andy said, "I never heard any trick of acoustics before."

"Have you ever listened closely from the foot of the stairs over there?" I asked.

He shrugged.

I said, "Anyway, Ms. Park has creative writing today, so you should go to her room when the bell rings."

Andy's eyes lit up, and he grinned broadly. Just then, the bell rang, and he was halfway to the stairs before I could call out to him.

"Andy, chairs."

He skidded to a halt and came back. He didn't bother to argue and quickly righted the chairs before hurrying off again. I tried not to feel offended that he looked forward to class with Allie but did everything he could to avoid it with me.

I said to Howie, "Okay, let's get our coats. We're going shopping."

# Chapter 8

Howie retrieved a gray, autumn-weight L. L. Bean field jacket and Yankees ball cap from his designated coat hooks just outside the common room. Then, we returned to my room, so I could get my bomber jacket. Apparently, he hadn't taken note of it when he was using it for a pillow because he eyed it appreciatively.

I shrugged into it, and he said, "Hey, Indiana Jones."

I said, "Yeah, it's a classic. You know who Indiana Jones is?"

"My dad and I watch all the movies about once a year, even *Crystal Skull*."

I eyed him. "Even *Crystal Skull*?"

"Dad's a real fan."

My hair was too long to pull off a fedora, but the combo would have been a good look. I'd actually bought the jacket not long after Novak and I had gone to the Olean Mall to see the third movie. Many years later, when he started dating Christie, I called her Elsa because she bore a passing resemblance to the hot Nazi lady.

We stopped in at the office for school van keys and both got a dose of Pam smiles too. When she referred to him by name, Howie blushed until he was the color of a fire engine. Pam's sunshiny smile had struck again. It seemed that another adoring fan was born.

Howie markedly avoided looking at the plywood-covered windows of Willow House as we walked past. Once it was behind us, he seemed to open up a little. The lot wasn't far, and it was about half empty. There were three twelve-passenger vans in a back corner. Two were white with green "Mannaz School" emblems on the doors. One was green with white emblems. That was ours.

Howie said, "That's a cool, old car," when we neared the Nova. He jogged over to it and looked into the window. He pointed inside and said, "Hey, it's a D20 on the shifter!"

The kid was gaining points left and right. I said, "It's mine."

"Can we ride in it?"

"Sadly, no," I said.

"Why not?"

"Oh, there are lots of reasons. It's not strong on safety features, and I don't have the right kind of insurance to drive kids."

I pointed to the green van. "That's us."

I don't know if Howie was actually disappointed or if I was projecting. After I unlocked the doors with the key fob, he climbed right into the sliding door and buckled up on the bench seat behind me. When I began my career at the Mannaz School, I wouldn't have hesitated to have Howie sit in the front seat of the van next to mine. Times had changed, though, and policy stated that twelve-year-olds couldn't sit in the front seat. He didn't seem to mind. But why would he? That's all he'd known.

The behemoth of a vehicle handled like a bag of wet sand, but it would take us down the road alright. I looked longingly at Lore as we drove by. It was still another mile into Geary proper. The town was little more than the intersection of 19A and Main Street. In town, 19A became State Street, but no one called it that. It was still 19A. There were more residential streets, but virtually all of the businesses could be found along the two main roadways. All told, Geary boasted a population somewhere around two thousand. We were headed to the Flower Shop. Yep, that's what it was called. There didn't seem to be enough emphasis on a good business name in Geary. Places were just what they were.

I parked the van on the street because if I used the little parking lot along the side of the building, I would have to back it up to get out. That was more trouble than I wanted to take. There was plenty of room curbside, which was good because the van took up a space and a half.

There was rarely much traffic in Geary, and today was no exception. The overcast sky was darkening even more as sunset approached, and a number of the cars which drove by had their headlights on. I noted that Howie zipped his coat higher as soon as he climbed out of the car, and I thought about how much I had acclimated to Western New York weather. It got pretty damn cold here.

The Flower Shop was a low building which had been a powder blue at one time. Now, it was a flaky, peeling gray. We walked along the sidewalk which was cracked and slightly buckled in a number of places. Random tufts of grass grew up through the cracks. I don't mean to imply that The Flower Shop stood out as an eyesore or anything. It blended in with the rest of the town. There was actually a brand-new sign hanging on the building, bright white and sporting primary-colored flowers. It was quite nice and did nothing so much as emphasize the shabbiness of its surroundings.

Howie followed me dutifully into the store though he was clearly puzzled by the destination. A bell chimed as we entered, and an overweight, gray-haired woman wearing a multicolored flower-print dress greeted us. "Afternoon. What can I do you for?"

Howie looked a question at me. I don't think he'd ever heard the "What can I do you for?" line before. I just gave him a nod, and he turned his attention back to the woman.

Because the Mannaz School was a boarding school which provided housing for employees, many faculty and staff didn't make much by way of connections in town. They were like tourists who needed supplies from time to time. People in Geary knew each other, often for several generations, so they usually took note when strangers were about. I fit into a strange, very narrow demographic. I had been around for thirty years, and my hair made me easy to identify and remember later. Not everyone would know my name, but they probably could tell you that I was that redheaded guy who worked at that crazy school.

I said, "Good afternoon. I would like to buy two dozen, long-stemmed red roses, please."

She looked first surprised, then pleased. "Comin' right up," she said and bustled away.

Howie stared up at me and asked, "Are they for Ms. Park?"

"Why would you think that?"

He shrugged. "She's the prettiest girl at school."

I said, "No, they're not for Ms. Park."

"Are they for Dr. Corman's secretary?"

I chuckled a little, and even though I was curious about who he'd guess next, I said, "These flowers are for our project. I'm not giving them to anyone."

He looked skeptical, but he didn't ask about any other potential recipients. He wandered around the shop a little as we waited, looking at the flowers in the coolers and little plush animals holding hearts and bows and such. The shop was small, and there was a bit of a rabbit warren feel to it. The warmth and soft lighting added to the coziness. Quietly from distant speakers, someone sang about being a common man and driving a common van.

Howie returned to the counter when the flowers were ready. The florist presented them with a flourish and said, "There sure is a lucky lady back home."

I'd definitely seen better roses, but I really didn't care how pretty or fresh they were. I don't mean to say they looked horrible or anything, but I had the feeling that the petals would begin falling off pretty quickly. They were plenty good for my purpose.

I thanked the florist and paid her in cash, which seemed to please her a great deal. I handed the bouquet to Howie, and we departed.

Roses are all full of symbolic value and historical significance, but there is also a supernatural potency to them. Their uses are broad, and they work well as substitutes for more exotic plants. I was not an expert in botany, supernatural or otherwise, but it's hard to be around as long as I had been and not pick up a few things.

Howie carried the bouquet of roses to the van. He cradled them carefully like a new-born baby, and I hoped that he wouldn't feel too bad when we wrecked them. I opened the door for him, and he handed me the flowers while he climbed in. I tossed them on the seat next to him, and he looked at me in shock as though I had actually tossed a baby or some other precious thing.

I kind of wanted to make an outing of it. As time passed since Howie's last episode, he seemed to grow more comfortable, and I liked the change in him. There wasn't much by way of quick treats in Geary. A diner, a supermarket, and a couple of gas stations were about it. Well, there were the bars. The Bar would probably even serve Howie. That was the joke among the residence of Geary anyway. If you could see over the bar, they'd serve you.

I chuckled a little at the thought of taking Howie to The Bar.

Howie asked, "What's funny?"

I buckled my seatbelt and said, "Platypuses."

"You were thinking about platypuses?"

"Nope."

"Then, why did you say they're funny?"

"Because they're like ducks and beavers mixed together."

He was clearly not sure how to respond to my silliness, so he picked up the flowers again and held them on his lap. He looked out the window as we drove, the buildings giving way to fields and trees. The sky continued to darken.

We'd been driving for a minute or so when Howie asked, "Are you going to tell me what our project is?"

"Sure," I said. "It's kind of an arts and crafts thing. We're going to make rings, like big hula hoop-sized rings."

"We're making hula hoops out of roses?"

"That's only part of it. I'll talk you through it when we get all of our materials together."

Back on campus, we parked the van and took the roses to my classroom. I retrieved a huge ring of keys from a desk drawer and handed over my four-cell Maglite to Howie. I asked, "Are you ready to hunt up some supplies?"

He flicked the flashlight on and off and said, "Check."

It wasn't four o'clock yet, but it was close to full dark because of the overcast sky. We headed along a wide trail, known to both the faculty and students alike as the Low Road. After about two hundred yards, we came to the outdoor archery range which was set up in a clearing with a steep gravelly hillside behind it. The all-weather, circular foam targets were backed up against the hillside to ensure that poorly aimed arrows wouldn't travel far. We weren't concerned with archery, though. We were collecting red-orange rocks which were mixed in with the gravel on the slope. Howie slowly swept the bank with the flashlight, and I picked rocks. Once I had a dozen or so good ones stuffed into the pockets of my jacket, we headed back along the path toward main campus.

Along the way we stopped at one of Noah's sheds. It contained mostly gardening supplies. It took me a while to find the key to the padlock. I had keys to pretty much everything, which I didn't use unless someone was with me. Moe could open virtually any lock.

There was no electricity in the shed, so Howie was on flashlight duty again. I really didn't need the light, but I had to pretend. The shed was neatly swept and organized, so it didn't take long for us to find what I was looking for, plant wire. I don't know if that's really what it's called. It was in a big spool and was used to train vines to grow a certain way. It seemed to be similar to electric fence wire, but the plant wire was coated in rubberized plastic. Noah had told me once that the wire was coated because it had a high iron content and was prone to rusting. I wasn't sure how much I'd need, so I took the whole spool. I was the type of guy to carry a bigger burden and make fewer trips. You know, macho.

The spool wasn't really all that big or heavy. I could have carried it easily in one arm, but I'm much stronger than I look. No use in drawing attention with acts of Herculean strength, so I used both arms.

We still weren't done, though. From the art room in Willow House, we took a four-foot-by-four-foot paint tarp and a big bottle of art glue. Howie carried them and wielded the Maglite. We managed the doors into Oak House and into my room awkwardly, but there was something fun about struggling with those simple physical challenges. It was like a Three Stooges routine, except that our third stooge had to sit out. Moe just trailed around instead of opening the doors. He has no mouth, but if he did, I bet he would have been laughing at us.

And we still weren't done. There was a lot of ranging and carrying, and Howie didn't complain once. We walked to the theater next. I kept the flashlight, but it was off because the way was lit well enough by the streetlights. The theater was one of the buildings off the square, so we didn't have all that far to go. I flicked on the lights as we went through the entrance, auditorium, greenroom, and scene shop. Howie was clearly impressed, his eyes round and trying to take in everything. I felt a wave of affection for him then for being so full of wonder. Kids can get cynical young.

I said, "Is this the first time you're seeing all this?"

"Yeah."

"Dr. Corman is a big fan of the dramatic arts. He usually shows this building off to any touring families."

Howie said, "My dad wasn't sure if he could afford to send me here. He got a windfall or something like that, and we kind of rushed the whole admissions thing."

So, it seemed that Howie wasn't booted from his last school. And relatively speaking, his family wasn't rich. I was liking this kid more by the minute. Not that I had anything against rich people. Despite my chosen lifestyle, I was one.

"Do you like to act?" I asked.

"Acting is okay. Mostly, I like to sing and dance." He looked a little embarrassed like he'd admitted to playing with Barbie dolls or something.

"That's awesome," I said.

"Really?"

"Yeah, we usually put on at least one musical every year here. You can try out. I think that Ms. Park might be directing this year."

His head bobbed and a goofy grin stretched across his face. "My dad and I like to watch old Gene Kelly and Fred Astaire movies."

"Maybe we can watch one on a movie night this year," I said. "In the meantime, I need you to help me carry a rug."

We worked our way past shelves of paint and flats to a corner full of rolled rugs. They were on end, and the smaller ones were in front, so we didn't have to dig. I didn't care what colors or pattern was on the rug and just grabbed one that was at least four feet wide. He took one end and I took the other. We shut off the lights as we exited.

It was a pretty easy weight to bear, so I stopped at the kitchen pantry before we returned to my room. When I emerged carrying a five-pound bag of salt, Howie actually said aloud, "What. . . but why?'

"It's for our project."

"We're making a hula hoop out of salt?"

I said, "Not so much. You'll see."

I stooped over and grabbed my end of the rolled rug with one hand and carried the salt in the other. "Let's go. Get your end, please."

We didn't have any doors to open until we got to my room, just a set of stairs to climb. We did a good job of it. We were getting the hang of the teamwork thing.

Once we were back in my room, we cleared the desks out of the way. There wasn't much room, but we were able to put two against each other and put another on top. We built one desk stack in the front of the room and one on the wall opposite my desk and ended up with a pretty wide space to work.

We laid out the painter tarp in front of my desk as close as we could get it. Using the art glue, I made a circle but left an inch unfinished. It was as big as I could draw and stay on the tarp, three and a half feet in diameter. Moe is good with geometry, so it was about as round as a guy with a squirt-bottle of glue could make it.

Because it was a team project, I had Howie carefully cover the glue ring with salt, leaving only the unglued inch unfinished. I was impressed with his fine motor coordination. The boy had some skills.

Moe helped a great deal with the next part, too, but of course, Howie didn't know that. To him, I was just really good at circles. We measured off eleven and a half feet of the plant wire, and I skinned the plastic coating from the last three inches on either end. The wire was malleable, and we easily bent it into a ring. We bent hooks into the ends of the wire, so the metal would be in contact when we connected them.

We looked at our metal ring on the floor next to our salt circle. They were of a size.

Howie said, "Mr. Brannon, do you ever read fairy tales?"

"Sure, I used to be an English teacher."

"This makes me think of something you might use to catch a fairy."

Howie was full of surprises.

I said, "We're not done yet. The next job will take the most finesse. Grab the roses and bring them over."

I took a bag of wire twist ties from the closet. Then, I sat cross-legged on the floor on one side of the metal ring and motioned for Howie to sit opposite me. He sat, holding the flowers on his lap. I demonstrated for him how I wanted him to twine the rose stems around the plant wire and secure them with the twist ties.

He cringed a little when he saw some of the petals come loose and fall to the floor.

"Boy, you really like flowers, huh." I said.

He looked at the floor and said quietly, "My dad used to bring a red rose home to my mom every day when he came home from work." He shrugged. "It was nice. She really liked it."

Shit. Normally, I would have read up on incoming students. Howie came late, and I didn't this time. I assumed that the mom was no longer in the mortal coil. This was tricky. If he wanted to talk, he could. If he wanted to drop it, he could do that too.

I said, "If you don't want to do this part, you can take a break."

"No, it's okay. I want to finish the fairy trap."

"Fairy trap? What are you talking about? Who catches fairies with roses?"

"Don't roses do something to vampires? I saw that in an old movie once."

Damn.

"What?" I said. "You don't believe in vampires, do you? This is arts and crafts."

Howie shrugged. "Why not?"

He deftly twined the roses around the ring, and we finished quickly. We tested the hooks at the ends of the wire. When they connected, overlapping rose stems crossed over each other completing the circle of roses simultaneously.

We stood and looked down at our work. It was good.

Now what?

Until the attacker was identified and dealt with, I wanted to keep Howie as safe as I could. There had been no episodes while he was in his dorm, so I felt that he would probably be safe there. I could chance the dorm.

The dining room was another story. All of the students and many of the faculty would be there for supper. Nothing had happened in the dining room yet, but all of the players would be there. The dining room just didn't feel safe. Maybe Moe and I could get Howie out before anything happened this time, but I didn't want to chance it. I wanted to control all of the factors that I could.

I said, "Hey, do you want to go back into town and get a burger? The diner there is pretty good."

"Aren't we going to finish?"

"What? This?" I waved at the rings on the floor. "We are finished."

He said, "I can help you lower the rug onto the salt ring. I doubt that the glue is really dry yet."

I said nothing.

He looked at me for a little while, and I continued to say nothing.

Finally, he said, "So, you're going to get someone to stand in the rings. Then, you're going to close the rings somehow without him knowing, and he'll be trapped. But you don't know what he is, so you did more than one kind of ring."

"He?" I asked.

Howie shrugged. "Or she." After a little. "Or it."

Damn.

"Let's put it together then," I said.

# Chapter 9

I told Howie that the rings weren't a fairy trap or a vampire trap or any other kind of a trap, and he didn't insist that they were. We went ahead and set up the non-existent trap together, anyway. My denial was really pointless in everything but technicality, but the Venator Council was pretty into technicalities.

If Morrey was anything other than a little boy, he wasn't a vampire. But roses bound things other than vampires. I didn't really know anything about him. This was a roll of the dice. I might get lucky. It was better than sitting around and waiting for another attack.

When we were truly finished with our project, I texted Corman and told him that Howie would be with me for supper. We returned to Geary and ate bacon cheeseburgers at Bettie's Diner. Bettie was still there almost every day. She used to be gorgeous, but a lifetime of smoking and diner food had taken its toll.

Howie and I talked over the meal, and I learned that his father was a widower. He was a modestly successful contractor in Buffalo. It had been just the two of them for over a year, and they watched a lot of movies together. There seemed to be a great deal of love between them but not much direction.

When we returned to school, we parked the van, and I walked Howie to his dorm, Beech House. Maggie James was a bit of a punster and had decorated the bulletin board in the kitchen with a tropical theme. You know, beach house instead of beech house. Most new dorm parents did some variation on that, thinking that it was a novel idea. It was a good idea anyway, a classic. It could handle some repetition.

After Howie went to his room, I spoke to Maggie in private. We went into her room which was messy without being dirty. The theme of the clutter was sports and leisure. One corner was mounded with an immense pile of athletic shoes. In another, a hockey stick and a lacrosse stick leaned against a pile of protective gear. Articles from no fewer than three different uniforms were scattered across her bed. The bed was neatly made, however.

She sat on her bed and motioned me to the chair in front of her desk. She looked a little anxious, and I wondered if it was because of Howie's explosions or if she thought she was in trouble for some reason.

I leaned forward, elbows on my knees. I was going for a casual, collaborative pose. "Howie's had a bit of a long day. We ended well, and I'm pretty sure you'll have a smooth night with him. If you need anything, though, call my cell. It doesn't matter what time it is."

She nodded and said, "Thanks, Mr. Brannon."

I thought it was a little funny when some of the younger faculty called me Mister even when there were no students around.

She chewed on her lower lip a little, and I could tell that she was taking time to form a question. "Is there anything wrong with him? Like epilepsy or something? I've never seen an epileptic fit, but some of what he did made me think of. . . you know. . . what people say about them."

"You saw one of his episodes?"

"Yeah, Terry and I had the soccer activity over the weekend."

I tried to think of some artful way to turn the conversation around to get the information that I wanted but decided that I just didn't have the patience for it. I asked for what I wanted. "Was Morrey Starr in the activity? The other new kid."

"Yeah, he was there, but he didn't play. He said he wasn't feeling well. I thought he was just being lazy, but I didn't want to push him on his first day. The kid looks like he could use the exercise, though."

"If he didn't play, what did he do?"

"He sat on the sideline. I was playing, so I didn't watch much. A couple of times when I looked over, he was watching the game close."

Morrey, the unknown factor, was present during all three of Howie's episodes. There was no guarantee that Morrey was the villain of this piece, but I was feeling more and more confident that he was. Maybe I was forcing the confidence, though, because if it turned out not to be him, I had nowhere else to go.

I excused myself and encouraged Maggie to call any time she needed a hand. Then, I left Beech House and went directly to Maple

House, the residence of Morrey Starr. None of the buildings were far from each other, but Beech and Maple were about as far apart as they got, maybe ten minutes.

I enjoyed the walk through the crisp autumn evening. Moe was with me, so I had no need for a flashlight. I really didn't like being separate from him for very long. There's no physical strain when he's away, but I feel uneasy, sort of incomplete. It was nice to be together.

When I came within sight of Maple House, I sent Moe ahead. I hadn't done much by way of spying for a long time, and I had to admit to feeling a little thrill. I was glad to be on the offensive instead of just trying to keep Howie safe. The thought caused a jolt of self-doubt. If I was wrong about Morrey and/or the safety of Beech House, Howie could be in danger. I couldn't know everything, and I wouldn't do anyone any good wringing my hands while Moe was on unending guard duty.

Moe didn't know exactly which room was Morrey's, but he's fast and not hampered by things like walls. He found the right place in only a few seconds. The boy was still wearing his jeans and shamrock t-shirt, but he wore slippers instead of sneakers. At first, I thought he was doing homework, but it was something else entirely.

Morrey was hunched over a yellowed piece of paper. The words written on the paper were not in any language that I recognized. In fact, I didn't even recognize the letters. The ink was brownish and faded and smudged. The paper had clearly been folded in quarters for a long time because the edges of the paper and the folds were brown with age. It looked very fragile.

So, I guessed I was getting somewhere.

I knocked on the front door of Maple House because it was polite, but I just walked in after the knock. It was standard operating procedure. Terry Brown, the dorm parent, sat at the kitchen table with a new student named James, no Jimmy. Jimmy was a fourth grader, and it appeared that they were working on long division.

They both looked up as I walked in and waited for me to speak.

I obliged. "Hey, Mr. Brown. I was hoping to chat with Morrey for a bit. Is he busy?"

In his room, Morrey's head jerked up at the sound of my voice. His eyes looked into the middle distance as people often do when focusing on listening. If he could hear me, he had some spectacular hearing. I proceeded as if he could.

Terry was thin in a fit way. He favored a hodge-podge retro look that worked well for him. He wore thick-framed Buddy Holly glasses and an olive-green Fleetwood Mac t-shirt with the band name in orange and yellow. His hair was a little long, not unlike my own but in a medium-brown shade. He spun a yellow pencil in his fingers like it was a tiny baton.

"Morrey's in his room. You want me to get him?"

I waved my hand. "I can find him."

At that, Morrey quickly and deftly refolded the paper and put it into the bottom drawer of his desk. From the same drawer, he removed a manga book that said *Astro Boy* across the cover. By the time I reached his door, he was reclining casually on his bed. He wasn't reading, though. He was very clearly listening to my approach.

When I knocked, he nodded his head three times. The old three count so he wouldn't seem overeager. Then, he yawned dramatically and said, "Yeah?"

I said, "Morrey, it's Mr. Brannon. I met you today in art class."

He was silent for another three count. "Come in."

I opened the door. Morrey would have looked just like a twelve-year-old boy lounging around in his room if Moe hadn't watched him so carefully arrange himself. His hair was still messy, and settled back into the pillows like he was, he created an image reminiscent of countless movie and tv portrayals of kids. I'd watched him set it up, so I knew it was contrived. But if I'd just walked in like a regular guy, I think he would have fooled me.

"Hey, Morrey," I said, putting on the old-buddy cadence. "I've fallen down on my job just a bit because I wasn't here over the weekend when you arrived. I was wondering if you could help me out."

He sat up and swung his feet off the bed. His Beaver Clever earnestness may have been a little overdone, but just a little. "What do you need Mr. Brannon?"

"Well, I have a little paperwork I need to fill out, and I'll need you to come to my office to answer some questions."

"Can't you ask me here?"

I grinned sheepishly. Both of us could act. "It would be easier in my office. See, there is no real paper in the paperwork. I need to enter the data directly onto the school's drive. It would just take a few minutes, and you can help me save time and effort."

"Gosh, I'm really tired. Why can't we do it tomorrow?"

His reluctance didn't come across as strange. He'd established himself as being on the lazy side. I thought that there was something calculating about it, though, something cautious. If I played the heavy, his guard would come up even more firmly.

I loaded up on the confidential air. After a deep sigh, I said, "May I sit down for a minute?"

"Sure," he said.

I pulled out his desk chair and sat in a pose almost identical to the one I'd used when talking to Maggie. We were collaborating. Leaning forward, elbows on knees, I said in a low voice as though someone might be listening, "I kind of have my hands full during the day."

Morrey put on his nervous, almost frightened face. "You mean the scary boy."

"His name is Howie, and I'd like to be able to focus on him during the day. You can really help me out by giving me a few minutes tonight. I would appreciate it a lot."

"That boy doesn't make me feel very safe."

My expression was as compassionate as I could make it without going into melodrama. "I'll keep everyone safe. I can do that better if I can keep from dividing my attention."

Morrey nodded bravely. "Can you give me a few minutes? I got to get my shoes on. And if I brush my teeth now, I won't have to do it when I get back."

I looked at my watch. It was barely seven.

I said, "Okay, I'll wait downstairs."

112

I went downstairs, but Moe stayed with Morrey. I lingered at the foot of the stairs because I wanted to focus on what Moe saw, and Terry and Jimmy might be distracting.

Morrey sat for a minute, his eyes unfocused. He was thinking hard, probably planning. Then, he stood decisively, went to his desk, and removed the yellow paper. He returned to the bed and knelt next to it. He reached underneath and pulled out a wooden box. It was dark, maybe mahogany, and its hinges and lock looked like brass. It was about twelve inches by nine inches and about four inches deep. A music box?

He placed the box on the floor and settled in front of it with his knees on either side. From beneath his shirt, he drew a chain with a small brass key hanging from it. He didn't insert the key into the lock right away though. First, he traced an X on the lid of the box with it. Top left to bottom right. Top right to bottom left. Then, he used the key in the lock and lifted the lid.

I felt my jaw drop open when I saw Morrey reach into the box, and I was glad that I hadn't gone into the kitchen where Terry and Jimmy were working. I might have looked a little funny to anyone who could see me just then. See, even though the box was only four inches deep, Morrey reached into it up to his elbow. I was like a stage magician gag, except it wasn't a gag.

He closed his eyes for a few seconds and came up with a little bundle of twigs tied with twine. There were about six twigs about six inches long, and there was some kind of grayish lichen on them. The twine just looked like the kind used for hay bales. He put them on the bed.

His eyes took on that unfocused look again. Then, he nodded once and reached into the box again, again up to his elbow. I couldn't help but to wonder how much space was really in there and how he found things. This time, he withdrew a long thin dagger. Thin enough to call a stiletto. It almost looked like a short rapier because the blade a good fourteen inches long. It was in a black leather scabbard with some sort of a leather truss setup.

I watched, fascinated, as he tied the weapon to his back so that it followed his spine. The hilt settled at the small of his back pointing downward. A little catch held the dagger in the scabbard. It was pretty ingenious. He stood and retrieved an oversized denim jacket from his closet. He slipped it on, and the harness and blade were invisible.

He placed the twigs in his inside jacket pocket and knelt again in front of the box. He put the yellow paper inside and relocked the box and retraced the X on its lid. He slid the box back under the bed and pulled out a pair of green and yellow Nikes. He wedged his feet into them without untying the laces and headed for the door.

I stood with my hand on the stairway's handrail, right foot on the first step. When Morrey reached the top of the stairs, I was looking up at him. He stared back.

I said, "I was just about to come looking for you."

"It's important to brush for two minutes," he said earnestly. "I couldn't find one of my shoes, too. It was under my desk."

I pretended to believe him. I knew that he was something other than what he pretended to be, and he was wary. The dagger was disconcerting, but I understood daggers. They were for killing close up. The bundled twigs were more of an unknown. I assumed magic. Whoever or whatever Morrey was, he seemed to know magic.

I walked into the kitchen to let Terry know that Morrey would be in Oak House with me. Back in the living room, Morrey was waiting at the door, a gap-toothed grin on his face.

He said, "Going out at night is cool and maybe a little scary."

"Don't be afraid," I said. "There's nothing out there scarier than we are."

I handed him my Maglite and said, "*Après vous.*"

He took the flashlight and said, "*Merci beaucoup.*" He walked out the door and jogged down the steps, and I followed. When we were outside the area lit by the porchlight, he flicked on the Maglite. Its beam carved a white cone shape in the darkness.

We walked in silence for a minute or two, and he said, "Will you walk me back? I'm a little afraid of the dark when I'm outside or in an unfamiliar place."

"Oh, sure. We'll stay together."

It wasn't long until we had reached Oak House. I'd left lights on inside, but the building was quiet. On weekends, there would be people doing activities until bedtime. On Wednesdays, George Ryan had a D&D group who played for a couple of hours after supper. On Mondays, though, the place emptied out not long after the evening meal.

As we walked up the main stairs, Morrey said, "This is kind of creepy."

"You think so?" I asked. "I find it pretty peaceful. It's a great time to get some work done."

I had left the light in my room on, and the door was unlocked, so we just walked in. Morrey gave me the flashlight, and I motioned him to the chair situated in front of my desk. He didn't sit down, though. He stood looking around the room. He clearly noted the desks stacked against two walls and the single chair on the area rug. The closet door was slightly ajar.

I sat behind my desk and watched him for a few seconds. The air of wariness about him clicked up a couple of notches. To my knowledge he hadn't seen the inside of my room before this, but it was obvious that things had been moved around. A boy might be curious about it, but a supernatural predator would be put on his guard. Morrey seemed to be deciding how to play it.

"I have some activities planned for tomorrow which require a little moving-around space," I said by way of explanation. "But this way you have a better seat to help me fill your data sheet."

He walked over toward the chair but stopped before he stepped onto the rug. He kicked at it with his toe.

"Your rug's lumpy," he said.

"Yeah, it was thrown down in a hurry."

"I can help you straighten it," he said and tried the grin again, but it was off, slightly like a grimace.

"Nah," I said. "It'll need to be taken outside tomorrow to be shaken out. The paperwork is more important for right now."

I was acting as casual as I could manage, but I needed him to sit down in the damn chair. If I tried to wrestle him into position, it would be harder to close the circles. And depending on which flavor of supernatural he was, he might just kick the shit out of me. Talamaur physical prowess is not superhuman. I needed to lull him into complacency.

I just proceeded with my questions. I actually had an old admissions document up on the desktop, and I began filling out the information. Morrey stayed where he was.

"Remind me what your middle name is," I said.

"Morris Anthony Starr."

"Your father's name is?"

"Louis Michael Starr."

He took a step closer. One foot on the carpet.

I continued to work my way down the list of questions. I never looked up from the computer screen, so I must have seemed thoroughly engrossed in my task. Moe was watching closely, though. Each time Morrey moved forward or even shifted in place, I knew it. I acted like I didn't know or care where he was in the room, just that he was answering my questions.

When we had gotten through about half of them, Morrey perched on the chair, only one butt cheek on. It was the way younger kids sat on their chairs when they were waiting to be dismissed. It was a "spring-into-action" pose. I continued with the questions, not acknowledging his movement at all.

After another four questions, he slid his butt fully onto the seat and hooked his heels onto the crossbar in front. His shoulders hunched a bit and he looked up at the *Highlander* poster behind my desk. On it, Connor MacLeod is in his sixteenth-century Scottish garb, kilt and furry leather boots. Morrey began to look a little bored.

I continued with the questions.

Moe carefully pulled back a corner of the rug behind and to the right of Morrey's chair. My familiar was silent, but moving fabrics were not, and many supernaturals had superhuman senses. He needed to be quiet and careful. Then, he retrieved a half cup of salt from the remainder of the bag in the closet. He didn't need a container or anything. A cluster of salt granules just moved through the air like a swarm of tiny white insects.

Moe moved fast for the next bit. He can't really do more than one thing at a time like he has two hands. He really doesn't have any hands. First, he arranged the salt just above the floor into a shape that would complete the circle. Then, he dropped the salt into place, not a grain amiss.

The change in Morrey was instantaneous. He suddenly sat bolt upright in his chair, his eyes wide. Knowledge was bright and clear on his face. He'd felt the salt circle close about him. He began to move in two seconds time, but it only took Moe one second to fit the wire hooks together closing both the iron and rose rings.

I don't know how far Morrey's leap would have taken him. It looked pretty powerful, but whatever mystical properties the rings possessed had created an impenetrable barrier around him. And apparently, that barrier was bouncy.

Morrey's leap carried him all of six inches, and his face mushed up against the barrier. It threw him backward, but he only had a couple of feet to go in that direction, and he was thrown forward again. There were five collisions in total. Three front. Two back. When he was able to check his motion, he used the chair to brace himself.

The situation was serious. I was confronting an unknown supernatural creature. He could be virtually anything and had expressed no qualms about hurting people. I knew that. I really did. But the pinball bit was freaking hilarious.

My God! I laughed so hard. I didn't make any sound for the first few seconds, just kind of spasmed with stomach contractions. My eyes were all squeezed shut. I had to steady myself on my desk. Finally, I had to take a huge gasping breath. I would have kept laughing, but I must have breathed in some spit or something and started coughing.

Through Moe, I could see the look on Morrey's face. It was part petulant twelve-year-old and part rabid wolf. I mean, he still totally looked like a kid, but there was murder in his eyes. Like crazy murder. Maybe I'm deranged, but something about that look was funny as hell too. Gap-toothed Norman Rockwell kid meets Norse berserker.

Eventually, my laughter trailed off to giggles. My stomach hurt, and tears were on my face. I breathed as evenly as I could through my nose. The return of the laughter was a close thing. I felt giggles bubbling up inside me. I needed to get a hold of myself. I had things to accomplish.

Morrey spoke evenly, his voice still that of a slightly lisping boy. "You think that's fucking funny?"

The image of Morrey's mushed face passed behind my eyes, and I started laughing again. This bout wasn't as intense as the first, but my poor stomach was rebelling against the contractions. This time, there was a definite braying donkey quality to it.

Morrey stood and said, "If you think that's funny, check this out." He then picked up his chair and threw it at me. When I say he threw it, I mean he threw it like Cy Young threw a fastball.

You see, while the ring trap wouldn't allow Morrey to pass, it had no effect on the chair. I was only about five feet away. Barring some fluke, I don't think that the thrown chair could have killed me, but it certainly would have messed me up badly. Two things saved me.

For one thing, Morrey was seriously pissed. I guess there must have been a sizable ego squeezed into the little plump form of a boy, and he didn't like to be laughed at. It's not so much that his aim was off. It's that he didn't account for my big black desk. One of the chair's legs struck the edge which caused the chair to flip. It still might have brained me if not for Moe.

Back in the old days, Moe saved my bacon a lot. He's not big on force, but he is big on physics. He's Judo Moe, using opponents' power against them and that kind of thing. I might have been rusty as hell on the action-adventure lifestyle, but not so my familiar.

He just added a little extra spin so that the backrest of the chair struck me soundly on my right shoulder instead of on my forehead. The blow hurt like hell and made me forget my stomach ache in a hurry. But the meat of my shoulder could absorb the impact a lot more easily than my forehead. I suppose it served me right for being so sloppy.

I couldn't hide my sharp intake of breath at the pain, but the sound of it might have been drowned out by the heavy wooden chair crashing against the wall. It was pretty damn loud. It actually caved in the drywall and puffed chalk dust into the air. The chair then bounced on the floor a few times and lay on its side. It didn't even break. Good chair.

My shoulder began to throb only moments after the shock of impact. Ouch. Fortunately, I had stabbed myself earlier in the day and had reacquainted myself with significant pain. Which reminded me, I still hadn't ripped the duct tape from my leg yet. Something to look forward to.

I played it as cool as I could. As I pressed my hand to my shoulder, I said, "Ouch! Shit! You little fucker!"

He flipped me two birds.

As he fumed, I smiled and said, "Now, where are you going to sit?"

My right arm still worked fine, but it didn't like to move and told me about it. Ambidexterity was not one of my abilities. I was right handed. I could have avoided some pain by fumbling with my desk drawer using my left hand. I had to prove my manliness, though. I very casually reached into the center drawer of my desk. I even did it without making flinchy faces or anything.

From behind boxes of paperclips and staples, I withdrew a stone. I'd had it for years. It was flatish, irregularly shaped, and about as big around as a drink coaster. The thing that made it special was the hole worn through it. The hole was off-center, and I could nearly fit my index finger through it. I'd found the stone in a creek about fifteen miles away. When I'd picked up the stone, another stone about the size of a cherry tomato fell out of it. The current of the water must have pushed the smaller stone against the larger one for years and years until it wore the hole through it. I still wonder how long it took to work its way in as much as it did and how much longer it would have taken for the littler stone to make it all of the way through.

I mentioned already that I don't know about magic. I do understand, though, that there are some natural phenomena which create magic. Something about the water and the earth acting in concert to create that hole made magic, permanent magic. Well, the magic would last as long as the stone was whole at any rate.

The magic of it was such that one could see through faerie glamours by looking through the hole. Moe could do it too if he could find the right frequency of the faerie's particular illusion. Digital cameras could even do it. They tended to show a double image revealing both the illusion and what lay beneath. The stone was classic, though, and I wanted to use it for the dramatic quality.

119

When Morrey saw the stone, he smiled widely, open-mouthed even. "Hey! It's a faerie stone."

I held the stone up to my face, so I could look one-eyed at Morrey through the hole.

He struck a jazz-hands pose and sang out, "Ta da!"

Through the magic of the stone, I saw Morrey as a dark-haired, freckle-faced, plump boy of twelve. He dropped the silly grin and put on a frightened wide-eyed expression. In a voice that sounded close to tears, he said, "Mr. Brannon, I'm ever so frightened. What are you doing to me. Why are you abusing me so?"

"What the hell?" I said and set Moe to dial though his frequencies of perception.

"Heh heh heh." Morrey chuckled and casually reached into his inside coat pocket and drew out the twigs.

I automatically tensed. I didn't think that any magic could pass through the barrier which surrounded Morrey, but I'd been wrong often enough that I didn't feel terribly confident about that. I would have sent Moe to snatch the twigs away from him, but my familiar would be unable to pass through the barrier either.

Morrey leaned his head backward so that he was looking toward the ceiling. He held the twigs over his eyes and broke them. They snapped like regular twigs, but a second later, they dissolved into glittering dust which fell onto the boy's face.

He'd managed to keep his eyes opened as the dust fell, and when he looked at me, I could see that his eyes had turned the color of gold. Not just the iris. The whole orb. The area around his eyes held the same color, so it looked like he was wearing a rough-edged, golden domino mask.

His brows came together in confusion, his weird golden eyes squinting. He tilted his head first to one side and then the other. Finally, he said, "What the hell are you? A human mage or something?"

I guessed that the twigs stored a sort of pre-cast true-seeing spell of some kind. Apparently, I looked human or close to it. Then, a thought came to me too late. Morrey swept the room with his golden gaze and saw Moe. The jig was up, and my familiar simply froze where he was.

120

Morrey looked from Moe to me and then back again. Then, he thrust one finger in the air. Seriously, he made the "ah, ha" gesture. Then, he grinned fiercely and actually said, "Ah, ha!"

He then pointed his already extended finger toward me and said, "You're a Talamaur." He waggled the finger in the air. "There are hardly any of you guys around. What the hell are the chances that I'd find one of you in some backwoods school for crazy kids?"

His weird golden eyes suddenly focused on me intently, and he leveled the finger at me again. "Why the hell are you old?"

I said, "It's not polite to point. Cut it out, or I'll break it off."

"Like to see you try," he said.

We stared at each other for a full minute, neither saying anything. Moe reached the end of his observational spectrum and called it quits. Morrey was clearly not a little boy, but he sure appeared to be one.

Morrey said quietly, almost to himself, "There are hardly any Talamaur around. Most of them are redheads. Well, the Talamaur-Moroi anyway. . ."

Morrey's eyes went wide, and his mouth came open in a chimp-grin. He pointed with both index fingers and shouted, "Caomhnóir!" He danced around in his circle, a passable jig. "Prince of the fucking Talamaur," he sang. "Living in the woods with crazy brats. Pretending to be a human guy. Looking old and getting fat."

"Holy shit!" he said and dropped down to sit cross-legged in his little prison. He drummed a pattern on his knees that sounded a little like the beginning of the "Wipe Out" solo. He said, "Take a seat, Caomhnóir. We've got some shit to talk about."

# Chapter 10

"I'm not a prince," I said.

Morrey waved his hand dismissively.

"I'm not fat."

Morrey tilted his head from side to side again while chewing his lower lip. "Yeah, okay. But you're getting saggy. That's for damn sure."

"Shut up."

"Are you going to sit down or what?"

"No," I said. I may have sounded a little sullen. I caught this evil little shit. He was at my mercy, but he didn't seem frightened. He acted as though he had control of the situation. I wasn't going to stomp my foot or anything, but I suppose I was feeling pretty peevish.

"Okay, stand. Suit yourself."

"What the hell are you?" I said.

"That's for me to know and for you to find out." The line sounded perfect coming from the from the little-boy guise. But, damn it, he wasn't a little boy.

And just then, I had a moment of frustration with myself. I wasn't going to slap myself on the forehead or anything, but it was one of those kinds of feelings. My instincts told me that Morrey was some kind of faerie. There were tons of different kinds of them, but most of them shared a weakness. Howie and I had even taken a little side trip to prepare ourselves to exploit it, and it just slipped my mind. I really had to step up my game.

I circled my desk to grab my jacket from the back of my chair. I felt around in the right pocket until I found one of the orange stones Howie and I had gathered from the archery range. Morrey was watching me closely as I did this. I didn't want to give him time to get ready for what I was doing, so as soon as I found one about the size of a golf ball, I tossed it to him. I didn't hurl it like a weapon, just a casual underhand lob.

Instinctively, Morrey caught it and his face went rigid. If he was a faerie, I expected him to cry out and drop the stone or fling it away from himself. He didn't. He held up his fist, clenched around the orange stone, and showed me his gritted teeth. I thought for a moment that he would say something biting, but he didn't.

My reflexes are fast, like Bruce Lee fast, when I don't have my head up my ass that is. So, the fraction of a second it took Morrey to draw back his fist was enough time for me to start moving. Moe was there to help too. The orange stone hummed past my ear, missing me by three inches. It would have missed anyway, I think, but Moe was able to exert some force and alter the trajectory a little. There was a popping sound as the stone went through the already cracked sheet rock wall behind me and rattled around inside the wall.

He opened his fist to show me the raised red flesh of his palm. Then, he squeezed his fist closed again so tightly that his arm trembled with the effort. He glared at me and spoke through clenched teeth. "Are you sure you want to play it like this, Caomhnóir?"

I know that Morrey was trying to intimidate me. He was clearly dangerous. The rock that he threw could have killed me. The velocity of it was incredible. I was in no hurry to die, but I felt the opposite of intimidated. Healthy fear is just that, healthy. So, yeah, I was afraid of Morrey. But I was also pissed off, and honestly, I felt energized in a way I hadn't in decades. I'd found the one who'd infiltrated my peaceful domain and preyed upon my charges. I now had a place to aim.

I sat back down in my desk chair and slouched a little. It was affected ease, but he had no more projectiles. Well, except the knife. Yeah, big exception, but Moe was watching him and could give me warning enough to get behind the desk before he could unsheathe and throw it. Morrey might still think that the knife was a secret despite knowing that I was a Talamaur. He would probably operate under that assumption anyway.

It was unnerving as hell to see Morrey's eyes tracking Moe's movements. I'd only seen that happen with other Talamaur before. Familiars actually sensed each other when they came into a certain proximity. This made it pretty much impossible to spy on other Talamaur, at least using familiars. I'd also heard that other creatures, even sensitive humans, could feel familiars in some way even if they couldn't really see them.

Moe flew in increasingly complex patterns until Morrey realized that he was being screwed with, and he flipped the bird at my familiar. I smiled and thought, *That's my boy.*

Because I couldn't keep Morrey in the circle indefinitely I finally spoke. "So now you know who and what I am. What are you?"

Morrey turned his attention from Moe back to me. He already had his middle finger up, and he simply aimed it at me instead of Moe. He smiled his gap-toothed smile at me. He also knew that I couldn't keep him here for long, and he was prepared to wait me out.

I would have to stop being the benign nurturer of children and be the. . . well, whatever I was before. I went to my big bottom desk drawer. I kept a bunch of stuff in there. Some of it had no business being in a classroom. One of those things I'd bought a long while ago just because it was cool. It was popularly known as a wrist rocket. A metal-framed slingshot which had a brace that lay across the shooter's forearm to lend extra support. It really was dangerous. Someone like me could even use it for small-game hunting.

Remember when I said that Moe was really good at physics? Velocity, range, wind, rates of decent: all of those things are familiar gold. He just needs some baseline data, and we're off and running. I was a world-class shot with pretty much any projectile weapon, and we'd been playing with the wrist rocket for years. It was a familiar tool, and I would be shooting from just a few feet away.

I very deliberately put the slingshot on the desk. Then, I rooted around in the pockets of my bomber jacket and came out with two handfuls of the orange rocks and placed them next to the slingshot.

Morrey was watching me closely now, and I felt satisfied with the look that flickered across his face. He was transfixed with the dull orange stones. He stood from his cross-legged position in one muscular movement. He took a sideways stance, hands held loosely at his sides.

I said, "Do you know why they're orange?"

His eyes flicked up to my face. I thought he wouldn't answer, but he did. "Iron."

"Yes, indeed. They're orange because they're rusting. Lots of old fairytales say that faeries cannot abide the touch of cold iron. What the hell is cold iron?"

The muscles of his jaw bunched, but he didn't speak.

I went on in full teacher mode. "Cold iron is iron which has not been smelted. It comes right out of the earth as it is. It's difficult to work, but I've heard that rudimentary weapons have been made from it."

I picked up the slingshot and one of the iron-rich stones, one about the size of a baby pea. I fitted the stone into the pouch affixed to the heavy rubber tubbing.

Morrey's eyes were focused on the weapon in my hands. I saw his tongue slip out to wet his lips.

I continued. "Something about the smelting process spoils much of the earth magic in the iron. Faeries still don't like it, smelted iron, I mean. It irritates them, and if they're injured by a smelted iron weapon, they heal much more slowly than usual. The cold iron, though, that burns. I heard that if it gets under a faerie's skin, it can even poison them. Have you heard anything like that?"

"Sounds like bullshit to me," he growled. His voice sounded rougher than the regular Morrey voice.

I brought up the slingshot, drew back the pouch, and let fly the cold iron missile in one fluid motion. Moe told me just exactly what to do, and he was virtually never wrong with that kind of thing.

Morrey was fast. He moved so fast that he seemed to blur, but it wasn't fast enough. The little stone dug a furrow along his left cheek about an inch and a half long and lodged under his skin. His eyes flew open and he fell to the floor thrashing. After only a few seconds, he visibly took control of himself and stood. There was already a large red swelling on his cheek that looked a great deal like a huge angry pimple. He stood, and with trembling hands used his thumbs to squeeze the swelling just as though it were a pimple. With an audible pop, the stone shot from the entry wound and bounced across the floor.

He bent over at the waist, bracing his hands against his knees. His chest was heaving, and I thought for a moment that he might vomit. I hoped it would stay on the rug, and I could just throw the whole mess out at once. He stayed in that position for a full minute. He was still trembling, but eventually, he was able to straighten up.

He glared at me. Then, he said in his non-Morrey, rough voice. "Okay, what the fuck do you want, asshole?"

"I want to know who I'm dealing with," I said. "You're clearly a true shapeshifter. The faerie stone or my familiar would have been able to see through a glamour, so you must really be able to change your physical shape. Are you a pooka or something?"

"Pookas change into animals, dumbass."

"Changeling?"

Morrey formed an X with his forearms and made a honking buzzer sound like I'd gotten an answer wrong on the *Family Feud*.

I snatched up another stone from the desk, fitted it into the slingshot pocket, drew, and let fly. I don't think I moved fast enough to blur, but it was damn fast and precise. Morrey threw himself to the side and bounced first from one side of the barrier to the other. He actually braced himself with one hand on the side of the barrier. The other was clapped to the side of his head.

"Mother fucker!" he hissed. "What the fuck is your problem?"

"Answer the question."

He took his hand away from his head, and I could see the notch carved out of his ear by the cold-iron stone. It was angry and red, but there was no blood. He looked at the hand for a moment. It was the same one that had the red welt from the first stone.

"I'm not a changeling."

"Okay," I said. "What are you?"

Morrey mumbled something under his breath. Moe hears really well, but I still couldn't make heads or tails of what he was saying. Then, I realized that it was the beginning of a chant of some kind. He repeated the same phrase over and over for about thirty seconds. He stopped abruptly, and there was a shimmer of orange energy around him.

Dismissing a glamour is instantaneous. Just a flicker and it's done. What happened with Morrey looked more like an animatronic effect from an eighties movie. Skin stretched as muscles and bones changed into different shapes beneath. Hair receded into his head, and the color of his complexion changed as though dark liquid was spilled onto a white tablecloth and bled out from several spots.

His clothes remained unchanged as did the golden stain on and around his eyes. His general size hadn't changed much either. Everything else was about as different as it could be and remain humanoid.

Morrey's skin was matte black like coal. His ears were large and pointed like a bat's, and his eyes were large and protuberant also like a bat's. His nose was little more than two nostril holes in his face, and his mouth was thin-lipped and impossibly wide, like he might have a flip-top head. He was no longer plump, so the denim jacket and shamrock t-shirt bagged comically. Thin, black wrists and wide-palmed, taloned hands hung past his cuffs. Apparently, goblins' arms were longer than human boys' arms.

His head sagged down between his shoulders and his chest heaved. The transformation had clearly cost him something. His injuries from the cold iron were still there but were less apparent because of his color change.

He lifted his head, which now seemed overlarge, on the wiry body, and said, "Happy?"

I said, "You're a goblin. Goblins can't shapeshift."

"Oh, really?"

I'd just watched him shapeshift, and I felt stupid for my statement of denial. He also had cast a spell on Howie and the other kids around him, a spell that seemed complex and elaborate. Compared to humans, I was old and had gained a lot of knowledge and experience. But in many segments of the supernatural world, I was kid. I would gain nothing from being narrowminded. Apparently, goblins could cast spells.

"A goblin mage?"

"Is that so hard to believe?" His weird face was expressive, and if his voice didn't convey his annoyance enough, his expression sure added to it.

I shrugged non-committally.

"Fucking Tolkien!" He spat. Literally, I mean. He spat a big wad of grossness on the rug.

"Excuse me?"

Morrey looked at me. Orange light danced across the gold of his eyes. "Yeah, you heard me. Tolkien and Gygax." He spat again.

"Cut it out," I said. "That's gross."

"I know what you're thinking. Goblins are wimps. They don't even have a whole hit die." His head bobbed in little agitated nods. "Am I right?"

The truth was that he was totally right. I'd never actually interacted with a goblin before, had only actually seen them at a distance. The thought of them getting bad press from fantasy novels and role-playing games had never occurred to me.

Ultimately, I really didn't care about goblin representation. He could go to the ACLU if he had a case. I wanted to know what he was doing at my school and why he was here. He was hurting my kids. Even though nothing would excuse him from his actions, I wanted to know the reason anyway. I wasn't sure what I would do about him yet. His answers to my questions would decide that.

I said, "What are you doing at my school?"

He held his spade-like hands palms-up and said, "It's a free country."

I grabbed up another stone, put it in the slingshot's pocket, and drew it back.

Morrey hands came up in a warding gesture, and he said, "For Christ's sake! Lay off!"

I said in a monotone, "Answer my fucking questions. It's the only way you possibly come out of this alive."

"I was just having a little fun." He smiled, and I saw that his teeth were crooked and pointed like a shark's.

"You came here just to torture children?" If I'd thought about it, I would have put more menace into the question, but I was truly baffled by the idea.

"Everybody needs a hobby," he said.

I shot him through the upraised hand. The stone didn't go all of the way through, and I have to admit to feeling a sense of satisfaction at his reaction. He waved the hand around while wheezing and moaning. He stumbled around in his little prison, rebounding a little when he contacted the barrier. Once again, he took control. He grasped the injured hand with the other and pushed the back of it against his knee. The stone emerged from the entry wound. He shoved harder and whimpered when the stone popped out and fell to the floor.

He stayed hunched over for a long while, and I waited. I casually picked up another stone and held it in the pouch of the sling. I had the sinking sensation that it might just be as simple as Morrey spelled it out.

Finally, he stood and said, "What the hell do you want to hear? I'm a monster. I get off on hurting children. It's a traditional thing. Don't you read? I'm a damn goblin!"

I said, "The children are mine to protect."

"Well, I guess I picked the wrong fucking school, didn't I?"

"You did."

He smiled his shark's smile at me and said, "Tell me that you never took a bite."

"I have never harmed one of these children."

"What a fucking wet blanket."

"What's your name?" I asked him.

He hesitated. Names are funny things in the supernatural world. There are all sorts of potential uses for them. I mean True Names, you know, with a capital T. Most humans don't even know their own True Names.

No, Caomhnóir is not my True Name. It's my real name but not my True Name.

I clarified. "Your real name, not your True Name."

"Why it's Morris Anthony Starr," he said in the little-boy voice. That was weird as hell, hearing that voice coming from the black misshapen creature.

I pulled back the slingshot.

"It's Melk," he said, holding up his hands in surrender. "Those things fucking hurt."

"I know."

He lowered his hands and stood waiting.

I said, "Tell me about the spell."

"You know magic?"

"Tell me in layman's terms."

He shrugged. "It's three spells layered together. The first part compromises the vessels."

"The children," I said.

"Whatever. They happen to be kids, but it works on everyone in the vicinity. Then, the second spell draws the lifeforce from the compromised vessels into the target subject. The third spell uses the lifeforce to fuel a specific emotion." He rubbed his hands together as though he were dusting them off and said, "And that's that."

"Why Howie?"

"He has anger issues. The subject has to have certain proclivities. Man, you should see what happens when one of them has lust issues. That's even better." This time the pointy teeth were bared in a lecherous smile. Those smiles just kept getting worse and worse.

"And this is fun for you?"

"Sure. Keeps me from getting bored. What do you do?"

"Music. Books. Movies. Food. Drink."

He waved a hand dismissively. "Anyone can do that."

"Can you?"

"Ha, you haven't convinced yourself that you're a human, have you? That's fucking funny." He slapped his knee causing the now baggy jeans to flap. "You don't see humans grazing in fields and crapping alongside the cattle, do you? Act like what you are. Quit being unnatural."

It was a variation of what I'd heard from every evil supernatural asshole I'd run across. They were as predictable as the Mannaz students. I said, "I am who I choose to be. I choose to have compassion."

He held up both hands showing the wounds on his palms and said, "Yeah, real compassionate."

It was my turn to point, impolite or not. "Those kids haven't hurt anyone. You, on the other hand, are a psychotic murderer."

"Rationalize any way you want. Killing is killing."

"I will rationalize, thank you. Regardless of legal and religious philosophies, all lives are not equal. Some make the world a better place. Some make it worse. Some make it a lot worse. Some like you.

130

Killing you saves innocent lives, and don't give me that crap about no one being innocent."

"Oh ho," Melk said, pursing his mouth. "You're innocent, I suppose."

"Not me, but I'm reformed. You are apparently incorrigible."

Melk struck a pose and suddenly his body was covered in bright-orange leopard spots. Moe could see that it was a simple glamour, as easy for faeries to do as breathing. Then, the goblin held up one finger, indicating that I should wait. I waited, and the leopard spots turned to a neon pink, then again to lime green. He ended his display with a little curtsey.

"Cute."

"So, are you letting me out or not?" Melk said. He put his hands on his hips and tapped a sneaker-clad foot. I couldn't help but to notice that the leopard spots matched the sneakers. A fashion-conscious monster.

"You tortured a twelve-year-old boy. You could have killed him along with any number of his classmates."

Melk shrugged. "Yeah, but I'm reformed now."

"Was that the attack on Howie the only trick you had planned or was there more up your sleeve?"

Melk pulled up the sleeves of the denim jacket to reveal thin but wiry black arms. Then, he turned his hands palms-up and palms-down a couple of times. Ha. No tricks up his sleeves, but I noticed that he didn't reveal the dagger hidden along his spine. I didn't think that he would reveal anything he didn't have to.

Caomhnóir of old was telling me to kill the little fucker and get it over with. No matter how much Melk joked about his current predicament, I'd pissed him off, and he was clearly too dangerous to have as an enemy. Mr. Brannon, however, was telling me not to act rashly, to consider the situation. There were people here counting on me, and the goblin was subtle despite the simplicity of his alleged motivations.

Melk crossed his arms over his chest and said, "Look, you're either going to kill me or you're going to let me go. I wish you would make up your fucking mind."

"I could turn you in to the Venator council," I said.

Melk burst out with a short harsh laugh. He looked at me with his huge predator smile for a moment. Then, he said, "Oh, wait. Are you serious?" He shook his head. "Why would the council give a crap about this? If anybody dies from my actions, it'll look like some weird sickness or medical fluke. Nothing supernatural. No, this is between you and me."

"I'm certainly not going to give you the opportunity to hurt these children again."

"I could give you my word."

"On your True Name," I said. It was possible to swear on a True Name without revealing the True Name. That oath would bind a supernatural creature, especially a faerie.

"Sure," he said without hesitation.

"I suppose you'd just find kids somewhere else to prey upon."

He shrugged. "But they wouldn't be the kids you've sworn to protect blah blah blah."

I didn't respond right away. Securing the safety of MY kids was tempting, but too much evil has been allowed by people who were content to protect their own and let others fend for themselves. Killing Melk would make the world a better place.

And apparently, I need to work on my poker face because the goblin was clearly able to infer my thoughts.

"Even if you kill me, Caomhnóir, who says all the little kiddies at his school will be safe from me?"

It sounded like a mad bomber kind of thing to say. Did he leave magical boobytraps around the school? Did he leave a literal bomb? I think I would have killed him then, but the cautious part of me wanted to cover all my bases, and killing him wasn't something I could take back.

I put on my bomber jacket, retrieved the Maglite, and headed for the door.

Melk said, "Where the hell are you going?"

"I'll be back in a few minutes."

"You're leaving me alone?" he said. "Like this?" He gestured at his goblin form.

132

"Moe will stay with you."

"Who the fuck is Moe?"

I pointed at my familiar who floated in front of the Django Reinhardt poster. Then, I turned out the light and locked the door behind me. Moe could see just fine. I didn't know about goblins, though.

I headed back to Maple House, the cone of light from the Maglite preceding me. My physical eyes couldn't see in the dark much better than a human's.

I wasn't totally sure what I was doing, but I thought I might like a means to exert more pressure over Melk. His magic box seemed just the sort of thing he'd value enough for me to use it as a lever. Now, I needed to figure out where I wanted to move him. What was my goal?

I found that goblins could see in the dark, or maybe that was included in Melk's true seeing spell. I really didn't know what the spell was called. I just cribbed "true seeing" from D&D. It's like when I refer to planets which can support human life as "M Class." You know, *Star Trek*ese.

Melk was amusing himself by spitting at Moe. What a disgusting creature. Obviously, he couldn't actually hit my familiar, but gobs of that phlegmy stuffy were dripping from my walls in several places. He could get good distance and he was very accurate. Too bad the ring barrier didn't block loogies. Well, at least he waited until I was gone before he started with that nastiness.

I wished that Moe were with me to help me sneak around. He would scout, and I would move quietly. I considered briefly pulling him from guard duty, but I liked having him where he could keep an eye on the goblin. I decided to be casual about going up to Morrey's room. If I could get in and out unnoticed, I would. If I couldn't, I would act with confidence. I could actually be honest. I was picking something up for Morrey.

My shoes were soft-soled, and I had a light touch. I was also familiar with all of the Mannaz buildings. So, once I found that the living room of Maple House was empty, I liked my chances. The door would squeak if opened quickly, so I took my time. I heard voices in the kitchen. My hearing is as sharp as a human's can possibly be, and I could tell by the conversation that Terry had a game of Hearts going. He was a huge Hearts fan.

I moved up the carpeted stairs silently. The second-to-the-last one groaned a little under my weight, but I didn't think the sound was noticeable. Once in Morrey's room, I gave the whole thing a once over. Aside from the mahogany box, everything I found looked like it belonged in a twelve-year-old boy's room. The box was my objective, though, so I left with it.

When I got to the bottom of the stairs, I saw that a boy named Larry was sprawled on one of the couches, reading an *Entertainment* magazine. He didn't see me until I was halfway across the room. He looked up, and I said, "Hey, Larry. See you tomorrow."

He gave me a nod.

I opened the door as slowly as I could manage and not look like I was purposely opening the door slowly. Larry had gone back to his magazine, and I thought that there was a good chance that he wouldn't even mention seeing me if it didn't come up. The door did squeak a little, but the Hearts game was pretty spirited, so no one seemed to notice.

Melk had tired of his spitting game and sat cross-legged and silent in the middle of his prison. Moe kept position in the back of the room by the closet. He seemed to like it there.

I held the box under my left arm and the flashlight in my right hand. I kept my pace slow because I needed to come with a plan. If I could get him to promise on his True Name that he wouldn't cause harm to anyone at Mannaz, I'd let him go, but I was sure it wouldn't be so simple. He would be like a genie in one of those Arabian Night tales, twisting interpretations of words and phrases or leaving other interpretations open.

The idea of the little monster simply moving on to his next group of victims grated on me as well. The thing is, there were monsters like Melk all over the world preying on humans. I couldn't stop them all. And he was right, at least my humans would be safe from him.

I imagined killing him anyway. Then, an image of Mannaz kids stepping on the magical equivalent of a claymore flashed across my mind's eye unbidden. That was unpleasant, and I felt a jab of potential guilt. I guess other kids would have to fend for themselves. Those hypothetical victims were faceless in my mind's eye.

I opened the door to my classroom and flipped on the light. Melk squinted in the brightness, but it didn't take him long to note the box under my arm. His strange face went hard, and he stood in one movement, glaring at me.

"That's mine," he growled.

I held up the box and said, "Is this where you keep your magical bombs?"

"Why would I tell you?"

I walked over to my desk and placed the box on it. I picked up the slingshot and a stone, loaded it, and shot him from five feet away. The stone struck him on the right side of his chest. The denim of his jacket and his partial dodge took away a great deal of the impact, but I didn't doubt that it hurt like hell. The stone bounced off and rolled away.

Melk made a sound something like, "Gack." He hunched over and dropped to his knees. He remained that way for a long time. I watched his shoulders rise and fall as he managed the pain. Eventually, he sat, legs splayed before him. He actually leaned his back against the ring's barrier.

He said, "At least I didn't have to dig it out."

"Swear to me on your True Name that you will not harm any of my students or coworkers at this school and that you will remove anything that might cause harm to them independently of you."

"And what do I get?"

I said, "I will release you with no further harm if you agree never to come back to this campus."

"What about the box?"

The words didn't want to pass my lips, but I managed to say, "You can have that too."

He nodded once and said, "I swear by my True Name that I will not harm any of your students or coworkers at this school and that I will remove anything that might cause harm to them independently of me." He smiled. "Now, you go."

135

I said, "I swear on my True Name that if you do as I ask, I will release you with no further harm. But you agree not to come back to this campus ever again."

Moe felt a pulse of energy. I'd never sworn anything by my True Name before. I didn't like it, but maybe that was just because Melk was the being to whom I swore.

"Great," he said and stood. "Let me out."

I'd told him that he could have the box but did not refer specifically to its contents. I guess that I'd learned from the Arabian Nights stories too or maybe *The Merchant of Venice*.

I said, "Toss me the key."

"Hang on a minute. You said that I get to keep the box."

"You can. I just want to see what's inside."

"I'll be embarrassed when you see my sexy underthings," he said and cocked his hip and probably would have made a pouty face if he had any lips to speak of.

I held my hand palm up.

"You can't make it work," he said.

"Then you won't lose anything by tossing me the key."

He looked at me for several seconds then said, "Yeah, okay." He drew the chain over his head, the key dangling from it. He tossed them to me.

Moe drifted nearer to me and the box. Melk pushed his face against the barrier which made his flat features flatten more. When he'd worn the Morrey face, it was funny. With the goblin face, it was just creepy.

With Moe's help, I traced the X shape on the lid of the box exactly as Melk had. The goblin's expression changed slightly, and I felt a little satisfaction. I probably should have paid more attention to the quality of the expression, but hindsight is twenty-twenty.

Moe, who was flipping through frequencies, sensed a hum of energy from within the box. The hum cycled up and then abruptly stopped. Was it some kind of magical engine that had turned on to disengage a mechanism?

The same hum pulsed when I inserted the key into the traditional lock and turned it.

136

I have to admit to feeling a little excited about the prospect experiencing the weird spatial phenomenon inside the box. What would it feel like to reach into that little box and feel all of that vast space within?

Leaving the key in the lock, I reached to lift the lid, and a number of things happened in the next second.

Moe reacts quickly, and fortunately, he was tuned into the energy moving around inside the box. There was a sort of magical click, and I dived to the floor. It wouldn't have been enough to save me, though, if Moe hadn't shoved at the bottom of the box. He couldn't lift it, but he could tilt it. The energy that burst from the box was mostly directed away from me.

There was no sense of concussion or heat. No sound. There was something though, an incredible force. The world seemed to turn orange for an instant, and I have only a vague idea of what happened over the next few minutes.

# Chapter 11

I may have lost consciousness for a few seconds, but mostly I was dazed and disoriented. My face was against the tile of the floor when my brain started working again. I wanted to get up right away, but my body wouldn't cooperate. When I realized that I wasn't getting input from Moe, a jolt of panic gave me strength enough to roll over. My familiar floated five feet away, but he seemed to be unconscious or something. I didn't even know that was possible. He looked whole, so my panic subsided to a barely manageable concern.

Next, I was able to move my head enough to see that Melk was gone. I couldn't tell if the circle trap was still engaged because that was the kind of thing that Moe told me about. Looking in the opposite direction, I saw the magic box was closed again and resting on its lid only about three feet away from my outstretched hand.

Why would Melk have left without the box? Was he coming back for it?

My mind went to the dagger that he wore under his coat, and my imagination treated me to a graphic scene in which he cut my throat with it while I lay helpless on the floor. That jarred a little more strength into me.

I rolled myself onto my front again, and my trembling arms managed one wobbly knee-pushup. I fell over in the direction of my desk where I came to an awkward sitting position with my back against the front of my desk. That seemed about the extent of my capabilities for the time being.

From my more elevated position, I could see that an imperfect square had been cut into the floor of my classroom right in the middle of the circle trap. I couldn't quite make sense of it at first. The rug, tiles, and floorboards were cleanly sheered through. The edges were perfectly smooth. They almost looked like they'd been sanded.

The dagger? As unlikely as a dagger that could cut through the floor like that was, I couldn't think of anything more likely.

If Melk had dropped down to the first floor, he might be circling around now to retrieve his property. My muddled mind couldn't recall exactly what we'd sworn to each other, but I knew that I'd told him that he could take the box. He'd be within his rights.

I really wanted to spring into action, but it just wasn't happening. I looked at Moe floating senseless just a few feet away. He couldn't scout for me. There we were, ignorant and helpless. Waiting.

Fear scrabbled around inside my chest when I began to wonder what I would do if Moe didn't recover. It's bad enough that I would be horribly handicapped, like a human losing his sight. Maybe worse. I wouldn't have to worry about that for long, though, because I'd starve to death no matter how much food I ate.

I wrenched myself away from that line of thinking. It was premature and wouldn't do me any good in my immediate situation.

I'd never heard of an unconscious familiar before. There'd never been an indication that Moe needed sleep or rest. As far as I knew he was always aware. I suppose that was mostly based on assumptions, though. When I sleep, I don't know what Moe does. Our communication is such that he can't simply tell me about it. We could probably manage a Lassie-and-Jeff type of thing. You know, "What is it, Moe? Do you want me to follow you?" Like that. I don't think that he does anything very involved while I sleep, but he makes a great guard or alarm clock.

I'm not entirely sure how long I sat there trying to keep myself calm. When it seemed that Melk wasn't coming back to kill me, I concentrated on getting up. I was able to twist around and get a grip on the edge of the desk. My arms trembled as I pulled myself up enough so that I could get my legs under me. My head swam, but I managed to stay upright. I wasn't going to let go of the desk, but I seemed to have conquered basic standing.

When I felt up to it, I took two shuffling steps toward Moe. No one could physically feel a Talamaur familiar except a Talamaur. Unless we willed it that is. The disconnect with Moe was difficult to bear, and I didn't know if touching him with my hand would alleviate my growing anxiety in any way, but I didn't think it would be worse than the blankness. I was at a loss and beginning to feel a creeping sort of desperation.

I stretched out my arm, and when my fingers came into contact with him, all of his perceptions snapped into place in my mind. It was like being slapped in the face with a giant ice-water hand. I collapsed and landed on my ass which hurt quite a lot. I didn't care, though, because the relief I felt was glorious.

Moe zipped around like a happy puppy. He had no tail and no tongue, but there was a definite wagging, licking quality to his behavior. His relief was equal to my own though I did no wagging or licking. Mostly, I tried not to fall over the rest of the way onto my back.

After basking in each other's company for a minute or two, we turned our attention to our screwed-up situation. There was too much for me to organize. I needed paper. Step one would be getting to my desk again. Maybe this time I could get onto the chair.

Standing and shuffling the few feet to my desk went more quickly the second time around. I must have been recovering from whatever that orange light was. I sat heavily on my desk chair and found a piece of scrap paper and a pencil. I wrote, "Melk." I definitely had to consider him. I suppose if he'd intended to kill me, he would have returned by now. It's not like I could stop him or anything. Since he didn't do that, I figured that he simply fled. Just to set my mind at ease, however, I sent Moe on a quick circuit of the campus. My familiar seemed fully recovered, and in just a few seconds, he verified that the goblin was gone, and my students and co-workers were safe.

Next, I wrote, "Box." It was on the floor where I'd seen it last. I would get it in a minute. For now, I was staying put.

My gaze meandered around the room, as I tried to make a synapse fire. The hole in the floor! That needed attention. I wrote, "Hole—Mess."

Moe checked it out. I couldn't help but to marvel. The dagger had been long enough to go all the way through the sheetrock ceiling of the room below mine. Even the puffy pink insulation was cut cleanly. Everything had fallen straight down.

Fortunately, the room below was Noah's supply room. It was a pretty big area containing mops, buckets, vacuum cleaners, and the like. There was a utility sink in one corner and a small metal desk in another. There wasn't much open space, but the debris had landed in the middle of an aisle between metal shelves. The chunk of floor and ceiling was mostly intact, like a two foot by two foot insulation sandwich.

I felt lucky because there was a better chance of hiding the damage in the supply room than it would have been in a classroom, office, or dining room. The lighting wasn't great, and kids didn't go in there. They would be the mostly likely to notice. Yeah, bored kids will totally stare at the ceiling.

I sat for what felt like a long while, but time can get funny in situations involving trauma. I wasn't physically hurt, but that orange light had done something to me. I think that a full blast would have torn the life out of me and not left a mark on my body.

I was about to push myself up from my chair to retrieve the box when it hit me. I had lost a student! Okay, really, I'd lost a faerie tale monster, but official paperwork said that he was a twelve-year-old boy. It didn't matter so much that parents or loved ones would come looking for him. They likely only existed on paper. But everyone at the Mannaz School would sure be wondering where he'd gone, and I had been the last one seen with him.

On the positive side, I could take my next step from the comfort of my desk chair. I'd need to call my only real friend in the supernatural community. Well, I'd try anyway. I doubted that the telephone number from 1986 would still work. Or if it did work, I doubted that it would connect me to Galen. He'd probably gone through a half dozen different aliases since I'd seen him last.

My father could, in theory, connect me to anyone who was possibly reachable, but nothing with him was ever simple or pleasant. I would avoid dear ol' Dad if at all possible.

Galen's number was not programmed into my phone. It was scribbled onto an old notecard which resided in one of the shoeboxes full of junk in my bedroom closet. My memory is good, though, and that phone number represented something important to me. A kindred spirit. I dialed it from memory.

I expected to hear that screeching warbling sound that signifies a disconnected number, but I actually heard the line ring.

After the third ring, a voice answered. It was female, a little quavery and a little rough, but not fragile. "Hello?"

"I'm sorry, ma'am. I must have dialed the wrong number."

My finger was halfway to the red phone icon when I heard her speak again. "Is there anything I can do for you?"

What a strange thing to ask someone who's just dialed the wrong number. I brought the phone back to my ear. What could I lose, right?

I said, "This was the number of an old friend. We lost touch. I found the number and thought I'd give it a try."

"What's your friend's name?"

What had Galen been calling himself in '86? I couldn't remember. I liked Irish, Scottish, and Nordic names. They worked well with the red hair. Galen was less distinctive looking, so his alias names were all over the board. I thought that it might have been Howden or Howard. It's funny that I could remember the phone number but not the name he'd been using. Memory is funny.

While I was rifling my brain for the elusive name, the woman on the line made a leap, and surprised the hell out of me.

She said, "Are you one of the friends who would know him by his 'special' name?" I could practically hear the air-quotes in the way she said "special."

I have to admit to getting a little twitchy then. There was no one around to observe, so it didn't really matter. "Special" name seemed a lot like "real" name. Humans weren't supposed to know our real names. To say that she sounded human would be silly, but well, she did. I had the sense that she was human. Maybe it was one of the countless things that Moe knew for very good reasons but couldn't quite translate to me.

She sounded a little old, but not all supernatural beings were immortal or even especially long-lived, but most were. She could be a human mage. They were considered part of the supernatural community despite being human. I was probably just being paranoid. Maybe she had a completely legitimate reason for knowing about Galen.

Throwing caution to the wind, I answered the question. "Yeah."

142

"Hold on," she said, and I could hear a drawer opening and closing. Then, there was a rustle of paper. "Okay, you give me his special name, and I can check for yours on the list."

"What list?" I asked. There shouldn't be a list of real names.

"The list of people who get his current contact information, of course. When I say 'special name,' does it mean anything to you?"

There was a little snark in the woman's voice that rang a bell in my mind. Something was familiar about it. I could almost draw an image, but it eluded me. Dark hair, wavy dark hair. Blue eyes and wavy dark hair. Almost black hair. A name flashed through my mind, and I said it instead of Galen's.

"Kelly Swan?"

The line was silent for a while. Well, mostly silent. I had good hearing, so her breathing still carried a little. Finally, she said, "Riley O'Brien?"

Wow. Apparently, we knew each other. Well, sort of at any rate. Kelly and Galen had been dating in the mid-eighties. She had been a retired model, probably all of thirty-two years old in '86. That would put her in her at about sixty-four now. Social security time.

She'd been a knockout when I'd seen her last. Wasp-waisted and generous in the hips and breasts. Her skin had been fair, but there was a dusky tone just below the surface like she had some Mediterranean blood from a couple of generations earlier. She'd had big hair. It was the eighties after all, but even when she didn't tease and spray it into that crazy style, it was still full and thick. Something about it always made me think that I could dive into that hair and get lost. The blue of her eyes wasn't like mine at all. Hers were almost indigo like new, unwashed blue jeans.

I said, "That's what I called myself when you knew me. Our mutual friend is Galen. My name is Caomhnóir." I knew it would be on the list.

"I thought you were just a regular guy."

"That's how I was supposed to look to. . ." I didn't know how to refer to her without sounding dismissive or disparaging.

I could practically hear the smirk in her voice. "To the mundane humans."

"Yeah. 'Mundane' is just the word we use, but I guess that is pretty crap sounding."

Kelly said, "Don't worry about it. I got the big talk. If I tell anyone about my immortal boyfriend, scary monsters will come and tear my head off."

"Hang on," I said. "Are you and Galen still together?"

She sighed, and there was an awful lot expressed in that one little sound. "I kicked him out not long after I turned fifty. He still comes to see me every month or so. He pretends to be my grandson for God's sake. How do you like that?"

"None of your friends recognize him?"

"I live in Albany now. We got the New York number transferred to a cell phone. This is the first time it's rung in ten years."

"Are you okay?"

She chuckled at that, but the sound was a little sad. "Besides getting old, I'm just fine. It would be easier to take if the love of my life didn't still look twenty-five. I love our visits, but the jealousy is beginning to bother me more and more."

"We had some wonderful times."

"We did," she agreed. "And I'll bet you're having wonderful times with some other young and beautiful woman nowadays, too."

I didn't reply, but Allie had leapt to my mind instantly. I imagined her in thirty years and wondered if what Galen and Kelly had experienced was the best-case scenario? Well, at least I knew that I could pretend to get old. You know, maintain the illusion for a while.

Kelly spoke again. "It seems that I'm getting a bit down. I am pleased to hear from you Riley, or do you prefer. . ." There was a pause and a rustle of paper. "How do you spell that name again?"

I spelled, " C-a-o-m-h-n-o-i-r."

"Is that Welsh?"

"Irish."

"Figures. It doesn't sound at all like it looks."

We spoke for a few minutes more. I didn't really have the time, but I had been very fond of her, and she was pretty clearly feeling low. She gave me Galen's new number. He was living in a little town in New

Hampshire, but I think that all of the towns in New Hampshire are small. I called.

The phone rang once and was picked up. I heard Galen's familiar voice say, "Hello," and thirty years fell away in a moment. Whether it was true or not, I felt that fixing my current situation was now possible.

I said, "Django Reinhardt or Wes Montgomery?"

I think I could hear him smile over the line. "Wes is the man! 'Airegin' still gets stuck in my head for days at a time. How are you doing Caomhnóir? Could this be a mere social call?"

"Hey, Galen. Sorry. No. I need help, and you're first on my list."

"How far down is Scathlann?"

"Far down." Scathlann is my father's real name. The truth of the matter was that he would be my next call if Galen couldn't help me, and I think Galen knew it.

"Where have you been? I think I was sporting a Def Leppard mullet and wearing really skinny ties when I saw you last."

I took a deep breath and said, "I'll have to give you the *Masterplots* version. Time is short."

"Kids use Shmoop now."

"I know. I've been teaching." I proceeded to give Galen a thumbnail sketch of the last three decades. It was general and light on details except for the last few days. After I finished, he didn't say anything right away.

When he did, he said, "You made yourself old?"

"Yeah, I know it's crazy."

"No, man. If it were in my power, I would have done the same thing."

"Yeah?"

"You talk to Kelly very much when you got my new number?"

"A little."

"Yeah, I would have gotten old for her."

We were quiet. I guessed that he was thinking about getting old with Kelly, but I was thinking about him breaking the only supernatural law that I'd ever heard of. Under penalty of death, we could not tell humans about us. We would talk about that later, though, because I had a more immediate problem.

I said, "Can you help me?"

"Yeah, yeah." He sounded like he was pulling himself from other thoughts. "I know a guy."

"You know a guy?"

"Yeah, I know a guy. He'll be coming out of New York. That's what, six hours at least? He's good at moving fast, though. He'll be there by morning. Just send me the address."

"You know this guy well?"

"Yeah," he said. "I know him from the old, old, old neighborhood."

"He's a faerie?"

"A changeling. Don't worry, Caomhnóir. He won't eat the children or anything like that."

"Thanks, Galen. I don't know how to repay you."

"Come by for a visit. We'll catch up."

"Absolutely."

We hung up. I wouldn't say that I felt energized *per se*, but I felt like I could stand up without too much trouble. So, I did. I walked over to the magic box and picked it up. My head alternately felt like an anvil or a helium balloon, but the sensation was equalizing as I moved. I put the box in my big desk drawer along with the wrist rocket. Obviously, the box wouldn't stay there for long, but I couldn't think of a better place at the moment.

I went down stairs to Noah's storeroom. The activity seemed to be flushing the effects of the orange light more and more, and I merely felt tired as hell as I unlocked the door and flipped on the lights. They were hooded florescent things, you know, that kind of lights that can make the healthiest person look tubercular. One of them was flickering. The falling chunk of ceiling had jarred a tube loose.

I gave the light tube a little twist, and the light steadied. Because the hoods directed all of the light downward, the ceiling a few inches higher was left pretty dark. I didn't think that I would have to do very careful work to pass general inspection.

I had a plan. I'd worn a lot of different hats at the Mannaz School over the years. For a number of them, I helped Noah with simpler maintenance projects over the summers. Big jobs were generally contracted out, but the two of us had done a good bit of work together. Some of that work involved hanging drywall, and more importantly, patching drywall.

The square of drywall which had been the ceiling had hit the floor first, and all of the other stuff had landed on top of it. I was not optimistic about its condition, but I was surprised to find that it was not entirely destroyed. I had been prepared to cut a new piece from Noah's supply of scraps, but it was nice to save some time by using the original piece.

I loaded the unneeded pieces of debris onto a blue plastic tarp which I found on a shelf. It was handy being able to work in Noah's supply room. Most of what I needed was right there. I gathered the tools and materials and set to work.

The job I did was of the Primitive-Pete variety and wouldn't pass more than a cursory inspection. I had more important things to deal with than subtle work, though. I thought it was pretty solid at any rate. The floor of my classroom was so sloppy looking that I decided to take another rug from the theater and roll it out on the floor. It was a short-term solution, but that's all I could manage.

I am as strong as a five foot ten, hundred-and-eighty-pound guy can be, but carrying a rolled eight-by-ten-foot rug from the theater was hard freaking work, mostly because one guy carrying a rug that big was just awkward. I was also not-quite-recovered from Melk's boobytrap.

At nine o'clock, repairs still hadn't been finished, but Moe and I took a break then to pull a little sleight-of-hand. We were good at that sort of thing. Familiars are misdirection kings.

I knew that Terry Brown was a conscientious dorm parent, so I didn't expect him to go to bed before all of his students were tucked away for the night. Moe scouted Maple House while I waited outside. The students in the dorm were pretty young, so all of them were in their rooms. One of them, a boy named Ronnie, was not going easily, though. He was a pain-in-the-ass a lot of the time, but this was the first time I was grateful for it.

While Terry wrangled Ronnie, I snuck up to Morrey's room and made a body shape under the blankets with pillows. Hey, it's a classic. Like my construction work, it wouldn't pass any real scrutiny, but before I left, Moe would add some verisimilitude.

I also searched through Morrey's dresser and closet to find an outfit. I stuffed a pair of jeans, a t-shirt, a sweatshirt, and a pair of low-top Chuck Taylors into a backpack. I opened the one window in the room and took out the screen. After tossing the pack out the window, I replaced the screen and closed the window.

I waited at the bottom of the stairs for Terry to come out of Ronnie's room. It seemed that the boy was finally down for the night, and the dorm parent looked like he had worked for it. His head hung and his eyes were aimed at the floor, so he didn't see me right away. He actually started a bit when he became aware of me.

"Jeez," he said and put his hand to his chest like a heroine in a silent movie.

"Sorry. I was just dropping Morrey off. He seems pretty done in."

Moe flushed the toilet in the upstairs bathroom. Who else could it be but Morrey, right? Terry glanced up at the sound. I didn't want him to go up to check on the non-existent boy, so I had to keep him engaged.

"How's Ronnie tonight?"

Moe opened and closed the bathroom door.

Terry smiled wryly and shook his head. "I'll need to wait in the living room for a while to make sure he doesn't sneak out to mess with the other kids, but that's been pretty typical. I intend to outlast this behavior. He only does this a couple of days a week now. For the first month, it was almost nightly."

Moe opened and closed Morrey's bedroom door.

"I'm hoping that he kicks the habit all together by Christmastime."

Moe flipped off Morrey's light.

I said, "Morrey was dead on his feet by the time we finished all the paperwork, so I wouldn't be surprised if he's sleeping as soon as his head hits the pillow."

"Yeah, you guys were gone a lot longer than I expected."

"We spent a while just chatting. I like to connect with the new students as much as I can right from the start."

"Well, at least Morrey won't need any attention while I'm guarding Ronnie's door. Some of these guys need constant direction. It's like herding cats, you know?"

"I do," I said.

After some commiseration and general small talk, I excused myself, retrieved the backpack of clothes from outside Morrey's window, and returned to repairing my classroom. As I walked back toward Oak House, Moe stayed behind for just a few minutes. He watched as Terry sat down on the couch outside of Ronnie's room with a copy of Steinbeck's *Wayward Bus* and began to read.

When I finished the repairs, I put the blue plastic tarp containing the remaining pieces of my classroom floor into the trunk of the Nova. Chances were that no one would pay much attention to that sort of thing in the dumpster, but kids could be very observant sometimes. Usually about the things I didn't want them to notice.

As I returned from the parking lot, I reminded myself once more that I needed to store the Nova soon. Snow in October in Western New York was not uncommon. Lake Erie and Lake Ontario were not so very far away after all.

I can get by on little sleep. Staying up for over forty-eight hours in a row was not untenable. Tonight was different, though. I wasn't used to the injury and healing process anymore, and the scissor-stabbing experience had taken quite a lot out of me. Also, I didn't think that I'd fully recovered from the orange light from the goblin box. I hoped that there wouldn't be lasting effects.

I retrieved the goblin box and Morrey's clothes from my classroom and took them to my apartment. I tossed the pack of clothes on the ten-minute chair and pushed the box underneath the ugly couch and sat down on it. I slipped off my shoes and leaned back, feeling like I might melt into the worn green cushions. Moe took one last pass by Maple House to make sure that Morrey's absence had not been noticed.

That's the last thing I remember for the night. I fell asleep sitting up with the lights still burning in my living room. I didn't even brush my teeth.

# Chapter 12

My cellphone warbled at a quarter to six in the morning. It rang three times before I was able to pull it from my pants pocket. My eyes were gummy and my mouth was pasty. It took an effort to focus on the number which I didn't recognize. After two more rings, I was able to figure out that it was probably Galen's guy.

I answered. "Hello."

With no introduction, the voice on the other end said, "I'm in a town called Geary. Google Maps says I should be there in ten minutes."

"Okay, call me again when you get to the sign that says 'The Mannaz School.' I'll tell you which place is mine." My voice sounded thick and raspy, and I regretted not brushing my teeth the night before when I got a whiff of my own breath. That's pretty bad, being able to smell your own breath.

Basic decency demanded that I clean up before my guest arrived. I drank a pint of water, washed my face, combed my hair, and brushed my teeth. I would have changed into fresh clothes, but apparently, Galen's guy was a fast driver. The phone rang and I picked it up right away.

"I'm here," he said.

"Drive around the square," I said. "Hang on to your phone, and I'll let you know where to go."

I stepped out of my doorway in my slippers and wished that I had grabbed my coat. It was pretty cold, frost on the ground and everything. I watched a silver Honda Civic drive slowly up the road. The car was so plain that it was practically camouflaged. When he neared the parking lot, I directed him to park next to the Nova. He backed into the space competently and climbed out.

I sent Moe to check him out. He was as nondescript as his car, standing 5'8" and of average build, neither handsome or ugly. His hair was a medium brown as were his eyes. He wore faded jeans, hiking boots, and a gray zip-up hoodie over a plain white t-shirt. He appeared to be about twenty-years-old, but that didn't really mean anything. He might be a thousand. There was no evidence of glamour, though. I was seeing his actual physical self.

I told him where to look for me. When he was generally facing in my direction, I waved at him. He waved back and walked toward me at an unhurried pace, hands stuffed into the pockets of his sweatshirt. This guy would have been virtually invisible on a college campus, in a supermarket, or sitting on a park bench.

He represented another supernatural type of façade. Melk-as-Morrey had looked innocent and vulnerable. There were also the seductively attractive types. This guy, though, was just forgettable. Even if someone did remember him well enough to give a description, it would be the kind of description that would fit every third guy.

When he reached me, he didn't introduce himself. He simply said, "Got any coffee?"

"Sure," I said. "I'm Caomhnóir."

"I know."

He just stood there. I wasn't sure if he was socially inept or if he was trying to be rude. He might have been helping me out of a jam, but I wasn't going to tolerate any sort of dismissive attitude.

"Here's the part when you tell me your name, and I invite you in. It's a civilized way to be."

"Is it?" He shrugged his shoulders. "Alright. Call me Rick."

"That's your name?"

"Sure."

I doubted that his name was really Rick, but I didn't see much of a point in making an issue of it. If Galen sent him, I could trust him. Up to a point, at least.

I stepped aside and said, "Come on in."

He entered and sat down on one of my kitchen chairs. When I closed the door, he asked again, "Coffee?"

"We don't have a lot of time," I said. I wasn't feeling frustrated so much as I was feeling anxious. Probably some of it had to do with fighting a goblin mage yesterday, sleeping sitting up, and waking up to entertain a stranger before six o'clock in the morning.

"We don't have time for coffee?"

"Morrey's dorm parent is going to be waking him up for school in about an hour. When I say Morrey, I mean you," I said.

Rick was so relaxed as to seem indifferent, and that did annoy me a bit. I had to remind myself that this was just a job to him, and he had driven through the night to do it. I couldn't get pissy because he wasn't all eager and earnest and whatnot.

I set about building a pot. The routine motions actually helped me to reset. I only ground about two-day's-worth at a time, so it was nice and fresh. The smell of it did good things to my mood. I brewed it moderately strong, normally only a mug's worth at a time. This time I made two-mugs' worth.

Rick watched the whole process, and as soon as I pushed the brew button, he said, "Have you got anything to eat?"

"Students eat at eight in the dining room." I didn't mean for it to sound as abrupt as it did. Stress.

"This thing that I do, it burns a lot of calories. I forgot to bring my Power Bars."

"I'm sorry," I said. "I need to do some shopping." The apology was in part for my tone but also because I didn't have much to eat. No beer. No food. Well, not much food. I reached into the cabinet and brought out a half-full box of granola bars. I placed the box on the table in front of him.

He unwrapped one of the bars and asked, "You have a picture?"

"No. Will that be a problem?"

"You're going to have to trust me a little."

I felt a fluttery sensation along my spine. Trust. Trust had never been a strong point with me. There were levels of trust. The trust I felt in Novak and Corman and Allie was significant, but it wasn't the kind of trust that involved life-and-death or supernatural subjugation or that kind of thing. Rick was a faerie, and faeries could be as dangerous and as tricky as anything. I did trust Galen, though, and he'd sent Rick to me. If I really trusted Galen, I was going to need to trust his guy.

I blew out a tight breath and said, "Explain, please."

He took a bite of granola bar and chewed thoughtfully. He swallowed then poked about with his tongue to dislodge a piece. "Okay. I need to get into your head. It's actually better for me that way

153

than with a two-dimensional, static picture. When I see in your head, I get the sound of his voice and the way he moves and that kind of thing."

"You want to read my mind?" I felt that flutter again. This time it was in my belly as well as along my spine.

"I only usually pick up surface thoughts. You know, what you're thinking about at the moment."

"So, you can't go rifling around for my debit card PIN or my Amazon password?"

"No unless you're thinking about them when I look."

Shit. Now, I was thinking about them. It's like telling someone not to think about pink elephants. Of course, they're going to think about pink elephants. That's just what happened.

Rick smiled. It's the first thing he did that seemed genuine. "I'm being compensated. I don't need to rob you or look at your browsing history." He took another bite and shifted around on the chair so that he was facing me more directly. After he chewed and swallowed, he continued. "Okay, here it is. The mindreading is just an aspect of my main power. Hypothetically speaking, say I wanted access to a bank vault."

"Hypothetically?"

"Yeah, hypothetically. I go into the bank and talk to a teller or someone like that. I ask about the manager or the president or someone else who can walk around anywhere and not raise suspicion, you know."

"Sure."

"The teller thinks about the manager, and I do a quick read. Physical contact helps, so maybe I hand over a fake business card or something and accidentally brush fingers. A handshake is great, but that can't always come across as natural."

He finished the bar and promptly began to unwrap another. It was a small price to pay, but they were really good granola bars. They had caramel and chocolate chips.

He waved the bar like a magic wand and said, "Ping. I get the right outfit, change into the manager, and walk into the vault. Easy-peasy."

154

"You just have to be sure that the real manager doesn't show up."

"Obviously."

Rick ate the whole second bar without saying any more. That was fine with me because I was busy pouring coffee. I kept cream for Allie if she stopped over for a cup. I offered that and sugar to my guest.

He chewed his lower lip briefly and said, "I don't care taste-wise, but the extra calories are always welcome."

I said, "Why don't you try the coffee black, and you can just eat the rest of the granola bars."

"Yeah, alright."

I placed his mug in front of him, and I took the seat on the opposite side of the table. The mugs were from the same set. Novak had gotten them for me several Christmases ago. Mine was yellow with the Starfleet command badge, and his was red with the engineering badge. He smirked when he saw his cup, held it up, and said, "You give me the redshirt mug?"

"Well, I'm sure not going to take it."

He sipped the coffee and then raised the mug to indicate his in approval. Then, he proceeded to dunk his third granola bar in his coffee. I considered taking the last one and doing the same. It looked good. I wanted to make sure that my guest didn't lack for sustenance, though.

Rick said, "Okay, scootch over here. In front of my chair."

He turned his chair to the side and indicated where I should place mine. When I sat, our knees were nearly touching. He dusted off his hands and shook them like he was trying to flick water from them.

He said, "Okay, I want you to think about the kid you want me to be. The more detail the better. If you can, replay specific interactions in your mind. Like mannerisms, speech patterns, posture, that kind of thing."

"What's it going to feel like?" I felt a little wimpy because I wasn't all fearless.

"You won't feel a thing."

"Sure?"

"Would it make sense for my power to give me away to the people I'm going to deceive?" He chewed on his lower lip briefly again and held up the middle and index fingers of both hands. "You will feel these on your temples, if that's okay?"

"If it'll help."

He leaned forward and placed the first two fingers of his hands on either of my temples. I replayed my interaction with Morrey in the art room the day before and braced myself for whatever was about to happen. Out of curiosity, I had Moe flipping through frequencies to see what he could see from the supernatural front. I kept waiting. I felt nothing, and either Moe hadn't landed on the right frequency, or there wasn't any discernable energy manipulation.

Well, what I actually felt was a little disappointed. Rick leaned back in his chair and casually unwrapped the last granola bar. And, apparently, that was that.

He held it up by its wrapper and said, "Sorry. Did you want this?"

"Go ahead," I said. "Did the mindreading thing go alright?"

"Sure. I told you that you wouldn't feel anything."

"You did."

Rick ate the last of his granola bar and washed it down with the last of the coffee. He stood and asked, "You have clothes."

I gestured to the ten-minute chair where Morrey's clothes were still in the backpack. Rick walked over to it and began to undress. He showed no signs of self-consciousness. He folded his own clothes and placed them next to the pack. When he was finished, he stood there wearing nothing but a bright blue pair of boxer briefs.

He shook his hands out again as he had done before the mindreading thing. Closing his eyes, he took a deep breath, held it, and breathed it out slowly. As the air left him, his skin began to ripple. The change which took place bore a striking resemblance to the change Morrey had made into Melk. In this case, a young man became a younger boy, so it wasn't quite as dramatic, but that type of thing is relative. Rick was faster than Melk, though, finished in something like ten seconds. Also, Rick's change was silent, no chanting.

Rick, who looked just like Morrey had, grabbed onto his shorts before they could fall down and began to dress. He didn't move the same as Morrey had, though. There was none of the awkward cutesiness. His manner was matter-of-fact. Business as usual. And entirely adult.

I pushed aside my squirmy reaction to having someone who looked like a twelve-year-old dressing in my living room. Hell, Rick was probably older than I.

I asked him, "Why didn't you need to chant? Melk chanted."

Rick pulled on his t-shirt. When his head popped through the hole, he said, "Melk was casting a spell. This is just something I do. I'm a changeling."

That made sense. Faeries used magic the way other people use their hands or their eyes. It just a part of the whole. I thought that the shapeshifting that Melk had done was more like the shapeshifting spells that human mages could perform, not innate, something learned.

I said to Rick, "I doubt that anyone had gotten to know Morrey very well, so you can just wing being a twelve-year-old boy. You can even play sick and hang out in your room all day. His laziness has been noted."

I paused before continuing. I hated to be rude, but some things just shouldn't go unsaid. "Three things:"

Rick looked at me expectantly.

I held up one finger. "Do not harm anyone."

He nodded.

I held up two fingers. "Do not disrupt the routine."

He gave me the double-thumbs up.

I held up three fingers. "Do not steal anything."

He said, "Sure. I'm a professional. I've already been compensated."

I said, "Okay, then. I'm not entirely sure how long the gig will be. I'll need to come up with a story and mock up some paperwork, but no one will look very closely at it. Can you sell a family emergency?"

Suddenly, Rick's Morrey face scrunched up, and in seconds, tears had beaded up in his eyes, just hanging there waiting to fall. His lower lip trembled and he said in a tiny, quavering voice, "Muh. . muh. . . my daddy. He. . . he had and accident." Both tears fell simultaneously, leaving clear tracks down his round, freckled cheeks.

I gaped.

He wiped the tears on his sleeve. The face he made looked brave, but his lower lip still trembled slightly. He sniffed and wiped his eyes again.

I said, "You are a damn acting genius."

"Master thespian," he said and bowed at the waist. When he unbent, his expression was entirely bland.

"You certainly are." I wondered how long he had been pretending to be other people. Was the average looking young man who arrived on my doorstep his true form or just one picked at random? Was he completely mercenary, or did he have any moral sensibilities? Galen sent him. I would trust him to do the job, but my curiosity was aroused.

We walked casually along the sidewalk toward Maple House. Within the first twenty paces, Rick's movements and manner transformed to fit his physical figure. Slightly awkward and out-of-shape but still energetic like a golden retriever puppy.

I said, "I'm going to try to get you inside without being spotted. If we're seen before that, just pretend that we met early this morning to go for a walk. If you're a little sheepish about needing to get more exercise, that'll probably sell it."

He nodded.

I sent Moe ahead to scout the dorm. Terry was in the shower. Yeah, yeah, I know. But it was just recon. All of the other kids were still asleep, except for Larry, who was lying in bed and reading a *Rolling Stone* magazine. I doubted that he would be stirring any time soon. We had a definite time window.

As we came to the steps leading to the front door of Maple House, Rick said, "How do I know where to go?"

In answer, Moe picked up a smooth gray stone about the size of my thumbnail. It appeared to float in the air about five feet from the ground. Rick's eyebrows raised, and he grinned in a very un-Morrey-like way.

I said, "Follow the stone."

The stone bounced in the air in a way that reminded me of those old singalong cartoons that had a ball bob along with the lyrics to the song. You know, like, "Mis-sis-sippi, it used to be so hard to spell. It used to make me cry." The stone reached the front door and waited there moving in a sort of figure-eight pattern.

Rick pointed at the stone and said, "Cute." He jogged up the steps.

"I'll check on you later," I said.

When the door closed behind him, I still waited until he reached Morrey's room. Once Rick was inside, Moe held the stone in front of him until he held out his hand. My familiar very carefully placed the stone on his palm and came back outside.

I was feeling pretty good. I would go back to my apartment to take a shower and change clothes. I wondered if I had time to grab a quick breakfast in town, but dismissed the idea. I hated to rush a meal, especially if I went out for it. By the time I reached my apartment, I had decided to have breakfast in the dining room with the kids. Yeah, I was feeling pretty damn good, all things considered.

That's when I saw the ambulance coming up the driveway. Its lights were flashing, but there was no siren going. I watched it make the turn up toward Novak's place. Corman's house was just beyond it. I ran after it.

# Chapter 13

Moe was in the ambulance in the blink of an eye. I would take a little longer to catch up. There were two paramedics in the front seats. A young, sandy-haired woman was behind the wheel. She wore square-framed, black glasses, and her hair was pulled back into a ponytail. The hair was thick and wavy and didn't look right pulled back, so I guessed that it was a pragmatic choice. She was cute, but something in her manner was serious, even grim.

The man in the passenger's seat looked equally as young, mid-to-late twenties. He was lean but boyish looking, his hair just a shade lighter than his partner's. He had Google Maps open on his smartphone. He pointed at Corman's house and said, "That's the one."

I can Usain Bolt when I want to, but middle-aged teachers aren't supposed to be that fast. I was still moving at a respectable pace, though, as I neared the house. The paramedics had gotten out of the vehicle but hadn't reached the door yet.

They looked back at the sound of my feet on the gravel. Just then, Novak opened the door to Corman's house. We all took turns looking at each other for a second or two.

Novak said, "He's in here." He stepped aside holding the door for them.

Before entering, the female tech said, "Can you tell us what's happened?"

Novak said, "He's responsive. He can tell you better than I can." He motioned them inside.

He closed the door after them but remained on the porch. He said to me, "We should give them room to work."

He was wearing sweats, dark-gray pants and a Geneseo State hoodie in a lighter shade of gray. His hairstyle didn't really allow for messiness, but there was something mussed about his appearance. His face still had the puffiness of recent sleep. The most remarkable thing about his appearance was the fear plainly visible on his face.

I said, "What's going on?"

Moe was inside with the paramedics, so I would get specific details. But I wanted to talk to Novak, if nothing else, to give him somewhere to focus. I don't know that I'd ever seen him so agitated. I think that Howie's explosions and the mystery illness of the students had been weighing on him. It would have been nice to tell him that the source of the recent problems was gone, but there was no way to manage it.

When he spoke, I could hear a tightness like his throat was a little constricted. "I'm not a hundred percent sure. Joe called me a half hour ago. I could barely hear him. He said he wasn't feeling well. That old man is tough as hell, so that's the equivalent of saying that he was dying, right? I ran over to check on him." He hunched his shoulders, stuffing his hands more deeply into the kangaroo pouch of his sweatshirt. "He was really pale and could hardly respond to anything I said. I was going to try to load him up in my car, but I figured that too much could happen between here and Warsaw Hospital."

Inside the house, Moe observed Corman talking to the paramedics. His skin was gray like ashes, and there were bruised looking hollows under his eyes. He wore striped blue pajamas and a heavy darker-blue robe. His voice was quiet and breathy, but he was understandable. He seemed a little embarrassed about causing a fuss.

I said to Novak, "But Joe can talk now?"

He shook his head but said, "Yeah, he rallied a bit while we were waiting for the ambulance. He said that he didn't want to go, but I think I talked him into it. That in and of itself shows how serious this is." He took a deep breath and blew it out. "He looked bad, Sean."

The paramedics reached the same conclusion, and in only a few minutes they had Corman on a stretcher and in the back of the ambulance. The man said to Novak, "Do you want to ride in with him?"

Novak looked at me. He clearly didn't want to leave Corman alone, and I didn't blame him. There was only one right response.

I said, "I'll make sure that your classes are covered."

"Thanks, Sean."

He grabbed my hand like he was going to shake it, but he just squeezed. Then, he let go, slapped me on the shoulder, ran to the back of the ambulance, and hopped in. The male paramedic followed and closed the door. The vehicle made a surprisingly tight turn and went back the way it had come.

I watched the ambulance until it rounded the bend and was lost behind the color-splashed trees. The horizon grew pink as I walked back toward my apartment. I played the day out ahead of me. Any institution, but especially the Mannaz School, has anchor people. People who hold a place steady, keep a place solid. With both Corman and Novak gone, I would be point-man. Others would step up. Pam and Allie came to mind immediately. Maybe Terry. But with both Corman and Novak gone, the school's situation would feel less secure.

I would send an all-school email telling everyone not to expect Corman and Novak in today. I would try to find a history sub. The Mannaz School didn't use outside substitute teachers. The list of reasons was lengthy. We covered absences in-house. Terry would be my first stop. He'd started college as an education major, so he had some coursework under his belt. He did a good job.

Normally, I would have been the first to fill in. It was my thing, but I felt a great need to be mobile today. You know, be able to spring into action at a moment's notice. I walked back to Maple House to speak to Terry personally about covering history classes. I could see in his eyes that he didn't want to do it, but he agreed to. I stayed in the dorm to help with the morning routine while Terry dressed in more teacher-ish clothes.

I walked with the group to Oak House and the dining room. Rick was doing a great job being Morrey, charming and clumsy and chattering in his lisping voice. The situation seemed pretty normal, not like there was a faerie mercenary pretending to be an adolescent school boy at all.

The Beech House students arrived at the same time that Maple House did. I greeted Maggie, Howie, and his dorm mates. They all seemed to be in relatively good spirits. I assumed that the morning in the dorm went well. I hoped that Howie's day would go smoothly. I planned to check on him regularly, but Moe would be on a regular, broader patrol.

Unless the evil goblin mage returned to exact his revenge, I thought that I could let Howie navigate the day without me. Yeah, Melk

162

swore to stay away and not harm anyone, but faeries are like super lawyers as far as exploiting loopholes. I wasn't counting that depraved little shit out the scenario.

I stopped off in the nurse's office before breakfast. Missy was gathering the morning meds when I arrived. Some Mannaz students did take medication. Newer students' dosages usually tapered until they were off them all together, but there were some exceptions. Not many, though, and those continuing meds were relatively mild. Most were just multi-vitamins or other supplements.

She looked up from her work when I entered the open door and said, "Hang on for a minute." She placed the last of the labelled pill envelopes into her little plastic bin and gave me her full attention.

I said, "Dr. Corman went to the hospital this morning."

Missy's face went still, and I could practically see her mind working. She was thinking of the kids who showed up at her door yesterday afternoon and wondering how closely she would need to watch them. After a little while she said, "What was the matter?"

"I'm not a hundred percent sure. He was weak, and his color was bad. Con went with him, so I expect news as soon as there is any to have."

She didn't say anything for a few seconds. Her eyes went back and forth as though she were reading invisible text. It was almost like seeing the plans come together inside her head. Eventually, she said, "After I hand out meds, I'm going to check in with the kids who weren't feeling well yesterday. Did anything happen with them last night?"

"Not that I heard of."

"If any of them are still feeling ill, I'll check in with you, and we'll go from there."

"Okay."

She looked at me appraisingly. "How are you feeling?"

"Right as rain."

"You look a little peaked."

I said, "No, I'm good." I had noticed that I wasn't looking great as I got ready for school. That orange light from the goblin box seemed to have beaten me up in a way that showed in a non-specific kind of way. "Let me know if you need anything. I guess I'm the go-to guy today."

As I left Missy's office, Moe checked on Kate, Todd, and Andy who seemed to be in pretty good shape. They were eating breakfast and talking to their friends, yesterday's bout of sickness barely a blip on the radar.

I flipped on the lights in my classroom and hung up my coat in the closet. I noted that the rug lay smoothly over my ugly patch job, and I felt some measure of satisfaction. I checked both Corman's and Novak's schedules and spent the next half hour shuffling, redistributing, and assuming their duties for the day.

I never made it to breakfast, and a little part of me regretted turning down that last granola bar. But once I'd gotten all of the metaphorical ducks in a row, the morning went without a hitch. The kids liked Terry and behaved pretty well for him in Novak's history classes. They behaved as well as Mannaz kids were likely to behave anyway.

With Moe on patrol, I managed to divert a punch-up between a couple of sixth graders before it really got going. I also learned who had been drawing penises on the elementary school artwork which was displayed in the common room. I just had to think of an excuse to search the culprit for the very distinctive, turquoise marker he had in his pocket. At this stage in my Mannaz career, I was good at manufacturing probable cause.

I decided to eat lunch with Howie again today. Just because Melk was gone, there was no reason to abandon the boy. I was less surprised to see Howie sitting with Paul, Jan, and Scott than I was to see Rick in his Morrey disguise also with the group. I shot him a look, and he smiled blithely. They welcomed me as I approached.

Today's lunch-table conversation topic was favorite Hogwarts professors. The Harry Potter books tended to be an area of common interest. It was rare to find a kid who hadn't read the books or at least seen the movies. I took joy in the appalled looks on the kids' faces when I told them that Severus Snape was my favorite. The debate got pretty spirited after that. The entire meal probably would have passed pleasantly if not for Duane.

164

Jan was going on about the merits of Professor MacGonagall when Duane shouted, "Hair trigger!" from across the room. It cut through the din of conversation, and the room went silent.

Howie became still as a statue, eyes downcast. The words clearly had meaning to him. He'd heard them before. What the hell did "hair trigger" mean?

It didn't take long for me to infer a probable meaning. Howie Tragger. Hair Trigger. Both go off easily. It was another way for Duane to mock someone. "Evolution" for a different victim. He must have gotten tired of tormenting Marty.

With Duane, it was difficult to know how to proceed. He loved to fight. He sought confrontation. I figured that we could try to ignore him first. If he didn't receive affirmation for his behavior, he might lose interest. Moe observed Duane's smirky grin as he tried to make eye contact with as many of his cronies as he could.

Andy and Brett sat to one side of Duane. His girlfriend, Sue, sat on his other side. She was a vaguely pretty blonde with dark roots and a perpetual hangdog manner. She looked even more miserable than usual. The mean-spirited smiles on Andy and Brett did not encourage my hope for a quiet resolution.

I tried to redirect attention by continuing the Harry Potter discussion. "Why do you like MacGonagall, Jan?"

"Are you kidding?" she said. "What is there not to like about her?"

The murmur of conversation picked up again. I hoped that the moment had passed, but Duane was just letting the volume in the dining room increase until it had nearly reached its former level. He wanted more drama.

The second shout was in a gameshow-host kind of a voice. You know, a "Come on down!" kind of a style. It was all drawn out. "Hay-air-trih-ger!"

The room went silent again. I stood up. It was time for phase two. Howie touched my arm, a pleading expression on his face. He clearly didn't want me to make a big deal out of it. I gave him a double thumbs up by way of encouragement.

I walked over to where Duane sat with his collection of lackeys and hangers on. The silence drew out as everyone waited to see what I would do.

Duane was popular in that strange high-school way in which few people really liked him, but they were afraid to get on his bad side. They preferred friendly relations with him rather than have his ill-will pointed toward them. It was easy to become frustrated with teenagers for allowing someone like that to acquire so much power over them. They only needed to choose, *en masse*, to refuse him power, and he would have none. In truth, though, it was only a microcosm of the wider world. The supernatural one too.

Duane looked up at me wide-eyed and innocent as I stood before him. He said, "Is there anything I can do for you, Mr. Brannon?" He twitched his floppy hair.

I kept my voice level and quiet. I didn't need any real volume to be heard because conversation in the room had not resumed. Everyone waited to see what would happen. "Please, stop shouting in the dining room. You're disturbing others."

I turned to walk away, and I made it two steps before he began again. He didn't shout, though. He began to chant.

"Hair trigger. Hair trigger. Hair trigger. Hair trigger. Hair trigger."

The words carried easily in the quiet room. And he wasn't shouting. The little shit.

I turned back again and said, "Please, stop."

All innocence again. "But why, Mr. Brannon?"

"I'm asking you nicely to stop saying 'hair trigger.'"

Duane stuck out his chin, as if daring me to hit it, and said, "There's nothing wrong with saying 'hair trigger.'"

That bullshit again. Great.

Howie had gone through serious abuse at the hands of a monster just because he had been a convenient target. He didn't deserve it. He didn't deserve this treatment from Duane either. I was fed up. I guess that's why I jumped my rail a little.

I should have simply removed Duane from the dining room so that he wouldn't have his audience. I should have, but something in

166

me had changed since yesterday. It would probably be fair to say that I had reverted a little. Talamaur tend not to confront problems head on. They're pragmatic and sneaky. I had learned to resist that tendency in my nature, but it was still there.

I said to Duane, "Really? Nothing wrong, huh?" Then, I turned my back on him to rejoin Howie and the others.

Kids are fascinated with power. Who has it? Who doesn't? When they push against rules and basic expectations, they're trying to find out the true edges of the envelope. They want to know how much power they have. The whole room had just witnessed Duane defying me, and I had done nothing. Unresolved tension hung in the air.

Sue looked like she wanted to get smaller until she just disappeared.

Andy and Brett seemed like they were watching a sporting event. Kids against adults. Duane seemed to have scored, but the ref hadn't yet made his decision.

Sean Brannon, the teacher, should have taken that teachable moment to re-establish expectations. Not have a knock-down, drag-out confrontation or anything like that. A summons to my office would have been sufficient. An indication that the problem would be dealt with later. Consequences, not punishment.

But just last night, I'd been shooting iron pebbles at a trapped goblin. I'd felt justified, but that was pretty clearly torture. No Geneva Convention for us supernatural types. I remembered then what it was like to be Caomhnóir, the Talamaur-Moroi. God help me, I kind of missed it.

I sat back down and smiled at Howie and company. I said, "What about Professor Flitwick?"

They weren't having any of it. We were all waiting to see what Duane would do. They were just being overt about it. I was trying to pretend I didn't care.

Duane tried to sing the next time. I thought he was going for a pop metal sound, but I didn't hear enough to tell. He only got as far as "Hair—".

Moe, in full spear mode, broke his concentration.

I wasn't going to feed on the little creep. It was just a negative reinforcement thing.

Just to clarify, there is no real damage from the spearing part of the feeding process. The only danger comes from drawing off lifeforce. That's how I rationalized my cruelty. In retrospect, it was flimsy. At the moment, I was fed up and mean.

Instead of singing, Duane hunched over with his arms around his middle. Stomach cramps are not an uncommon reaction.

Sue said, "Hey, are you okay?" She put her hand on his back and began to rub in a circular motion.

Duane swatted her hand away and said, "Quit it, Sue!"

She held the hand to her chest with the other, and her shoulders hunched even more. The tautness of her face made tears seem imminent. I thought that she might get up and leave, but she stayed. Her head drooped even more than usual, and from the top, the dark roots of her hair stood out starkly.

In a minute or so, Duane's pain seemed to have subsided a little. He began to inhale again like he was going to burst into song. I had been dealing with his pathological stubbornness for two years. He wouldn't quit if I stabbed him a hundred times. Guilt was already beginning to creep up on me, so I decided to change tack.

Moe overturned a half-full class of cran-apple juice from Duane's tray onto his lap.

In full voice, he sang, "Hair--Fuck!" and stood up abruptly. He looked around for someone to blame, but no one could have reached the glass but him.

Sue flinched at his shout and abrupt movement, but she kept her head lowered.

The mean smiles on Andy's and Brett's faces were suddenly aimed at Duane.

Duane glared at them, but they didn't seem cowed. He stalked away dabbing at his pants with a paper napkin. The kids watched him go, and I saw nothing like respect or affection on a single face.

There seemed to be a universal feeling of relief at his departure. Well, in everyone except for me. I needed to get ahold of myself. Melk was one thing, and Duane was another.

168

# Chapter 14

I climbed the back stairs on the way to my office. I needed to avoid people for a while until I could wrap my mind about this new development. Really, it was more of an old development. Regression. Backsliding. Whatever you wanted to call it. It was something I thought I had left behind me. I had exerted my power to cause pain to someone who was helpless to stop me. Was Duane a douchebag? Sure. Did he have it coming? Maybe. Was it my place? That one was harder.

The creased brown leather of my brogues flexed easily, the soft soles silent on the wooden steps. Moe saw a couple of girls coming down the hallway toward me, so I stepped into the restroom at the top of the stairs and locked the door before they rounded the corner. They were talking about Duane's fearlessness as they walked by the closed bathroom door and descended the stairs. The sound of awe in their voices caused my fists clenched of their own accord.

I willed my hands to loosen, and I took in a lungful of air and let it out slowly. I did that a couple of times. The muscles of my forearms ached, and I was glad that I kept my fingernails closely trimmed, or I probably would have gouged my own palms. I shook out my hands and focused on breathing in and out for a full minute.

What the hell? My anger was flaring instantly and intensely. It seemed that the taste of Caomhnóir I'd gotten last night had affected me. It unnerved me how appealing the violence had become. How natural it felt. This required some thought. Later.

When the hall was clear, I walked directly to my office. I didn't lock the door, but I left the light off. That way, I wouldn't feel like I was shirking my responsibilities, but I really hoped that passersby would assume that I wasn't in. Slouched in my chair with my legs splayed out before me, I sent Moe on another quick circuit of the campus. It was a job of seconds.

I felt like having a whiskey and listening to some Wes Montgomery. It would be relaxing. I could take up smoking again too. It's not like it would kill me or anything. I just didn't like the smell getting stuck in my clothes. It was different when everyone else's clothes smelled like smoke. And furniture and carpets and car upholstery and. . . Hell, everything used to smell like cigarette smoke. But if I took up smoking again, I'd just be one of those guys shivering in the parking lot next to the funny genie-lamp-looking ashcans. That'd take all the fun out of it.

Moe found business as usual on campus. Most of the teachers were competent, even with Mannaz students. Kids had acclimated to the program for the most part, and things were going pretty smoothly.

I honestly didn't know how humans could go through their lives so uninformed about their immediate surroundings. I guess they couldn't miss familiars they never had. Normal, for them, was not knowing what was around the corner until they turned it. What a pain in the ass that would be.

With that in mind, I decided then to send Moe to Warsaw Hospital to check on Corman and Novak. It was over twenty miles, and I didn't really like him to go so far away. There was no reason why he couldn't, aside from my separation anxiety that is. At short distances, it seems almost like Moe can teleport. He can't. He's not even faster than a speeding bullet. The twenty miles would take him something like five minutes to cover, which seems like an eternity to me.

He can fly right through solid objects, so a bee-line makes the most sense for quick travel. We're not always sensible, though. Sometimes, I like to play. It's fun to zig and zag around things. It's kind of like the camera work in *Return of the Jedi* when Luke and Leia fly the speeder bikes on Endor. No, there was no practical point, but frequent, simple amusements were good for the soul, and I thought my soul needed some *Star Wars*.

Despite messing around a bit on the way, Moe made the trip in good time. Once in the hospital, he was able to find Corman's room in just a few more seconds. There wasn't much to see, but I felt better touching base with my friends than sitting around and wondering how things were going.

The room was just like any hospital room. It wasn't private, but the bed closest to the door was vacant. I really didn't like the smell of hospitals. Fortunately, Moe didn't have to share all of his sensory information, and he considerately kept that back. Hospitals also have

170

this bustling hushed sound. There is a ton of activity, but everyone does it quietly. It's not regular enough to be white-noise, but I always thought that there was something similar about the quality of sound.

Corman slept and Novak stared into space while holding a *National Geographic* on his lap. It was open to an article on climate change. He occasionally glanced down at it, but his eyes didn't seem to track, and in over ten minutes, he didn't turn the page once. His sweats were looking pretty wilted, and I couldn't help but to wonder if he'd slept in them.

I thought that Corman looked better than he had at his house that morning. There was still a vague grayish undertone to his complexion, but he looked more natural. The IV running into the back of his hand probably had something to do with that. The bruised-looking hollows under his eyes were less pronounced as well. He breathed normally and seemed to be sleeping comfortably.

A youngish nurse came in wearing blue-green scrubs and checked in on him. She had medium-brown hair and wore little wire-rimmed glasses, pretty in an unassuming way. I paid attention because she drew my attention away from Corman and Novak, who barely noticed her coming and going. She had a cute bottom, and Novak didn't even glance, so I knew that he wasn't himself.

I was about to bring Moe back to school and turn my attention elsewhere when Corman stirred. It wasn't anything dramatic, just a subtle shifting beneath the bed covers. His eyelids fluttered a bit before opening, but when they did, his eyes were sharp, aware. They settled on Novak who hadn't yet noticed he'd awakened. There was something tender in his expression that made me feel like an intruder in the moment. I considered the three of us the heart of the school, but Corman and Novak seemed almost like father and son. They had something that I couldn't. Maybe it was just being human.

Corman didn't speak right away. His gaze traveled from Novak to take in his surroundings. He didn't move his head, but his eyes moved from one corner of the room to the other. When he came to Moe, the sweep stopped abruptly. His eyes narrowed. A funny sound came out of me then. It was less of a movie heroine gasp than a clipped "hut" noise. He was looking at my freaking invisible familiar. Then, his eyes unfocused like he was trying to see a hidden 3D picture or something. Moe stayed absolutely still, deer-in-the-headlights style.

After a few seconds, Corman didn't literally shrug, but something in his manner suggested a shrug. He turned his attention to Novak then.

He said, "Are you still here, Conrad?"

Novak started, and the magazine nearly fell from his lap. He caught it absently and leaned toward Corman.

"Yeah. Do you need the nurse?" His voice was hushed, gentle in a way I rarely heard from him.

"No, but if you would incline the bed so that I can have a drink, I would appreciate it."

Novak found the control for the bed and started the small quiet mechanism which raised the upper end. He stopped it when Corman was nearly sitting upright. Novak then handed him a plastic cup of water with a straw sticking out of it. The wrinkles around the old man's mouth stood out starkly as he drew on the straw. When he handed the cup back, I could see that his arm trembled a little with the weight of it.

Novak seemed to see the tremble as well and took the cup quickly before it could fall. He placed it carefully on the tray next to the bed. He didn't say anything, but I could tell he was preparing to express something weighty and important. The intent was in his eyes, and he rubbed his palms on his thighs. It was a familiar mannerism which indicated that he was going to launch into something.

Corman spoke before Novak did. His voice was quiet, but it was even and precise as was usual. "Con, you should go back to school and check on things. I appreciate the moral support, but—"

Novak interrupted, "I'm sure that Sean's got things under control."

"I'm sure that he does. He's a good man."

I felt a little tightening in my chest at his casual words of praise. A little affirmation from Corman went a long way.

He reached over the tray and patted Novak's arm and said, "You need to get out of here. I do appreciate your support, but you need a change of scenery. You can check on my school and report back to me tomorrow after you get a good night's sleep."

"Maybe you'll be okay to come home tonight?"

"I doubt that will happen," Corman said. "If it does, I'll call you. You need a change of clothes and a meal. You and Sean can go to that place that you like."

Novak shrugged his heavy shoulders. "I don't know if I could concentrate on anything."

"Then, don't."

Novak looked at him for a moment and asked, "Don't what?"

"Don't concentrate on your shower or your meal or your sleep. Just have them."

"What if—"

Corman interrupted him. "I appreciate your support. You are a good friend, but you're not doing me any good by watching me sleep." He reached across the tray to pat Novak's arm again. "Go home. Call if you need to but go home."

Novak didn't say anything. He just nodded and stared at his tennis shoes.

I considered calling Novak then and impressing him with my prescience. Sometimes I like to show off. But I remembered the last time I'd showed off and had Andy looking for bugs in the common room. I resisted the impulse.

Moe stuck around long enough to observe Novak stepping into the hall to call Christie for a ride. Apparently, she would have no problem leaving her job for a couple of hours. A part of me wanted to pick up my friend and give him whatever support I could, but it was better that I stay around the school. That's where I could do the most good.

I would do good, damn it. I wanted to blame Duane for the way I was feeling about myself, but I knew that was bullshit. I made my own choices.

While Moe made the return trip to the Mannaz School, I decided to check in on the teachers and students with my regular old eyes and ears. It was good for me to get used to it so that I wouldn't always feel so handicapped when my steadfast familiar was not

173

nearby. Despite my seeming age, all of my senses were pretty much perfect. My body was as fit as a fifty-something man's body could be.

I strolled up and down the halls looking into the little windows of the classrooms. I observed Allie asking her students questions about the nature of Griffin, the protagonist of *The Invisible Man*, and his reaction to the power of invisibility. Sure, it was nice just to watch her, but the topic resonated with me as well. Griffin is selfish, and he uses his power to take advantage of others. He has fits of temper in which he lashes out at those around him. Throughout it all, he is able to rationalize his horrible treatment of others. It almost seemed that some higher power was speaking to me through the book, saying, *Don't be like Griffin!*

Moe was back before I'd finished my circuit, and even when he stayed by my side, his senses added markedly to my physical ones. From Ms. Hart's math class, we heard very clearly, "There's nothing wrong with saying 'Hair Trigger'!" The speaker was clearly not Duane, which caused me to feel even more angry than if it were. It was Andy.

Andy was a chameleon kid. He seemed to have no self-identity, incapable of introspection. When he was around nice kids, he tended to be pretty nice. When he was around thugs, he tended to be aggressive. When he was around devious kids, he tended to be sly. I knew that Duane wasn't in his class, so the display in the dining room must have made a pretty strong impression to have such lingering effects on Andy.

Damn it! I should have dealt with Duane like a teacher and not like a Talamaur. Set boundaries and stick to them in a firm but respectful way. But no, I had to give in to my baser nature. I'd given him horrible stomach cramps because I was pissed off. It's not as though he would learn a lesson from such a seemingly random experience. Well, I would need to be better this time.

I knocked on the math room door and opened it.

Andy was in the middle of the statement again. "There's nothing wrong. . ." His look of defiance was so similar to Duane's that I thought that he should probably pay him royalties. The difference between the two was that Andy blanched and dropped his eyes immediately after seeing me. I didn't know if he really felt ashamed, but his expression conveyed a good approximation of the emotion. Maybe I was just feeling cynical, and the look on his face was genuine.

Howie had been looking down at the top of his desk, like he was trying to make himself small enough to avoid detection. When I opened the door, his eyes came up as Andy's were going down. He gave me the same look of pleading that he'd given me in the dining room. He didn't want me to make a big deal out of the teasing. He was just the kind of kid who didn't want his misery to impose upon others.

Laura Hart twitched all over. It was her main mode of expression. She was a thin, birdlike woman who seemed at once tightly wound and also vague and distant. I wouldn't have thought that the combination was possible, but she did it. Her movements were kind of herky-jerky at the best of times and got more pronounced as she became more anxious. She also always seemed to be one step behind everyone else, like her processing speed was especially slow, and she seemed unable to focus on anything well.

She managed to hang on at the Mannaz School because other teachers had the tendency to bail her out of difficulties. I'm all for community spirit, but I was pretty tired of Laura. She never expressed gratitude to those who helped her. She seemed to think it was owed to her.

And there I was about to fix her problem. Part of my motivation was community spirit, but part of it was the opportunity to have a do-over. I would handle Andy better than I'd handled Duane.

I said in a casual tone, "Ms. Hart, would you mind if I borrowed Andy for the rest of class?"

The corner of her mouth twitched a couple of times, and her shoulder shrug looked like old stop-motion film effects, kind of like a visual stutter. "He'll be responsible for today's lesson."

I said to Andy, "Grab your stuff. We've got places to go."

While Andy shoved his book and notebook into his backpack, I gave a small nod to Howie who returned it. He looked relieved. The strain in him melted away, and by the time Andy and I left, Howie's back had straightened and his shoulders squared.

Andy trailed along behind me as I finished my tour of the classrooms. He didn't say anything. I'd never punished him for anything before, but there had been some natural consequences for misbehavior on a couple of occasions. But now, he was acting like he expected the guillotine or something.

We ended up in the dining room. He seemed a little confused. I gestured to a small side table. "Take a load off. Do you want some tea?"

He wouldn't look at my eyes. "I don't like tea." I thought he wanted to add something else like, "Tea is for old ladies," but he didn't.

I said, "I'll brew two cups of the apple spice. If you really don't want yours, I'll drink it too."

There was a hot-water dispensing machine, so I didn't need to heat a kettle or anything. I typically liked a big, chunky diner mug, but I used real teacups this time. It would be easy to drink two of them if Andy didn't want his. I brought the cups with their teabags in them over to the table and put one in front of him, and I sat down across from him.

We sat for a bit. I saw him lean forward a little to smell the tea. It smelled a little like hot mulled apple cider. I put a spoon and a sugar packet next to his cup. He reached for them right away.

I said, "You should let it steep for a few minutes."

"Steep?"

"Yeah, just give the water time to draw out some flavor and color."

He starred at the tea, probably because he didn't want to look at me.

"That won't make it go faster, you know," I said.

"Okay." He shifted his gaze to the spoon and sugar a few inches away.

I asked him, "Do you like Duane?"

His eyes rose to meet mine for a second. Then, he looked away and shrugged. "Yeah, I guess."

"How about two years ago?"

Andy didn't say anything. When Duane had showed up at Mannaz, he'd quickly established himself as the alpha dog. That meant putting all of the other dogs in their places. I knew some specifics, but

I didn't mention any. Because Andy was one of the other dogs, I was pretty sure that he was thinking about them, though.

"It's tough to be new, and no one likes to be targeted."

He said, "Yeah."

"And what do we learn from Spiderman?"

Andy looked up and the corner of his mouth quirked. "Really?"

I held my hands out, palms-up. There were still some guys who pretended to think that comic books were just kids' stuff. I persisted in treating them with a certain amount of cultural seriousness.

He sighed dramatically. "With great power comes great responsibility."

I said, "Use your powers for good." I reminded myself to do the same. To be a superhero, not a supervillain.

He picked up his spoon and looked to me for affirmation. I showed him how to squeeze the teabag by wrapping the string around it and the spoon that held it, so he wouldn't need to use his fingers. He dumped in the sugar and began to stir it distractedly. He picked up the cup and held it under his nose. It was a good smell.

He sipped at his tea. His bottom lip protruded in consideration, and he bobbed his head in approval. He held the cup up and said, "This is good."

I said, "It is." I would have rather had regular black tea, but that had caffeine, and Dr. Corman had rules about students drinking caffeine. I didn't think it would have been as palatable to a twelve-year-old anyway.

We sipped our tea in silence for a few minutes.

Andy said, "I'm sorry for making fun of Howie."

I nodded but didn't say anything.

"Do I have to apologize to him?"

"I never really saw the point of forcing someone to apologize. I think that only genuine apologies have any validity."

"Yeah. I'll tell him I'm sorry when I see him after school."

I felt a little of the darkness lift from me then. The tension that had been bunching in my shoulders since lunchtime eased a little. This moment. This is why I did this whole Mannaz School thing. I didn't think that Andy was magically fixed or anything. We would likely have similar conversations in the future. For a moment, though, I saw his decency and potential. I'd brought that out of him, to some degree at least, and I didn't need superpowers at all. Mostly what I needed was patience and a level head.

Andy and I hung out until the next class change, which wasn't very long. He continued with his classes, and I spent the afternoon checking in now and again with everyone. Rick seemed to be having a lot of fun being Morrey, which seemed strange to me. But I was thinking like a human. Some creatures were designed to do special things, and they really enjoyed doing those things. Otters like to swim, right? Horses like to run. It made sense in those terms. Rick was a changeling. He could look and sound like anyone. That's just how he was built.

Allie stopped in to my office after my creative writers had gone at the end of the school day and asked about Corman. I told her all that I would know if I didn't have a familiar. She showed concern, but I could tell that it wasn't the same for her as it was for Novak and me. That's natural. Corman was a good boss to her. He was a friend of long standing to me. I couldn't very well hold it against her.

Thinking about my great fondness for Corman, I felt a little snubbed because neither Corman or Novak had called me yet. That was self-centered of me, and I acknowledged that without the feeling going away. Intellectually, I understood that they were fighting their own battles. I would focus on that and ignore the abandoned feeling that kept creeping in.

I half expected Novak to show up after school to meet up for a drink, but Lore was closed on Tuesdays. I sent Moe around to his house and found that he was sleeping deeply at a little after four. He clearly needed it, and I didn't begrudge him some rest. Moe lingered just a little. The care had eased out of Novak's features, and his chest rose and fell with deep slow breathing that was not quite heavy enough to call snoring.

I would have called Allie to hang out, but she had to work on Tuesday nights. All teachers had some nighttime and weekend duty. She'd actually picked Tuesday as her duty night because Lore was closed. Ah, the girl had priorities after my own heart.

Normally, I'm just fine with solitude. I need it on a pretty regular basis, but right then, I really didn't want to be by myself. The current situation and the decisions ahead of me were big. I don't mean to indicate that I hadn't been in more dire, even life-threatening, situations at other times in my life. When I thought of it in those terms, my anxiety seemed silly. My priorities had shifted, though, and berating myself about my concern for others wasn't going to help anything.

I ate dinner with the students in the Oak House dining room. Afterward, I stopped in to Maple House to thank Terry for covering classes, and I took the opportunity to check in on Rick as well. He was playing Magic: The Gathering with Larry in the living room. He waved distractedly and said, "Hey, Mr. Brannon." He was so damn good at being an adolescent. Moe seemed unable to identify any kind of power signature in truly shifted creatures, so I felt like I had to learn some tells or something. I hated being so easily fooled.

I also visited Howie in Beech House. He gave me more attention than Rick had, but he was also engaged with his dorm mates. Maggie actually had a full-sized foosball table in the basement, and the students were playing an informal tournament. I could tell that Howie wanted to spend more time with me, but when it was his turn to play, I left to let him have fun with the other kids. It was good to see him happy.

I was just stepping through my apartment door at about half past nine when my phone rang. Novak wanted to know if I was interested in having drinks. I thought that he meant at my apartment, and I told him of my limited selection of potables. But he wanted to go out and suggested The Bar. I didn't sigh aloud, but I felt a sigh in my soul. But I didn't want to deny my friend's request, so I agreed.

Novak was a Geary native, born and raised. He'd gone to Geneseo State College after high school, and his first teaching job was at the Mannaz School. He was smart and relatively open-minded, but I found him to be an exception to the Geary rule. Despite his education and some travel, he still felt a great deal of affection for his hometown. The Bar was an institution, overserving locals for something like four generations. If not for my friendship, I doubt that he ever would have given Lore a chance. He genuinely liked The Bar.

I didn't change out of my school clothes. I just retrieved my car keys and headed back out the door. Allie was returning from her dorm visit, and we met on the sidewalk. She had taken the time to change into a more casual outfit after school and was wearing jeans and a red sweater under a black, thigh-length overcoat. The coat also had a hood which she had up. She looked cute as hell.

"What's shakin'?" she asked.

"Con and I are going out for a couple of drinks."

The contemplative crease appeared between her brows. "But the pub's closed."

I smiled wryly. "But The Bar is open."

She rolled her eyes.

"Don't blame me," I said.

She chewed on her lower lip for a few seconds and said, "Do you think Con would care if I came?"

"I think that you would be a welcome addition. You'll doubtless save us from giving in to our baser impulses."

"Hold on," she said. "Don't expect miracles from me."

# Chapter 15

We walked toward the parking lot. I casually flipped the keyring around my finger, gunslinger style. They made a rhythmic clinking sound. Ching-ching. Ching-ching-ching.

When we got ourselves situated in the front seats of the Nova, Allie wrinkled her nose a little. She looked pointedly at me and said, "Your car smells a little funky."

I shrugged. "She's old."

"She needs an air freshener."

I shrugged again.

The Nova rumbled up the short drive to Novak's house. Allie and I got out of the car and walked toward the house. Novak and Christie met us on the porch. I was struck again by the physical contrast between them. There was something a little comic about it, but over the years I saw how well they fit in most other ways, and except for rare moments like this, they looked natural together.

Christie stood five inches taller than her husband. He was a little swarthy and dark-haired, except where it was gray. She had creamy white skin, pale-blue eyes, and ash-blond hair. He was stocky. She was slight, small-breasted and narrow-hipped. She was aging well for someone so slim. There was still a softness to the lines of her face and a straightness in her bearing.

She said to Allie, "Are you going to drive these guys home if they get tipsy?"

Tipsy? Who was I, Nora Charles?

Allie looked at me expectantly and I said, "Why not?"

Christie said, "Good. I'll worry less, now."

Allie, Novak, and I climbed into the Nova. Novak wanted the back seat for some reason. Maybe he was being gentlemanly. This outing was for him, so who was I to deny him his choice of seat?

Allie watched my right hand as I shifted into reverse and backed into my three-point turn.

I asked, "Can you drive a stick?"

She didn't answer right away. Moe showed me that she had a huge open-mouthed smile on her face, and her eyebrows were raised high. So damn cute. I glanced at her for a second while I pretended to have to focus on navigating the driveway.

When she spoke, she affected a smoky voice and put on a heavy Mexican accent. "I can drive the hell out of your stick, señor, for miles and miles."

Novak snorted from the back seat which set Allie off into laughter. I couldn't help but join in. We weren't howling or anything, but there were still occasional chuckles and we drove along the square and past the school sign. I felt grateful to Allie for the levity. I didn't know how long it would last, but every little bit would help.

Once we were on 19A, I asked again. "Can you drive a stick?"

She rolled her eyes. "I know that back in your day things were different, but now-a-days, some people might consider that question sexist."

I rolled my eyes as well. I was sure to make it really broad and dramatic, so she couldn't miss it. "Yeah, but can you drive a stick?"

"I wouldn't have told Christie that I would drive if I couldn't do it."

"Good enough."

She gave me the look and the voice again and said, "I love to drive the stick."

"Uh huh," I said keeping my eyes on the road.

"Si, señor. For miles and miles, I drive the stick."

Novak chuckled in the back seat.

Allie said, "Miles and miles." Then, she was quiet, but she was smiling.

Geary was pretty dead on a Tuesday night. Actually, it was pretty dead every night, but it's a relative thing. The exceptions were The Bar and, to a lesser extent, the Silver Creek bar. The clientele at The Crick tended to be older, and they didn't stay out so late.

We pulled into the parking lot of The Bar which was sort of paved. Potholes had been filled in with dirt and gravel and never seemed to be level. There were so many of them that the dips and bumps were impossible to avoid. The only option was to drive slowly or beat the hell out of your undercarriage. Well, a large number of the vehicles in the lot were trucks, so the extra ground clearance probably proved beneficial.

Even on a Tuesday at almost ten at night, there were six vehicles in the lot. One belonged to Bob Mueller, the owner and primary bartender. I think that he and Novak were distantly related, but from what I'd been able to glean over the years, most people in Geary were distantly related.

Before the Nova even came to a stop, Moe was scouting the bar. Sitting at the bar were three middle-aged guys wearing barn coats and baseball caps. The heels of their work boots rested on the rungs of their stools. Cans of Genesee and Genesee Light sat on the bar in front of them. They had been talking to Bob, but when the Nova turned into the lot, they leaned in their seats to get a look and the new arrivals.

Bob was paunchy and had a head of thick gray hair which could do with a trim. He wore a Wyatt Earp mustache and sported a couple-of-days-worth of stubble on his cheeks and chin. He wore a western-style shirt, jeans, and cowboy boots. His belt buckle was large, and his big belly made it tilt toward the floor.

The man at the bar who was closest to the window said, "It's Con Novak and his faggy friend." He paused, considering, and added, "And a girl too. Looks kinda dark."

Another who couldn't see said, "The street light on that side's busted."

"The girl is dark, dumbass."

"She from the rez?"

There was a Seneca Reservation not too far away where the locals liked to buy cheaper gas and cigarettes.

"How the fuck do I know?"

Moe moved on.

There were a couple of younger guys playing pool. They were dressed similarly to the men at the bar. One was dark, and one was blond. Aside from that, they were of a type. The blond one had a huge wad of chew in his lower lip.

Three couples were gathered around a table in the corner farthest away from the door. They were eating Buffalo wings, and drinking pilsner which they poured from pitchers. They all wore green and gold satin bowling shirts and were talking and laughing together.

As Moe flitted by, he heard one man say to another, "You just couldn't find the sweet spot."

The woman next to him said, "He ain't never been able to find the sweet spot."

They all laughed louder.

"Sweet Home Alabama" was playing on the jukebox at a fairly low volume, but loud enough that people needed to raise their voices a little to be heard.

Novak climbed the chipped cement steps and pulled the door open. He couldn't stand on the top step when he did it, though, because the door opened out too far to leave room. He had to reach up from the next step down. The door was heavy and splintery. Allie entered after him, and I brought up the rear.

It's not as though the place went silent when we entered, but conversation stopped for a couple of beats while everyone gave us the once-over. Actually, the men looked Allie over more than once. I understood. I really did. I just didn't like the predatory glint in some of their eyes.

Bob and the men at the bar nodded to Novak as we approached. I wouldn't say that they ignored me. They accepted me as Novak's friend, but that was about as far as that went. I'd only lived in the area for thirty years, so I was clearly still an outsider. And I talked high-falutin'.

We bellied up to the bar, and Novak asked for a Genny.

Bob said, "Can or draft?"

Novak turned to us and said, "You guys want a pitcher?"

Allie didn't look thrilled at the idea, and she asked Bob, "Do you have any stouts or porters?"

Bob looked like he swallowed a bug. "We just serve regular beer here, honey."

Novak said, "She ain't from around here."

"Gee, that ain't obvious or nothin'" Bob said.

"We'll get a pitcher o' Genny and three glasses."

While Bob drew the pitcher, Allie leaned over and whispered into my ear, "Ain't?"

I whispered back, "He does that here."

"Why?"

"I think he doesn't want to seem high-falutin'."

Novak carried the pitcher, and I carried the stack of glasses to a small table near the back door, as far away from everyone as we could get. Allie followed. Moe hovered near the ceiling, taking in the room.

Novak is a great guy. Smart, knowledgeable, and morally sound. I'd spent more time with him in the last thirty years than I had with anyone else. He was my best human friend. A good man in every sense of the word. Better than me, I guess. I just didn't understand how he could have such affection for this town and the people in it. Admittedly, they'd never given me much trouble, but I was a white man who looked like I could handle myself.

Novak poured the beer and set the pitcher down in the center of the table. He said, "Thanks, guys. I know that this wouldn't have been your first choice, but I really need to be away."

I said, "Sure, Con."

"You said, 'ain't.'" Allie's tone was serious. "Why?"

Novak shrugged.

"Will you avoid doing that in the future, please?"

Novak drank off half of his beer, wiped his mouth, and said, "Does the word 'ain't' cause you pain or something?"

She said, "When it comes from you? Yes."

I repeated, "He does that here." It annoyed me too, but I wasn't going to make a thing of it.

We drank and chatted about everything but Corman. The Genesee was insubstantial, and we drank it fast. I mean Novak and I. Allie did her sipping thing. If I didn't know what to look for, I'd have thought that she was drinking right along with us. I guess it's a natural smart/pretty girl adaptation. Don't want to get drunk with horny guys around.

"Sweet Home Alabama" gave way to "Shook Me All Night Long" and then "I've Got Friends in Low Places." I was far from a regular at

The Bar, but I came in sometimes with Novak, and it seemed like the same songs were played on the jukebox every night for the last thirty years.

When Novak got up to get another pitcher, Moe spotted the two pool players swaggering toward our table. I turned in my seat to watch them advance. They smirked and grinned and elbowed each other. When the blond one smiled, the tobacco in his lip was plainly visible. They took up position in front of Allie.

She glanced at me, and I nodded. You know, the "I got your back" nod.

The dark-haired guy spoke, but he didn't speak to Allie. He spoke to me. "I was wonderin' if the little chica here would wanna dance."

"Achy Breaky Heart" was the current jukebox selection.

I said, "Ask the chica."

"Well, you know, I didn't know if she could talk English."

Allie smiled sweetly and said to me, *"¿Están bromeando estos chicos? Son dibujos animados."*

I said, *"Si, lo sé."*

Dark-hair said to me, "You talk Mexican?"

"I do."

"Why? We're in America."

I said, "Mexico is in America too."

His mouth fell open, and he puffed his chest up. "No, it ain't!"

I let it go. Basic geography was clearly not his thing.

The blond guy lightly punched Dark-hair on the arm. "You was right. She's Mexican." He turned to me and said by way of explanation, "I thought she's a slant." He grinned, showing his tobacco again and said, "Ya know, 'Me so horny. Me love you long time.'" He made hip-bumping motions.

I was a teacher at a private boarding school. I couldn't go pounding the shit out of assholes willy-nilly. I could stab them with Moe. These idiots deserved it more than Duane had, but I really didn't want to start sliding down that particular slippery slope.

Novak was heading back our way with the fresh pitcher in hand. I thought that he could use his townie powers to defuse the situation.

That would be best. I didn't want to earn the school bad press by getting into a brawl, and I didn't want to use my familiar as a torture device. I resolved not to do those things and congratulated myself heartily.

I can be petty, though, and a little juvenile, so I chose to fuck with the rednecks. Physically, Moe can't do much. He can exert some force, though, so tapping Dark-hair on the shoulder was easy.

Dark-hair turned to Blond and said, "What?"

Blond said, "What do you mean, what?"

"Can't you see I'm talkin' to the chica?"

"So, talk."

Dark-hair turned back to Allie. This time, Moe put a lot more force into his "tap," and the force was concentrated like a stiff finger jab. He aimed right for the kidney. Dark-hair's eyes went wide, and he jumped forward almost bumping into Allie who deftly moved in her chair to avoid contact.

Dark-hair spun around and faced Blond with fist cocked. "What the fuck do you think you're doin'?"

Blond took a double-step backward raising his fists into something like a John Sullivan pose. "The fuck?"

Novak barely avoided being backed into by Blond, but he was able to move himself and the pitcher of beer out of the way in a looping spin. The man wasn't really graceful, but he was physically competent in a competitive athlete kind of way. Not a drop was spilled. He put the pitcher down on an empty table.

In a voice that was loud enough to carry, he said, "Dylan? Cody? What's up with you guys?"

Dylan, the dark-haired one, and Cody, the blond, glared at each other. Neither one of them seemed willing to lower their fists. It wouldn't take much to set them off, and a part of me wanted to have Moe goose one or the other of them. I didn't want Novak to get involved in an altercation, though.

Novak said, "What's going on, guys?"

Dylan said, "This fucker's got to learn to keep his hands to himself!"

187

Cody didn't lower his fists, but he looked at Novak as if for help. "I got no idea what's up his ass. I didn't touch him."

"Are you callin' me a liar?" Dylan was trembling.

By this time Bob had come from around the bar. A cynical part of me wondered if he would have bothered if Novak hadn't gotten involved. I guess the point was moot, but there he was next to Novak. He didn't look as formidable, but the two of them together would give any troublemakers pause.

Bob said, "Enough of this horse shit! If you gotta go fisticuffs, take it to the parkin' lot."

I thought that Dylan and Cody would both rooster-strut out to the parking lot, and I expected that everyone in the bar would gather around the windows to watch the contest. "Flirtin' with Disaster" came on, but that was the only sound. Everyone, including the bowlers, was watching to see how this would play out. I couldn't help to think about Laura Hart's math class. Conflict was fascinating.

Before Cody and Dylan could take action, the door from the parking lot opened. Moe took note, but no one involved in the impending fight did. Every other man in the place did, though. There was an almost gravitational force surrounding the woman who entered. The lady bowlers were the next to note the arrival because they couldn't help but to follow their husbands' or boyfriends' gazes.

The woman was dressed casually in snug jeans, sneakers, and a tight white t-shirt bearing an American flag. Despite the cold, she wore no coat, nor any bra from the look of the erect nipples pushing at the thin cotton fabric. Her breasts were not large, but they were prominent, and their unfettered movement was hypnotic as she strode across the floor. Her auburn hair looked tousled and thick like a lion's mane, giving her a look of the wild. Her skin was a tone or two darker than I would expect from a redhead, but there was still a light dusting of freckles along her cheeks and nose. Her smile was mischievous, even a little naughty.

And she moved right toward the knot of potential combatants.

Allie was the first of the group to notice the woman approach. She said, "Wow!"

All heads swiveled, and every man looked the redhead up and down at least once. She struck a hip-cocked pose and actually put her hands on her hips and arched her back making her breasts push harder against the material of the t-shirt.

"What's a girl gotta do to get a drink around here?" Her voice was all Jessica Rabbit. It was the kind of voice Allie had tried to affect when we left the school. But Allie had a wholesome kind of sexiness, like a Gil Elvgren pinup girl from the '50s. The redhead would have no qualifiers. She was just sex personified.

No one responded right away. We all just stared, stunned and slack-jawed. Bob, to his credit, was the one who spoke up first. "You just gotta ask, honey."

"Jack Daniel's."

Bob hurried back around the bar, Dylan and Cody forgotten. If he had a tail, it probably would have been wagging. There was almost a bounce in his stride.

The redhead gestured at Dylan and Cody and said, "You guys going to keep me company at the bar?"

Their conflict was forgotten, entirely. They looked hypnotized. Neither said anything, but they walked side-by-side like sleepwalkers toward the bar. Before following them, the redhead turned to me and winked broadly and gave me the double-thumbs-up. Then, she turned and followed the men, her smoothly rounded bottom as alluring as her breasts had been when she'd approached.

"Wow!" Allie said again. "When I act sexy, that's what I'm trying to do."

"You know her?" Novak asked me. He sounded impressed already.

"I don't." Even as I said it, I wondered if it were true. The double-thumbs-up was one of my things, like the double-point-and-grin, à la Bruce Campbell. Why would a stranger make a face at me and use one of my signature gestures on me?

As Novak placed the pitcher on the table, he said, thoughtfully, "That girl looks kind of like Tawny Kitaen in the Whitesnake video. You know, rolling around on the hood of the Jag."

Moe zipped to the bar for a closer look. She really did look like Tawny Kitaen, if Tawny's Whitesnake-era sexiness had been bumped up a couple of notches. And that's no insult to Tawny. The woman was in full flirt mode. I didn't know what Cody had said, but the woman gave him a playful little shove and said, "I will not!" But she smiled as though she might.

I noted that even her voice was similar to the actress's. I wasn't a major fan, but I'd seen her in *Witchboard* and on the Hercules TV show. The voice was really, really similar, just bumped up a couple of sexiness notches, more velvet in it.

Her Jack Daniel's was already gone, and I expected to feel my old rescuer complex kick in when Dylan slid another double in front of her. She grinned impishly and looked at him out of the corner of her eye and said, "You guys aren't trying to get me drunk, are you?"

I knew then, on some instinctive level, that she was playing with them. Not like a woman using her charms to get free drinks, but like a cat who swats the dazed mouse around to see if it will try to run again.

I would check in again, but I didn't feel all that concerned for the woman. Maybe this was one of those cases when Moe could see things that I couldn't interpret, on a conscious level at least.

Allie, Novak, and I went back to our conversation. Speculations on the redhead gave way to a little history on Dylan and Cody. Novak had gone to school with Cody's parents. Dylan's dad was from Belfast just a few miles away. He insisted that they were really good guys at heart.

To which Allie responded, "Yeah, for racist, misogynist morons."

"They didn't mean anything by it," he said.

There was some heat in her tone. "No, Con, they really did."

I caught her eyes, tightened my mouth, and gave one small shake of my head. I thought that she was going to push it, but she gave an equally short nod. We both knew that this outing was for Novak, and he was protective of Geary and its people. An argument would accomplish nothing.

She seemed unable to resist one parting shot at Dylan and Cody. "I shudder at the thought that they will one day reproduce."

190

Novak looked down at the nearly empty beer in his hands and smiled wryly.

"Are you serious?" Allie said. "What are they twenty-one, twenty-two?"

Novak said, "Dylan's twenty-two, and he's got three kids."

"And his wife doesn't care if he's hitting on *chicas* and redheads at the bar?"

Novak said, "Dylan's not married."

"Oh?"

"He just knocked up a couple of girls."

"Right. Thanks for the clarification," Allie said.

We were quiet for a beat or two, and Novak added, "Cody's married, though." He smiled broadly and said, "Yeah, okay, they're assholes."

Our talk wasn't as spirited or varied as usual. There was the ease of friendship between us, but we didn't seem able to get into the groove of things. We were on the third pitcher when Novak said out of the blue, "I don't think the school can survive if Joe doesn't make it."

Allie and I just sat silently, waiting. He looked at the two of us and our expressions and waved a hand dismissively.

"I'm sorry," he said. "I don't know where that came from."

"Is it that serious?" Allie asked, hunching forward a little.

"I don't know. No one knows. The doctors sure as hell don't know."

I knew. Or had a vague idea anyway. He'd had the lifeforce sucked out of him, and he wasn't regenerating it. It hadn't been a Talamaur feeding, but there were plenty of similarities to one. I thought he would have a chance if he made it a couple of days, but Novak's concern was legitimate.

I put my hand on his shoulder and said, "We'll deal with things when and if we need to."

Allie put her hand on his other shoulder.

Novak drank the last of his beer and stood abruptly. He said, "One more pitcher," and hurried back to the bar.

I knew that all the GMO corn sugar wasn't going to kill me, but I worried for Novak. The Genny wasn't very satisfying, and I thought

191

about how much more I would have enjoyed a gathering in my apartment. I'd never considered myself a snob before. Maybe I would need to reassess.

When we left, the redhead was still looking sharp and alert, but Cody and Dylan were decidedly bleary. They didn't quite track our progress as we headed for the door, their eyes just a step behind us. The woman gave me the Bruce Campbell, double-finger-point and waved at Allie and Novak.

As we negotiated the cement steps, Novak said, "Are you sure you don't know that woman?"

"I think I would remember her," I said.

In an offhand way, Allie said, "I've never really thought about being a lesbian before."

Novak and I stopped and gaped. Allie continued until she reached the Nova. She held up her hand and said, "Keys."

I tossed them, and she snagged them out of the air. We climbed in, and she adjusted the seat and the rearview mirror. The Nova came to life with her deep, throaty growl. Allie said, "I have to admit that I've been looking forward to this." She revved the engine, and the chassis shivered with the power of the V8. Allie's smile at me was wicked.

I thought, *That redhead has got nothing on you.* Of course, I was biased.

She drove well. Her innate caution kept her speed conservative, but she shifted like a racecar driver, and the Nova never sounded better.

We were a couple of miles down the road when Novak swore in the back seat. "Shit!"

"What's the matter?" I asked.

"Joe wanted me to meet with the parents of a prospective student tomorrow."

Allie said, "How soon would the student arrive?"

Novak said, "Not until after Christmas break. I don't think I have it in me to make nice with prospective parents tomorrow."

"I'll do it," I said.

"Yeah?"

"Sure. I'd have to cover your classes while you did it anyway. You teach your own classes, and I'll talk to the parents."

"Thanks, Sean." Novak sounded genuinely relieved. "You're better at that kind of thing than I am anyway."

# Chapter 16

I took extra time getting ready on Wednesday morning. Truth be told, I kind of liked dressing up. The '30s and '40s had made quite an impression on me, and those were years when a lot of men could wear the hell out of a suit. I had some good ones myself, but I liked to dress to fit my environment, and with the exception of Corman and Pam, the Mannaz School was not much of a suit-wearing kind of place.

I wore a single-breasted, charcoal gray number with a cobalt-blue shirt that could almost give my eyes a run for their money. My tie was dark purple with a dark-blue diamond pattern that could only be seen when the light hit at just the right angle. I even took the time to brush and polish my black oxfords. When I combed my hair, I tried to emphasize the white over my ears with the subtle use of some styling product.

I "accidentally" ran into Allie not long before classes. I didn't even need to go that far out of my way. Moe helps me to bump into people just as well as he helps me to avoid them. We didn't literally collide, but I did round the corner dramatically like I was in a hurry to get somewhere. I took a great deal of pleasure when she looked me up and down. See, I'm all for sexual equality.

She said, "Goodness, Mr. Brannon." Then, she punched me lightly on the shoulder and said, "Good luck with the parents."

"Thank you," I said and bowed slightly at the waist.

She smiled at me and continued on to her classroom before the students arrived.

My meeting with the parents wasn't until ten, and I'd read through the application materials the night before. Since I had nearly an hour and a half to prepare, I meandered a bit on my way to the teachers' lounge and another cup of coffee. I took it to Corman's office where I planned to drink it while rereading the prospective student's paperwork.

Pam's outfit today was a russet-brown suit over a rusty-orange blouse. Her earrings were shaped like jack-o-lanterns, and the ends of her blonde hair were tipped with pale orange.

When she saw me, she flashed her hundred-watt smile and gave me a onceover. "What's the occasion?"

"I'm interviewing the parents of a potential new student."

Concern tightened the soft lines of her face, which was just all wrong. Her face was made for smiles. Even when at rest, a potential sunny smile seemed to wait just below the surface. That's why the look of worry she gave me was so dramatic, so earnest, so heart-breaking.

She said, "Have you heard anything more about Dr. Corman?"

"He's still at Warsaw Hospital. I don't think he's getting worse. Con would be the person to ask."

"Okay," she said.

Her face was strained with care. I didn't want to leave her looking down like that, so I concocted my most absurd crystal-ball theory yet, totally juvenile gross-out stuff. I said, "It's not a crystal ball. It's a petrified snot bubble from a triceratops." The corner of her mouth bent upward.

"The triceratops was Joe's childhood pet, and the snot bubble is a keepsake. The only thing he has to remember his beloved pet because it fell into the backyard tarpit."

It was, hands-down, my worst crystal ball backstory, but she smiled all the way then anyway. It was still a bit sad looking but better.

"Thanks, Sean. Good luck."

I touched a hand to my chest. "People keep wishing me luck. Do I really seem that in need of luck?"

"You'll charm their socks off," she said, and her smile dialed up a notch. Not back to normal by any stretch but better still.

I entered Corman's office and closed the door behind me. I patted the crystal ball as I passed it and said, "I know you're not a snot bubble." I felt a little pulse from the ghost within it, rather Moe did. I expected confusion. Ghosts were often confused, but what I felt was concern, awareness. I think it would have talked to me if it could.

There's a pretty wide range of ghosts existing on this plane. Some are not much of anything but a lingering feeling or a dim memory. Others are almost like the people whom they had been in life, just you know, minus the body. To my knowledge, though, ghosts faded. This one in the crystal ball was old, but it was also sharp. Moe could feel its perceptions. Strange. I'd never seen anything like it.

I had heard stories of ghosts who were so connected to a place or a family that they were able to somehow draw energy from the living. A little vampiric, I guess, but I don't think that ghosts would require a lot. Supposedly, that kind can stick around for centuries. I'd never seen one, though, and I'd done a good bit of traveling.

Through Moe, I conveyed my feeling of concern for Corman and any comfort I could give to the ghost. My familiar doesn't use words. I can hear words through him, but if I can't hear them myself, he can't tell me what's been said. Because of that, I can't have conversations with ghosts. No séances for this guy. I think they can tell Moe things, but he works in feelings, and to some degree, intents, so that's what I get. I assume the same works from me to ghosts.

I took off my jacket and hung it on a hanger in the closet. The closet had Corman's smell in it. I'm not sure the exact combination of scents that made it, but there was leather and pine and the kind of sweetness that comes from certain pipe tobaccos. It had been pretty consistent over the years. It was a manly smell but also refined. Evocative of sitting in highbacked club chairs and drinking old scotch while playing backgammon.

My coffee was gone, and I'd almost made it through the paperwork for the second time when there was a knock on the door. On pure reflex, Moe checked and found Pam on the other side. I glanced at the wall clock to find that I still had over forty minutes until my meeting. I hoped that the new parents weren't that eager.

I said, "Come in."

Her smile was a bit impish, her eyes creased at the edges. "Do you have a secret you'd like to share?" Her eyebrows came up in inquiry.

I had thousands of secrets, but I wasn't really prepared to share any of them. What I said was, "I'm an open book Ms. Wesley."

"Maybe a little summer love at Lollapalooza?"

"What?" I wasn't able to follow her insinuation. My first instinct when I was at a loss was to get my familiar moving. I didn't always know what to do with him, but he was fast, and his perspective often made mysteries plain. This was one of those cases.

Moe was out in Pam's office in the blink of an eye where another Talamaur familiar did the equivalent of a chest bump with him. Oh right, when familiars interact with each other, they behave as if they have mass. Well, more significant mass anyway. Three ghosts orbited around the other familiar. I wished I didn't recognize it but I did. There was a crackle of metaphysical energy within perimeter of the ghosts' orbits.

Sprawled negligently in a dark-blue suit, crisp white shirt, and red power tie sat my douchebag cousin, Doru. He looked an awful lot like me when I wasn't pretending to be middle aged. If anything, he was better looking. His hair was cut in a trendy kind of style, shaved on the sides and a little floppy on the top. His goatee was so neatly trimmed and combed that it looked fake. His suit cost ten times mine, and his shoes looked hand-sewn. The tie matched his hair almost perfectly.

Without raising his arm from the chair's armrest, he flicked a little wave at Moe. He didn't smile. He smirked. He was a smirky kind of guy.

His familiar bumped Moe again. We clenched up in frustration, Moe was like a dog on a leash. My familiar is as tough as they come, but Doru's familiar had the ghosts to tip the scales. Familiar fights are mostly pointless, but Moe didn't seem to care about that.

The dismay that I felt must not have appeared in my face or manner because Pam continued. "Or do you have a whole family hidden somewhere?"

I faked a serene smile and said, "Do I have a visitor?"

"I'll say." She shook her hand as though she'd touched something hot.

If she'd told me how pretty a scorpion was, I would have had a similar feeling.

"Well, let's reveal the mystery. Send in my visitor, please." I glanced at the wall clock for effect. "I have an appointment in a little more than a half hour." But it wasn't like Doru would care about anyone enough to try to keep to a schedule.

She returned to her office and said to Doru, "Mr. Brannon has a few minutes before an appointment, so you can speak with him briefly."

Doru conspicuously shook a gold Rolex from his cuff and examined it long enough for Pam to get a good look at it. He stood and moved across the room as if there were a camera on him, and he was walking in slow motion through a layer of ground fog. Some John Woo kind of thing. He pointedly did not look back at Pam as he entered Corman's office and closed the door behind him. His familiar, I noted, took a quick detour under her skirt, though.

I would have said something about his lack of class when he came in, but he did things like that specifically to pick fights. It was his way of controlling interactions. I suddenly wished I could spend some quality time with Duane. Even Dylan and Cody would be preferable.

"What the fuck did you do to yourself?" His tone was thin with a kind of laughing mockery. "You look like shit. Who ever heard of a fucking geriatric Talamaur?"

"What do you want?" My voice was as flat as I could make it.

He dropped into the chair that I usually used and crossed his legs, ankle to knee. He slouched with a studied sort of dismissiveness. The coolest guys don't care about anything, right? The effect was spoiled somewhat when he squinted at the crystal ball.

"Now that's a fucking waste," he said after a moment's study.

"What are you talking about?"

He pointed at the crystal. "Trapped mage ghost."

I just stared at him.

"Ha!" It wasn't a laugh, only an exclamation. "Smart guy doesn't know something. Imagine that."

"Why don't you edify me?" I said.

He smiled, but it wasn't a smile that conveyed humor. It was a gloating smile. A one-upsmanship smile.

It was pretty clear that he wasn't going to explain, so I repeated, "What do you want?"

"Can't I just want to check in on my dear cousin?"

"It would be the first show of concern for another being I ever saw from you," I said.

Doru's familiar floated behind him like a bodyguard with its ghost satellites. Doru tried to wait quietly, but that was never his strong suit. He liked to hear himself talk. After about thirty seconds, he spoke.

"When I heard about your appearance and your behavior toward my associate, I became concerned."

I squeezed the bridge of my nose like I had a headache. I didn't, at least not a literal one, but I felt like I was about to enter into a world-class headache type of situation. I sighed gustily and said, "Are you kidding me? You're associating with goblins now?"

"Melk and I have similar aims."

"And what aims might they be?"

Doru made a dismissive gesture. "This and that. It's more of a shared philosophy."

"To have a philosophy, one must be able to think in an organized and reasonable way." I maintained my flat delivery. A show of emotion was exactly the thing he wanted.

This time he treated me to a smile of the threatening variety.

"There you go again acting all superior. You're not better than I am."

"Sure, I am," I said. "In every way."

He uncrossed his legs and placed both feet deliberately on the floor. He leaned forward and said, "We both know that I could kick your ass right now."

I scoffed, which is something I rarely did. He brought that out in me. "What? Because I won't subjugate ghosts to supercharge my familiar, you think that makes you better?"

"I use all of the tools at my disposal. Every Talamaur does it."

"Your absolute statement is incorrect."

Doru's brow furrowed. "What the hell are you talking about?"

"I am Talamaur, and I do not subjugate ghosts. Clearly 'every' Talamaur does not subjugate ghosts."

"There you go again. You know what I mean. Every Talamaur but you."

"Do you know every Talamaur?" I asked. "There aren't many of us but. . ."

"You are such a self-righteous snob."

"Ghosts are the life essence of sapient beings," I said. "Their souls." I felt the hook set. I knew that my explanation was pointless, but I couldn't seem to resist trying to make him understand.

Doru slouched back in his seat. "Yeah, the only part we can't eat."

"Yeah, but you do," I said. "Your familiar does anyway. It just takes him longer to devour spirits."

"So?"

"So, whatever is left when your familiar is done is unable to move on to the afterlife. They're doomed to wander with just enough self to be frightened, lost, miserable."

"You don't even know if there's an afterlife," he said. He flapped his hand as though being pestered by a fly.

"You don't know there's not."

He leaned forward again, but he wasn't trying to look intimidating this time. He was aping interest. "Is this going to be one of those times when you explain compassion to me and giving a shit about people even when they can't do anything for me?"

"That's the one."

"Think it'll take this time?"

I shook my head while looking at the desk blotter in front of me. "What do you want, Doru?"

He touched both of his hands to his chest in a "who-me?" pose, face innocent.

"I would have thought you'd be better at this after so many years," I said.

"Better at what?"

I just looked at him, and he looked at me. I couldn't think of any reason to try to outlast him, so I spoke.

"You know, pretending to be something aside from a psychopath. We both know that you don't care about people who can't do something for you. You pretty much just said it. So, what do you want, Doru?"

"But it's not for me. It's for the good of everyone in the whole world."

200

I shook my head in disbelief. My mouth even sagged a little while I did it. Some people would say something like that to be funny because it contradicted what they'd just said moments before. I might do something like that because I understand verbal irony. But despite "knowing" Doru for over a century, I really didn't know if he could understand irony of any kind. He might not even realize that he'd contradicted himself. He was kind of like a two-hundred-year-old toddler with superpowers.

Have you ever tried to explain to toddlers why they can't have what they want? But I still couldn't seem to help myself. I spoke with exaggerated patience. "You can't admit that you don't care about anyone who can't do something for you and then convince me that you have altruistic motives. If you want to fool me, you have to lie consistently, not flip-flop from moment to moment."

He held his hands palms-up. "Can't I want something that will help me and others at the same time?"

"In theory," I admitted. "My default, though, is to assume that anything you want is somehow corrupt or depraved."

"This time, you would be wrong. You can help me to make the world a better place."

I snorted and laughed. It wasn't a belly-laugh or anything, but it was pretty hearty.

Doru's jaw clenched. I could see the muscles of his jaw bunch, and his hands grasped the arms of the chair so hard that I heard the wood creak.

I would never understand him. He didn't bat an eye at being called a psycho or corrupt or depraved, but a little chuckle made him tense as a bowstring. I guess he didn't mind being crazy or evil but not the butt of a joke.

I really shouldn't have, but I pushed a little more. "You're not supposed to start with the punchline. You tell me about the plan first. Then, you tell me that you want to make the world a better place. See, then, that's when I laugh."

His eyes bugged dangerously, and he said quietly, raggedly, "Why don't we give that blond out there a little thrill."

Doru's familiar blurred into action, but Moe is just about the badest-ass familiar around, and he caught up with it just shy of Pam. To say that they wrestled wouldn't be accurate. They pit themselves against each other. Doru's familiar, with its ghost batteries, was stronger than Moe, but it was unable to disengage and get to Pam. When it wrenched free, Moe just caught it and battened down again. They couldn't hurt each other, so Moe just put all of his strength into tangling up Doru's familiar so that it couldn't accomplish anything.

Moe was strong enough that the other familiar had to exert a significant amount of will to contest with him. Moe was so distracting, in fact, that one of the ghosts began to drift away. Doru's familiar snagged the ghost, and Moe surged against its hold. It was the spirit-world equivalent managing greased piglets, I think.

Pam, of course, was oblivious. A part of me wondered if Corman would have noticed, though. With that thought, I glanced at the crystal ball. With Moe in the next room, I had no idea how the ghost inside was reacting to the happenings.

I looked up to see Doru glaring at me. Things hadn't gone the way he'd planned.

Subjugated ghosts are really only good as batteries. They make familiars stronger, able to lift more, exert more force. In theory, they could perform minor tasks, but why would they? And they'll escape if they can. The longer a ghost is enslaved, the more docile it becomes, but it's also becoming weaker. Standard operating procedure for a Talamaur is to rotate ghosts, usually three: old, middle-aged, and young. The old and middle-aged ghosts might not take orders, but they're unlikely to rabbit. The young ghost gives a lot more power but takes some wrangling. Classic trade-off. Trying to wrangle three young ghosts would keep the familiar so busy that it couldn't do much of anything else.

Doru loved to be dominant. He was a swinging dick. Even though my body was aged, and my familiar had no ghosts, we were left with a stalemate. And it pissed him right the hell off.

I said, "What do you want?"

There was a sharp crack of splintering wood, and one of the heavy arms of Corman's guest chair came away in Doru's hand. He held up the jagged pieces and then dropped them onto the floor where they clattered dramatically.

Pam looked up from her work at the sound. I hoped that she wouldn't investigate. I wasn't afraid of what Doru could do to me, but I wasn't the most vulnerable person around. Going fisticuffs with my dear cousin might not reveal my supernatural nature, but it certainly would not be becoming behavior for a man in my position. He seemed to be pretty close to violence.

When he said, "Fine," and leaned back in his chair, some of the tension left me.

His familiar stopped struggling to reach Pam, and Doru tried to strike a nonchalant pose, but the broken chair arm made it look awkward. He had to lean to the left side because the right was no longer quite structurally sound. I decided not to comment on the contrivance.

The casual way in which he spoke was equally unconvincing, but at least he was moving past the conflict. I hoped.

"The Venator Ex Hominibus Council is meeting before the New Year to vote on a new measure. I want you to give me your vote. Make me your proxy."

"No," I said.

His jaw muscles bunched. "You haven't even heard what the measure is."

I resisted the urge to attack his character again. Doru would get something out of the passing of this measure which automatically made me want to oppose it. From experience, I knew that this was reasonable reaction, but I also knew that continuing a confrontation wasn't going to get me what I wanted: Doru gone and my friends safe.

I said, "So tell me about it."

I could see him considering how to draw out his minor victory but not knowing how. He settled for the self-satisfied smirk.

"The measure would allow the Venator to reveal themselves to specific humans for the purpose of facilitating. . . certain activities. It would take some of the burden from our shoulders as we move among them in our daily lives, and we could, you know, make more meaningful connections with the humans."

I said nothing.

"Come on," he said. "What could be wrong with that?"

"Let me get this straight. After hundreds of years, the strict prohibition against revealing ourselves to humans would be lifted—"

"Only to specifically designated humans," he interrupted.

"To facilitate 'certain' interactions." I made air-quotes with my fingers around "certain." I continued, "And to make meaningful connections with humans."

"Right."

"Okay, what do you get out of it?"

He made an encompassing gesture. "What do we all get out of it?"

Of course, I knew he was full of bullshit. Doru liked to feel superior to others. He liked to have more privileges, more status, more material possessions than anyone. For my entire life, that superiority was the only thing that Doru seemed to care about. I didn't believe that he would do anything for the good of the community. If everyone were elevated equally by this proposed measure, he wouldn't see it as an improvement for him.

I didn't want him to go after Pam again, or anyone else for that matter, so I chose not to call him out. It was really hard. There was no way that I would give my vote to him.

Venator society is not a democracy. Most other countries, especially in Europe, had pretty complicated hierarchies. The United States' structure was basic, though. There was a council of elders made up of a representative from each of the major types of venator. If any proposals for change are made, they come from the elders. The next tier down is known as the nobles. I honestly don't know what makes a noble a noble, but I did know that I was one, and Doru was not. Nobles could vote on changes, but they could not propose them.

Oh, right. Doru wasn't a noble because he was a bastard. So legally speaking, he wasn't my cousin. His parentage was common knowledge, but my uncle did not make him legitimate before getting himself killed. Talamaur are some of the most secretive of the venator, you know, the most secretive segment of the secret society. Anyway, Uncle Magon died almost a hundred years before I was born, and no one talked about it. Of course, status conscious Doru was bitter as hell about it.

I really didn't have to feign interest at that point. I'd just been thinking about the venators' one and only law a few days ago. Now, there was a possibility of it changing. I was wary of Doru's motives, but I was intrigued at the potential of the measure.

I said, "Why, after hundreds of years, would the Venator Elders want to change their one and only law?"

"I don't know. Times are changing."

"What kind of interactions are you hoping to facilitate with informed human assistance?" I asked. I really didn't expect an honest answer, but sometimes Doru just couldn't lie effectively.

"This and that."

"Give me a 'for example,'" I pressed.

"Identification papers."

"Since when do humans need to know about our supernatural natures to forge some documents?"

He made his encompassing gesture again. "Other venator could benefit more than I. Vampires could have daytime protectors who are in the know. Werewolves could have game wardens who look the other way."

"Right," I said. "And police officers and coroners could hide or spoil evidence of sloppy kills."

"I suppose."

I took a moment to consider before I spoke. Doru was not subtle, especially considering that he was a Talamaur. But for the life of me, I couldn't see what he would get out of having this measure passed."

Finally, I said, "A Talamaur kill, sloppy or not, looks like death by natural causes. What could you have to gain by this?"

I thought he was going to launch into his 'good-of-the-community' spiel again, but his face changed, went hard. He stood abruptly and the chair wobbled. He said, "Are you going to make me proxy or not?" He tried to affect a kind of Clint Eastwood tone, but the upward pitch change in his voice made him sound like a petulant child.

I looked at him for a long three seconds. It was enough time for me to squash the "Hell no!" that was rising to my lips. With our history, I was baffled that he would ever believe I would consider his proposal. He was an unrepentant bad guy. I just couldn't follow his play. I would, however, try to be as discreet as I possibly could for the sake of my friends and my students.

I said, "It's important for me to make informed decisions. I'll need to look into the measure more closely."

He glared down at me. "Have you ever used your noble vote before?"

"No."

"Have you ever even gone to a session?"

"No."

"So, you've wasted your influence for your whole life."

"My political influence."

Doru chuckled then, the sound as cold and hard as ice cubes falling in an empty glass. He spread his arms to encompass the campus. "You mean this? You starve yourself for years, so you can convince a bunch of humans that you're one of them. Why? They have no power or influence or wealth."

"You couldn't understand."

"Maybe not, but I know a lever when I see one." He shook his watch out and tapped the crystal with a finger. "Voting on this measure is time sensitive. You better get informed quick and tell me where you stand on my offer."

"Offer?"

"Yeah, do I need to spell it out?"

"Maybe you should," I said. "I like to know where I stand."

He only said, "Humans are fragile." Then, he stalked out of Corman's office. He didn't slam the door. He didn't even close it. He said nothing to Pam as he walked through her office and out her door. She was retrieving a ream of paper from her supply closet, and she turned to see his retreating back. The smile on her face faltered like a flickering light.

I should have anticipated the familiar, but I didn't. It goosed Pam's bottom as it flitted by. Her faltering smile was replaced by a look of shock as the paper fell from her spasming fingers. It thumped to the floor. She spun to scan the space behind her.

Moe harried the other familiar and its ghosts as they followed Doru out to the parking lot. He opened the door of a new black S-Class Mercedes, but before he got in, he flipped both his middle fingers at Moe and, by proxy, me.

He didn't obey the ten-mile-per-hour signs. His tires actually squawked when he gunned the car from the parking lot. Moe watched until the car, Doru, and his familiar were several miles down the road.

Pam looked shaken from her encounter with the familiar. Considering what Doru could have done, I suppose she got off easy. Still, being grabbed by an invisible man would be hard to reconcile. For a full minute she stood where she was. Her eyes moved methodically around the room as she turned slowly in a circle.

I considered going out to see if she needed anything, but I really didn't know how to go about it. The moment passed. A well-dressed couple who looked to be in their middle thirties knocked on the frame of the open door.

Pam wrestled a welcoming expression into place and smiled at the newcomers. She really was a champ, working past her first supernatural experience like that. Well, I assumed that it was her first time.

She said, "You must be the Whiteheads. I'll let Mr. Brannon know that you're here."

I stowed the broken chair and its detached arm in a corner and answered her knock.

"The Whiteheads are here."

"Before you show them in, may I borrow one of your guest chairs?"

Her smile turned uncertain and her brow creased. She leaned a little to one side and was able to see the damaged chair. She looked back to me and said, "Okay." She was clearly full of questions, but they would go unanswered. I hoped that she wouldn't be too disappointed.

# Chapter 17

I pretty much sleepwalked through the interview with the Whiteheads. I must have done an okay job of it because they began the official application process and scheduled a visit for their son, Edmund. Obviously, I was still interested in the school's future, but I thought that there would be other more significant things to worry about than a mid-year addition. But what did I know, maybe Edmund was another fairytale monster or some kind of were-creature. We had precedent now after all.

After the visitors left, Pam didn't actually ask any questions. I thought that she would want to know about Doru's identity and the broken chair. I'd been trying to come up with some plausible lies, but it turned out to be unnecessary. I was bothered, though, by her distracted manner, staring into the middle distance for several minutes at a time. My guess was that she was doubting her senses, trying to figure out why she'd felt something that clearly wasn't there. I hoped that she'd be able to dismiss it as a fluke, but sometimes things like that could stick in people's minds like a burr.

After shuffling papers for a few minutes, I came out of the office to asked her, "Is there anything else which requires my attention this morning?"

She tapped at her desktop keyboard and stared at the screen for a few seconds. "The only thing I see here is that Morris Star is sick and staying in his dorm this morning. It might be nice to check on him."

"Thank you," I said. "Is anything up with Todd, Andy, or Kate?"

"Not that I see. They're all in class."

"I'm off to Maple House. I'll be back by lunch, but text me if anything comes up before then."

"Okay, will do."

To go with the suit, I'd worn a black wool overcoat which was too warm for the weather but looked awesome. I left the leather gloves in the pockets, but I looked forward to wearing them in a couple of weeks. Trim my hair and put a fedora or a homburg on me, and I could've fit in in the '40s. The cut of the suit wasn't really right, but the overcoat would hide that.

As I walked toward Maple House, Moe lingered in Pam's office for a minute. She sat motionless for some time. Then, she got up and began to look around her office. In the supply closet, under the printer table, in the narrow place between the bookshelf and the wall. I don't know what she thought she'd find, but I'd leave her to it for the time being. I have no idea how I would handle an intervention if she weren't able to come to terms.

The temperature outside was chilly but not cold, and the sun was only occasionally obscured by the clouds. I began to feel the draw of Rochester again, somewhere to see a show, live music at least, and have some expertly made cocktails. Yeah, it was probably the suit and coat talking. When I was dressed like that, I felt like going out on the town.

Moe zipped ahead to Morrey's room in Maple House. The blinds in the room were drawn, and the main illumination came from a gooseneck desk lamp which was aimed at the bed. That's where Rick sprawled, propped up on pillows and reading an *Astro Boy* manga.

He brought a juice glass containing dark liquid up to his mouth. I was curious, so Moe checked out the contents. Bourbon. A brief scan revealed a 750 ml of white label Jim Beam stowed in the space between the bed and the dresser. The changeling was sipping whiskey alone in his room before noon. It hardly seemed professional to me, and I felt a little jealous.

I knocked on the front door of Maple House and entered. Terry, wearing jeans and a blue t with a smiley face on it, was sitting at the kitchen table drinking coffee and reading *Cannery Row*. He must have been on a Steinbeck kick. Nothing wrong with that.

He looked up when I entered and said, "Hey."

"I'm just here to check in on Morrey."

"He's in his room. Been pretty quiet. Might be sleeping."

"I'll be unobtrusive," I said and headed up the stairs.

Rick obviously heard my steps, but I'm not sure that he knew who I was. He placed the glass on the desk and casually waved a hand over the bottle and glass. Both vanished. The smell of the whiskey disappeared as well. Interesting.

Moe flicked through the frequencies until he found Rick's glamour. Then, he was able to perceive the booze again. I like to be aware and informed. It's in my nature.

I knocked lightly on the door.

Rick groaned piteously. After a pause, he said, "Yes."

"It's Mr. Brannon."

In a more natural voice, he said, "Come in."

I entered and closed the door behind me. I picked up a cup which read "Darien Lake" on the side and dumped the pencils it held onto the desk. I wiped out the empty mug with a pocket handkerchief and held it out to Rick.

"Give," I said.

He smiled broadly. The bottle and his glass reappeared along with the sharp, sweet smell of bourbon. He unscrewed the cap from the bottle and poured two fingers into the mug. He put the bottle back into its little niche, retrieved his own glass and held it up in salute.

"To moving unseen among mortals," he said.

We clinked glasses and sipped. I would have preferred Maker's Mark or Bulleit, but there was nothing wrong with white label Jim Beam.

I pulled out the desk chair and sat. "Where'd you get the booze?"

"Dylan and Cody."

"I wasn't sure that was you."

"Jeez," he said. "Really? I was giving you signs like semaphore."

Rick drank again. It was so strange to see what looked like a twelve-year-old kid wearing sweatpants and a Pokemon t-shirt drink neat bourbon.

"How'd you get to town?" I asked.

"Ran."

"Where'd you get the clothes?"

"Borrowed them."

"Borrowed really?"

He smiled big again, gap-toothed and freckle-faced. "Why would I keep them when I was done? I didn't think that people would still be using a clothesline this late in the year. Handy, though."

We sipped our drinks in a pretty comfortable silence, but soon my curiosity inspired me to speak.

"Why'd you decide to be a woman to get drinks?"

He shrugged and splashed a little more whiskey into our glasses. "Easier free drinks. Women rarely buy drinks for men no matter how good looking I make myself."

"Were you inspired by Tawny Kitaen?"

"I like that Whitesnake video."

I nodded. Of course.

"What's it like? Being a woman, I mean?"

He moved his whole upper body in a way that said to me "I don't know" or "It's hard to explain." He gave it a whirl, though.

"I spend a lot of my time as a woman. I've been doing this for a long time."

"Do you mean "faerie" long time or. . ."

"Anybody long time."

"Hang on," I said. "Do changelings have a specific gender?"

"Sure, I was born a guy." He swirled his drink and sipped at it. "Some changelings are tied more closely to their gender than others, so much so that they can't really do the other very convincingly. I've heard stories of some who can't even manage to change sexes at all. If that's true, I bet it's just psychological."

"Are there faerie therapists?"

"We don't use the word 'therapist.' But healers have all kinds of titles."

He sipped again and looked into his drink while he thought. I wasn't sure a hundred percent what he was thinking about, but it turned out that he was going to tell me more about being a woman.

He said, "Anyway, as a woman, I feel simultaneously weaker and more powerful than a man." He thought. "Let me amend that. An attractive woman has power because the promise of sex makes men stupid."

"So, you. . ."

211

His smile was mischievous, even a bit lecherous. Really strange on that Norman Rockwell face. "Wouldn't you be curious about what sex is like for the other half?"

"I never really have. I like women. I've always been totally satisfied by them."

A thought occurred to me, and I spoke without thinking. I'm sure that I made a yucky face when I said it too. "Dylan and Cody?"

Rick stared at me. Just flat nothing in his eyes. Finally, he said, "Seriously? That has nothing to do with sexual preference. That's a taste and self-respect thing. I picked those guys mostly to help you out. But also, they were young and unaccompanied. More likely to buy drinks."

"Couldn't you just glamour some money and pay for yourself?"

"Yeah, I could, but I'm a changeling. It's a kick to convince people that we are someone else. We're like actors and then some. Plus, glamour money disappears. I don't want to screw up somebody's job."

That gave me pause. A deceptive faerie who was concerned about a human's livelihood. Maybe I should be careful about my preconceived notions.

"So, Dylan and Cody didn't expect a return on their investment?" I asked.

"Heh, there's not a human out there whom I can't outdrink. They were barely conscious when I left them. That bar will keep serving as long as you're able to get your money out. But that brings me to the other side of the female-power coin. A lot of men feel superior to women and have an entitled or dismissive attitude toward them."

"And they think they can have what they want."

"Yep."

"But you're probably stronger than any human man."

"Meaner too," he said. "Anyway, I have a wider perspective than most, but because of my power, I'm never really oppressed. I don't entirely know what it's like."

"So, if a guy gets handsy, you can just break it off."

He held up his glass in a salute. "Sometimes broken but none broken off to date." We both drank again.

212

I said, "What I really came to tell you is that I'll have Morrey's paperwork together by tomorrow, so your gig is nearly up."

Rick scooted forward and swung his legs off the bed. The look he gave me wasn't necessarily intense, but it was probing. He reminded me of Missy.

He said, "These kids might not act like it, but they think a lot of you and the headmaster and the guy who looks like a bulldozer. What's his name? Novak. They know that you care."

"It's good to hear."

"So anyway, I'm going to butt in a little. Even though it's not my job, not even my business at all, I'm going to make a suggestion.

"Okay."

"Talk to Galen about whatever happened to the headmaster."

"How do you know about what happened to the headmaster?"

He gave me an exasperated look that managed to also look good-natured. "Everyone knows that something serious happened, and I happen to have greater insights into possible causes."

"It wasn't faerie magic that hurt Dr. Corman. It was mortal magic that happened to be cast by a faerie. Would he know anything about human spells?"

Rick tilted his head, and his smile was amused. "You don't know?"

"Apparently not," I said.

"Galen has no faerie magic. The magic he uses comes from his human father. All he knows is mortal magic. What he got from Lady Bronwyn was a long life and a strong constitution."

I just sat there like a lump. Galen was my best friend in the supernatural world, but it seemed that I had a lot to learn about him still. I felt excluded like with Corman and Novak. Like a second-tier friend.

Rick seemed to intuit my thoughts and said, "Galen's not very talkative about his father or his human heritage. I've known him ten times longer than you have, so don't take it personally."

I'd known him since the end of the Second World War. Ten times longer?

"I knew he was half-human," I said, and I hated to hear a slightly defensive tone in my voice.

"Maybe he can give you some insights into how to reverse the effects of the spell. Another perspective couldn't hurt anyway. I think that these kids need the headmaster. They sure think they do."

Sometimes someone says something that opens up my thoughts. Reveals other avenues. It was like that now. I'd been viewing what had happened to Corman in terms of a Talamaur feeding, but that perspective was too narrow. Maybe he wasn't doomed to fade away. I felt a tiny bud of hope bloom in my chest. It wasn't until then that I realized how fatalistic my outlook had been.

"Thanks, Rick. I'm going to call Galen now." I emptied my cup and put it on the desk when I stood up. "Thanks for the drink."

He said, "Don't breathe on anyone. You have whiskey breath."

I said goodbye to Terry from across the kitchen where he was still reading, and I headed back to my apartment. I figured that I could talk more freely to Galen there, and I could brush my teeth and mouthwash before heading back to Oak House.

I hung my coat over one of my kitchen chairs and sat down in another. I dialed the number and tried to think of how I would word my questions. He answered before the second ring, so I still didn't have them quite formed yet.

"Hey Caomhnóir, how are things going with Rick?"

"His name is really Rick?"

"It's a diminutive."

"Yeah, he's been great. He actually suggested that I call you to ask about the spell that Melk, the goblin, used on the kids here."

"What can you tell me?"

I described what Moe had seen about the movement of energies when Melk cast the spell. The passing of energy out of the students and Corman and into Howie. I related what Melk had said by way of explanation when I'd had him in the circle. I ended by telling him about the spell being written down and locked in the boobytrapped magic box. When I finished, I noted that I'd been able to get through the entire narrative in less than five minutes.

214

He didn't respond for a long time. It's not as though I expected an easy answer, but maybe I hoped for one.

Finally, he said, "If I could see that spell, I might be able to make something out of it. I don't want to get your hopes up too much. I'm not a hardcore mage or anything. I'm more of a longtime dabbler."

"How long is longtime?"

"Oh, the sixth century sometime."

It was my turn not to say anything. I knew that Galen was old, but he must be close to my father's age. I guess that was just life in the supernatural world. Assumptions were hard.

"Can you bring me the box?" he asked.

"I hate to be away for that long. How long would it take me to drive to. . . where is it. . . Keene?"

"It's about eight hours."

"You just know the travel time off the top of your head?"

"I looked it up after I talked to you."

"Sixteen hours roundtrip. I really don't want to lose that much time."

I heard the smile in his voice when he spoke next. "I stumbled onto a place totally by accident in Utica, New York."

"Utica? Really?"

"Yeah, I needed a rest on a long drive. The place is called Delmonico's. Happy hour specials are great, and the female staff wear short skirts. There's a Holiday Inn and a Hampton Inn close by. I'll get a room. We'll catch up a little at the restaurant. Check out the box in the hotel. I'll stay, and you can make your return trip."

"I'd like to make this as fast as possible," I said. Really, the thought of catching up with my old friend sounded great, so I wasn't hard to persuade.

"That's the cost of my insights. Will an extra hour or two make a difference?"

"I have no idea. I'm out of my depth in this. What time do you want to meet up?"

"I can be there by five," he said.

I asked, "How long will my drive be?"

"It's almost halfway. I'd say four hours."

"Okay, I'll meet you at Delmonico's in Utica at five. I haven't had the Nova on a road trip in a while. It might be fun despite the errand I'm on."

"You still have that car? It must be fifty years old."

"Fifty-two."

"Will it make the trip?"

"She'll get me there alright."

We hung up. The reason for the trip was dire, and that was not lost on me, but I was excited to see Galen after so many years. I had to leave in an hour, so I had a lot to do in the meantime.

# Chapter 18

I talked with Novak just before he went to lunch in the dining hall and let him know that I had to run an important errand but would be back by the following morning. He seemed less concerned with my absence than just plain exhausted. He wished me luck. Just after that, I found Allie and asked her to cover my creative writing class. She agreed but made it clear that I would owe her. . . a lot. It was never easy to anticipate her expectations on things like that.

I didn't plan on staying the night, but I packed an overnight bag. It's just a thing I did, always prepared like a boy scout. I dressed in blue jeans, brogues, and a dark-purple sweater-vest over a white button-down. I slipped into my bomber jacket and was about to head for the door when the Gibson caught my eye. I stared at it on its stand for a full two minutes. It really bothered me that I felt the need to take it with me. I wasn't going to run away. I wrenched myself away from the "always prepared" rationalization, and walked out the door without my guitar.

I was on the road by 12:30.

I liked to drive, especially the Nova. She was powerful, and she was pretty, and she wasn't typical. Mustangs, Camaros, and Chargers seemed to get all of the attention. Most people forgot that Novas ever had been muscle cars.

There were no real decisions I could make regarding Corman or Doru until I got more information, so I resolved not to fixate on those problems while I drove. I would try my best at least.

I took 19A to 408 to 390 to 90 again. It was the way that I usually drove to Rochester. I'd just stay on 90 for another two and a half hours until I reached exit 41. I listened to the engine and the wheels on the road and watched the familiar sights go by. I really didn't need to think about the route.

My memory is pretty sharp, and I unspooled over seventy years of it as Moe and I negotiated the road. I'd first met Galen in a jazz club in Chicago in 1946. We were both there to listen to a clarinetist named Sidney Bechet. The club was small and pretty full, and as we were a couple of single guys, we shared a table. We really hit it off, and after the show, we talked all night in various bars and clubs around the city. Neither of us had a clue about the other's supernatural nature.

We must have really made a strong impression on one another, though, because we instantly recognized each other when we met again. That was in a New Orleans restaurant called Tujagues in 1971. It was pretty clear from the second meeting that we weren't human. Physically, we still looked in our middle-twenties. And try as they might, normal humans can't pull that off.

Despite my trusty familiar, he saw me first. I blame the red hair. He leaned on the bar next to me and said, "There are a ton of great jazz musicians to hear in this town."

That was that. Relatively speaking, we spent a lot of time together over the next fifteen years. We didn't move in together or anything like that, but we kept tabs. Music was our most obvious connection, but it went well beyond that. We actually liked the society of humans and respected them as sapient beings. We loved their art. Books, movies, paintings, all of it.

Apparently, he hadn't been completely forthcoming, though. It was foolish to expect that, but I really had felt jealous when Rick clearly knew much more about him than I. I knew that he was half-faerie, but I hadn't known that he was fifteen-hundred years old or that he'd told his human girlfriend about his supernatural nature. I couldn't be too pissy about that, I guess. I'm the one who vanished without letting him know where I was going. That markedly curtailed sharing opportunities. But what's thirty years to a guy halfway through his second millennium?

The sky had grown dark enough to call for headlights as I neared my exit. Sputtery drizzle required occasional passes with the windshield wipers. Moe zipped ahead to note the best lane changes for turns and such. It was all pretty direct, and I was pulling into the parking lot of Delmonico's Italian Steakhouse in just a few minutes.

The sign for the Holiday Inn was visible just on the other side of the parking lot. I could imagine the setup being pretty appealing for people needing a good stopping point for the night. Cocktails and a steak within easy walking distance of a cozy room.

I parked as close as I could. I don't like my leather jacket to get wet if I can help it. I'd neglected to condition it recently, and it didn't smell great when it got wet these days. Moe checked the bar to find Galen while I sat wondering if the rain might taper off more.

The restaurant was dimly lit and there was a lot of polished, dark wood. What struck me most, though, were the caricatures of famous Italian-Americans which were painted on the buff-colored walls throughout the establishment. Frank Sinatra even had his own booth full of framed photos and other memorabilia.

The second strongest impression came from the waitstaff and bartenders. They were mostly women wearing short black skirts and white dress shirts. Some also wore black fedoras. Moe spotted a few men dressed similarly in slacks instead of skirts, but women outnumbered them by a wide margin. They were all quite attractive.

The bar was square, having a segment that flipped up to allow access for the staff. It was made of dark wood and surrounded on three sides by tall upholstered stools. Galen sat at one of them with two drinks in front of him. Had he ordered for me? The bartender was staring at him with rapt attention. She looked so beguiled that it was hard for me to believe that he didn't have some kind of fae magic.

The bartender was that kind of pretty which is almost cute. Maybe it was just her size. She was tiny, all of five-feet-tall. If she weren't so curvy, one might have mistaken her for a young girl. She was Asian, her skin dark and her hair black, pulled back into a high ponytail. She wore a dangerously short skirt, and her dress shirt was unbuttoned low enough that the black bra she wore beneath could be glimpsed occasionally, depending on how she moved.

Galen had always gotten attention from the fairer sex, but he wasn't overtly handsome. He had a Harrison Ford thing going on, distinctive and appealing but not regular enough to be classical. He looked like an everyman, but the chicks sure dug him. And he looked twenty-five. Fashion choices aside, he was like I'd seen him last. Ah, the life of the quasi-immortal.

He wore black work boots and black jeans and a burgundy cable-knit sweater. On the back of his stool hung a hooded gray raincoat. He was fairly big but not big enough to draw much attention.

Muscular in a way that often goes unnoticed. His brown hair was cut close and his hazel eyes seemed to change color depending on the light. As he talked to the bartender, they were practically glittering.

When Moe drew near, I could hear Galen saying, "My friend will be here soon."

The bartender asked, "Is she a new friend?"

He smiled. "*He* is an old friend. This is actually a reunion of sorts."

She smiled in return. I think she was encouraged by the knowledge of my gender. I hated to interrupt their flirting, but time was short.

I left the warm dryness of the Nova and jogged through the drizzle to the entrance. It wasn't five o'clock yet, so there weren't many patrons. A pretty blond at the hostess station asked me if I wanted a table.

I pointed at Galen at the bar and said, "I'm meeting that guy."

She made a dramatic sweeping gesture to indicate clear passage to the bar.

When Galen saw me, his eyes went wide. The stare was so overt that the bartender quickly looked over her shoulder to see the cause. The surprised expression turned into a broad smile. He hopped from his stool and came over to hug me.

"My God, you got old."

"I told you," I said.

"Yeah, I know. Imagine if you hadn't. I might not have recognized you."

Galen sat back down on his stool, and I took the one to his right. He said to the bartender, "This is my new friend, Daksha. She makes a hell of a Sidecar."

I knew that Galen was sharp, but I didn't want to leave him hanging if he'd forgotten my current name. I said, "My name is Sean."

She nodded her head. "It's nice to meet you, Sean. Would you like a drink?"

I think that she was surprised at my apparent age, but as a bartender, she was good at covering that sort of thing. How many twenty-five-year-olds hang out with fifty-five-year-olds?

"That's not mine?" I pointed at Galen's second drink.

"Happy hour drinks are two for one," she said.

"At the same time?"

She nodded.

"This place is great," I said. "I'll have two rye Manhattans, please."

Her workstation was at the opposite corner of the bar. We both watched her go to it. Her heels were horribly high. I marveled that she could spend a whole shift wearing them. They looked like torture devices, but they did wonderful things to her legs. And when she reached for glasses in the overhead rack, her already-high skirt rose a little higher. She put the glasses on the bar and tugged her skirt back into place.

Galen and I looked at each other and then back at Daksha.

I said, "That must get old. Every time she reaches up, she's got to tug the skirt back down."

He said, "Looking never seems to get old, though."

"Says the fifteen-hundred-year-old man."

"I guess you made friends with Rick."

"Yep."

He said, "I'm closer to sixteen hundred."

The lovely bartender returned with my drinks, walking smoothly on the high heels as if she were performing an acrobatic dance. A stilt dance or something. I asked her, "Daksha? Is that Indian?"

Her head bobbed as she carefully placed both drinks in front of me. "But my mom is Filipino."

"And you ended up in Utica?"

Galen said, "Daksha is a student."

"Polytech," she said.

I sampled the first of the Manhattans which was excellent, and I told her so.

"Thank you. Now, if you'll excuse me, I still have some prep work to do before the rush. I was distracted from my duties at the beginning of my shift." She smiled at Galen, showing how much she'd enjoyed the distraction, then returned to her work station.

"She reminds me of someone," I said. She didn't look like Allie, but she reminded me of her anyway.

"That can't be a bad thing."

"I don't know," I said. "How was it with Kelly all those years?"

His face dropped a little, and I felt bad about it, but I really wanted to know. His response could strongly affect my choices in the near future.

He drank the remainder of his first sidecar and pushed the glass away. Then, he slid the new glass into the vacant spot. I drank more of my first Manhattan and waited.

He said, "It was good, really good, until it wasn't." He swirled the drink and looked into it. "I didn't want to get old with her. People say that kind of thing, but I don't get it. I have never gotten tired of life, and old age looks like total shit to me. I would have faked it with her, though." He gestured at my middle-aged face when he said the last part.

"What about your honesty? The full-disclosure thing."

He shrugged his shoulders. Then, he said, "She wasn't bothered by my. . . otherness. I think that we could have stayed together for the rest of her life if she hadn't had to look at my eternally-young self everyday. It really bothered her that she just had her three score years and ten, and I would just keep going on in my prime, partying forever."

I sighed.

Galen said, "So tell me about the woman you are obviously thinking about."

I started talking about Allie tentatively, but fifteen minutes later, it was obvious that I had it bad for the girl. I ended by saying, "I never really considered telling her anything about the supernatural world. Venator beheadings and all that."

"It's like prohibition," Galen said.

I just looked at him.

"Making, transporting, buying, and selling alcohol was illegal, right? Everyone knew it, and they knew they could be punished for it. But alcohol consumption actually increased. Unless law enforcers had some ulterior motive or some lawbreaker was too overt to be ignored, the powers that be usually looked the other way."

222

"So supernaturals tell humans about themselves all willy-nilly like people went to speakeasies in the '20s?"

"Not willy-nilly," he said. "The Venator Council chops heads when supernaturals get willy-nilly, but there's a big difference between willy-nilly and not at all."

"And no one told me?" I felt a bit petulant.

"You're a kid."

"I'm a hundred twenty-seven."

He chuckled just a little and said, "I'm over ten times older than you. You're ten times older than a twelve-year-old." He patted my shoulder.

"So, there are humans walking around who know that vampires, werewolves, and faeries are real?"

He said, "Yeah, humans who can keep a secret. It's not information to be shared lightly." He sipped his drink and added, "And supernaturals tend to police their own misjudgments before things come to the attention of the Venator council."

"That's just lovely," I said, but I understood the practicality of it. If you shared your secret with a blabbermouth, it would be best to shut him or her up asap.

I drank the remainder of my first drink. Galen and I had important things to discuss, but I decided to give us the rest of our drinks and dinner to just be friends. It had been thirty years after all.

We settled our tab with Daksha and moved to a booth. Patrons were arriving at a pretty good clip by then, but there were still plenty of seating choices. We remained bar adjacent, but we couldn't see much of Daksha. She was so short that only her head and shoulders were visible as she moved quickly and efficiently to deal with more numerous orders.

Galen suggested the sixteen-ounce sirloin in a wine-mushroom sauce with garlic mashed potatoes. I normally like my steaks with nothing but salt and pepper, but I followed his lead. We drank a table red wine which turned out to be pretty nice and chatted about the last thirty years. The steak and the conversation were wonderful. Among other things, we found that neither of us had really gotten into grunge, and both of us crushed on Kate Beckinsale pretty hard.

Gears shifted to business as we waited for the bill. Galen said, "So, where's the box?"

"In the trunk of my car."

"Why don't you go get it, and I'll pay the check and meet you outside."

A thought struck me as I was shrugging into my jacket, and I said, "You're going to put moves on Daksha."

He didn't answer but took his smart phone out of his pocket. He poked at the screen a few times and held it out so I could see. There in his contacts list was her number.

"Fast work," I said.

"I was here for forty-five minutes before you showed up."

"You don't need to brag," I said and headed out to the parking lot.

The rain had stopped, but the night was still cool and damp. The traffic noise on the wet roads was somehow pleasant. I opened the trunk and took the box from where it was nestled in my travel blanket. Yeah, I'm always prepared: toolbox, road flares, flashlight, the works. I also slung my overnight bag over my shoulder. Brushing my teeth before the return trip seemed like a good idea.

I closed the trunk and was halfway to the restaurant entrance when Galen emerged. He'd almost reached me when Moe sensed a slight hum of energy from the box. I stopped instantly and held up a hand for Galen to do the same. He did. I felt like I'd just heard the click of a landmine trigger under my foot.

"What's the matter?" he asked.

"Some kind of power has activated."

"Hold up the box so I can see it."

I did as he asked. Galen closed his eyes and breathed deeply in and out, in and out, in and out.

After half a minute, he opened his eyes and said, "It's okay."

"How could you see it with your eyes closed?"

"See, sense, perceive, whatever."

"It's okay?"

"Yeah, yeah. I've seen others like this before, maybe even this one exactly."

The memory of the orange light flickered behind my eyes. "You're sure?"

"Yeah."

He came nearer and the hum increased. Nothing intense, but the box was clearly responding to Galen's closeness. He put a hand between my shoulders and held the other out toward the hotel. "Come, Caomhnóir. I brought beer that I want you to taste, and we'll try to unravel your mystery."

We walked across the parking lot to the Holiday Inn.

# Chapter 19

The hotel room was nice, not opulent or anything, but it was clean and spacious and had all the amenities I would want. After Galen flipped on the lights, I placed the goblin box on the desk. He went directly to the little refrigerator and withdrew a couple of bottles. He popped the tops with an opener on his keychain and handed one to me. We clinked bottles and almost simultaneously said, "Sláinte."

The beer was a little malty and a little hoppy, really well-balanced. Biscuity sweetness met an earthy, grassy bitterness. Nothing dramatic, just good. I would have liked to see it in a glass, but beer tasting was not the priority of the moment.

I noted the label: Ishmael American Copper Ale by Rising Tide Brewery in Portland, Maine. I'd never heard of Rising Tide and assumed that it was small and didn't ship far. If my life didn't unravel in the not-too-distant future, I might need to take a weekend trip to Maine.

I held up the bottle and said, "Why allude to such a slog of a book? This is great."

He shrugged. "It was on tap at my local and became my favorite. Thought I'd share."

"Thank you," I said and took another pull.

"So, you know what that is?" I pointed at the goblin box with my bottle.

"Pretty sure."

"You sounded sure in the parking lot."

He grinned at me. "You looked like you were going to shit a brick. I thought you could use some comforting."

"I did not," I said, but I was smiling back because it was probably true.

He put his bottle on the corner of the desk and picked up the box. He examined it on all sides, touching it in certain places which seemed random to me. After a minute or two of that, he placed the box flat on the desk in front of him, squaring off the corners. He sat on the chair, his back straight, shoulders level, and held his right hand over the surface of its lid. In a voice nearly inaudible to my mundane sense of hearing, he spoke rhythmically, but I couldn't detect the repetition of a chant. Moe could hear every syllable and inflection, but it didn't matter much to me because I didn't know the language. It could be some weird beat poetry for all I knew.

Stopping abruptly, he turned the chair to face me and said, "Do you have the key?"

I drew it from my pants' pocket and held it out to him.

He said, "I'm not going to do it."

"What? Why?"

He said, "Moe saw the pattern that Melk traced on the lid, right?"

"Yeah."

"And you have total recall of what Moe sees?"

"Not total, but it's good. Anyway, it was just an x."

Galen considered for a moment and said. "Precision is important with things like this. You unlock it, and I'll open it."

Only a tiny bit of the orange light from that box had messed me up in a way I'd never experienced before. I'm a kind of guy who likes to have a handle on things. Know what to expect. The orange light wasn't in that category. I'd lucked out before. Maybe it was more Moe than luck, but it sure felt like it had been a close call.

I only hesitated a little before I moved closer. I said, "I did not look like I was going to shit a brick."

Galen grinned and rolled the chair to the side to give me room.

I traced the X pattern on the lid. Moe felt a little hum of power like a small motor activating. I inserted the key and turned it until I felt the mechanism click. I wasn't trembling at all. Totally brave. I left the key where it was and stepped back.

Galen rolled the chair forward and reached toward the lid.

My voice was a little thin when I said, "Don't you have to disable the boobytrap?"

"I think it was a one-shot deal."

"You think?"

"Yeah, that kind of thing has to be recharged."

"Couldn't it have more than one charge?"

He chewed on his lower lip for a few seconds and said, "Maybe. Probably not." He began to reach for the box again.

Without meaning to, I said, "Hey!" and flinched away a little.

He turned the swivel chair to face me and said, "What?"

I said, "You're just going to open it?"

"I'll point it away."

"That's it? You'll point it away?"

"Yeah, I'll point it away. You took an oblique blast. It was mostly pointed away, and you survived. If it's all the way pointed away, we should be okay."

"Should be?"

"I could lie and tell you that I'm positive."

"I think you're missing the point of a lie," I said.

"Okay, then. When it went off before, you said that there was no physical damage, no visible sign of it on your body or the room?"

"Right."

He turned to the box and tipped it onto its back, so when the lid opened, the interior would be facing the wall and not us. He muttered, "I think I know what it is," and nudged the lid. It swung open, falling to the desktop with a clunk.

*He thinks he knows?* My flinch and eye-squint were involuntary and would have been embarrassing if anyone had seen them. I was behind Galen, though, and thought the movement escaped his notice.

He sat and I stood in silence looking at the bottom of the box. Eventually, he leaned forward and quickly passed his hand in front of the opening. Nothing happened. He did it again but made a couple of quick passes. Then, he held his hand in front of the opening for three seconds.

"Oh, for the love of Pete," I said and set the box upright. The heavy wood made a decisive clunk again. The lid remained open.

He looked at me narrowly and said, "That was a dangerous thing to do."

"You said it only had one charge."

"Apparently, that's all it did have. Lucky for you."

"Okay. Why lucky for me?"

228

He didn't answer. He smiled again, and there was something mischievous in it. "What did Melk do then?"

I repeated, "Why lucky for me?"

"Between the two of us, who knows more about this?" He waved at the upright box.

Assuming that the question was rhetorical, I didn't answer.

He repeated, "What did Melk do then?"

"He reached in up to his elbow and pulled out things too big to fit in there."

Galen rolled the chair out of the way again and gestured to the box. The smile never left his face. I didn't think he'd let me get hurt, but I couldn't help but to wonder if I were about to be the victim of a kind of supernatural whoopee cushion or joy buzzer.

I prepared myself for a mystical sensation. A charge. A hum. A zap. Something. Gingerly, I stretched out my hand toward the opening. My teeth were gritted. My weight was on the balls of my feet, my legs bent slightly. I was poised like a cat. My hand entered the box and continued down until my palm contacted the cool, polished wood of its floor. It felt like wood. Moe could detect nothing interesting either.

I removed my hand and showed it to Galen like it was some sort of foreign object.

He waved me back and asked, "What did the spell paper look like?"

I stepped back and described it in detail.

He repositioned his chair in front of the box and closed his eyes for several seconds. Without opening them, he leaned forward and reached toward the opening of the box. When his fingers neared, the interior of the box shimmered, the light behaving something like heatwaves but also like slow-moving mist. His hand, wrist, and forearm passed unhindered into whatever little pocket-dimension it held. After only a moment, he withdrew his hand with the paper held between his thumb and forefinger.

He opened his eyes, looked at me, wagged the paper and said, "*Et voilà.*"

"*Pourquoi ça n'a pas marché pour moi?*" I asked.

"Faerie box only works for faeries." He wagged the paper again. "May I?"

"Damn racist box," I muttered. "Of course, I'd like you to read it. Anything you can tell me will be appreciated."

"Don't speak too fast." He pushed the box to the edge of the desk and carefully opened the paper on the flat surface. After a short inspection, he said, "Will you open another beer for me?"

It was only then that I noted that we'd emptied the first ones. It was like magic. I opened another bottle for each of us and gave one to him. He drank and hunched over the paper. I assumed then that he knew the language. His focus was tight, and he said nothing for nearly twenty minutes, only occasionally making sounds of frustration or revelation.

I wandered the room a little, drinking the tasty ale as I did. I stared out the window across the parking lot for a while. The rain had stopped, but the blacktop was wet and reflected streetlights and the red Delmonico's light less than two hundred yards away.

I toed off my shoes and kicked them in a corner. Then, I put my empty bottle on a nightstand and lay down on one of the two beds in the room. It would have been nice to doze, but the longer Galen studied the spell and didn't say anything, the more my anxiety grew. While I had been drinking, eating, and looking at pretty girls, I could keep the object of my visit to the back of my mind. Now, though, we were into it, and Corman's plight was in the forefront. When I could wrench my mind away, it just went to Doru and his Venator measure. And the only thing I could do was lay there and worry.

In order to give me something else to focus upon, I was about to send Moe back to Delmonico's. Watching people enjoy food, drink, and each other's company would make a decent distraction. Moe could share a pretty clear impression of the smells too, and I did like the smell of seared beef.

Before I sent my trusty familiar away to find amusement, I heard the squawk of the desk chair across the room. Galen was leaning back rubbing the heels of his hands in his eyes. The mechanism in the reclining backrest made a quacking, duck-call kind of sound.

He said, "Damn, this thing's going to make me go cross-eyed? Did you drink all the beer?"

"The second four-pack is untouched." I got up and retrieved two more beers from the fridge. He leaned forward with another duck call and took one from me. I sat on the corner of the bed closest to him.

He drank and didn't speak right away. He seemed to be ordering his thoughts, probably trying to dumb down his explanation of magic so that I could understand it. He took a deep breath and blew it out slowly. "Okay, first of all, that is intimidating as hell." He jabbed his thumb over his shoulder to point at the spell. "It's three spells twined together to create a very specific result. There are countless simpler ways to torture and cause mayhem. This seems needlessly complicated."

I said, "Melk claimed that he was just looking for kicks. Maybe he was bored with easier methods."

"Great. If he felt he needed to challenge himself, it must be that others haven't been able to challenge him for a while. This is just the kind of guy who would love to distract himself in a contest with a worthy opponent. You got the drop on him, and he's not going to forget it."

Those were not encouraging words, but I said, "I made him swear to stay away from the Mannaz School campus and not to harm anyone there."

Galen gave me a skeptical look and said, "I know faeries. It's not that simple. What did you make him swear to exactly?"

Casting my mind back a few days to pick out a specific memory was a piece of cake. I really should have spent more time dissecting Melk's vow before this but better late than never. Galen's perspective as a really old faerie would be extremely valuable.

"Okay," I said. "His exact words were 'I swear by my True Name that I will not harm any of your students or coworkers at this school and that I will remove anything that might cause harm to them independently of me.'"

Once I said it aloud, I saw that I'd made no provision for myself. I gave myself points for being selfless which eased my feeling of dumbassedness. Never mind that it was accidental. I said, "I guess I'm still wide open for retribution."

"Yeah, there's that. And your school is now something of a wildlife preserve."

"What?"

He smiled indulgently at me and made air quotes. "'I will not harm any of your students or coworkers at this school.'"

"Shit." I saw it plainly.

He nodded. "You meant 'at this school' to describe the people, as in the people who reside at the school. You didn't want him to harm a specific group of people."

"That's what I meant. But 'at this school' could also describe the conditions for not harming the people. As in, he can't harm these people while they're at the school."

Galen nodded. "That would be a legitimate interpretation, so if any students or teachers leave the school, he can consider them fair game."

I should have taken more time to think that through. That's just the kind of thing a faerie would do. I saw a glimmer of hope, not long-term but a respite. I said, "I don't think Melk will do anything more to antagonize me. At least not yet."

"Why?"

"I had a visit this morning. From Doru."

"That asshole." Galen made a disgusted face.

I sighed. "Yeah, he described Melk as his 'associate.'"

"Melk gave away your hideout."

"Yep."

"He could tell anyone he wants about your location and not break his promise."

"I know."

Galen made a "come on" gesture and said, "Anyway, why do you think Melk will leave you and your friends alone?"

I told Galen about the Venator measure and about Doru's request to be the proxy for my noble vote. I didn't leave anything out, and even though there was no need, I emphasized my skepticism of Doru's motivations.

Galen looked thoughtful. Then, he got up and opened the last two beers. It was only then that I realized that I was holding an empty bottle. Autopilot drinking. Talking is thirsty work. He handed one to me and took a pull from his own. He said, "That's very interesting. And by interesting, I mean ominous."

I waited for him to elaborate, and after taking a couple of turns around the room, he did.

"I had a visit the day before yesterday from a red cap who lives in Boston."

My eyebrows went up. I was hearing about an awful lot of faeries lately. I knew that some were still around, but it was common knowledge that modern technology had caused a mass exodus back to their homeland. Those who didn't look human would be revealed by cameras. Analog or digital would see through any glamour. Maybe not clearly, but enough to put up red flags.

Galen continued. "The red cap's real name is Soulis, but in the human world, he goes by William Rufus. From what I've heard, he's a bit of an old-school gangster. He has legitimate businesses, but also has interest in some criminal enterprises. Anyway, he came to me in person to talk about the same Venator measure."

Without thinking, I said, "But you can't vote."

His smile was wry. "True. We half-breed bastards aren't allowed."

"Sorry."

He waved a hand. "Lady Bronwyn does dote on her little rape-baby, though."

The shock on my face, must have looked funny because Galen laughed.

"Relax, Caomhnóir. That's the way she talks, and I do too because something about the dismissive attitude takes power away from it. Mom has never withheld affection, but she also likes to remind me of my origins. It is what it is."

"Okay," I said. I felt awkward as hell and didn't know what else to say.

"All of that happened not long after the Roman Empire fell. It's just a bedtime story to me."

233

"Bedtime story, huh?"

"Sure, a traditional faerie tale—father rapes mother, mother kills father and raises bastard son in Tir-Na-Nog."

"I think I saw the Disney adaption."

"Anyway, the faerie community knows that Lady Bronwyn denies me little, so Soulis clearly believes that I might bend her ear toward his cause. She is an Elder and could exert a good deal of influence."

"What did he offer you?" I asked.

"Everything. . . but he emphasized the benefits of passing the Venator measure. As an Elder, he'd composed it and proposed it. It's his baby."

"Is there something we're not seeing? If I'd heard about the measure from anyone one but Doru, I probably would have thought of it in a much more positive light. On the face of it, it doesn't seem like a bad idea. Now that I know a red cap gangster is the originator, it's even more dubious. Do bad guys think that we'll forget that they're bad guys?"

Galen chuffed a laugh. "People often do. Humans more than we, but we're not immune. I was going to look into this measure anyway, but learning that Doru has a stake in it as well. . . that means that I'm going to make this a priority."

"I feel like I should do something to help."

Galen said, "Right now, it's a matter of getting information, and it seems that you no longer have any contacts in the supernatural community."

"Except you."

"Except me. For now, you should take care of your friends and your school. We'll keep in touch. Presently, we'll attend to immediate concerns." He put his beer bottle down on the desk and picked up his overnight bag from the floor and tossed it onto the bed.

"Corman," I said.

He nodded. "Corman." He sat on the bed next to his bag. "I honestly don't know if I can help there. I have one idea that you can try, but it'll be a Hail Mary.

"Okay."

234

"Melk's spell manipulates lifeforce and human vessels, but it's really not like a Talamaur feeding. A familiar makes a single breach, a small point-of-entry that can heal with relative ease. The goblin spell weakens the overall structure of the vessel, making the metaphysical membrane porous. The children seem to be more resilient, their membrane more flexible, more elastic."

He paused, thinking. I waited.

"I think that Talamaur might have something in common with blood-drinking vampires. Only more incorporeal. Blood drinking vampires' saliva contains a sort of time-release coagulant. Nature's way of saying 'Waste not, want not.' Why let resources bleed out when they can be saved for later? Talamaur may do the same kind of thing."

"May?"

"It's not as though Talamaur have submitted to any tests. You guys are the most mysterious people I've ever heard of. By a lot. Like I said, this is a shot in the dark. I'm drawing a parallel. Maybe there isn't one. But in the absence of any other option, you might as well try it."

"What am I trying exactly?" I thought I knew, and it made me feel a little ill.

"You can do nothing and hope Dr. Corman recovers on his own. Or you can you can feed on him, just a sip, and hope that Talamaurs produce a metaphysical coagulant that jumpstarts the healing process."

"The healing process that you're not sure exists."

"Shot in the dark," he said. "I'm sorry that I don't have more options."

"You did all you could." I hadn't realized how much I'd gotten my hopes up until they were dashed. Okay, not totally dashed. I had a Hail Mary.

"Regarding Corman, yes, there's not much I can do, but I'd like to offer more assistance of a martial nature. I planned on this when I only knew about Melk. Now that Doru and Soulis are in the mix, I feel even more strongly about giving you some aid."

He unzipped the overnight bag he'd dropped on the bed and brought out a black leather drawstring bag. It was the kind of bag I used to hold D&D dice, but this one was big enough to hold three good-sized grapefruit. He held it up and turned it from side to side like he was a stage magician. Then, he opened the mouth of the bag and showed me the inside. It looked empty.

He looked at me with his eyebrows raised, apparently waiting for a response.

I said, "An empty bag."

"Listen closely," he said and whispered into the mouth of the bag, "Eladoon."

"Does it make magic shortbread cookies?"

"That's Lorna Doone, wiseass." He reached into the bag and withdrew a damn sword. Granted it wasn't very big. The sheathed blade and hilt together were two feet long. He reached in again and withdrew a holstered blued revolver. Twice more he reached in to bring out boxes of ammunition. He drew the bag closed and carefully put it aside.

It was a cool trick, but I'd just seen it with the goblin box. I made a circular gesture with my hand to take in the items on the bed and said, "What's all this?"

"I'm going out on a limb here," he said. "I'm guessing that you no longer carry arms."

"Not much call for them at boarding school."

"You've got nothing?"

I shrugged. "I have caches hidden all over the country."

"Anything close?"

"New York is the closest."

"You'll take these then," he said and lifted the sword. "And I guarantee that you have nothing like this." He drew it from its plain black leather scabbard.

The blade was two-edged and eighteen inches long. Though the steel was matte gray, it seemed to shimmer somehow, nonetheless. Along the center of the blade on both sides, runes ran from the hilt to about the midpoint of the length of it. They looked similar to the Elder Futhark but were not the same. The runes were shiny and black like obsidian. The cross-guard was straight, and the grip was wrapped in supple black leather. The pommel was wrought in the shape of an acorn.

The weapon looked like the ideal combination of artistry and practical function. And though it looked new, there was a sense of age and power about it.

Moe flicked through the power spectrum and quickly found the right pitch. The sword pulsed slowly, like a dynamo which has yet to cycle up. It made me think a little of the Nova when she's warm and loose from driving, and the engine is idling comfortably at a stoplight. That feeling of power in repose.

Galen said, "This is Fetann."

At the mention of the name, the rhythm of the pulsing power changed almost as if it recognized the word. Could it be cognizant?

"This was forged specifically for me when I had grown enough to use it. It's nearly as old as I am. It is virtually unbreakable and is always sharp. The most important thing about Fetann, though, is that it has the power to cleave energy and spirit."

Moe backed away from the weapon, and Galen laughed at me. I really needed to put more effort into minding my facial expressions. Poker-face practice. I'd never thought of Moe being hurt before. I really really didn't like the idea, and it must have shown.

He snapped the sword back into the scabbard and said, "Yes, this could potentially injure or destroy a familiar. I've never tried, but it has dispatched a few ghosts. It can also unravel the power which is manipulated to cast spells. When you described your experiences with Melk, I thought of how useful Fetann would have been to you."

He lowered the sword to the bed again but kept a hand on it. "It is also potent against corporeal supernatural beings. Any injury dealt with it, which does not kill outright, will heal slowly, at least as slow as a human would heal. Like iron to faeries or silver to were-creatures and vampires."

What I felt at his offer was difficult to classify. Gratified clearly. Awed. As he described Fetann, it was one of the most powerful melee combat weapons I'd ever heard of. I was also horrified at the responsibility of possessing something like that. Also, I was just really touched in a sappy Hallmark kind of way. That Galen held me in such high regard was staggering.

When I got my face under control, I said, "Nuh uh."

"What do you mean? 'Nuh uh?'"

"I'm not taking that."

"Why not?"

"What if I lose it? What if someone takes it away from me? What if I get dead? That thing is too potent to let Melk or Doru or someone get ahold of it."

He stroked the sword hit like it was a pet or a child. "Fetann and I will always find each other. Eventually."

"In the meantime?" I asked.

"Fetann will only serve me or, in theory, one whom I choose to empower."

"Say again."

He took a moment to respond, and he did so with a question. "Can anyone make Moe do anything either you or he doesn't want to do?"

"No."

"Fetann will do my bidding. He's mine. If I ask Fetann to do your bidding, he will. My wishes would, of course, always trump yours, and I can always revoke your permission. This is strictly a loan."

"What will you use to defend yourself?"

"Fetann is my greatest weapon, but I have others at my disposal. You should really begin your own collection."

"Yeah, sure. I'll go straight to the magic shop."

"To use Fetann, I will need something from you, though."

"Like what?"

Galen looked a little unsure when he said, "Your True Name would be best."

"Uhm. . ." I didn't know how to respond. True Names. Wow. I mean, he was trusting me with his artifact-level sword and all, but—

Before I could tell him "absolutely not," he jumped into the gap. "But some of your blood will probably work."

"Probably?"

"I've never lent Fetann to anyone before."

I didn't speak right away because of the instant lump in my throat. I couldn't seem to speak around it. After I'd managed myself and thought I could trust my voice, I said, "After fifteen hundred years, you're going to loan out your custom-made god sword for the very first time. . . to me? Why?"

The intensity of his look made Missy's look whimsical. He said, "That should indicate the regard I have for you."

I looked down quickly and blinked really fast. I'm surprised that there wasn't a hurricane wind generated by my eyelashes. After I got myself under control. . . again, I thought with great satisfaction, *Take that Rick! I got the super sword and you didn't!* Petty, I know.

Galen drew Fetann again. With care, he drew the tip of the sword across the meat of my forearm. The cut was short and shallow, and I barely felt it. He held the sword to catch drops of blood as they fell from my elbow. When he'd gotten enough, he said, "Go wrap that. There are bandages in the bathroom."

Moe stayed while I went to the bathroom to deal with my scratch. I thought that there might be some kind of spell, a ritual or something. But it was much more like a conversation between a parent and a child who was being left with a babysitter. As Galen smeared my blood with his fingertips along the length of the sword's blade, he talked to it. The blood actually soaked into the steel which was just a bit disconcerting.

"This is my friend, Caomhnóir. You will be going with him, and I want you to aid him just as you would me. He is worthy to wield you, and he has need of your power."

That went on for a little while. Sometimes people talk to things, inanimate objects. I talked to the Nova and my Gibson. I think a lot of people do. It doesn't make us crazy, right? The thing is, the sword talked back. Moe was already dialed in to the right wavelength to pick up its power signature. It was easy to pick up the fluctuations in it when they began. The rhythms made me think of the adults' voices in the old Peanuts cartoons.

The communication went beyond that, though. There was also an understanding of emotion and intent, much like when Moe helps me to communicate with ghosts. Fetann was experiencing some anxiety. I kid you not. It really was like a little kid about to go on his first sleepover. Galen continued to speak quietly to the sword in not much more than a murmur. Finally, there was an easing of tension and then a sort of galvanizing pop.

Suddenly, I could feel the sword without Moe's perceptions. There was a wary acceptance. A trust more in Galen than in me. At that moment, I understood, without a doubt, that Fetann was alive. The significance of this was amazing. The trust. I was glad I'd stayed in the bathroom while Galen and Fetann had their conversation. I wouldn't have to struggle to hold back tears in front of anyone. . . again.

I entered the room showing the two-by-three-inch bandage on my arm like a war trophy. Galen still sat on the bed with his hand on Fetann, which was back in its scabbard. I nodded to the gun on the bed. "So, did that once belong to Wyatt Earp, and it now contains his steely determination and shoots hellfire bullets or something?"

"It's a Colt .38," he said. "The official police model. I bought it from a guy in Chicago in 1935, I think." He picked up and rattled a box of shells and said, "These are hollow points."

"Magic hollow points?"

"Sure, they transform from lead cones into blooming lead flowers." He shook the box again. "There aren't many things that can just shrug off a bullet. At the very least, a gun might buy you some time, and you can strike from a distance."

He put down the box of bullets and picked up the holstered revolver. He unsnapped the strap, took it out, and handed it to me, butt-forward. "It's loaded."

It was blued steel with wooden grips. The barrel was four inches. I dropped and spun the cylinder, noting the six, unmarked, brass casings. I snapped it closed again. The gun was well-worn but sound. The bluing was new, and there was no sign of cracking in the wood. It felt pretty good. I handed it back.

"Joking aside, is there any special significance to it?" I asked.

"Nah, it's just a good, dependable gun. Easy to use. Easy to maintain. Shoots straight."

"I know guns."

He opened the magical bag and put the gun and ammo back inside. "When's the last time you went shooting?"

"Ten years, probably."

"It's a perishable skill."

"Not for Moe," I said.

Galen placed Fetann back into the bag and drew the strings closed. When he said "Eladoon" over the opening, my new awareness of the sword abruptly vanished. I started a little.

"What the hell? I whispered.

"Oh, right." Galen held up the bag again. "This is just a portable doorway. Fetann and the Colt are in another dimension."

"Yeah, I know." I did too. The concept wasn't new to me. I just didn't have much first-hand experience with other dimensions, even little pocket ones which were basically storage rooms. I made a mental note to keep Moe far away from the bag when it was open.

He tossed me the bag which I caught. I said, "This just seems like too much."

"It's a loan."

"Don't you have a magic sword which isn't an heirloom of power and whatnot?"

"I actually do," he said. "I want you to have Fetann."

"But—" I began, but he held up a hand to stop me.

"This is a time when you should yield to my greater experience. Something is happening. You're my friend and you're involved. I would rather you had too much firepower that you don't need. This is the part when you accept graciously."

"Thank you, Galen."

He stood up and hugged me, all manly with the back slaps and everything. He said, "Now, you have some miles to drive, and I have a tiny, sexy woman to flirt with."

I was on the road again before eight o'clock, and I was pulling into the Mannaz School parking lot by midnight. Eight hours in a car wasn't quite as effortless as it once was, but I felt pretty good all told. I wondered if I'd be able to sleep.

241

# Chapter 20

I retrieved my overnight bag from the back seat and slung it over my shoulder. I stood next to the Nova for a few minutes just breathing the chilly air and looking across the square. The car's hot engine popped and pinged as it cooled, and a little breeze rustled leaves which had not yet fallen. Because I felt strangely awake, I decided to take a walk to Oak House and check out my office. Sometimes people left notes for me on my desk, and I wanted to see how much work Allie had gotten out of my creative writing students. I didn't need a light to make my way through the building because Moe didn't need a light. All was quiet except for the soft shush of the heating vents. The only illumination came from the exit signs over the doors.

I did flick on the overhead once I entered my room. After my eyes adjusted I checked my desk. On the center of my blotter was a neat stack of supervillain character sheets topped with a lavender note written in dark purple ink. Allie liked purple. It read, "Mr. Brannon, your students behaved pretty well. Effort on the assignment varied. Ms. Park." Brett's "Fart Man" and Andy's "Dr. Lemon Tofu Monkey Toes" were about as expected. Karen and Todd had produced more viable antagonists for their comic book project. Looking over student work took my mind from more weighty issues, and I felt a little sad when I'd finished with it.

Sleep is necessary for a Talamaur, but we need less of it than humans. Since I had been aging myself, I found that the gap was shrinking. I could operate without it, but I'd gotten used to sleeping like a human, and without it, I tended to get a bit grumpy and less focused. Being focused would be of great importance in the immediate future. I had no idea how things were going to play out. Best to try to get some sleep.

As I walked past the bulletin board outside of Pam's office, a paper flapped. I'd almost gotten to the exit door before the strangeness of the flapping paper settled into my brain. Pam was neat and orderly. Everything on her bulletin board would be spaced evenly and stapled at all four corners.

Moe found that the flapping paper wasn't stapled. It was held in place by two thumbtacks in the upper corners. It was an old yellow newspaper clipping, a review of the George Melvin Jazz Combo which was performing in Buffalo, New York, in June of 1952. There was a grainy picture of George sitting behind his piano and six men standing in a semi-circle behind him. On the far right was a fresh-faced, grinning guitar player holding an old Gibson ES-150. It was my main guitar until Gibson put humbuckers on the 175. My image was circled in red magic marker. The ink smelled fresh.

I carefully removed the tacks and the clipping. This was just the kind of petty shit that would give Doru his jollies. I'd hoped that he might go away and give me some space to decide what to do about my vote. I can be foolish sometimes. I'd have to stop doing that. My cousin wouldn't give me a respite. He'd pester me and annoy me at the start and get worse from there. I just hadn't expected him to start so soon.

Walking back to my apartment, I felt more and more sure that I knew from where the clipping came. Of course, it would be unwise for a semi-immortal being living among humans to have a keepsake box in his closet. And that semi-immortal being would have no reasonable excuse whatsoever. Yeah, I'd beat myself up about that later.

Doru didn't even bother to be subtle. That would be in keeping with the Talamaur way of doing things, but he seemed to have missed that trait. Papers and photographs were scattered around my bedroom. A box of thumbtacks was overturned, half on my desk and half on the floor. The cap of the red Sharpie was left off the pen and lay amongst the spilled tacks. The keepsake box was in front of the open closet door, its lid leaning against the wall.

The album which I used to hold paper mementos was laying open on my bed. The adhesive plastic cover of one of the pages was pulled back. The George Melvin clipping had come from that page. That book must have weighed the better part of four pounds. Go, ghost power. Moe sure couldn't have lifted it.

I assumed that Doru's familiar had done the work. It made more sense than Doru coming in the flesh and sneaking around. I normally didn't think of familiars doing so much heavy lifting, but I didn't imagine that Doru would have qualms about running through ghosts like triple A batteries.

It didn't take long for Moe and I to clean up the mess. Nothing was broken, and I should have felt more grateful for that. The pettiness of the thing bothered me, though. Doru's familiar hadn't needed to move anything to search my apartment. They don't have eyes to see. If there's a pile of things, a familiar just needs to come in contact and sink through it for the contents to be revealed.

Doru was just trying to shake me, make me feel threatened, off-balance. Damn it to hell. It was working. He wasn't smart. He really wasn't, but he had a good instinct for finding vulnerable spots, causing fear or frustration or anger. An idiot savant.

As I replaced the clipping in the album and the album in its box, I reflected on how atypical Doru was for a Talamaur. My people keep to the shadows, gather information, develop long-term strategies. We strike from ambush or, better yet, we strike through proxies. We have power, but it's subtle. Talamaur did not seek attention of any kind, let alone glory. Then, there was Doru, the swinging dick. He needed to prove his superiority, to dominate, to bend others to his will. He wanted others to know and admit that he was better than they.

An idea flitted through the edge of my consciousness, but I couldn't get a hold of it. Something about the nature of Doru. The harder I tried to capture it, the further it seemed to fly. I knew how well chasing the thought would work out, so I turned my attention back to the task at hand.

I put the keepsake box under my bed with the case for my Fender Super Strat on top of it. There was no space between the case and the box springs, and I doubted that any familiar would have the muscle to dislodge and maneuver the pieces around. With Moe back on campus, I doubted that another familiar could escape his notice, and he'd be on patrol in the coming days.

I actually did sleep. I got a good four hours but found myself staring at the ceiling by five o'clock. At six, I was showered, shaved, and dressed in another sweater-vest combo. It was standard winter attire, and winter was looming in the darkening skies. This outfit combined a dark-blue vest over a purple-gray button down and black slacks. After lacing up a chunky pair of black Skechers and throwing on my black wool overcoat, I headed out the door.

Before I closed it behind me, I thought about the weapons Galen had entrusted to me, and I went back inside. The magic bag was small enough to fold over and fit into the inside breast pocket of my overcoat. I certainly wouldn't be doing any quickdraw moves with it, but it would be better to have my resources close at hand. The slight bulge wasn't very noticeable.

If I was going to be up, I might as well have some breakfast. Bettie's Diner put on a good one. I didn't always have the same thing, but the western omelet with home fries and salt-rising toast was a frequent choice. I nodded to the retirees who pretty much owned the counter seats. They nodded back. Bettie took my order herself, and I pretended to read a paperback copy of *The Maltese Falcon* while I drank coffee and waited for my food. I didn't feel like chit-chat, and reading a book seemed to discourage that.

Moe made rounds of the Mannaz campus. The school was just waking up as I sat in the cozy warmth of Bettie's, listening to the quiet conversation of other early risers. Noah was the first in Oak House, vacuuming the carpeted areas with an ancient upright. He refused to discard anything until it was beyond the hope of repair, and the vacuum had both red and blue parts and was duct-taped in several places. Raymond, the kitchen manager, came next and fired up the gas range. Novak arrived shortly after. He looked like he could have used more sleep.

I didn't interact with anyone at the diner more than necessary, but I often just liked to be among people. The retirees mostly talked about the good ol' days. They were obviously not very objective in their recollections. The coffee was okay and the breakfast was very good, especially the salt-rising toast. It was extra buttery. I lingered after I'd eaten all I was going to. Others came and went in the time that I sat and eavesdropped on Bettie's patrons as well as the people at the Mannaz School. The retirees outlasted me. I thought that some of them were also regulars at The Crick, and I wondered if they just migrated there when it opened.

I was back in my own kitchen by 7:30 and would have stayed there for a while longer if Moe's attention hadn't been captured by a group of students in the common room of Oak House. Relatively responsible students were allowed to arrive early to play cards, work on assignments, or generally socialize. This morning, they'd found something of interest.

Karen, Katie, Jan, and Paul stood hunched over a large book open on one of the table tops. Jan rotated it so that she could see a two-page picture right-side-up. A bright pink sticky note marked the page.

She said, "It really does look like him."

Paul slid the book so that he could see the page more clearly. He poked his index finger at the text beneath the picture. "1919? How old do you think Mr. Brannon is anyway?"

Jan put her hands on her hips and sighed gustily. "I didn't say that the guy in the picture is Mr. Brannon. I just said it looks like him. A lot."

The picture looked like something from the introduction of *Cheers* except that this pub scene was in New York instead of Boston. There I stood, my back to the bar with a dozen or so other people. I was hoisting a mug in salute to whomever held the camera. I wore a derby hat and a dark suit, and a giant grin dominated the lower half of my face. Luckily, the picture was black and white, so my red hair couldn't be used as further identification.

Where the hell had my cousin found that book? It wasn't mine. I hadn't taken off my coat yet, so I simply about-faced and headed to Oak House. I would have like to have brushed my teeth, but I thought it best to remove the book from circulation as quickly and surreptitiously as possible. Kids had this troublesome capacity to believe the impossible, and I would rather have fewer than more adolescent brains working on the weird old-timey picture.

I casually strolled into the common room, hands in the pockets of my coat. Paul looked up first and started. One of those "speak of the

246

devil" reactions, I guessed. The vaguely guilty expression quickly changed to one of good-humored amusement.

He said, "Hey, Mr. Brannon. Jan thinks you're a hundred years old."

The three girls looked up at me as well.

"Uhg," Jan growled at Paul. "You make me crazy, you dumb boy."

Karen rotated the book, and Katie stepped aside so that I could see the picture clearly. Karen tapped her finger on my smiling black-and-white image. "Is that your grandfather or something?"

Details about my family were relatively scarce even to me, but there was no reason for the kids to know that. See? Talamaur really are closed-mouthed. I said, "It might be. Or it could be a great uncle or something. I've never seen that picture."

Paul said, "See, Jan, I told you that Mr. Brannon wasn't a hundred."

Karen's comment was characteristically snarky. "I can give you some help with basic subtraction if you need it."

Paul smiled broadly. "I was rounding down to save Mr. B's feelings."

"Does anyone know where this came from?" I asked the group.

They all took turns shrugging and grunting negatives until Karen said, "It was just lying open on the table with the Post It in it when I walked by."

I closed the book and picked it up. "We had visitors yesterday. I think that one of them might have left it. The book's pretty clearly expensive, so I'll put it away for safekeeping until I can make some calls."

None of them seemed terribly bothered, and Paul took a pack of playing cards out of his pocket as he walked toward another table. The girls followed. My guess was Hearts. It was pretty popular recently.

I took the book to my classroom and would have put it in the bottom drawer of my desk, but it was too big. I stowed it in the closet instead. Procrastination with the coffee pot in the faculty room had been my plan. Seeing Allie couldn't help but to brighten my day. But the damn book spoiled that idea. Doru was going to escalate, and I wanted to knock down all the ducks I could while I could.

I retrieved the mocked-up withdrawal paperwork for Morris Starr and considered taking it right to Novak. He was the acting headmaster, sort of. But I guess I was too. I didn't feel much like trying out my atrophied lying skills this morning, so I sent Moe to check out Corman's office. Pam wasn't in yet, so I decided to take the opportunity to put the paperwork into her inbox.

On my way down the stairs, I noted the time and wondered about the last time Pam hadn't been behind her desk by 7:30. A worm of unease turned in my stomach. My first reaction was to send Moe to look for her, but I didn't know where she lived, and my familiar was needed here. I forced myself to relax. People sometimes ran late. I had a plan, a step-by-step plan. After putting the paperwork in the proper place, I headed to Maple House and hoped to catch Rick before his dorm arrived at the main building.

Hands thrust deep into the pockets of my overcoat, I ran my script through my head. Terry Brown was pretty bright and generally observant. It would have been nice to work on my lying with someone a little less astute, but my lying was probably better than I credited it. Also, there no reason for him to expect deception. It was boarding school, not the French court.

At the dorm, Terry was busy trying to convince Ronnie to put on his shoes before going to breakfast. It seemed that, in an act of defiance, Ronnie had thrown all of his shoes out of his bedroom window. Rick and Larry were outside retrieving them.

In a few terse sentences, I told Terry that Morrey would be leaving because of a family emergency. He nodded, thanked me, and turned his attention back to Ronnie.

Just then, Rick and Larry came back inside carrying armloads of shoes of varying styles. Rick and I shared a look. He appeared appropriately concerned when I told him that I would need to speak to him in private. Moe kept tabs downstairs while we went up.

Rick sat at his desk chair smiling his gap-toothed Morrey smile. "It's been a fun couple of days. Are you sure you don't need more help? My rates are reasonable."

I said, "We're not quite finished. You need to seem all nervous and scared or sad. Some kind of anxiety anyway. We need to cross campus, and anyone might be watching."

"Okay, sure." He stood and straightened up his clothes and said, "There are a couple of empties under the bed. You should probably take care of those."

"Thanks."

"No problem. How do I get my car?"

"You can drive it yourself."

"Glamour?"

"If it's not too much trouble. It'll be a basic shuffle. Once you no longer look like Morrey, no one will pay much attention to you."

I sketched out a rough plan. It was simple but all we really needed.

Rick rolled his shoulders and turned his head from side to side like he was about to step into a boxing ring. He breathed in and breathed out and whispered, "And action." His face went taut with imminent tears. His lower lip quivered, and he actually paled. With those Campbell's-Soup-kid features, it was heart-rending. Rick was talented as hell, and I wondered if he would teach lessons.

When we walked through the living room, Terry and Larry took one look at that grief-stricken face and looked away. Ronnie looked as though he would burst into tears himself, his battle over the shoes forgotten.

As we walked toward the parking lot, Moe saw the real Rick veer off when we neared my apartment, but he had gone invisible. An illusion of Morrey continued to walk next to me. The real Rick opened and closed my apartment door, but to my mundane eyes, the door appeared static. I'd seen more supernatural phenomena in the last week than I'd seen in the last thirty years, but I was getting used to it quickly. Seeing Rick's ability to maintain multiple illusions was really impressive, though.

I had to open the van door for the Morrey illusion which climbed onto the middle seat and sat motionless. I wondered how much willpower and deliberate intent Rick had to use to keep it going. I'd been told that glamours were nearly effortless for faeries, which was probably a good thing for us because Rick was also shapeshifting at the same time.

After a minute or so, Moe showed me Rick, approaching the parking lot. He appeared as he had when we first met, but he was invisible to my mundane senses. Now, that would be really handy. Invisibility to anything but cameras. Rick obviously knew that I had a familiar, but he still jerked a little when I turned to look at him. I guess Moe slipped his mind.

I lowered the window, and he said, "I'll keep the Morrey illusion going until you're off campus."

"Awesome."

"Can you see anyone watching?"

Moe rose about forty feet into the air and made a 360 scan. I said, "I don't see anyone obvious. Someone could be looking out a window or something."

Rick said, "Good enough," and suddenly appeared to my regular eyes. He held out his hand and we shook through the window. He looked at me for a while, and I waited for him to say what was on his mind. Finally, he said, "I think I understand a little bit of it."

"What's 'it'?"

"Why you stay here. You really matter to these kids, and on some level, they know it. Even when they call you an asshole, they say it with a kind of reverence, you know? And when they talk about Corman, you'd think they were referring to some benevolent king or something."

"Asshole?"

He shrugged, arms partially outstretched. "They're kids. Human kids even."

"You like humans?"

"Some," he said. "I'm a case by case kind of guy." He patted my forearm which was resting on the open window. "Anyway, good luck with. . ." He waved toward the central cluster of buildings. ". . . all the shit going on."

"Thank you, Rick."

He gave me the double-finger-point, turned, and climbed into his car. He pulled out first, and I followed. The image of Morrey vanished when we neared 19A. Rick turned toward Geary, and I turned toward Warsaw. The lumbering behemoth of a vehicle was not fun to drive, and I had no music to listen to.

I was headed to the hospital to sip off some lifeforce from a dying friend in the hope that it would jumpstart some kind of healing response. Longshots were not unknown to me. The problem I was having was whether or not my actions would cause the opposite result of the one I intended. I didn't know if he could recover on his own or not. He'd shown little evidence of improvement, but what did I know? None of my degrees were in medicine. If he could recover on his own, and my little sip made him take a bad turn, I would have a really hard time with that. I didn't want to make the wrong call.

I hadn't gotten more than a couple of miles down the road when my cell phone rang. Moe was on guard duty at the school until I sent for him, so I pulled off the road before answering. I didn't want to crash a school vehicle with a nonexistent student on board. That would sure be hard to explain.

The number on my screen wasn't on my contact list, and I didn't recognize it. When I picked up, I recognized the voice, though. It was Corman likely calling from his room phone.

"Sean? Are you busy?"

"I was just coming to see you," I said. "Be there in a half hour."

"Good. I would rather talk to you in person."

"Anything serious? Have you felt a tremor in the force?"

He didn't answer right away. He was quiet long enough for me to take a quick glance at the phone's screen to make sure that the call hadn't dropped. His voice had a pensive quality when he said, "Maybe. I've felt something, at any rate. We'll talk when you get here. Until then."

He hung up. I put the van back into gear and wondered what was up with Corman and if I were about to make things better or worse for him.

# Chapter 21

Moe wasn't with me to scout out Corman's room at the hospital. I didn't know if there was much practical purpose in leaving my familiar at school, but I felt better having him there to keep an eye on things for as long as possible. Unless Corman had been moved, I had a pretty good idea of where his room was located, but I made like a normal person and asked the woman at the information desk.

She was middle aged with dark hair going gray. Something about her, from the gravelly voice to the brusque manner, evoked a truck-stop waitress more than a hospital receptionist. She directed me to the third floor. When I told her to have a good morning, she looked at me suspiciously, like I was being sarcastic or something. Apparently, I seemed genuine enough because she gave me one curt nod before turning back to her computer screen.

Corman had his bed raised entirely in the upright position, and he was looking directly at me the moment I stepped into the doorway. Did he sense my approach? Was it just chance that he happened to be looking my way? I really missed Moe. If there were anything special to observe, he could have done it. What would it be like to walk around like a human all of the time? Lots of surprises and fewer informed choices for sure.

"Welcome, Sean," he said and gestured to the chair near his bed.

He was alert, and there was no quaver in his voice though it was quiet. His skin still had the grayish undertone that made me think that his condition wasn't improving. The bags under his eyes looked bruised. He rested his hands on his lap before I'd taken note of any tremors or marked strain.

I lifted the chair and moved it as close to the bed as I could and still leave room for my knees. My sitting position made Corman seem to tower above me, but I didn't mind. It seemed appropriate. We sat that way for a long time it seemed. I just wasn't sure what to say, and he'd called me after all. I'd already been on my way, but he hadn't known that.

When he spoke, his words seemed a little random. "I was a bit of a fluke in my family."

"Oh?"

"Yes, my mother's side of the family was pure Romani. My grandmother was highly respected. She had 'the sight,' you see."

"The sight?" I asked though I understood.

He waved a hand, the movement a little weak. "Precognition, empathy, the ability to see spirits. Apparently, the ability doesn't hit each generation equally. My mother had none of it, but my grandmother insisted that it was strong in me. I am, apparently the last in a long line of gypsy fortunetellers." He smiled a little and added, "I use the term 'gypsy' for its dramatic effect, not as a pejorative."

This was the story I'd wanted thirty years ago. And now, I had a strong suspicion about the identity of the ghost attached to the crystal ball on Corman's desk. Loving gramma felt about right.

I smiled back. "Here I thought you were a medical doctor and headmaster this whole time."

"Fooled you," he said. "Seriously though, I didn't believe any of it. I read a great deal from a very young age, and I chose science over superstition.

"My mother's family immigrated to the United States when she was young. My father was American, the son of Dutch immigrants. He was Christian, and I considered his religion another form of superstition, another of the numerous mythologies of the world. My parents were a strange pair, but they loved each other. They were good parents, but I quietly looked down on them because they couldn't see that science held all of the answers we needed."

Corman stopped for a moment and took a deep breath. "Will you pass me that cup of water?"

I stood and handed him a blue plastic cup from the movable tray which had been pushed to the side. He took it, and I could see that his hands were a little unsteady. He drew a mouthful from the straw and handed it back.

"If you need to rest, I can come back later," I said.

"No, I want you hear my story."

"Okay."

"When you came for your interview all those years ago, you asked me about the crystal ball. It was my grandmother's. She said that it had been in her family for generations. It still makes me think of her though I don't have many specific memories. I know I loved her. My mother said that my grandmother talked at length about my power. My ability to 'see.'"

I was interested in the things that he was telling me, but I still wasn't sure what point he was working toward. Corman would never talk this long without having a point. That's just the way he was wired. There was nothing to do but sit back and let him get where he was going.

He said, "There have been times when I've experienced things which defy my understanding. That doesn't mean that I stopped believing in science, simply that science hasn't gotten around to looking at everything yet. As I've been lying here these past few days, I wonder how much we don't know and if my parents' superstitions might have some basis in fact. Unrecorded and unexamined, maybe, but facts nonetheless."

Corman looked at me hard, trying to make a decision. Maybe his speech wasn't entirely planed after all. His shoulders sagged a little, and I was pretty sure that all this talking was taking a toll on him. I knew better than to ask again if he needed rest, though.

He went on. "I spent my life denying any strangeness I experienced. There was a reasonable explanation for everything, even if I couldn't see it. When I first met you, however, I felt something, almost saw something, that shook me. I could accept that I had excellent intuition, that I had a way with reading people and anticipating their actions. I was simply perceptive. But when you met Charlie Worthington after your interview, and he was having a tantrum, I think I perceived on an entirely different level. Almost as though I were seeing a different world, at least a glimpse of it.

"I think I knew, on some level, that you were different, somehow 'other.' My intuition told me that you were a good man, though. Once I had driven away the. . . strangeness of the experience with the light of reason, I felt confident in hiring you."

"Thank you," I said.

He nodded in a little truncated bow. "I felt something again just a few days ago when Howie Tragger had his episode in the math room. It was similar in some ways but much more unpleasant. Even painful. Without any empirical evidence or any structured system of reasoning, I know that whatever happened is the reason that I am in this bed."

He was silent then except for his breathing. I guessed it was my turn to speak.

Would the Venator council care if I told a dying old man about us? It seemed to be less of an issue than I'd, until recently, believed. I wanted to risk it, but something, maybe my secretive Talamaur nature, compelled me to evade.

I said, "I don't doubt that science will one day get around to explaining virtually every superstition from every culture. In the meantime, we probably shouldn't assume that they are entirely baseless." Noncommittal, that's me.

Corman gave me that probing look again. I had the feeling that he was switching to Plan B. He said, "My mother used to tell me stories of creatures who looked human but weren't. For the most part, they were fairy stories, but there was another creature that comes to mind now, the strigoi."

I felt a little internal jolt, but I didn't let it show. I hope I didn't anyway.

He said, "There were two types of strigoi, the strigoi-mort and the strigoi-moroi. The former undead, the latter living. They're vampires of a sort, but they don't necessarily drink blood. They can simply absorb life from others by a type of osmosis. One of the things that made them stand out was their red hair and bright blue eyes."

"Wow," I said. "That is strange."

Many of those tales did, in fact, refer to my people. We were never undead, but we could survive grievous injuries, so I understood how observers might take away the impression that we could rise from the dead. I felt trapped, but that was silly. I could get up and walk away whenever I wanted.

"It's a good thing I wasn't around then," I said with the most genuine smile I could manage pasted across my face. "Someone might

255

have taken it into his head to drive a stake through my heart or something."

"Yes, those were different times," he said. "Hopefully, in these more enlightened times, we wouldn't assume that one is evil simply because of his race or appearance. One of these strigoi might even be a benign influence, even the protector of a community. If he existed, that is, and wasn't just an element of folktales."

"It sounds like a show on the CW," I said.

Corman settled back into his pillows. The talking seemed to have taken a lot out of him. His eyelids looked heavy. I think that his reserves were close to exhausted, and he would sleep soon whether he wanted to or not.

"I would rest easier if I knew there was someone who could protect my school and the people there," he said.

"Rest easy then."

He looked at me and nodded once. He closed his eyes, but I didn't think he'd drifted to sleep. If Moe were here, I'd have a better idea.

I said, "If there were a chance to make you well again, would you take it, even if it were dangerous?"

He smiled bleakly, but his eyes remained closed. "As opposed to dying slowly?"

"Who says you're dying?"

"I do," he said so quietly that I had to strain to hear.

A part of me wanted to argue with him, but my optimism was on the wane, and I doubted I'd fool anyone, especially Corman.

His voice sounded a little fuzzy when he said, "It doesn't seem like much of a dilemma. I would live if I could. Seventy-two years still doesn't feel like long enough."

He was asleep in seconds.

I sent for Moe and waited for him to arrive. Corman's breathing deepened. The quiet bustle of the hospital went on around me.

I felt definite relief when my familiar returned, but I also felt sharp anxiety at what I was about to do. A queasy stomach, sweaty palms, and a vague sense of dread topped it all off.

Corman was sleeping soundly, and I hoped I wouldn't spoil that. Moe shifted to pointy mode, all ready and waiting. I'd done this thousands of times. I had all kinds of finesse, precise control. I knew that, but I was so afraid of screwing up. I couldn't think of anyone whom I respected more than this wasted old man sleeping on the bed in front of me. What if I was the one to snuff him out like a candle? What if I spoiled whatever chance he had to recover on his own?

I'd seen plenty of people die in my day. Sure, this specific situation was unique, but it wasn't all that different from what I knew. Lifeforce and death were my specialty. Looking at him there, I believed that if something wasn't done, Corman was going to fade away. I proceeded on that premise. It was either that or stand around wringing my hands.

Moe pierced the old man. He flinched a little in his sleep but didn't awaken. I drew out a drop of life and stopped. My eyes went wide at the jolt I felt when it touched my aura. It dispersed throughout my being, leaving a little humming tingle as it went. I'd never experienced anything like it. Moe disengaged and observed Corman's reaction to the process.

I didn't know what I was looking for, so I gave Moe his head. He could flip through frequencies and focus his attention where he wanted. Maybe he would notice something and bring it to my attention.

I would have Moe check me out later. That zap I got from Corman could probably stand some analysis. It didn't really feel so much like more nutrients. More like a spice, like habanero lifeforce or something. I'd have to make a mental note to look into it later.

My father could doubtless edify me on the whole of Talamaur knowledge if I had a crowbar strong enough to pry it from him. He loved to acquire information because it was power. I never knew him to take any pleasure in it, though. Shouldn't fathers teach their sons all they have to offer? No, Scathlann, my sire, sat on his information like a dragon sits on a hoard of treasure.

I found myself getting pissed off at him. I felt sure that he would know how to save Corman if anyone did. The truth of the situation, though, was that I hadn't asked. I could have sought him out instead of Galen. I just assumed that he wouldn't share, but maybe he'd changed in the last three decades. I should really visit him again so that my anger at him would have more legitimacy.

Moe and I stayed for another half hour, trying to observe some change in Corman. He slept the whole time. When I was convinced that I wouldn't learn anything more, at least for the time being, we headed back to the Mannaz School. My familiar zipped ahead, and I chugged along behind in the school van.

Moe began a circuit of the campus and quickly became aware of Doru's familiar mucking about in my apartment again. Range varies depending on numerous factors, but familiars always detect other familiars if they are within thirty feet or so. Moe attacked which resulted in the typical familiar clinch. The ghost-powered familiar was much stronger, but Moe was too tenacious to allow any constructive activity to take place.

Doru's familiar retreated and Moe harried it and the ghosts for a mile or so before breaking off and returning to school. My cousin had little in the way of imagination, and it appeared that his familiar had been trying to remove the keepsake box from its wedged position beneath my bed. To the familiar's credit, it'd made good progress.

I couldn't assume that Doru would continue with his annoying but harmless torment. He would escalate. But how? He was difficult to predict because he had so little concept of scope and degree. He would find pushing someone in front of a moving train equally as funny as throwing a pie in someone's face. I suddenly wished that I'd made it easier for him to get to the newspaper clippings.

I felt discouraged. My path was unclear. I might protect the people at the Mannaz School by simply leaving. The everyday operation of the place would take a hit from losing both Corman and me in short order. Even with my ego firmly in check, I wondered if the school could survive the loss. All things being considered, though, everyone would be alive, right?

Then, I thought of Doru's ability to find and exploit weaknesses. Maybe he couldn't grasp the idea of caring for people on a personal level, but he could still use it against me. He would know that I cared about the people at the school even if I left them behind. He could use one or two people as hostages as easily as he could use the whole school.

I could give him what he wanted in order to protect my own. I remembered how well that worked with Nazi Germany not too long ago. Anyway, I didn't understand Doru's part in this Venator measure. I couldn't shake the feeling that people would be hurt or killed as a part of the plan. I didn't want to sacrifice other people to save my own though that was exactly what I'd done in my bargain with Melk.

Simply killing Doru seemed like a viable solution, but it wouldn't be simple. Not really. What would the fallout be in my own family? What kind of allies might he have, and would they try to avenge him? Would the Venator council involve themselves? Could I even beat him in my weakened condition?

I zombie-walked through the day, my vague exterior belying the army of over-stimulated hamsters running on individual wheels inside my head. Mostly, I avoided people if I could. The creative writing kids didn't do much of anything constructive, but to be fair, I didn't either.

Moe was ever vigilant, always on the move. I admit that he checked in on Allie and Howie more than others. Pam looked like she could use some sleep. She drooped a little, and her smiles were forced, a bit distracted. Novak was clearly taking Corman's ill health harder than anyone. He seemed older, not as hale, and as distracted as I.

Novak stopped in my room not long after the creative writers had gone. He absently kneaded the back of his neck with one hand while he spoke. "Hey, Sean. Can you be point man tonight? I haven't seen Joe since Wednesday, and I'd like to look in on him."

"Sure," I said. "I stopped in to see him this morning."

"How'd he look?"

I shrugged. There was no point in lying if Novak was just going to see him in an hour.

He nodded and said, "Thanks." He began to leave but turned back. "What happened with Morrey Starr? Pam said that you signed off on his withdrawal papers. Why did he leave?"

"There was some kind of family emergency. I think that one of the parents is in a bad way, and they want him home."

He stood fidgeting for a moment. He seemed to want to say something but didn't know how. Novak was not a fidgeting kind of guy, so it looked strange on him. Finally, he said, "Thanks again," and left.

He was gone for a couple of minutes when Doru's familiar entered the room. Moe was going to give chase, but I held him back. My phone buzzed in my pocket, and I answered it.

It was Doru. Apparently, he wanted to have eyes on me while we talked. "So, are you going to make me your proxy or what?"

"I haven't had time to look into the measure," I said. "It's not as though I can look it up online."

"The bastard faerie didn't have any info either?" He sounded smug.

I clenched inwardly. I didn't think that his familiar could spy on me without Moe being aware of it. Not closely at any rate. I suppose it was possible at a distance, but familiars' senses had maximum ranges. They couldn't really see or hear much farther than a human. Their speed and intangibility just allowed them to get close in a hurry.

He seemed to guess my thoughts, and it was more important for him to gloat than to keep a secret. He really wasn't a normal Talamaur. "Ha! You're such a dumbass. Didn't you ever think of hiring regular detectives? Jesus, you've got all these tools you can use, and you don't. You have some moral problem with hiring PIs too?"

"None at all," I said.

I relaxed a bit, now that I could see how he worked it. I doubted that it was just a single PI. Probably a team keeping in contact with cell phones. It's hard to spot a tail when it's constantly changing. If they were any good, they would cost a lot, but Talamaur, as a rule, could have virtually limitless financial resources.

In theory, his familiar could have done the job. Gotten a bead on the Nova and followed from a couple hundred feet in the air. But that would mean sending his familiar two hundred miles away and being separated from it for eight hours at least. He wouldn't like that any more than I would. It could be done, but there would be a kind of tension. Very unpleasant.

He chuckled coldly. "Damn, Caomhnóir. This is too easy. You've been out of the game too long. Pretending to be human. We both know you're going to give me what I want."

"You know that do you?"

"Yeah, because you're weak. Why do you associate with people who can't give you anything and need to be protected? All weak and fragile and shit. I don't need to beat you. I just need to threaten your little human pets."

I felt like something heavy and rotten sat low in my stomach. I said, in a flat tone, "Careful you don't overplay that hand."

"Why?" he said, a snicker just under the surface. "You've got like eighty of them. I could do that thing that the terrorists do in the movies. You know, 'We'll kill one hostage every hour until you comply.' Like that."

He was right. He could do that. The question that I had was why wasn't he? Certainly not moral compunctions. Something was staying his hand, at least for the time being. Doru wouldn't be the brains behind any outfit. But Melk seemed to be pretty damn smart. And from what Galen had said about the red cap, he was an honest-to-God crime boss. Doru was probably just a flunky following orders.

I reminded myself that a pissing contest with Doru would benefit no one, not even Doru. I said, "I need more time to look into the measure. You said that the vote isn't until the New Year. There's still time for due diligence."

He scoffed. "I said 'before the New Year.'"

"That still leaves about two months," I said.

"Yeah, but I'm not patient." Doru hung up, and his familiar bolted.

I just sat for a long time because I had no idea what the hell to do.

# Chapter 22

Novak called me after supper but before I left for a dorm visit. It was probably a good thing because I'd been looking longingly at the Maker's Mark bottle which I'd carelessly left on the counter.

He said, "Hey, Sean. How are things going?"

"Fine," I said. "As smooth as they ever are."

"Good. Joe's drifted off, and the nurse said that he'll probably be out for the rest of the night."

I asked, "How's he doing?" If he were doing well, Novak probably would have led with that, but the optimist in me still hoped that my efforts earlier in the day had done some good.

He sighed. "I don't know. I'm not a doctor." I heard him breath on the line some more. "But he looks. . . fragile."

"Sorry."

The line was quiet for a bit. Then, Novak said, "Anyway, I wanted to make sure that you put together a crew for the Haunted Forest setup. I didn't get around to it."

I'd forgotten all about the Haunted Forest. It was a bit of a Mannaz School "conditional" tradition. If there was no snow, sleet, or pouring rain, we would set up a sort of spook house along a path through the woods. The work crew was usually made up of Novak and I and some of the veteran Mannaz students. Sometimes other teachers and dorm parents pitched in as well, but we were the core of the effort.

"Of course," I said. "I'll recruit a crew tonight from the usual suspects." A thought occurred to me, then, and after a second's consideration, I voiced it. "I know we usually don't put kids on the crew until they've walked The Haunted Forest a couple of times, but I'd like to invite Howie along."

"Fine by me. You sure seem to have a way with the kid. He's been the ideal student for the last few days."

"I was thinking the same thing."

"Be sure that Paul is there. He could probably direct construction himself."

"You do know that the work crew is entirely voluntary, right?"

"Don't let Paul know. See you tomorrow," he said and hung up.

Keeping Howie close by felt like the right thing to do. Doru might not be very smart, but he was a predator. He had the instinct. He would go for a weak spot, and I was sure Melk had told him all about my protective attitude toward the boy.

I stopped by each dorm for a short time and asked specific students if they wanted to help out. Each of them said yes. Part of the allure was the fun of building things to scare schoolmates, but there was also the bonus of missing classes and the gravitas of being one of the school's "elders." It seemed that most of the kids would rather hook a plastic skeleton to a zipline than learn about the Reformation or how to balance equations.

Howie was clearly touched by the invitation and was all full of bounce when I left him at Beech House. I guessed that he would be even more buoyant when the other kids made a big deal about a new kid going out with us.

I went home as early as I could and not feel like I was shirking my responsibilities. To my surprise, I only picked up the Maker's Mark to put it back in the cabinet. I expected to go into one of my worry and fret routines. You know, I would have every intention of going to sleep, but instead, I would stare at the ceiling and second guess everything I'd ever done. Then, I'd worry about how I would probably screw up the next day.

To my surprise, I washed my face, brushed my teeth, and went to sleep. Just like that.

Moe is a good guard while I sleep, but he can't do anything elaborate while I'm unconscious. I don't think he can anyway. I'm unaware of him, but he has awoken me in times of need, so he must have been on the alert. Before I'd gone to bed, I instructed Moe to continue making rounds of the school and to rouse me if there was any sign of Doru or his familiar. I felt confident that he could and would do it, but I didn't want to ask for anything more complicated.

Apparently, nothing of note happened throughout the night.

I woke the next morning rested and looking forward to some work in the woods. As coffee brewed, I checked the weather app on my phone. Low of 39 and high of 55. Chance of precipitation 4 percent.

I dressed in jeans, hiking boots, t-shirt, green flannel shirt, and an old gray Columbia fleece. Galen's magic bag barely made a bulge in the inside pocket of the fleece.

I ate breakfast in the dining room with the work crew. Paul was there carrying himself in that quietly competent way that made him an excellent student helper. He didn't brag or try to lord his privileges over anyone. Howie looked a little nervous and a lot excited. Kate, Jan, and an eighth grader named Stevie had worked on set up in previous years, and they seemed glad to be included again. A good crew.

On the surface of things, Stevie didn't seem like a good choice. He was a slow processor and a slow executer, and he had a childlike quality without being childish. But his mind was a steel trap, his problem-solving skills were excellent, and his detail work was first-rate. He just couldn't do anything quickly. He almost seemed to be stuck in slow motion. The Mannaz School was good for him because adjustments were made which allowed him to reach his potential. We all knew he would never make it in a fast-paced environment, though, and hoped that he would continue to find places where he could fit in.

Novak met us after breakfast, and we headed to the theater where the Haunted Forest materials were stored. Noah had backed the school pickup to the wide back door which opened off the scene shop. The boxes that we needed were stacked in a corner. Howie seemed to know instinctively to follow Paul's lead. All of the kids did. The kids carried the stuff out and handed it to me. I passed it up to Novak who stood in the truck bed waiting to stack.

Between loads, I said, "I wonder if Paul would like to come here to work after he graduates from college."

"Not if he wants to make any money." The chilly air and exercise were bringing color into Novak's face, and I was glad to see it.

"Paul doesn't seem like a 'get rich' kind of guy."

"Then he's perfect."

When everything was loaded up, we headed off to the Low Road. There were two main hiking-trail loops at the school: the High Road and the Low Road. The High Road was for more athletic, fit students. It was rocky, winding, and had some pretty steep grades. The Low Road was relatively broad and flat and short, not much more than a mile. It was good for starting out young or generally short-winded hikers. Also, it was great for the Haunted Forest.

There was a clearing at about the half-way point of the Low Road which would be our base of operations. Noah would drive the truck up a seasonal access road that skirted Mannaz property and bisected the clearing. He would wait for us to unload everything and then go about his day.

Our breath clouded before us as we walked down the driveway to the trailhead. It was still the fun kind of cold that was zingy but didn't hurt. Our cheeks were pink, and our strides were brisk. Leaves had been falling hard over the last couple of days, but there was still a good bit of color in the trees including the rich blue-green of evergreens. Spirits were good in our little party.

Stevie tended to lag, and Novak and I expected it. Through unspoken agreement, Novak stayed with him as I kept up with the others. They were exchanging stories of the best scares they could remember from past Haunted Forest treks. Paul had the most, but Kate was really good at impressions, and she could imitate the voice and manner of everyone at the school. I occasionally had to remind her to keep her portrayals nice, but that was only after I got my laughing under control.

We reached the clearing and found that Noah hadn't yet arrived with the truck. We shuffled around as Paul asked me questions about how we would divide up and who would have what jobs. Core elements of the Haunted Forest were yearly staples, but we usually tried to mix things up a little. We probably wouldn't get very elaborate this year, though. On some level, Corman's situation was on everyone's mind, and we were all in conservation mode.

After we'd stood around for a few minutes, I had Moe veer from his guard duty route and check on Noah. The old guy was talking to Pam outside of her office. Apparently, the light was flickering in the faculty bathroom, and she wanted to let him know in person. Judging from the dopey grin on his face, he didn't mind Pam distracting him from his other duties. If he felt compelled to deal with the light immediately, we might be in for a longer wait.

I was about to suggest a game of tag or chopsticks when I heard a scream. It was raw, abrupt, and terrified. The kids heard it too, their eyes going wide, heads swiveling to locate the direction from where it came.

With barely a thought, Moe flickered across the distance. The whole dreadful experience would be over in a handful of seconds, but Talamaurs and their familiars can pack an awful lot into just a few seconds.

A hundred yards back down the trail, Moe found Stevie rolled up like a hedgehog in the middle of the trail. Novak stood over him, stance wide and knees bent. His eyes were riveted on something further down the trail. A huge black bear was reared on its hind legs, roaring, and flailing around with it clawed paws. Dry leaves and twigs clung to the animal's thick fur. It shook its head as though it were being assaulted by stinging insects.

I turned to Paul and grabbed him by the shoulders. He flinched away, startled by my abrupt movement. I said his name sharply. He looked me in the eyes.

I said, "Take everyone back to the school. Keep going the rest of the way around the loop. Go fast."

Howie, voice trembling, said, "Mr. Brannon—"

I let go of Paul and pointed up the trail. "All of you, go back to Oak House, now!"

The students began a jogging run up the trail, and I turned the entirety of my attention to the conflict a hundred yards back down the trail.

The bear charged Novak and Stevie. Something was off about it. Never mind that it should have been hibernating. Never mind that black bears generally weren't aggressive, especially to humans. It just wasn't moving right. It snapped its jaws at empty air and swung its head from side to side as it rushed forward. That didn't seem to slow it down any, though.

There was no time to fumble with the magic bag to get to the weapons it contained, so I took off at a sprint. I could travel the distance in seconds, but I knew that I would be too late. Moe was already there, though.

My familiar couldn't affect the physical world with much force, but he could maximize what force he could exert. He was like a judo master, and he could buy me some time. He slammed into the bear's front paws just at the moment before they struck the ground in its galloping run. It wasn't much, but it didn't take much. The bear's front legs folded under it, and its throat and jaw came down hard on the packed surface of the trail. Its teeth clacked together, and it grunted explosively.

Before Moe had made contact with the bear, I understood the animal's unnatural behavior. Moe saw Doru's familiar harrying the creature, maddening it with painful jabs to its nose and eyes, prodding it from behind, and aiming it directly at Novak and Stevie.

After Moe's initial move, he could do nothing else to help. Doru's familiar took him in a clinch. Moe gamely tried to escape, so the struggle would remove both familiars from the combat equation. It would just be me against an enraged, clawed, fanged, three-hundred-pound animal. I would basically be fighting with my eyes closed, too, because I depended so much on Moe's sensory input, especially with precise physical movement.

Without my familiar to guide me, my footing wasn't as sure on the trail as it could have been. My time might have gotten me into the Olympic 100 meter, though. It'd been a long time since I'd gone all out, and I wasn't confident with my physical competence anymore.

The bear was up from its fall in three seconds. Doru's familiar was no longer antagonizing it, but the animal was thoroughly enraged. Insane. Novak was the closest thing to attack, so it continued its charge.

I don't know what Novak thought he would do, but his fists were clenched, and he did not budge from his position between the bear and Stevie. My friend looked formidable, broad-shouldered and heavy-armed, but he was overmatched. Stevie was lying silent and still on the ground, his arms wrapped around his head, his chin tucked to his chest, his eyes squeezed shut.

I saw a branch jutting into the path ahead of me. It was a couple of inches across, and its curving end was about six inches off the ground. I sacrificed a tiny bit of speed to stoop and grasp the end as I passed. As soon as my fingers closed over it, I knew it was punky with dry-rot. Better than nothing. Maybe.

Novak roared in challenge and crouched as though to launch himself.

But I'm the one who actually leaped. Despite slowing to grab the branch and being unbalanced by its unwieldy weight, I cleared over twenty feet. I missed colliding with Novak by inches and landed a few feet in front of him. The branch came down on the bear's head with all the strength I could muster. The rotted wood fragmented, and the bear tumbled.

I heard a startled exclamation from Novak just before the animal rammed into me. That much mass moving with that much momentum doesn't stop on a dime. I'm the one who changed direction. It was just a matter of physics. We went wide of Novak and Stevie. The impact jarred me, and my body screamed with the force of it. I hit the ground hard, and the air exploded from my lungs. I writhed for just a moment until I could push the pain away. My lungs didn't want to draw air yet, but I couldn't wait around for them.

The bear recovered before I did. The blow to the head had just enraged it further. Before I could get moving, it clubbed me with a huge paw, its claws parting fleece, flannel, and my skin with equal ease. I felt the impact, and I knew the pain would follow close. I didn't know how bad it was, but at the moment, it didn't matter. I had to keep moving.

I scrambled away on hands and knees. Not far, just to have room to maneuver. This fight needed to be over fast, or I would be screwed, maybe Novak and Stevie too. I bet on the bear pursuing me and rolled to the side. A half second later, it passed me, missing me by a hand's breadth.

Before it came to a stop, let alone was able to reverse direction, I'd dived onto its back. Yeah, I know. What the hell was I thinking? I wasn't thinking. I was instincting. I think that there may have been a half-formed image of me putting the bear into some sort of full-nelson type hold. If I'd ever wrestled a bear before, I would have known that it was way too massive for me to get my arms under its front legs and then around the back of its neck. I didn't know till I tried, though.

I did manage to get my arms around it, but I couldn't quite get my hands to clasp firmly. I found a lot of thick hair, though. I grabbed as much as I could and threw myself to the right side. The bear overbalanced and lost its feet. Now, I was clinging to a bear's back by its chest hair, both of us on our sides in the middle of the path. We probably looked like we were spooning or something. He was mad and thrashing, and I was scared. But kind of elated too.

Fortunately, I was more flexible and was able to get first one knee and finally both feet under me. It wasn't as easy as it sounds. I was standing in a broad stance, feet wide apart and knees bent around the bear's mass. The animal was throwing its weight around, and I thought I might lose my grip every time it did. I was still instincting, and I was pretty sure that losing my grip would be a bad thing.

No plan came readily to mind. In my defense, this was all new territory. But something happened to take decision-making out of my hands. I lost my balance. I felt myself start to go backwards. If I fell, I would hit the ground first, and the bear would land on top of me. I didn't think that I could hang on after that, and I wasn't sure that I should either.

Not knowing what else to do, I threw myself backward hard. As I did, I lifted the animal as much as I could manage and arched my back. Yeah, I might have had one of those half-baked pro-wrestling moves in mind again. You know, when the one guy lifts the other guy and falls backward. Then, the other guy lands hard on his shoulders and neck.

It didn't work out like I planned.

Two things happened, the second as a result of the first: I felt a lot of pain in my back and lost my grip on the bear's fur.

My body is basically a human body, but a human body can do some amazing things. You know, the mom lifting the car to rescue her child and that kind of thing. There are consequences, though, especially for a middle-aged body. Muscles, tendons, and ligaments have their limits, and in my case, throwing a three-hundred-pound bear over my shoulder exceeded those limits. Something came loose in my back, and my pain receptors lit up like a pinball machine. That jolt jumpstarted the pain of the claw gashes on my side too.

My whole body spasmed, including my hands. I'd done a good job of lifting, so instead of a body slam, I managed a short toss. The location of the half-dead pine tree just a few feet behind me was just blind luck. It did a lot of damage and saved the day. Bad luck for the bear but good luck for the rest of us.

The collision of the bear's head with the tree trunk might have been enough to discourage it from further combat, but the short, sharp, broken branches which jutted from the trunk definitively decided the issue. I heard the meaty impact and the snapping of dry branches and the yowl of the bear.

From my position flat on my back, I turned my head and saw the animal struggle to its feet and swing its head back and forth. A broken branch protruded from between its shoulders. It took two faltering steps and fell. It got up again and managed to keep its feet. The whole time it made the most pitiful groaning, whining sound. It staggered drunkenly back the way it had come. It fell again and got up again continuing around a bend where I could no longer see it.

Even through the agony in my back and the surging adrenaline, I felt a wave of pity for the animal. It had done nothing but be a convenient tool for my cousin. Apparently, its usefulness was done because the familiar and its ghosts released Moe and fled. My trusty familiar made no move to pursue them and, instead, came to me.

Novak also rushed over to me as well and knelt by my side. "Holy fuck, Brannon, are you okay?"

He reached for a pocket which I was sure held his cell phone. I grabbed his arm and said, "Don't call 911."

"What?"

"Check on Stevie. Give me a minute." My voice was tight and probably not very convincing. It might have even sounded like a person going into shock.

"Fuck that!" he spat.

"Conrad!" I shouted and had Moe "slap" him across the face. It wasn't hard, but the dramatic value of an invisible slap was significant.

His eyes went wide, and he put his hand to his cheek. "The fuck?"

I said in a level, reasonable tone, "There are things that you don't understand. Trust me."

Novak looked down the path in the direction the bear had gone. Then, at the site of combat, then, at the lucky pine tree, then, down at the bleeding rents in my clothing. I thought that he was replaying the battle. He ended up at my eyes and nodded once. He stood and went to Stevie. His hand absently rubbed the place where Moe had struck him.

I hadn't been hurt so badly in a long time, definitely not since I'd been starving myself. I didn't know what would happen. Talamaur can heal from anything that doesn't kill us, but we need fuel. Life force. I was in short supply. I would need some but how much? I didn't want to bleed out or be crippled up, but I didn't want to rejuvenate myself too much either. In light of my current situation, my apparent age was low on the list of priorities, but there it was in my considerations none the less.

I'd just about managed the pain when I felt the diagnostic buzz assessing my injuries. I knew instinctively that whatever I'd done to my back was far worse than the gashes from the bear's claws. Gritting my teeth to hold back the agony, I maneuvered myself into a sitting position. I mostly used my arms. I thought I could stand and eventually walk, but I wasn't quite ready to make the attempt. I didn't want to let Novak know that I was hurt as badly as I was. I'm a pretty good actor, but there are limits.

Through the riot going on in my body, I felt something I hadn't experienced for a long time. I was ready to begin the super-accelerated Talamaur healing process, but I simply didn't have the reserves to make it happen. I wished that there was a bad guy around. Not even necessarily a really bad guy. Cody or Dylan would do. Unfortunately, there was just my best friend of the last thirty years and a fourteen-year-old boy.

Novak came back over and knelt next to me again. He looked at me, and I could see that there was a lot going on in his head. Having made some decision, he shook his head in the negative. "Stevie is okay. He's just scared. We can have Missy look at him back at the school. I've got to call someone to help you. You're hurt bad."

271

I was going to argue, but the blood which soaked my side and the harshness of my breathing made it too hard to sell. The jig was up. I'd already had Moe slap him. I would have to reveal a little more of my nature. I couldn't think of any other way.

He brought the cell phone out of his pocket, but before he could even unlock the screen, Moe plucked it from his fingers. Novak made a sound like "Whaga?" Then, he watched open-mouthed at his phone floated ten feet above the ground. He looked back at me with real fear in his eyes. "Are you doing that?"

"Yeah. You can't call, Con, but you can help me."

He'd just faced down a bear with nothing but his bare fists. But now, he looked ready to run. His head began to shake a negative again, just little short movements.

I said, "I'm the same guy you've known for the last thirty years."

He stared at me for a three-count. "What do you need?"

I could feel my healing ability waiting in standby mode. If I were a phone with an update, my screen would read, "Connect to External Power Supply." I was in a lot of pain and more than a little scared about what was going to happen to me, but I was also terrified of hurting my friend, maybe even killing him. I had excellent control and a desire to take care, but denying the danger to Novak would be a lie. There would be a slight gamble, and I was just selfish enough to take it.

"I need a little life."

He didn't respond and instead, looked up and down the path. Stevie sat with his knees drawn up to his chest, staring up the path in the direction the other kids had gone.

Novak whispered, "Are you some kind of a. . . vampire. . . or something?"

"Yeah."

"How long—" he began, but I held up my hand to cut him short.

"I'll answer your questions later. You need to decide now."

"Could you take what you need without asking?" he asked.

"Yeah."

He took a deep breath and let it out slowly. "Okay, what do I have to do?"

"Nothing," I said.

Moe set Novak's phone on the path and did his thing. I felt a rush, a relief, a satisfaction. I knew, despite my best effort to deny it, that this was the natural way of things. It wasn't a thing that I would need to re-adjust to.

Novak flinched and squinted one eye. Then, he looked down at himself, probably to see evidence of what he was feeling. "Shit. It's like a pukey hangover."

There was no way for me to know exactly how much to take. I decided to err on the side of caution. I didn't want to hurt Novak. That was my main consideration. My first normal, if restricted, feeding in over a decade and a half was over in just a few seconds. Hell, less than five minutes had passed since I first heard Stevie's scream. A lot can happen in a really short time. If I was going to keep a lid on my part of the whole situation, I was going to need to keep up the pace. What was my next step?

Novak had the classic nauseous guy look. He burped quietly a couple of times while looking into the middle distance, letting his stomach settle. He breathed slowly in through his nose and out through his mouth.

He said to me, "That's it?"

"Yeah."

"I'm not going to turn into a vampire now, am I?"

"No. Look, I'll answer all of your questions later. Now, we need a story."

"You mean one that doesn't involve you jumping around like Spiderman and levitating my phone?"

"Yeah," I said as I had Moe return Novak's phone to him.

He instinctively held out his hand when it neared him. Staring at it in wonder, he whispered, "What the actual fuck?"

"What about our story?" I asked.

Novak said, "We'll keep it simple. You and I were able to scare the bear away. I don't think that Stevie really saw much of anything. We'll play dumb about anything else, like the bear getting speared with a pine branch."

"Good."

The healing began then. There was heat and a sensation like an entire colony of ants stomping on the lower half of my back with little ant-sized cleats. A similar but less pronounced feeling was also present around the claw marks. The seeping blood slowed markedly.

"Help me up," I said.

"I don't know," Novak began.

"I'm a vampire, right? I've got to be standing before I can turn into a bat."

He just stared at me for a few beats, then said, "You can? You know."

I smiled. "No, but I can walk if you help me get started."

He stood and offered me his hand. I gripped it and got my legs under me. He hauled up as I straightened my legs. Mission accomplished.

It was my turn to feel a little nauseous. I waited with my eyes closed for it to pass. It did, and I felt steadier.

"I'm okay," I said. "You and Stevie continue around the loop. I sent the other kids that way. Maybe you should call Pam and give her our story before the kids scare the hell out of her."

"What are you going to do?"

"I'm going to sneak back to my place and get cleaned up before anyone sees me."

Novak said, "I'm going to have to call Sandy too."

"Who?"

"Ed Sanders, county conservation officer." Novak waved his hand at the scene of battle. "It'd seem weird if I didn't. I don't want to ask any of these kids to keep a secret. I won't do that."

"Give me a little lead time if you can," I said.

I turned away and began walking back down the trail. I put all of my will into looking casual about it. I think I managed. The stabbing pain I felt at each step caused a little hitch, but I minimized it as much as I could.

"The bear went that way," he shouted.

"I'll just kick its ass again if it shows its face," I said without turning back. Turning back would have required my torso to pivot. I

274

had no doubt that that would hurt, probably more than I would fake away. So, I walked and concentrated on not flinching with each step.

As far as the bear was concerned, Moe had already found it lying thirty feet off the path in a drift of fallen leaves. It was still breathing but unconscious. I doubted that I would wake it by walking past. Ed Sanders would probably have to put it down, and I hoped that the poor thing never woke up.

As soon as I was out of Novak's sight, I cut the act. I knew that I had to keep moving, but I didn't care how I looked doing it when there was no audience. I thought that I would have to pull it together again when I was out in the open. Then, the absurdity of the idea struck me. Most of my left side was soaked in blood, and strips of my sodden fleece hung in tatters almost to my knee. I was pale, gaunt, and disheveled. I doubted that hobbling could draw any more attention. Hell, if I exaggerated the stagger, I could pretend to be trying out my Romero-era zombie costume.

Moe scouted for me. I wasn't very worried about being spotted until I got to the square. The driveway to the school was flanked on one side by trees, and I kept to them. Once main campus opened up, though, there would just be the square on the left and buildings on the right. I didn't know if Moe could give me enough notice to avoid being seen if a car came along, and there was no way that he could ensure that someone wouldn't happen to look out of a window and see me.

I stopped when I came to the edge of the trees and had to wrestle with a great big pile of aggravation. Despite being the middle of first period, Andy and Brett were on the square throwing the football back and forth. I wanted to blame someone, but my brain refused to draw up their class schedules. Not that focusing my frustration on a particular teacher would help my situation in the least. I could have blamed Andy and Brett, and I was pretty sure that they shared some of it, but I had to remind myself not to hold teenagers to the same standard that I had for adult professionals.

Even though I had all sorts of negative emotion crashing around in me, I couldn't help but to note that both of them actually had pretty good arms. They were varying their throws: guns and long bombs and tosses. I waited until Andy, who had his back to the driveway, threw a long, high one. Moe just gave it a little extra umph, and it went higher and longer. So much so that it cleared the roof of the theater.

Brett had stopped backing up when he knew catching ball was a lost cause, and he just watched it arch over the building. "Holy shit! That was far."

Andy stood slack-jawed, baffled by the distance. I couldn't actually hear him say, "Fuck," but I could see his mouth form the word as he looked down at the hand on the end of this throwing arm.

Andy ran over to Brett, and the two of them jogged around the theater building together. They shoved at each other playfully. Seeing them behaving like kids helped me to redirect my peevishness toward their teacher even though I still couldn't remember who it was.

Now, I had to move fast. The boys wouldn't be out of sight for long, and I had a lot of ground to cover. I had to hope that no one would see me and that my injured body would cooperate. I was smart enough not to launch into an all-out sprint, but I ran. It almost caused me to collapse into a face-first slide when the first lance of pain hit my lower back like a lightning bolt. I staggered and kept my feet, though, and I was able to force the pain away more with each step.

No one sounded an alarm, so I assumed that I wasn't spotted. Moe had my apartment door unlocked and opened by the time I reached it. I didn't throw myself in and collapse, but it was a close thing. I stood trembling, braced against the back of a kitchen chair. All of my concentration went to managing the pain. It was less of a traditional throb, and more like rhythmic stabs with an icepick.

The itching sensation of healing had begun as soon as I'd taken life from Novak, but the feeling was starting to gain momentum, and it distracted me from the pain. Exchanging one discomfort for another at least gave me some variety. As soon as I was able, I stripped out of my clothes right there in the kitchen. Blood would be easier to clean from linoleum than any other surface.

I was out of the shower and toweling dry in just a few minutes. I hoped that no one would note that I was wearing different clothes when I reappeared, but there was nothing to be done for it. The pile of bloody rags on the floor was destined for the garbage. Maybe the hiking boots could be saved, but there were some dark spots on them that I wouldn't want to explain today.

My back was healing at a pretty remarkable rate, and the claw marks were already forming scabs, I decided not to bother with a bandage. I hadn't really fed in such a long time that I'd forgotten what I was capable of. That thought gave me pause. I wiped the condensation from the bathroom mirror and examined myself. I didn't think that I looked any younger or older, but I definitely looked rough. Grayish. Gaunt-cheeked. Dark circles under my eyes. An observer might think that I'd caught whatever Corman had.

Moe could keep tabs on my appearance, but I needed to get to Oak House soon. Wearing another pair of jeans, brown brogues, a purple flannel shirt, and my bomber jacket, I headed over to Oak House. My trusty familiar found everyone from the work crew but Stevie in the common area. Pam and Novak sat with them. Stevie was in the nurse's office with Missy. She fussed over him and had him lie down on one of the infirmary cots.

When I entered the common area, Paul, Howie, Jan, and Kate were playing cards. They seemed fine, which made sense because they hadn't seen anything. They'd heard a scream, and I'd yelled at them. They'd all had more stressful days at the Mannaz School.

Pam and Novak looked up when they heard me. Pam had a listless look, and Novak appeared positively haunted. I felt a jab of guilt. I approached. I had no excuse for my late arrival. Coming up with something that wouldn't sound stupid or incredibly suspect was more than my frazzled mind could manage. I would improvise if I had to, but if no one brought it up, I'd leave it alone.

Novak said, "Sandy's on his way over. He'll want to talk to us about what happened."

"Okay," I said. "He's your friend. I'll let you do the talking."

Pam stood up then and touched my shoulder lightly. "Are you okay? You look peaked."

"Fine as paint," I said.

She looked at me for a moment longer and said, "I have to get back to the office." After a brief shoulder squeeze, she left.

I sat down gingerly in the seat she'd vacated. I winced a little.

Novak said quietly, "Not too bad for being mauled by a bear." His expression was wary.

"Fringe benefit." I didn't want to get into anything yet. I needed time to figure things out. Changing the subject seemed like a good idea. "What does the rest of the day look like?"

"The kids go to class starting second period. I relieve Terry from his subbing duties after we talk to Sandy. That's as far as I've gotten."

"Why don't you come over to my place after school?" I asked.

He hesitated, not long but long enough for me to notice. "Why don't we go to Lore? I could use a Pooka."

"Yeah, okay." Did Novak not want to be alone with me? We would have to drive together, right? I would defer my hurt feelings unless he suggested that we drive separately. "I guess we can sit at a table for some privacy."

# Chapter 23

I sat with Novak in Corman's office while he talked to Ed Sanders. Sanders wore a uniform that looked like a green version of a state trooper's. His campaign hat was perched on one knee. He was a blond, rawboned man with big, chapped knuckles and a bony chin and brow. He seemed pleasant enough, but something in his look made me think of primitive man. A hunter/gatherer type. He took notes as Novak told him our version of the bear encounter. Apparently, we'd waved our arms around and made a bunch of noise to scare it off. Trust Novak to create a no-frills, completely plausible account.

As with everyone I'd met from the area, Sanders seemed to have a friendly, respectful relationship with Novak. They were just a couple of old friends chatting for a bit. I might as well not have been there. I only sat and nodded at appropriate places in the narrative, which was just fine by me.

When the tale was finished, Sandy stood up and said, "I'll call in some guys to take a look in the area. I know where you're talking about. What you described isn't normal behavior for a bear, especially at this time of the year. I suggest you keep the kids out of the woods until I get back to you."

"Will do," Novak said.

Sandy shook his hand. Then, he shook mine. His eyes lingered on my face for a moment, and he said, "You look like you should take a rest. Maybe see a doc. Your color's bad."

"Thanks," I said. "I'll check in with our nurse."

Novak walked with Sandy to the door. I stayed where I was, but Moe followed them out. Sandy put on his hat. It was set forward shading his eyes, a strap anchored it on the back of his head. Sandy slapped him on the shoulder and said, "It's been too long, Connie. We got to get together soon."

"Give me a call in a few days. Things are a little crazy around here recently."

Sandy nodded and was about to turn away but stopped. He looked uncertain for a second and said, "That redheaded friend of yours?"

"Yeah?"

"We don't have a lot of hard drugs around about, but he's got that kind of look."

Novak smiled, but there was strain in it. "Naw, something's going around the school. The headmaster is actually at the hospital with it. I'll be sure he gets checked out, but I guarantee you it's not drugs."

They shook hands again, and Sandy walked out the door.

Novak took a deep breath and looked at the office door with clear trepidation. I couldn't help but to feel hurt. He'd known me for thirty years. That seemed like it should count for something. I suppose that it did. He was keeping my secret, at least for the time being. He was giving me a chance to explain myself. I was going to need to make some choices about that. You know, how much to tell and how to tell it.

He took another deep breath and returned to the office but only came as far as the door. He leaned on the doorframe affecting a casual air. I let him think that it fooled me. He said, "Well, I'm going to relieve Terry. There's no reason why he shouldn't have a few hours off."

"Okay. I'll find the bad-weather Halloween decorations in the theater. We'll Plan B it."

Novak continued to stand in the doorway. He was pretty clearly making a decision. "So, I've got some errands to run after school. Why don't I meet you at Lore at five or so?"

"Yeah. Okay." I felt a clenching in my chest. Maybe I was just expecting too much. You know, him not being afraid of me. Then again, Novak's friend Brannon had been a middle-aged teacher, not a vampire. Anyway, I could affect casual as well, and I did. "I'll see you then."

He turned and headed back to his classroom. I sat and felt sorry for myself.

When I was finished doing that, I pushed myself up from the chair. My back felt like one big knot, but the pain had receded a good deal. I could move normally if I thought about it. I took a couple of turns around the office. I didn't know what to do after that. I placed my hand on Corman's crystal ball hoping that it would provide comfort for me the way it did for him. Moe just picked up worry from Gramma. I had enough of that already. I tried to express some positive vibes to the ghost, but she wasn't fooled, and I knew it. Moe and I couldn't lie to ghosts.

Moe recommenced his patrol of the campus, and I went to the staff lounge for coffee. Not because I wanted coffee. I was just wandering, looking for solace in routine. "Making-a-pot-of-coffee" therapy. The bell rang for class change just as I was taking my first sip of indifferent coffee. I planned to drink it back in my room, but Allie came in before I'd quite made it out.

It was her prep period. She must have been on starting blocks to get to the lounge so quickly. Had she been looking for me? The concern on her face nearly broke my heart. Maybe she only felt concern because she didn't know I was a monster. I chose to believe that it wouldn't matter to Allie if she did know because I needed to believe it.

She walked directly to me and lay her hand on my cheek. "Are you okay? I heard something about a rabid bear on the Low Road. That's crazy, right?"

Her touch did something to me. I felt a relief, a comfort, and I really needed that. I put my hand over hers holding it more tightly against my face. Screw propriety. I said, "I don't think that bears are very prone to rabies."

"There really was a bear?"

"Yeah."

"But are you okay?"

There was tension in her face, real anxiety. Her warm brown eyes were shiny, and she'd squeezed her lips into a tight line.

"Yeah, I'm fine. Just a little scare."

She put her other hand on the other side of my face and examined me. I was glad that I still had my coffee mug in my hand then.

Otherwise, I might have kissed her or hugged her or both. She said, "You don't look good. Has Missy had a look at you?"

"No."

"Go see her."

"I'm fine."

She sighed. "He-man, Ugg." She dropped her hands. "Try to get some rest or something. I know it's close to Halloween, but you'll scare the kids if you go walking around looking the way you do."

I was going to protest, but she poked me in the chest. "Get some rest. I'll cover your creative writing class." She was trying to look tough, but I could still see the shine in her eyes. She was worried for me. She cared.

At that moment, I felt a terrible fear that she would find out what I was and would look at me the way Novak had. Like I was some kind of wild animal that might bite or a leper who might infect. I wasn't going to see Missy or a doctor. I wasn't going to take a nap either, but I might lie about that. Allie had a point. My appearance was drawing attention, and the Talamaur, as a rule, don't like to draw attention.

I said, "Thank you, Allie. I'll head to my apartment now."

I was going to dump my coffee in the sink, but Allie took it from me. "Get out of here already."

I got. After snagging a big, black garbage bag from the custodial closet, I did actually go back to my apartment but not to nap. I needed to find some way to reset my system. I didn't know exactly how to do that, but the situation warranted some experimentation.

I still felt some nagging discomfort at the small of my back, but the pain was mostly gone. But my body felt heavy, lethargic. The energy I'd taken from Novak seemed to have gone specifically to my injuries, but something was still off. There was a weakness that was not simply from a middle-aged body pushed to its limits. I needed to get more lifeforce and hope that it went where I needed it. I didn't think that waiting around for a leaky juice box to have a tantrum was a safe bet, so I prepared to go out.

I stuffed my ruined clothes into the garbage bag. Only a little blood had gotten onto the linoleum, and that came up with Windex and a paper towel. I knotted the bag closed and left it by the door.

Galen's magic bag didn't fit into the bomber jacket's inside pocket as well as in the fleece's, but it did fit.

I tossed the bag of ruined clothes into the Nova's trunk, noting that the debris from Noah's storeroom ceiling was still there. It was easy to lose track of things like that. Since I was going in to Geary, I'd get rid of it there. Yeah, I was going to Geary to do some day-drinking. A couple of different kinds.

There was no way for me to rationalize preying on one human over another without acknowledging the whole "playing God" thing, so I didn't try. I'd taken a gamble on Novak because I was in a desperate spot. Now, I was just choosing. I would still be as careful as I could be. I didn't want to hurt anyone. I would just be gambling with the lives of strangers, or even better, people whom I didn't like. Real bad guys were the best, but I wasn't sure where to find them.

I pulled Moe from guard duty. I would need him. There was nothing I could do about that.

My first stop was The Bar. The place opened at 11 for the lunch crowd though few people actually ate there. Moe scouted ahead while I drove the Nova along 19A. There were actually quite a few people there, most at the bar and a few at tables. Some were actually eating too. Dylan and Cody weren't among them. Yeah, in the universal scheme of things, being offensive to Allie wasn't a big deal. That didn't keep them off my shit list, though. I'd have to find another likely candidate. It turned out to be pretty easy.

When I maneuvered the Nova through the rutted parking lot, the old guys at the bar who had a view out the window started up about me. Again, in the universal scheme, not a big deal, but I was looking for an excuse to target someone.

A weathered old guy with a straggly beard said to Bob, "It's Con Novak's faggy friend, but Con ain't with him."

Bob said, "Go easy on the fags. I met a couple in Olean once. They were nice, even bought me a drink."

"They's prob'ly just trying to get you drunk. You know how they are. I think they all oughta be shot. It says so in the Bible."

"The Bible talks about shootin' people?" Bob asked, crossing his arms across his chest.

The old man scoffed. "They used rocks or somethin' back then."

Bob said, "Henry, opinions are like assholes, and I'm sick of yours. It stinks."

"It's a free country."

"We'll my bar ain't, so shut up or get out."

Henry shook his head sadly. "I never took you for liberal, Bob." He said liberal with withering disdain.

Bob didn't respond but moved to the taps to draw a Genny for another customer.

I was surprised to have an improved opinion of Bob. I'd never felt one way or the other about him before. He'd just seemed like a Geary guy, but at least he didn't hate gay people for being gay. Point one to Bob.

I left two stools between Henry and I when I sat down at the bar. I didn't want to scare him away with my apparent gayness. His eyes did shift nervously in my direction. He was obviously a narrow-minded idiot, but I couldn't help but to wonder what it was about me that made him think I was gay. What with my sickly appearance and all, he probably thought I had some contagious gay disease.

Bob asked, "What'll it be?"

"Double Jim Beam on the rocks."

My drink was deftly assembled and placed in front of me on a napkin. Napkins were not a regular part of service at The Bar, and I wondered if Bob was trying to be especially nice to me.

Moe can draw lifeforce quickly or slowly. I'd never really tried to be extreme about it. I didn't see that it made much difference. I was going to try for slow this time around. Maybe I'd have a sense of how much was enough or could maybe tell how the energy was being used. I didn't want to get young. I just wanted to look less consumptive.

I took a sip of bourbon. Then, I took a sip of Henry. I imagined him as an IV bag instead of a juice box, just drip drip dripping. Lifeforce doesn't have a flavor or compatible types or anything. Men, women, young, old, black, white, Christian, Muslim: they were all the same to me. Well, that's what I'd thought before the drop from Corman anyway. Boy, that had some zing.

284

Different people did respond differently to being fed upon, though. Some became extremely sick to their stomachs or developed horrible headaches. Others barely noticed anything. I know that it reflects badly on me to say that I was disappointed to find that Henry was one of the oblivious kind. I didn't want to really hurt him or anything, but making him ralph in the parking lot might have given me a certain satisfaction. Bigots bring that out in me.

The mirror behind the bar was handy. I took a bit of life from Henry and waited, sipping my drink and looking at my reflection. Despite his clearly not liking me, the old man showed no signs of vacating his stool, so I continued to take my time, just little sips. About halfway through my second double Jim Beam, I could clearly see that I had better color, the gray fading away. The dark circles had lessened as well. When I saw the wrinkles around my eyes begin to fill in, I stopped and hoped the process didn't continue. It didn't. Not much anyway. My intake had been gradual enough to monitor effectively. My gamble seemed a success.

I stood up from the barstool and found that the pain of my strained back was gone. I gave Bob enough money for my drinks and a good tip. I hoped that Henry wouldn't keel over in the next couple of days, but I couldn't muster up a great deal of concern. Physically, I felt much better, and that actually helped my mood too.

Bob said to me before I walked to the door, "Looks like you really needed them drinks."

"I really did." I waved and said, "Have a good day."

Bob said, "You too."

Henry grunted discontentedly.

After a diner lunch at Bettie's, I went back to Mannaz. I suppressed the urge to go to Lore and drink until Novak showed up. It would only be four hours or so, but I didn't want anyone to think I was a lush. That was a good sign, you know, that I still cared.

Noah had left the school truck parked behind the theater, waiting for someone to unload the Haunted Forest gear and put it back in the scene shop. I was so inspired by my lack of pain that I obliged. I stowed the boxes back in their place. Then, I found the more-fragile indoor decorations in their loft storage area and hauled them down. I went ahead and loaded them in the truck, but I decided not to take them to Oak House where the party would be held. I didn't want to get caught with whiskey on my breath. I didn't want Allie to catch me at all, especially after I'd let her believe that I was going to rest up.

I went back to my apartment to think some things through. Restlessness tugged at me to go somewhere, but with the help of the Gibson, I managed to settle in. Strumming familiar chord progressions and riffing in familiar scales provided a backdrop to my thoughts. Thoughts of my other life overlapping my current one.

Reasonable or not, Novak's wariness toward me made me feel less inclined to share my story with him. Over the years, I'd often imagined what it would feel like to let my new friend know who I really was. I envisioned a feeling of liberation, an unburdening. My hypothetical reveal had clearly been much too optimistic. Novak was a good man, a smart man, but his thinking probably wouldn't be flexible enough to deal with this other reality. I had to tell him as little as I could. It was the Talamaur way after all. We were enigmas. Cue dark, dramatic orchestral score.

The real source of Talamaurs' power came from the acquisition of information. Information could be extremely valuable. Sure, any Talamaur could win virtually any Olympic event, but that put us nowhere near the top of the supernatural dogpile of strength and speed. No, we were superspies with the finest means of surveillance connected directly to our brains. A few creatures were able to sense a familiar, and a mage or group of mages could set up wards to bar familiars or fields to sense them. Otherwise, we could watch and listen to anyone or anything. Letting anyone know who we are and what we can do would lessen our effectiveness and make us potential targets. Thus, the secrecy.

Obviously, many in the supernatural community knew of our existence. Our specific powers, though, tended to be more legendary, matters of supposition. As a people, we were known to adhere to a specific set of ethics regarding the use of information, and our usefulness tended to win us potent allies if we treated them right. See? We don't want the community to know much about us except that we're useful and that we are people of our word.

With that in mind, naïve scenarios of telling Novak all about myself were dismissed, and I got down to my checklist. What did Novak know? One, he had seen me fight the bear which involved some impressive speed and strength. Not many people could clear twenty feet in a long jump, but maybe he hadn't seen that very clearly. He'd definitely witnessed me overpowering the animal by main strength. It certainly wasn't from the cartoony wrestling moves. Two, I actually told him that I was a vampire, pretty clearly not the blood-drinking kind. Three, he knew that I'd been injured, and in short order, I wasn't anymore. Four, Moe had slapped him and taken his phone away.

Was there anything else? That was all I could remember. I strummed an Em7. Then, an A7. Then, a Dmaj7. I thought some more. Nope. That was all. I absently strummed the progression a few more times, but I pretty much had my script set for my conversation with Novak. To celebrate, I decided that I would have some beers and flirt with Jeannie. It's the small things, you know.

I left Moe to his regular patrol of the school. He never showed any signs of dissatisfaction or fatigue, but that didn't seem to keep me from feeling a little guilty for keeping him on constant guard duty. It was entirely possible that I was feeling bad for myself because relying on my mundane senses for long periods of time caused me a bit of emotional strain. Sure, he was my security blanket, but in a real, practical way, being without him blunted the best edge I had for basic survival.

The Nova and I headed toward Lore, and Moe checked on certain people before recommencing his regular rounds. I wouldn't say that the crisp air and color-splashed trees were entirely lost on me, but I wasn't in much of a mood for aesthetic delight.

When I pulled into the parking lot, even the familiar and much-loved sight of Lore was spoiled a little, definitely off kilter. As the gravel of the lot crunched under my shoes, a gallery of faces fanned through my mind. Imagination isn't always a pleasant thing. It showed me Jeannie, Coop, and even Vernon wearing expressions just like the one on Novak's face before he'd marshalled his resources to face me alone in Corman's office. Fear, trepidation, disgust.

I knew that everyone in Geary wasn't the same. Everyone wouldn't react the same way, would they? I wondered who would hate me because of what I was and not who I was. My brain just wouldn't stop speculating.

Jeannie waved and called out to me when I came through the door. Her smile was warm and wide. Vernon and a middle-aged couple sat at the bar. They looked over their shoulders to see who was arriving. Vernon waved as well.

I was very aware of my role: the good-natured teacher of difficult children, the flirt, the musician, the lover of beer. None of those things were incorrect. I was the same guy I'd been all along. At that moment, though, thoughts of my other nature eclipsed it all. I wasn't a complete fraud, but I was lying by omission.

After taking a moment to settle myself, I built my own smile and strode toward the bar. I would enjoy the nearly two hours I had before my meeting with Novak. There was no reason not to. I exchanged smiles and waves with a number of familiar patrons who were scattered among the tables.

Then, the magic of Lore happened. I drank a Red Cap, a Boggart Brown, and a Green Man IPA. I flirted with Jeannie. I met the couple who were from New England and visiting family in the area. I talked to Vernon and the couple, mostly about the similarities between western and detective fiction. Somewhere along the way, something unclenched inside of me, and I breathed a little easier. Abracadabra!

The downside of relaxing was the more-extreme beartrap kind of feeling I had when the door opened and Jeannie called out, "Conrad! Come join us."

Two hours had passed. I'd been lulled by companionship and beer into forgetting my troubles. My brain took a disoriented moment to recollect my script. To remind myself what I would tell Novak and what I would keep to myself. To center myself.

I pasted on my smile and turned along with the others at the bar to see Novak walk toward the bar. The couple offered to move down to give Novak room to sit next to me, but he said, "We're going to be taking a table tonight."

Jeannie made a funny face and said, "Whaaaat?" She drew out the vowel extra-long. "You guys always sit at the bar."

"We've got some stuff to talk about," he said. There was no meanness in his tone, but neither was there any friendliness. It was flat and cold as a tombstone. The joking expression on Jeannie's face faded and turned moderately puzzled.

I was suddenly pissed at Novak for spoiling my pub experience. For bringing this stupid conversation here when it should have been private. If he was really so afraid of me, why not have this talk at The Bar or the Silver Creek where he would have more redneck friends to protect him from me? It's not as though he could spoil those places for me. I hated seeing Jeannie's expression change like that. I hated Novak's lack of faith in me. My feelings of betrayal, sadness, and fear were quickly turning to anger.

I reined all of it in and locked it away. Deception was in my nature. At that moment, I accepted that my whole "out of practice" schtick was bullshit. I wasn't out of practice being a Talamaur. I was in denial. I liked being Sean Brannon, the benign teacher and nurturer of children, but I couldn't stop being a Talamaur. Whatever I eventually became, that would always be part of me.

See? I was so good at deception that I had even deceived myself. All things come to an end, so the saying goes, even my delusions it seemed.

Vacating my stool, I said to everyone at the bar, "Thanks for the craic!" I made an open-mouthed, "waiting-for-the-applause" face.

The couple just stared at me. Jeannie and Vernon shook their heads simultaneously both wearing small smiles.

Vernon said to the couple, "Craic is Irish for pleasant companionship. He uses that line on new people."

"You're welcome," said the woman.

The man said, "No problem."

I shook hands with the man and woman and settled my bill with Jeannie after I'd ordered an Old Shuck for me and a Pooka Pale for Novak. On a whim I also settled the tabs for the couple and Vernon. I gave Jeannie an absurdly big tip.

Holding up the cash, her eyes a little wide, she said, "Are you sure?"

"Of course." If I'd been a stranger, she'd probably have been more reluctant to take it, but no one in the Geary area was rich. Well, except me, but no one knew that.

I picked up my pint of roasty, black lager and headed for a corner table. Novak followed.

I sat with my back to the wall so that I could see the room. Novak sat across from me. His eyes flicked toward my face briefly then settled on his pint of beer. He didn't say anything and began to turn his glass in slow circles. I considered waiting him out, making him begin, but I couldn't think of what the point would be. I'd indulged my emotions quite a lot in the last few decades which was all well and good, but I was now grooving on the emotional distance thing. I would figure out if it was healthy for me later. Now, I was just going to get through this. . . thing.

"What do you want to know?" I asked.

He didn't answer right away. He sighed, and with his eyes still fastened on his beer, he asked, "Did you hurt Joe?"

*Fuck you!* I thought. I didn't say it, and I didn't pause more than a beat before saying, "No." I drank then followed up with an observation. "So, you're a Geary guy after all."

He spoke quietly, but there was heat in it. "What the hell does that mean?"

"You're judging me based upon my race and not the content of my character. It's a good thing that I'm not Muslim too, maybe gay."

"I don't care about that stuff."

"Really?"

"Vampires eat people."

"Really? How are you feeling, Con?"

He took another of those flickering looks at my face. Then, back to the beer that he still hadn't tasted. "I felt sick to my stomach."

"How about now?"

He shrugged a little.

"Just because you watched the *Blade* movies doesn't make you a vampire expert."

"So, tell me about it."

"I don't have to kill anyone if that's what you want to know." I didn't have to tell him that people did occasionally die. "You experienced the process first-hand and don't seem the worse for wear."

He was quiet again. Another kind of person would be eaten up with curiosity. I guess that he was more of a sports and politics guy. I drank more beer while waiting for him to form another question.

"Do you know what happened to Joe?"

Novak was certainly loyal to Corman and really concerned for him. There was no denying that. I considered lying but didn't.

"A monster got him."

He looked at me for longer this time. "Are you serious?"

"Yeah. The little creep would have taken out a bunch of kids too if I hadn't stopped him."

"So, you're a hero vampire?"

"Yeah. Nick Knight and I."

"From that Canadian cop show?"

I didn't figure that I really needed to answer, so I drank instead.

Novak asked, "Can you help him? Joe, I mean."

"I tried, but I don't know if it'll take."

I saw the muscles in his jaw bunch before he asked, "Did you kill it? The monster?"

"No, but I drove it away."

"Can it come back?"

I didn't feel like going into details if I didn't have to. Basically, he wanted to know if there was a potential supernatural threat to the school. I decided to treat Melk and Doru as one entity. Melk couldn't come back, in theory at least, but Doru could. Why not keep it simple?

"Yeah."

"Why don't you leave? Then, the monsters would have no reason to come here."

That hurt despite my best effort to maintain emotional distance. Leaps of logic aside, my friend of thirty years wanted me to go. He clearly blamed me for the strange things going on lately, and he seemed to have no desire to understand me. How could I have misjudged him so badly?

I kept my voice flat which took some effort. "The monster who hurt Joe didn't know I was here."

"Why did he come then?"

"He wanted to hurt kids, and we had some."

"And that kind of thing just happens all the time?" He was a little louder.

"Sometimes."

I wanted more beer. Mine was empty. Novak's was still full. I considered asking him if I could have it.

Novak brought his fist down on the table and spat, "Why?"

The action and vehemence took me by surprise, and I flinched just a little. It seemed that Novak had been suppressing his emotions too.

"As far as I know, it's always been that way."

He sneered. "And no one has ever noticed?"

"Humans can't know about us. If they find out, it's bad for them. Monsters don't advertise."

"You would know."

I stood and said, "I'm getting another beer while you get yourself together."

He stared at me flatly. I'd seen worse. I was the scapegoat. He didn't seem to want to understand me, just blame me.

I paid Jeannie for another Red Cap.

"Is everything okay over there?" she asked, worry clear on her face and in her tone.

"No," I said and smiled sadly. "I appreciate your concern, but your worry won't help anything. I'm sorry that we brought this here. I'll try to wrap it up soon."

She bobbed her head once and said, "Okay, Sean. Thanks."

Novak was talking on his phone as I approached. He looked close to tears, his face ready to collapse. His hand visibly trembled. I thought he might actually drop his phone. My resolve to be distant began to soften. We'd been friends for a long time, and he did have an awful lot to deal with lately.

292

Something happened then which was completely unprecedented as far as I knew. So of course, I was unprepared to deal with it.

A sudden jolt of panic caused me to spill half of my beer, but I didn't drop the glass. Moe hadn't expressed distress, but I reacted to what happened to him. Things didn't normally happen to him at all. He observed. I was used to him observing and completing simple errands for me. Things didn't happen to him.

When Doru's familiar and its ghosts pounced on him as he made his rounds of the school, it shocked the hell out of me. Familiars can't sneak up on each other. Could they? I would figure how that happened later.

I sensed Moe's attempt to struggle against his attackers, but something had immobilized him. I knew that familiars could be barred from places, but immobilized? I tried to will him from his paralysis, but I only managed to shake more violently, sloshing more beer onto my sleeve and the floor.

I don't know how long I stood there, straining against whatever was happening to my familiar, but eventually, I felt a hand on my shoulder. Jeannie had come to stand beside me and eased the pint glass from my hand. She put it on an empty table. Taking my wet hand in hers, she tried to maneuver me onto a chair.

I took a couple of steps with her before I was able to get ahold of myself and start processing again. I said quietly, "No. I'm okay. I have to go."

She released my hand reluctantly, and I hurried over to Novak. Adrenaline made me quiver, and I tried to still myself. I needed self-control, but the thing with Moe was terrifying, a threat to the core of who and what I was.

Novak stood stunned, looking at the screen of his phone. His mouth worked silently for a moment. When he looked up at me, he said, "The hospital said that Joe is bad. He's dying."

The clamp that tightened on my chest threated the calm façade I'd been presenting. I'd feared this would happen, but I guess I'd been harboring more hope than I thought. I'd seen a lot of friends die over the years, but it was never a casual experience. Flying apart wouldn't help anyone, so I pushed everything into its appropriate compartment and spoke calmly.

"Something's happened at the school. We have to get back now."

His eyes focused on my face, and his jaw tightened. Through clenched teeth, he said, "Did you hear what I said?"

"I did, Con. It sucks, but something bad is about to happen at the school, and we're needed there."

He didn't shout at me, not quite. But it was loud, and people were already watching us. "What? Do you have some fucking vampire-sense or something?"

I quickly closed the space between us, grabbed him by the front of his shirt, and jacked him against the wall. Buttons popped. I was faster than he could track, and he hadn't been able to react in the least.

His look of shock turned to rage in half a second. His position was off. I was too close, but he swung his right fist in an awkward roundhouse. Even without Moe, my reflexes are fast. I caught his fist. The impact jolted me, but I didn't show it. He tried to yank free, but I squeezed and twisted, straightening his whole arm and threatening to hyperextend his elbow.

I might not know how to fight a bear, but I had plenty of experience with men.

I thought that the hold would be enough to subdue him, but he jabbed his left fist into my side, just below my floating ribs. He wasn't able to get a lot of power into it, but it still hurt. Once again, I was able to downplay the pain. Since I was out of hands and didn't want to let him go, I pulled him six inches from the wall and slammed him against it again. He rapped the back of his head a good one, and his teeth clacked together.

While he was a little dazed, I hissed into his ear. "Calm the fuck down, dammit, and listen to me. If you tell anyone about me being a vampire, monsters right out of a horror movie will show up and rip you into pieces."

His eyes came into focus again, and he glared at me. "Are you threatening me?"

"I'll have nothing to do with it," I said. "That won't stop them from killing you and maybe Christie, too. Anyone you tell will be in danger."

Novak was clearly not used to being manhandled, and I could see that he didn't want to yield. That was more pride than I was used to seeing in him, but bringing Christie into it seemed to get through to him.

He said, "Let me down."

I said, "You take a swing at me again, and I'll stop being nice."

He nodded once, and I released him.

He wouldn't look at me, but I stayed close, crowding him. I wanted to be sure to make an impression. "If you tell anyone about my nature, you will be killed along with whomever you tell. I won't hurt you or Christie, but I can't protect you from what will come for you." I took a slow breath and said, "You were a good friend, Con."

Without Moe, I could only see what was in front of me with my mundane eyes. I pretty much knew what I was going to see when I turned around, though. Every eye in the place was on us. Someone, probably Jeannie, had gone downstairs and gotten Coop. He hadn't yet stepped in, but I saw that he had gotten halfway across the room on his way toward us.

I headed toward the door. When I came abreast of Coop, I said, "Sorry, Coop. I didn't want to bring this here."

I didn't give him time to respond and continued on my way. I would have spoken to Jeannie if I could have, but I wasn't going to change course. I walked out the door without a look behind me. Having Novak by my side when I faced Doru would have been a comfort, but that didn't seem to be in the cards. Somehow, Doru had tied up Moe. I could still see and hear what my familiar could, but he was helpless to do anything. The other familiar and its ghosts had done something I'd never even heard of before let alone seen. One familiar had ambushed and paralyzed another.

I knew, without a doubt, that Melk was behind it, and I regretted like hell not killing him when I had the chance.

Being proactive seemed prudent, so once inside the Nova, I took out Galen's magic bag. I said, "Eladoon." Instantly, I felt the presence of Fetann through the open portal. There was some measure of comfort in that. I withdrew the sword, the .38, and a box of ammo. The ammo went into my left coat pocket. After I checked the cylinder of the revolver, that went into my right coat pocket. I hadn't practiced for years, and hoped that I would be able to hit the broad side of a barn. If I had Moe to guide my hand, it wouldn't matter, but I didn't. Fetann lay thrumming on the seat beside me. It'd been even longer since I'd practiced any blade-work.

Novak hadn't come out of the building yet, and I resigned myself to going it alone. If I kept moving, I wouldn't get weighed down in the significance of all of the crap going on. The Nova started easily, almost as if she were eager to go. I drove faster than I should have without Moe's perceptions, but I needed to protect my familiar, my kids, and my friends.

# Chapter 24

I scanned the adjacent fields for deer as best I could, but the headlights revealed little that wasn't right ahead of me. When I'd covered half the distance back to school, I felt my phone buzz in my pocket. I wasn't going to try to wrestle it out while speeding along a dark, country road. The damn thing made me crazy, though, because it just kept ringing. My anxiety began to creep again. I almost pulled over to answer the call, but the need to rescue Moe was first in my mind. I would deal with other things later.

I forced myself to slow down when I reached the Mannaz driveway. Running over students wouldn't help anything. Admittedly, I drove faster than ten, but it was a lot slower than I wanted to go. The extra time helped me to remind myself that Moe was probably bait for a trap of some kind. Bait and hostage combined.

Before I was able to cut the engine after parking in my usual space, I saw movement in the rearview mirror of the Nova. It was Allie jogging toward the car. The tails of her unbuttoned overcoat flapped behind her. She stopped short of the back bumper to give me room to climb out. The door popped and groaned open. My eyes darted to the sheathed sword on the seat. Moving to hide it now would just draw attention to it, so I left in in plain view hoping that she wouldn't notice it. The gun and ammo felt heavy and bulky in my pockets.

She began hurriedly speaking before I could even straighten up, let alone close the door. "Isn't Howie with you?" She didn't wait for a response. "Maggie said that she saw him go off with you toward the Low Road trailhead, but Con said that no one was supposed to go into the woods because of the bear. I tried to call you both, but no one would answer."

I took her by the shoulders firmly and said, "Slow down. He's not with me. When did Maggie see him?"

Her eyes were actually jittering, like spasming. "Uhm, just before the dinner bell."

I let go of her, and she began to lean toward me before getting ahold of herself. I held my watch up to the lamppost so I could see the time. 6:13. I said, "So, he's only been gone about twenty minutes."

"But he left with you going toward the woods where the bear was! And you're here. Who's he really with?"

Her agitation was contagious. I could feel it crawling up my spine and tightening everything up. I shoved it all away and kept a calm voice and a composed expression.

I asked, "Maggie actually saw me with Howie? She's sure it was me?" Could Melk have broken his word and returned with his shapeshifting routine?

"She said that she saw you from down the driveway and that you waved to her."

"It wasn't me."

"Then, who?"

I was suddenly aware of Moe moving but not of his own power. Doru's familiar was towing him like a tugboat pulls a barge, only much faster. They zipped along the Low Road toward the clearing halfway around the loop. It seemed that my familiar and my student had gone in the same direction. Following Moe would probably lead me to Howie. I just needed to get rid of Allie. I wanted to comfort her, but there was no time.

I said, "Go back to Oak House. If he's going to return on his own, that's where he'll go. Keep trying to reach Conrad. He may be headed to the hospital. Joe's taken a bad turn."

"Oh, no!" Her hand rose to cover her mouth.

I didn't think that her face could have looked any tenser, but I was wrong. Too much was being dumped on her shoulders. She was a young second-year teacher, and I was leaning on her pretty hard.

"Has Pam gone home yet?"

"I don't think so."

Good. I said, "Let her know what's going on. The office will make a good command center. Also, tell Terry. He's solid. I've got an idea about where Howie might be. I'll get back to you as soon as I look into it."

She seemed heartened to have specific tasks before her. She looked no less tense, but she was less jittery. More focused.

Impulsively, I kissed her lightly on the mouth and said, "Go on. Let me see if I can fix this."

"Thanks, Sean." She turned and jogged back toward Oak House, her coattails flapping.

I zipped up my jacket and made sure that the pockets were securely fastened. I didn't want the gun or the ammo to bounce out as I ran. Then, I reached into the Nova's front seat and took out Fetann. Its scabbard had no frog, and I wouldn't have wanted to mess with it if it had. I just gripped it in my left hand and took off. I didn't go full out because it was dark, and I didn't want to twist my ankle or something without Moe to guide me. I moved pretty damn fast, though.

Only moments after his capture, Moe had begun flipping through power frequencies so that he might learn something about whatever bound him. He'd found that he wasn't actually paralyzed, simply imprisoned in a sort of force field. At his normal density, he'd seemed unable to move, but familiars can contract and expand a great deal becoming more or less dense. If he contracted, he could move around within his prison though he'd found no way to escape it.

I could still see through his perceptions, and what I saw almost made me despair. Doru stood in the clearing on the side of the path opposite Mannaz property. He held Howie by the back of the neck. The boy stood on tiptoes to relieve the pressure and trembled visibly. The collars of both his field jacket and his button-down shirt were torn, and a drying blood-trail ran from his nose and down his chin. At some point he must have tried to run for it. Up close, he would have recognized that Doru wasn't me.

The charade was clear now. Doru wore jeans and a brown leather jacket over a green sweater vest. He hadn't changed his trendy hair style, but he'd used something to whiten the short-buzzed hair over his temples. I could see how the deception would have worked at a distance, especially when the sky was darkening.

Melk was there as well, all black-skinned and orange-eyed. His dark red tunic, gray leggings, and low black boots were tailored to his true form. The long knife that had cut so easily through my classroom floor hung openly from his wide, black belt. Gold dust had created the harlequin mask shape of his true-seeing spell, and it became quickly apparent that he was responsible for Moe's predicament. The goblin made a couple of gestures, and Moe moved toward them and rose from near the ground to Doru's eye level. It was unnecessary. I could see just fine before, but the drama of it was supposed to get my attention.

Doru smiled unpleasantly at Moe and me. He said, "This is your own fault, Caomhnóir. You should have just given me what I wanted when I wanted it. You thought you were better than me, but now, you'll learn how wrong you were."

He lifted Howie by his neck and shook him a little. The boy's grimace was his only expression of pain. His bravery inspired me to keep my head. He weighed a hundred pounds, which was a lot to straight-arm, but Doru must have thought that the spectacle was worth the extra effort. He clearly wanted Howie to react more strongly, and tightened his grip. Howie whimpered, added strain clear on his face. Frightened as he was, he also looked exhausted. He must have struggled hard when he'd tried to get away.

Doru said, "I have your Achilles' heel right here, cousin. My associate has the proxy paperwork waiting for you to sign, too."

The cowardice of the two gloating monsters kindled a hatred in me deeper than any I could remember. I wanted to kill them, but not quickly like putting down a rabid dog. I wanted them to regret what they'd done. I wasn't naïve enough to believe that their regret would be moral. But I wanted them to regret ever crossing me, harming what was mine to protect. I trembled with it, the desire to mete out retribution for their transgressions.

But even if I could take the two of them, which was highly questionable, the fight would definitely put Howie in greater danger. I sure as hell didn't want to sign over my vote. But whatever crap Doru had planned with the Venetor measure wasn't worth Howie's life, not to me anyway. I wouldn't go in guns-blazing. I would swallow my pride and sign the fucking papers. They'd win in the short-term, but I'd get them for it later. I had time. And if Soulis, the red cap, was the one holding their leashes, I'd get him too. I didn't care how scary the fucker was.

I stopped running long enough to get my anger in hand. I needed to be level-headed, to think before acting. Howie was too important to endanger more than he already was.

I jogged into sight of the clearing. The night was fairly bright with moonlight and star-shine, but that didn't matter a great deal because everyone but Howie had supernatural sight of a sort. At least I did once I came into range of Moe's perceptions. I still held the sword, but I carried it in its sheath at my side, the most non-threatening a way that a person could carry a sword in his hand.

I must have been closer than they expected because both of them started a little as I neared. Melk raised the taloned fingers of his right hand and began muttering a second later. The little shit was casting a spell. In a fraction of a second, I instinctively grabbed the sword's hilt and began to draw. I might have gotten it clear, but I checked the movement instead. I would not meet aggression with aggression. Howie's life was at stake.

I stood frozen, Fetann's blade half-way clear of the scabbard, when five beams of orange light shot from Melk's splayed fingers. Each beam struck one of my limbs, both wrists and ankles, and also my neck. The light encircled them and somehow became solid, like steel covered in warm buzzing foam. Instinctively I strained against them and didn't budge them a millimeter.

With a flick of his wrist, I was spread-eagle and floating in the air five feet from the ground. Fetann slipped from my grasp as my arms were jerked wide. It lay in the tall, dry grass, its partially exposed blade glimmering faintly.

So much for good faith. But if they needed me bound and helpless, I would do it to save Howie. I have pride, but I've gone a long way toward taming it. I'd lick the mud from their boots if I had to.

After leaving me to hang for a few seconds, Melk giggled, then he twiddled and flicked his fingers, making me dance in the air. At first, I tried to resist, but it was useless, so I conserved my strength, letting my limbs move like a marionette's. Being jerked around by one's extremities causes a great deal of strain on connective tissue and muscles trying to compensate for unnatural movement. It wasn't a fun kind of dancing.

Melk was pretty clearly having a grand time of it, as payment for being my slingshot target while trapped in my classroom, no doubt. His cackling laughter accompanied first the squat-and-kick part of the Russian Hopak dance, then a Rockette routine. He began to dance along as well, which caused me to be wrenched around even more aggressively.

After an Irish jig and some kind of a variation on the Charleston, Doru shouted, "That's enough."

Melk ceased my movements but gave Doru a look that showed clear disdain. My cousin may have been in charge of this particular operation, but the goblin certainly didn't feel subservient.

The goblin said to Doru, "What? Has it been too long since you were the center of attention?"

My breath was coming harshly from my activity, but I wanted to get this situation back on track and finished as soon as possible. Between breaths, I said, "What's all this?" My eyes flicked to my magical bonds. "It'll be hard for me to sign proxy papers like this."

Doru took a few steps nearer to me, but we were still fifteen feet apart. He dragged Howie along with him which was better than being held in the air by his neck. The boy grunted and whimpered but tried gamely to keep his feet. His eyes were red from crying which I hadn't heard.

Howie looked up at me, blood on his mouth and chin, tears on his cheeks, and bruises beginning to darken under his eyes. In a rough whisper, he said, "Mr. Brannon, are you okay?"

I blinked hard, but that didn't stop the tears that ran down my own cheeks. Even after being abused and terrorized by fairytale monsters, Howie was concerned for me. This kid needed to survive. He had to. He's where hope came from.

My voice cracked just a little. "I'm okay. We'll be done here in just a minute."

"Somebody, call Hallmark," Doru sing-songed while wiping away imaginary tears with his free hand.

Melk stayed where he was, his hand held before him to keep me still and hovering. The spell was obviously potent, not for magical lightweights, but he showed no signs of strain. He could be acting, or he could be strong. I went with strong.

Doru puffed up his chest and looked me in the eye. He said, "You are such a pussy. The great Caomhnóir, Scathlann's favorite. Crying like a baby just because I get a little rough with your pet. It's not like you don't have more."

"His name's Howie."

"I don't care." Doru must have squeezed Howie's neck again because the boy hissed in pain.

"Do no harm to the boy," I said. "And I'll sign the papers. There's no need for this."

"What?" Doru said. "You're not going to condescend to me? Tell me what a degenerate I am? Immoral? Unable to understand decency?" He batted his eyelashes at me.

I'd gotten used to his reptilian smile, but the eyelash thing was unnerving on a whole other level, like a psychotic coquette. A thousand and one biting retorts came to mind. I had only to point out what he was doing at that very moment to support every characterization I'd ever made of him. Predators were predators, but they didn't have to be petty and cruel. Doru knew what I thought of him. There was no need to rehash any of it, so I simply said, "No. You win. Let the boy go in safety, and I'll sign the papers."

A muscle in Doru's cheek twitched. He didn't look shocked, not quite, but a little confused and at a loss. This clearly wasn't how he expected things to play out, and he didn't know what to do. Simply taking what I offered didn't seem good enough because he wanted more. He wanted to hurt me.

He said over his shoulder to Melk, "Do you hear this guy? What's his game?"

If he expected Melk to support further conflict, he'd misjudged.

The goblin said, "Yeah, he said you won. I guess you won. Just give me the word, and I'll let him down to sign the papers."

"I'm in charge here," Doru shouted. His hand must have clenched on Howie's neck again because the boy yelped.

"Let the boy go," I said. "He's too scared to run."

"Quit telling me what to do!" he snarled. Spit flew from his mouth.

But then, Doru's smile widened, like to Joker dimensions. I knew my cousin was mean, and I knew he was stupid. The smile was those things, but it was also crazy. Mean, stupid crazy.

"I've got a whole school full of these." He held Howie up one-handed again. It must have hurt the boy, but I think that Howie was too worn out, too numb to show it. Doru gave him a little shake and said, "He's not the whole show. That's why I think he'll make a good object lesson."

"No, Doru!" I didn't know what he was going to do specifically, but I knew it would be bad.

Melk's eyes flicked to Doru nervously. The tension in my bonds decreased slightly. He said quietly, "Soulis isn't going to like this. We've got what we wanted. Just let him sign the papers, and we'll leave. It's the smart play."

"You're not smarter than me!" Doru screamed. More spit flew. Then, his crazy smile returned.

Melk's eyes found mine and stayed there longer this time. The wheels were turning. He was calculating. He was clearly a bad guy, but he was smart and, in this case, practical. Hope began to grow in me. Maybe I could win an ally if I worked it right. I was about to make a play to Melk when Doru made a comment which was meant to sound offhand. But it made a shudder run through me.

"My old ghost is getting pretty tired, I think. I need a new one, young and full of spirit. Hang on, just a minute. Look what I've got!" He patted Howie's head with his free hand.

"No!" I barked. Then, in a more even tone, I said, "If you hurt the boy, the deal is off."

A Talamaur can only subjugate a new ghost, freshly dead. Usually, the ghost is the victim of a feeding. The familiar empties the victim, and before the ghost can depart, the familiar binds the ghost to it. The ghosts typically struggle. Some stories actually claim that ghosts have escaped, but those stories have the flavor of legend. I'd never heard any verifiable account. No, the ghosts would be slowly drained much like their bodies had been drained until nothing but a memory remained. It might take several years, depending on the ghost, but the end would be the same.

I said, very distinctly, each consonant clipped, "If you hurt that boy, I will never sign those papers."

"Ha!" Doru gave Howie a jiggle. "There are so many more. I'll just pick another. I'll be too full to eat, of course, so I'll just have to kill them, but that's pretty fun too."

I would have bucked against my restraints but there was no give to them. I roared, "Give me the papers, you sick fuck!"

"Ha!" Doru pointed a finger at me. "There we go. Make with the name-calling. You know how I love it. You know, the part where you look down your nose at me." He took a step closer. "Why don't you laugh at me? How about that?"

I turned my attention to Melk who was looking more and more nervous. His eyes were fixed on Doru. I said, "Hey Melk, if this goes sideways, what's Soulis going to do?"

The goblin didn't answer.

I said, "Red caps aren't known for being very understanding."

Doru said, "Melk will do as he's told. Soulis needs me. I'm too valuable to cross. That's why I get to be the one to. . . negotiate with you."

He tittered then. I was at his mercy, and he was going to make me suffer. Beating me wasn't enough. I'd never realized the extent of his insecurity. I didn't want to imagine what he would actually have to do to prove himself my better.

"Doru!" I shouted. When he looked at me, I spoke softly, calmly. "You've won. You beat me. There is no need to hurt the boy."

"Oh, but there is. If I don't make an impression on you now, you'll forget your place. It's all your fault for acting better than me."

Melk hadn't spoken or moved, and his face was blank. He wouldn't look at me again. I guess he decided to take orders from Doru. He maintained my bonds, and that was it. It seemed that there was no one to hear my plea. I was helpless.

My regret at approaching the clearing passively was overwhelming. Could I have fully drawn Fetann when I had the chance?

Could I have beaten both of them? I didn't know, but if I had known how this would play out, I would have given it a hell of a try. I would have rather failed in action at least.

"Now, see what your attitude brought?" Doru said.

He walked closer, another five feet or so and held Howie up so that I could see his tear streaked face clearly in the moonlight with my physical eyes and hear his hitching sobs with my physical ears. Through Moe, I saw the Doru's familiar dart forward and stab into the boy. Howie screamed and bucked in Doru's grasp. It seemed that the boy had grabbed a livewire. This familiar clearly excelled at causing pain.

I roared and strained with every ounce of strength I could muster. There was no give in the bonds, but that didn't matter to me. I would spend myself pointlessly, but I wouldn't just watch the murder of a child. My student! He was my charge, my responsibility.

I felt Fetann's consciousness. On some level the sword was aware of what was happening too, and it didn't like it. Through our connection, I tried to will the sword to my hand. Galen hadn't indicated that the sword could move on its own, but I was casting about for anything that might help. I didn't know if I was doing it entirely right, but I felt and could actually see the sword quiver. But that was all.

Doru, eyes glittering, held Howie easily and bared his teeth at me. The boy still writhed, but his movements were slowing, weakening. "I don't want you to ever forget this."

Through gritted teeth, I said, "I never will." My takeaway was very different than Doru intended, however.

Rage was the main thing I felt, but unfortunately, not the only thing. That would have been easier. Easier than powerlessness. Failure. Fear. Loss. All of Howie's potential would amount to nothing. His future endeavors, his contributions to the world, his happiness were all being needlessly erased. All because of the petty vanity of an empty little narcissist.

I saw the moment when Howie died. It had been a while, but I'd seen too much death during my lifetime to miss it when I saw it. His eyes went vacant, glassy. His mouth fell slack. A long slow breath wheezed from deep in his lungs. Maybe he could have been revived at that point if there was an AED handy, but he probably wouldn't have survived for long.

Doru dropped the body without ceremony as if the boy were a piece of trash, a paper cup. It fell in an awkward, boneless heap, legs folded under and torso sprawled to one side. It was completely still, just so much inanimate organic matter. I stared at the heap which had been my student so that I would remember. If I ever lacked the resolve to act decisively against my cousin, this would be what I remembered.

As horrible as the sight was, it wouldn't be the last horror for Howie and probably not the worst either. He had been a fighter in life, and his spirit would be the same. To struggle futilely to survive twice, body and soul, in quick succession went a long way toward taming new ghosts. And there was still nothing that I could do.

"Now, we just have to wait a little while. It won't be long." Doru giggled and looked at me in a pointed sort of way. "Do you see now, Caomhnóir, that I'm better than you are?"

I didn't say anything. I was wrung out. I'd been worthless in this whole situation. I'd played it wrong, assuming that giving Doru what he demanded would satisfy him. If I'd come in with guns blazing, would it have turned out better? I didn't see how it could have been worse.

Howie's ghost detached from the body. It was inevitable and normally followed death pretty quickly. Through Moe, I saw the shimmering mist, only vaguely human-shaped, begin to rise. Doru's familiar created a sort of dome shape over the slowly rising ghost. I don't know why familiars had to wait, but they did. Instinctively, Howie resisted his ascent. This wouldn't be quick or easy for Doru's familiar. When the spirit reached a certain height from the body, the familiar would envelop it entirely, and the real spiritual struggle would begin in earnest.

I resigned myself to watch every moment of this just as I had the death of Howie's body. So near despair, I almost missed the sound. But it wasn't really a sound. It was something that I sensed through Moe. It was like a rumble in the distance, like a big engine. Maybe a semi rig. And it grew in intensity.

Doru looked up and around. He'd sensed it too, but Melk seemed oblivious. A strange shudder ran through Doru's familiar as well. It seemed that Melk's true-seeing spell didn't include all aspects of perception. He couldn't hear the engine, but he could clearly see our reactions.

The goblin asked, "What is it?"

Neither of us responded. We were both preoccupied. The sound that wasn't a sound continued to grow and set up a kind of resonance that I felt as a pressure in my head. I would have shaken it to clear it, but my neck was still bound. I was sure that it wouldn't have helped anyway. Moe contracted within his prison, trying to move away from whatever approached.

Doru was free to shake his head, and he did with one hand pressed to the center of his forehead. His familiar was rippling like the water of a pond on a breezy day, but it remained intent on Howie's ghost and would not flee as I thought it wanted to.

Doru's eyes, squinted tightly in pain, came up and found mine. "What are you doing?" he asked, his voice rough.

Too busy managing my own discomfort, I didn't respond.

The familiar had almost entirely enclosed Howie's ghost, but the strange ripple going through it had somehow compromised the familiar's integrity. Howie's ghost was making a contest of it, effectively striving against his would-be captor.

When I thought I could take no more of the metaphysical pressure, I saw what was coming and so did Melk. The nearness of the thing must have made itself detectable to the goblin's spell. Doru didn't see it, probably because his familiar was engrossed in the subjugation of a new ghost. I don't know that it would have mattered. I don't think that the familiar could have dodged. The thing might have sounded like a tractor trailer, but no truck ever moved so fast.

Much of what I sense through Moe is not physical, which makes it difficult to describe. Analogy is as close as I can come. So, this thing sounded like a big rig, but it looked like a comet, a golden sphere with a magnesium-white center trailing an orange and red tail behind it.

It flew directly at Doru's familiar and Howie's ghost. When they collided, there was a concussion like a lightning strike. Not like the rumble of thunder in the distance, a deafening whip-crack detonation that sent out a shockwave of metaphysical force. It was like that to

Doru and I anyway, and Melk seemed to experience some measure of it too.

Howie's ghost was borne away, but the familiar flew apart, scattered by the convulsion of energy released by the impact. There one second and then simply gone. Could it have been destroyed? I had no idea what happened to the familiar, but Doru's reaction was immediate and extreme.

He went rigid, his eyes wide, protruding like marbles. His mouth gaped, but no sound issued from it. A handful of seconds passed before the sound came. It doesn't seem right to call it a scream, but that's technically what it was. It was like a bandsaw ripping at a heavy oak board, and it just kept coming. I didn't understand how his lungs could hold so much air. There is a finite space in lungs, though, and eventually there was just no more. Even after his breath and the sound of his scream died away, his stance and expression didn't change.

Though Melk's perceptions were more limited, he still seemed to see plenty. And he couldn't help but to cringe and stagger away from the sight of the collision. His binding spell wavered, but to his credit, he didn't drop it entirely. The orange energy still bound my wrists, ankles, and neck, but the beams coming from the goblin's fingers seemed to go slack like loosened chains. As I fell toward the ground, I straightened my body like a diver's. It was a close thing, but I managed to bring my left wrist down upon Fetann's exposed blade. Either the sword miraculously shifted in the tall grass at the perfect moment, or Galen's sentient blade was able to intentionally move itself a critical inch.

Fortunately, cleaving the energy of the spell blunted some of the impact against my flesh, or I might have amputated half of my hand. As it was I received a deep gash that didn't hurt initially. The orange energy cracked like glass, the fissures traveling up the beam toward Melk. In the space of three seconds, they reached him, and there was a blast, an energy feedback which knocked him on his ass. The rest of my bonds vanished suddenly.

I pushed myself up to my knees, my right hand wrenching at my pocket flap and diving for the .38.

309

Using one of those martial arts kick-up moves, the goblin was back on his feet almost instantly. Almost was the operative word. He was up just in time to see the gun aimed at his center mass. I shot three times in quick measured succession from twenty feet away.

The first two were wide. The third tugged at the material of the blousy, red tunic. The bullet might have creased him, but it wasn't a significant hit. With Moe's help, I wouldn't have missed, but he was still imprisoned.

After a shocked second, the goblin turned and ran. He clearly hadn't expected a gun, but he adjusted quickly. He moved fast.

Ignoring the blood running freely from my left hand, I used it to steady my right hand. I didn't take the time for a slow breath, but I aimed deliberately and squeezed off the fourth shot. Fifty feet away, Melk's body jerked, and after two faltering steps, he fell first to his knees then directly onto his face.

The gunfire had shaken Doru from his strange paralysis, and he'd run in the other direction toward the tree line. By the time Melk had fallen, Doru was thirty yards away. I sent my last two rounds after him. I don't know if I hit him, but he didn't stop regardless.

My first and strongest impulse was to chase Doru down and torture him to death. I wanted to hurt him more than just about anything, but I can be pragmatic. I comforted myself with the possibility of him living without his familiar. If it had been destroyed by the comet, Doru would effectively be a human. A human who would starve to death no matter how much food he ate. That sounded pretty horrible. Not horrible enough but better than nothing. Also, a Talamaur without a familiar just isn't that valuable to anyone, so he would be absent of allies and other resources.

I put the gun back into my pocket and retrieved Fetann. I had to put the scabbard under my arm in order to draw the sword because my left hand was too numb and slick with blood to grip it effectively. I let the scabbard fall to the ground and went to free Moe. My familiar's prison was intact, so Melk was still alive though he lay motionless on the ground. I struggled to my feet and stood still for a few moments until I was sure that my wobbly legs would cooperate.

Moe and I were both aware that Fetann could destroy him, so we were careful about having them in close proximity. Moe compressed himself on the far end of his prison. It turned out that I didn't have to hack at the spell or exert myself at all. I just brought the tip of the sword in contact with the binding energy, and it cracked and fell away like dust. Nice trick that.

I breathed easier with Moe free, and we turned our attention toward Melk.

I'd only taken a couple of steps, though, before I heard the big engine again. The comet-thing had apparently atomized a familiar, and my protective instinct tried to force Moe to flee. He resisted though. That had never happened before. Instead of trying to force the issue, I trusted Moe and chose to believe that this was one of those times when he'd perceived and understood something that I hadn't.

The comet-thing came into sight again. This time there was no fiery tail because it wasn't moving like a bullet train. It looked different in other ways as well. The golden sphere with its intense white center had gained a shimmering pearlescent halo. Moe understood what it was, but it took me a few seconds to grasp.

I first recognized that the halo was Howie's ghost. Once I understood that, I knew that the white center was also a ghost. But I'd never seen a ghost so bright. The sphere took longer to figure out, but it shouldn't have. It was lifeforce. I perceived lifeforce every day, but never like this. Lifeforce behaved kind of like a liquid or a gas, or so I'd thought. This was different. The bright ghost was carrying the lifeforce with it in a field of some kind. But ghosts couldn't do that. Could they?

Doru had mocked me for not recognizing the ghost in Corman's crystal ball as a mage's ghost. I hadn't, but eventually I perceived a similarity between that ghost and the one hovering before me now. It was like seeing a family resemblance.

Joseph Corman's bad turn at the hospital must have gone all the way bad because here was his ghost. It hadn't moved on to the great beyond. It hadn't wandered about in confusion. It had sped immediately across thirty miles to rescue me and Howie's spirit if not his body. Ghosts didn't tend to behave so decisively, and they also didn't have the power to atomize Talamaur familiars.

311

Corman's ghost sent intent to me through Moe in that empathic sort of way that ghosts communicate through familiars. He demanded to help, more assertive than ghosts usually were.

I believed that he'd already been incredibly helpful, and I wasn't sure what else he could do. I expressed as much.

Impatience wasn't really what the ghost expressed in return. It was more like frustration, probably because of the limitations of our form of communication. He wanted me to understand something, but it was too complicated to articulate through feelings.

Once again, Moe acted independent of my command, and he moved toward the ghosts. My heart hitched. The memory of Doru's familiar flying apart into little familiar-particles was still very fresh, but I didn't try to hold him back.

I wished that I'd braced myself before Moe came in contact with the ghosts and that sphere of lifeforce. I don't know that it would have made any difference, but I like to think that I wouldn't have looked like such of a spaz. I absorbed all of that energy all at once, not like drinking through a straw at all. It wasn't like the firehose experience I had with Howie on his first day of classes at school either. Imagine if you will, drinking an entire gallon of water in one swallow. Outside of cartoons, where the characters' throats swell and contract to allow passage, it just doesn't happen.

There was that kind of strained-elastic kind of stretching sensation. Then, I was amidst the most intense part of the Talamaur healing process. I was used to a particular sequence. You know, the tickly diagnostic. The buzz. Then, the intense itching that was almost a pain of its own. Yeah, I went right to that part, but it was unexpected. I had no warning. Thus, the spaz part.

I hadn't realized that my muscles had deteriorated so much over the years. Not until they started to inflate like they'd been partially empty water balloons reattached to a flowing spigot. My whole body became tauter, denser, and straighter in just a few seconds. It was not a comfortable sensation, but at least it was over quickly. I didn't mean to collapse afterward. I didn't pass out or anything. My body just didn't want to stand up while it was thrumming.

I might have stayed down longer, but Moe let me know that Melk was not done struggling. The goblin was moving again, not fast but moving nonetheless. My fourth shot had taken him in the spine, and nothing below his waist seemed to be working. He was pulling himself along by grabbing fistfuls of tall, dry grass and dragging himself along.

I pushed myself up with surprising ease. Fatigue was entirely absent, and holy crap, I felt strong. Fetann lay where I'd dropped it. I bent and cleaned the blade in the grass and retrieved the scabbard. It was then that I realized the deep gash in my hand was entirely healed despite being made by the magical blade. It hadn't been a matter of hours. It was seconds.

I re-sheathed the sword, and after loosening my belt a notch, I was able to fit it between the belt and my hip. It felt awkward, but I wanted my hands free.

My whole body was still pulsing gently and I realized that my movements were defter, more precise. My vision was sharper too. I didn't bound like a deer after the retreating goblin, but there sure was a spring in my step.

Moe was watching the goblin closely. Corman and Howie followed me, just a little behind, one to the left and one to the right. Corman no longer glared like a miniature sun, but he was still brighter than any ghost I'd seen before.

I had a sudden realization, then, and there was a little stutter in my step. I was aware of the ghosts without Moe's perceptions. Moe was focused on Melk, but I knew where Corman and Howie were.

I knew because they were mine. It came to me then, an understanding. Corman and Howie had bound themselves to Moe. There'd been no struggle because they'd volunteered. Moe didn't have to wrangle them because they were acting independently, not like slaves. More like teammates.

I made a mental note to visit with my father no matter how much of a condescending jerk he was. I needed to understand more about my nature, my potential. What was possible and what wasn't. I might need a crowbar to pry information from him, but I was going to try my damnedest.

Melk heard me approach and stopped his slow flight. He smelled like blood and shit. I didn't know if he'd soiled himself or if my bullet had just ripped up his guts. He was leaving quite a trail. I didn't know about goblins' healing abilities, but he seemed in pretty rough shape. I wasn't dropping my guard at any rate.

Before I got too close, I emptied the spent brass from the .38 and dropped them into my right pocket. After reloading, I took the last few steps and drew the hammer back, all dramatic like in the movies. He rolled over, and his eyes went to the gun first. Then, in quick jittery movements, they darted to my face then to the ghosts on either side of me. The golden dust around his eyes was still doing its job.

He didn't say anything for a long while. I'd hoped that he would try to fight, or even better, beg for his life. He just stared at me, flat and entirely without emotion. I wanted to make him express something, fear or remorse or defiance. Instead, he just waited. I wasn't going to get anything out of him. I doubted that I could do anything to him that hurt more than his scrambled guts anyway.

Eventually, he said, "You better hurry. The sound of those shots is going to draw attention."

"Are you kidding? In the woods of Allegany County?" I downplayed it, but there was a chance that he was right, especially with the recent bear thing and a missing student.

"Maybe you're right," I said. "Quiet is better." I replaced the gun and drew Fetann.

Melk's eyes flicked to the shimmering blade. He said, "So Galen is backing you?"

I didn't answer. I stood looking down, still hoping for some kind of reaction. This wasn't going to be as satisfying as it could be.

He said, "I'm not going to beg if that's what you're hoping for."

"I know," I said and placed the tip of the blade at his throat.

"I killed him, you know."

"Dr. Corman?"

"That's not who I meant," he said. "I mean Mr. Brannon, the kindly teacher. Nurturer of children. That guy is long gone." He smiled.

"I know," I said and drove the blade into his throat. There was a muffled crunch as Fetann's tip bit through vertebra. I flicked the blade first one way and then the other. Melk's head came away, but there was still a smile on the little fucker's face. Blood pumped out onto the grass but not for long. The smile stayed though.

# Chapter 25

So, I had a big fat mess to sort out in very short order. I would consider my whole "killing in cold blood" thing later. I was fine with tabling that. I didn't feel bad about it and would get around to contemplating it when I had more time. First things first.

I shut off my phone, took out the SIM card and the data card, and destroyed both of them. I was now incommunicado and untraceable. Probably anyway. I only knew about this stuff from *NCIS*.

Next, there were two bodies to deal with. They would need very different kinds of attention.

Howie's first. There was a hitch in my breathing when I thought about him, but I didn't look at the body. His ghost was suddenly near and communicating comfort, trying to console me. That made it worse. My throat constricted with grief and regret. Squeezing my eyes shut, I focused on my breathing and locking feelings away in favor of sensible action. Howie seemed to understand that he wasn't helping and moved away. I sent gratitude in his direction.

Howie's body would have to be found, preferably soon. It was now only so much meat, but I hated the idea of scavengers getting to it. I also didn't like the idea of one of the other kids finding it. Options were relatively few, but I thought I had an idea.

Melk's body was a different matter. It had to disappear. Not disappear by hiding it. Disappear by destroying it. If hikers were to find it twenty years from now, it would be examined. Even if reduced to bones, it wouldn't take much to deduce that it wasn't human. The Venator council wouldn't like that one little bit. And contrary to what some mystery writers would have you believe, disposing of a body is no mean feat. I thought I had an idea for that, too. Not perfect, but passable. And gross as hell.

I picked up the Howie's body. It was entirely limp and still felt warm. It seemed that so much had happened, but he'd really only died a few minutes ago. A fireman's carry would have made the most sense. It was practical. Hell, I'd carried him like that once when he was alive. This time, though, I carried him across my chest like a parent would hold his child. Then, I ran. I ran all out, Moe showing me exactly where to put my feet every step of the way. I was the wind, covering six hundred yards in little less than a minute.

We were at Noah's garden shed, not far from the archery range. I didn't have the key to the padlock, but I never really needed keys. I had used them for show, but that was all. Moe is good with little mechanisms like tumblers and bolts. He unlocked the padlock, lifted it from the eye-latch, and opened the door for me. I placed the body on the floor, curled up like he was when he'd slept on the floor of my classroom. It was quite convincing. He looked like a tired boy who had lain down after a busy day. I didn't know how the whole situation would be interpreted, but looking natural would probably go a long way.

I left the lock on the ground but made sure that the door of the shed was closed securely. It didn't look like it would swing open on its own or anything, but the image of that happening and an animal getting to him... not him... just the body. Damn it. I pushed that image aside. If the door remained unlatched, whoever found him might assume that he'd entered under his own power. Howie had been handled roughly before he died, but none of his physical injuries had been life-threatening. The medical examiner who performed the autopsy would try to form a reasonable theory. The fewer signs of foul play the better.

Moe and the ghosts ranged ahead of me as I took off toward my apartment. I had ghosts. This new development would take some getting used to. I said that I would never subjugate ghosts, and I hadn't. I shouldn't have this squeamish feeling, right? They'd volunteered. That would go onto the list of things to consider later. Recent days were just rich with fresh experiences and moral questions.

My initial plan had been to get to the parking lot, hop into the Nova, retrieve the goblin's body, and drive away. I wasn't a hundred percent sure where I would be going, but I'd figure that out when I got some distance. With Moe's help, I could likely keep to the shadows and avoid detection. At least until I got to the car. The Nova just couldn't sneak.

Yeah, I'd decided to take the Nova instead of the Subaru. That wasn't really a reasonable choice. The Subaru would draw much less attention than a fifty-two-year-old muscle car as I escaped one life to start another. Unfortunately, that wasn't the only unreasonable choice I was going to make.

My choice to retrieve the Gibson was based purely on sentiment. Practically speaking, I could easily replace the guitar with something just as good. I could probably even find another 1959 ES-175 specifically. I didn't want another one, though. I wanted mine. I was able to rationalize this foolish indulgence, though, because I really did need to get that keepsake box. A record of my nomadic life over most of the twentieth century. That sort of thing would make a great exhibit at my Venator trial. Actual documentation of my vain stupidity.

There was no way for me to enter my apartment while staying in the shadows, so I would have to minimize my exposure. Moe would see that the coast was clear as best he could, and I would move quickly and quietly.

Dinner was over, and the students were back in their dorms with their dorm parents. Moe found that Oak House was empty except for Pam and Allie. Pam was on the phone, tears ran freely down her cheeks. Allie stood just inside the door of the office, shifting her weight from one foot to the other. She clearly wanted to be moving, doing something. Her face was taut with tension, but her eyes were dry.

Pam said into the phone, "Well, I haven't seen him. Allie said that he went to check on something, but he hasn't come back yet."

Moe moved in close to hear the voice on the other end of the line. It was Novak. His tone was tight. "I won't leave Joe. I have to stay here."

Pam's face, the one made for smiles, went hard with anger. The change was even more dramatic than her worried face had been. Her tone was just as hard. "Damn it, Conrad, he's past needing you. We need you, now. Howie needs you."

Novak said nothing.

Pam said, "Dr. Corman would want you to look after the children. That's been his first consideration since the day I met him."

Silence on the other end of the line continued, and I wondered if Novak had hung up. The downside of talking on a landline was that you couldn't just check to see if a call had ended. Finally, he said, "No one has seen Sean?"

"Allie saw him when he first returned to campus. But no one since then."

Novak said, "You better call the cops. I'll be there in a half hour."

"Howie's only been missing for a little more than an hour. Will they come for a kid who's only been gone for an hour?"

Novak blew a breath. "He was seen in the company of a stranger in a potentially dangerous area."

Pam sounded uncomfortable when she said, "Maggie told us he was with Sean."

Allie's eyes squinted. She clearly didn't like the uncertainness of Pam's tone.

Novak said, "Sean was with me. I met him at Lore. He'd been there for hours. Whoever Maggie saw, it wasn't Sean."

I annoyed myself a little by feeling gratitude toward Novak for backing me. Why shouldn't he back me? I'd never given him reason not to.

There was something sharp, a little insistent, in Pam's otherwise calm voice when she pushed for affirmation. "But will the police come for that? So soon, I mean?"

Novak said, "I'll call Sandy before I leave the hospital. He'll get something moving. An AMBER alert. Some troopers."

Police response time is not great out in the country, but I needed to get going. The further away I was when Howie's body was found the better. I couldn't stick around looking twenty-five-years-old and all that. I had to leave, but leaving at the same time a student died would be highly suspicious. Sure, I had an alibi for the abduction but not the beating and not the death, even if it looked like natural causes. Healthy twelve-year-old kids didn't typically die of natural causes. I would definitely be a person of interest.

The smart thing to do would be to ditch all of Sean Brannon's possessions and burn the damn memento box. Hell, I was a twenty-five-year-old kid, and no one would believe that I was Sean Brannon, physical likeness or not. Maybe hanging on to things wasn't smart, but I knew I would regret it if I didn't retrieve my guitar. Sentimental monsters. Go figure.

Moe returned from Oak House to help me move around in the dark. He couldn't be everywhere at once, and I needed him with me more than I needed him to keep spying. I skirted the back of Birch House which was mostly dark, but there was a streetlamp right outside my apartment door. It wasn't a spotlight, but it might as well have been.

Moe opened the door for me, and I moved as fast as I could through the light and into the darkness within. I didn't turn on the lights inside but kept Moe close to show me what I was doing. A downside of using him as a seeing-eye familiar was that he couldn't keep watch at the door. Oh well, there was nothing to be done for it.

I left Fetann on the kitchen table and hunted around in the back of my kitchen cabinet for an old tea tin. It didn't hold tea. It held two rolls of bills: five thousand in hundreds and two thousand in twenties. It'd been stowed there for so long that all of the bills were old designs. But they'd spend just fine. I left the tin on the counter and stuffed the rolls of money in my left-hand jacket pocket with the .38 ammo.

In the bedroom, I took the Gibson's guitar case from the closet and tossed it on the bed. Then, I got down on my hands and knees to drag the stupid keepsake box out from under the bed. What the hell was I thinking keeping that thing around? It was wedged under there with the Fender's case, and I tilted the bed up to free up some space.

The Gibson's guitar case slid from the mattress. Gee, who could have foreseen that? I made a grab for it and missed. The case hit the bedside table and knocked it and the lamp it held to the floor. Surprisingly, the lamp didn't break, but there was quite a thumpy racket. The first three thumps were from the case, the table, and the lamp. But the fourth thump was loudest. That was the bed falling back to the floor when I let go of it to grab at the case. Good thing I didn't turn on the light and draw attention to myself, right?

I didn't pause or even slow. Box under one arm and guitar case in hand, I moved into the living room. In seconds, the Gibson was packed away, and I was heading toward the door. My ears were good, and they'd just recently gotten better, so I heard the footsteps nearing my door. I went still as Moe locked the door and continued outside to investigate.

Allie stood on the other side of my door for a moment, anxiety plain on her features. She squared her shoulders and her lips tightened to a line, her resolved look. She knocked three times and waited.

I didn't respond. I stood in the dark not knowing what to do. I could crash through window maybe and take off like the proverbial bat out of hell. That seemed entirely too dramatic, and that kind of behavior would make me way more interesting to the police. I could let Allie in and put her in a sleeper hold. Make her pass out long enough for me to make my escape. But I wouldn't do anything to hurt her or scare her any more than I had to, not to save my life.

After half a minute, she tried the door and found it locked. She said, "Sean, I heard you moving around in there. I don't know what's going on, and I'm scared as fuck. Please, open the door."

I couldn't let her see me like this. There would be no rational explanation to cover it, and I didn't have time to explain anyway. The brief "I'm a vampire" approach hadn't worked well with Novak, and I wasn't willing to try it again.

Then, she did it. Damn it! In a voice so quiet that a human wouldn't have been able to hear it, she said, "Sean, I need you."

Well, hell.

I put the guitar and the box on my kitchen table with Fetann and opened the door. She peered into the dark room, probably only able to make out general shapes. "Where have you been?"

I didn't answer. There was too much.

She said, "Pam finally got ahold of Con." After a pause. "Dr. Corman died."

"I know," I said.

"Did you find Howie?"

There was so much hope in her voice. She seemed to have accepted Corman's death, but Howie was just a kid, and she thought I could save him. Hearing, in that one question, her belief in me did something to my insides. I'd failed. I couldn't see it any other way. My confidence in myself and my understanding of virtually everything was coming apart.

I made the mistake of trying to speak. I said just one word, but it came out as a sort of honking sob. I'd meant to say, "Yes."

I don't know if Allie understood what I'd try to say or not. I don't know if it mattered. In an instant, she was in my arms, her face on my chest, her arms locked around the small of my back. She must have felt the gun in my jacket pocket, but she said nothing as wept. It wasn't pretty or manly in any way. It was mostly quiet, just shuddering and trembling, but occasionally I had to take breaths. They sounded harsh, like a rasp on hardwood.

It felt like a long time that we stood like that, but it was probably less than a couple of minutes. I got myself under control, and drew back.

Allie couldn't see in the dark, and it made sense that she'd want some light. She probably just wanted to get me cleaned up and find out what happened. I could have stopped her when she reached for the overhead-light switch, but I didn't. In retrospect, I wonder if I was testing her. I guess I always would have wondered if I hadn't.

The kitchen light flared, illuminating the bulk of my apartment. . . and me. In just a couple of seconds, her eyes adjusted, and her mouth dropped open. Then, her mouth moved like she was trying to speak but no words came out. Her right hand came up and pointed vaguely in my direction. She began, "You. . ." Nothing else.

While she stared and pointed, I turned to the counter and tore off a couple of paper towels. I wiped my eyes with one and my nose with the other. I'm sure that I still looked like hell, but at least there was no longer snot on my face.

She looked at me like I was a puzzle that she had to figure out, a maze with a twisting path. I'd never seen her worried expression combined with the inquisitive little crease between her brows before. Finally, she said, "Sean?"

"It's me," I said.

"I don't understand."

"I know," I said. My voice was a little rough but mostly back to normal and under control. "I can't explain. I'm sorry. I just have to go."

To my surprise, she just gave a short nod. She accepted it just like that. "You'll tell me later."

"I can't—" I began.

She interrupted, "Later." Her right hand touched my left forearm lightly. "Where's Howie?"

I felt my face begin to collapse again, but I managed not to start bawling and blubbering. This tough-guy shit is exhausting. I said clearly, if a little quietly, "He's dead."

Her hand tightened on my arm. "What happened?"

I just shook my head. The question deserved an answer, but I couldn't say anything. My next words came of their own accord. I said, "I didn't do it." It was pretty obvious that I feared she would assume the worst about me.

Novak had, and I wouldn't get over that soon.

Alejandra Park, bless her, placed her hands on my cheeks and looked up into my face. Her dark eyes were shiny, and a sad smile touched her mouth. She said, "Of course you didn't." She kissed me lightly on the mouth. Her lips were soft.

I loved her. I doubted that I'd ever see her again, but facts are facts. No need to lie to myself.

Her simple words of faith were one of the greatest kindnesses I'd ever experienced, and she even repeated them. "Of course you didn't." Then, she stepped back to give me space.

I thrust Fetann beneath my belt again. Allie looked with curiosity but said nothing. I put the memento box under my left arm and picked up the Gibson case with my right.

"What do I say when people ask me about all this?" she asked.

The only lie I wanted her to tell was the one that would save her from the Venators. The rest didn't matter. Melk was right. Sean Brannon was dead. He had no more to lose.

I said, "Tell it the way it happened. Just don't tell anyone how I look. It would be bad for you if anyone found out."

"The way you look? You mean, younger than me?"

"Yeah."

"I was going to leave that part out anyway."

"Thank you, Allie. You deserve an explanation, but—"

323

"You'll tell me later."

I shook my head, but there was a tiny smile on my face. The smile didn't mean that I wasn't a hair's breadth away from crying again, but it was there nonetheless.

"Where's Howie?" she asked.

"Noah's garden shed."

She nodded.

I was about to ask her to shut off the light before she opened the door, but she was already doing it. The room went dark. She opened the door and stood aside.

As I moved past, she said quietly, "'Gator."

I stopped and was going to tell her that I could never see her again. She would just contradict me anyway, so after a little pause, I said, "Crocodile."

I hurried to the parking lot, not a blur or anything, but going fast.

I didn't know if there was much point in trying to be stealthy at this point, but I figured that it was better to err on the side of caution. I only opened the driver's-side door of the Nova. It often takes a repetition of noises for people to take notice, so it seemed worthwhile to limit the racket my creaky old car made. I tossed the guitar over the front seat into the back where it bounced a couple of times and landed on the floor. The keepsake box went onto the new floor mat in front of the shotgun seat. Fetann went on the seat itself, within easy reach.

Keeping the Nova's low growl from roaring took some finesse, but I managed. I knew her well. I feathered the gas to get her out of the parking lot. There was a slight downgrade on the driveway, so I was able to push the clutch in and let the engine idle while coasting past most of the buildings. The headlights were on, so I would look less like a person sneaking if someone did take note of my passage.

Moe ranged ahead, finding the clearing as we had left it. I did turn the lights off after I turned onto the utility road which ran near the Low Road and skirted the clearing. Moe showed me the way, and I still tried to go easy on the gas though we were no houses close by.

Near the clearing, there were signs of some inexpert driving. The soft earth and grass just off the road were torn up where someone had made a hasty U-turn. Some bushes had actually been driven over, and the smooth bark of a birch tree was scraped off about two and a half feet up. Shiny, black paint showed where the smooth white wood had been scored.

My guess was that the paint came from the Mercedes I'd seen Doru driving on his first visit to the school. He drove expensive sports cars, but I guess that he couldn't handle a car very well without his familiar.

I maneuvered the Nova so her nose was pointed out, and I would be ready to go as quickly as possible. I could have continued on up the utility road, but it became narrower and more overgrown as it went for several miles before reaching a main road. I wanted to be gone fast.

From the Nova's trunk, I took a couple of bungee cords and the blue tarp I'd used to transport the debris from my classroom floor and Noah's ceiling. I had to leave that mess on the floor of the trunk, but building materials would be easier to clean up than decapitated goblin.

Moe had checked Melk's corpse over and found it still warm. A lot of blood had run out of the stump of the neck, and the grass was dark with it. In retrospect, beheading was probably unnecessary, indulgent even. Yeah, well, safe and sorry and all that. Supernatural types sometimes shrugged off serious injuries, or apparent death, and Melk seemed the type who might do that sort of thing. Plus, I'd been really pissed at him.

With Moe around, I didn't need to rifle pockets or anything. I knew what I wanted and took the goblin's knife and the seven hundred dollars and change I found in his pocket. Everything else was rolled in the tarp along with the body. I tied off each end of the bundle with the bungee cords to lessen the likelihood that body fluids would leak onto the floor of my trunk.

I hefted the body and was about to head back toward the car with Moe to guide me when I heard the rustle of leaves. Glancing over my shoulder, I saw Corman's and Howie's ghosts pushing leaves over the bloodstains. I gaped. Like a full-on kind of gape.

Ghosts usually didn't have the power to manipulate the physical world. And before you say it, poltergeists are a different kind of a thing. Also, they were acting with complete independence and intent. They weren't following orders. They were taking initiative. I was sure that it was really Corman who was setting the goals, but Howie was choosing to help as much as he could.

The leaf cover wouldn't withstand much scrutiny, but Howie's body was a third of a mile away. There would be no reason to examine this area, and if no one noticed the blood for a few days, it would stay unnoticed. Moe conveyed my gratitude to the ghosts, and my troop of spirits and I headed to the car.

After depositing my burden into the trunk, I put Fetann, the .38, and the ammo back into the magic bag. My smartphone and its broken cards were also in my jacket pocket, and I decided to toss them in the bag as well. Let's see the FBI track a signal to a pocket dimension. The bag went back into my inside jacket pocket.

The goblin knife I left out. I was sure to keep the scabbard too. Anything that could cut cleanly through my floor like it had might just require a magical scabbard. I would find out about my new toy in short order. I planned to use it soon. Moe scanned it for any indication of booby traps or other unpleasantness while we headed toward Short Tract, a little community that made Geary look like a thundering metropolis.

My method of goblin-body disposal relied upon context, or a lack of it. Body parts could only really be identified if there were big enough pieces in close enough proximity. It would be a nasty bit of work. The goblin knife, Moe, and the carnivorous wildlife of Western New York State were going to scatter tiny piece of Melk so far and wide that no one would have any idea what they were looking at. Especially after they'd been eaten and shat out by coyotes and crows and whatnot.

I found a little turnout not far from County Road 15 which would keep me out of sight of anyone on the road. Not that any cars drove by anyway. The area was "quiet" and "out-of-the-way" in the land of quiet and out-of-the-way places. Mostly, Moe helped me to see in the dark, but every minute or so, I sent him on a quick little circuit of the surrounding area.

I lay the tarp on an open, flat, grassy area. Melk's body had cooled more, and the surface blood seemed to have coagulated. Boy, I had hated the little shit, but this was going to be difficult. Body mutilation was yet another new experience for me. So many new things. I just had to find the right mental space. I would imagine myself as a meat cutter. You know, like at a supermarket. This was just meat that I was going to give to all of the hungry animals of the woods and fields. Right? No, I couldn't really convince myself, but I managed to get through it anyway.

I stripped off my coat and noted for the first time that Fetann had cleanly sliced the left sleeve halfway to the elbow. I sighed and rolled up my sleeves and got down to it. I won't go into detail. You're welcome. But three things I will mention. One, the goblin blade cut through bone with about as much effort as I might have needed to cut celery with a decent kitchen knife. Two, the Melk pieces were very small. And three, most of the blood was still liquid. . . and warm. My trusty familiar took care of most of it though.

Moe transports liquid as easily as he transports anything else, and he sopped up most of the blood at intervals. Each little quantity he would take high into the air several hundred yards away and basically atomize it, a little red mist which dispersed on the breeze. He couldn't get all of it, but he got quite a lot of it.

The more. . . solid matter stayed on the tarp, in the middle as much as I could manage it. When I was finished, I tied up the four corners with one of the bungees and put it back in the trunk. The package was still juicy, but it didn't think it would leak out if we got a move on. The second bungee I used to tie the trunk lid so that I could leave it unlatched with a four-inch gap to the outside.

I washed up with some moist towelettes and drove at a sedate pace along 15. For several miles there were lots of woods, and lots of fields, and hardly any houses. Moe removed fun-sized servings of Melk the goblin from the Nova's trunk and distributed them to out of the way places where animals were likely to come across them. It took about six miles of me put-putting along to get all of it. Then, I had only a bloody tarp, not all that uncommon in hunting country. And a bloodstained, kid-sized medieval-looking outfit, just a few days before Halloween.

I stopped in a small town called Angelica and pulled behind a little grocery store which was already closed. I wrapped up Melk's clothes in the tarp and tossed them into the store's dumpster. Since I was there anyway, I threw in the floor debris as well. The dumpster had been locked, but Moe took care of that and even locked back up when we were through.

I-86 would take me across New York. Of course, I was going to Galen. He was my best friend, and he'd always been willing to help. I'd stop for gas as soon as possible, and I'd pick up a pre-paid phone, maybe even at the same place. I remembered his number. I would call him for his address. I had to give back his stuff anyway, and he could help me with perspective and more pragmatic things like setting up a new identity. What fun.

I was also considering a reunion with Scathlann, dear ol' Dad. He was a cold, condescending dick, and I wasn't looking forward to seeing him, but I needed him. There was too much that I didn't know, and he had a lot of knowledge and that backroom-deal kind of clout that Talamaurs can build up.

I would find Doru. If misery and a lingering death by starvation were all he had to look forward to, I'd leave him alone. If he was happy and well, then I'd have to do something about that. He would answer for his offences at any rate, and there was no mercy in my heart for him.

I felt a little flicker at my side. Howie's ghost hovered next to me like he was riding shotgun. He'd been a pretty gentle kid, but he was expressing a concurrence with my vengeful feelings. I guess that being murdered is an effective way to lose one's innocence.

Corman was flying with Moe up above the car, and I had the sense that he was learning from my familiar. I didn't know how, only that there was some kind of inquiry and response going on. I hoped that they were planning and that they could share it with me somehow. I supposed that knowing the next couple of steps I'd take was technically a plan, but I sure couldn't see very far ahead.

# About the Author

Edgar Washburn was a teacher for many years. He enjoys drawing, playing guitar, and drinking craft beer. He spent most of his life living in New York State and New Hampshire but now resides in Oregon with his wife. *Incognito: Preternatural Pedagogy* is his first novel.

Made in the USA
Columbia, SC
15 August 2021